# MY LADY LUDLOW AND OTHER STORIES

THE WORLD'S CLASSICS

ELIZABETH GASKELL

*My Lady Ludlow*
*and Other Stories*

*Edited with an Introduction by*
EDGAR WRIGHT

Oxford   New York
OXFORD UNIVERSITY PRESS
1989

Oxford University Press, Walton Street, Oxford OX2 6DP

Oxford New York Toronto
Delhi Bombay Calcutta Madras Karachi
Petaling Jaya Singapore Hong Kong Tokyo
Nairobi Dar es Salaam Cape Town
Melbourne Auckland

and associated companies in
Berlin Ibadan

Oxford is a trade mark of Oxford University Press

Introduction, Note on the Text, Select Bibliography,
Appendix and Explanatory Notes © Edgar Wright 1989
Chronology © Oxford University Press 1981

First published by Oxford University Press as Round the Sofa 1913.
Mr. Harrison's Confessions first published in
Cousin Phillis and Other Tales 1911.
This arrangement first issued as a World's Classics paperback 1989

British Library Cataloguing in Publication Data
Gaskell, Elizabeth, 1810–1865
My Lady Ludlow and other stories.—(The World's classics).
I. Title
823'.8[F]
ISBN 0-19-281838-4

Library of Congress Cataloging in Publication Data
Gaskell, Elizabeth Cleghorn, 1810–1865.
My Lady Ludlow and other stories / Elizabeth Gaskell ; edited with
an introduction by Edgar Wright.
p. cm. —(The World's classics)
I. Wright, Edgar, 1920– . II. Title. III. Series.
823'.8—dc 19   PR4710.M9 1989   88–18134
ISBN 0-19-281838-4 (pbk.)

Printed in Great Britain by
Hazell Watson & Viney Ltd.
Aylesbury, Bucks

# CONTENTS

# INTRODUCTION

In 1859 Elizabeth Gaskell published a two-volume collection consisting of a shortish novel, a number of short stories, and a brief narrative account of a curious historical episode. Taking account of an old method recently popularized again by Dickens and others, she presented them as a 'chain' of stories introduced by a scene-setting prologue, and furnished with brief 'links' between each story. The whole collection, taking its name from the semi-autobiographical prologue, was titled *Round the Sofa*. The reality was that the stories were originally published at various times and in various periodicals during a three-year period; collected together they represent all her shorter work since a previous collection in 1855. This reality was recognized on republication, when the title was changed to *My Lady Ludlow and Other Stories*. The collection demonstrates much of her range and interests as a talented writer of shorter fiction.

Gaskell was a born story-teller. While recognized today mainly for her work as a novelist, her novels deploy at greater length the narrative skills and themes presented in the shorter tales. Telling stories and recounting incidents came naturally to her. Her letters are alive in their depiction of her reactions to people and events, whether in snippet sketches of local and domestic trivia or, to take a famous example, the detailed and penetrating 'warts and all' account of Charlotte Brontë at their first meeting. As a writer she rapidly acquired the technique needed to support a creative imagination. Yet she never lost, and rarely ignored, the gift of accurate and clear narration, or the easy and natural style of story development, often from an initial personal note or recollection, that seems simple yet can range without effort from humorous incident to sensitive feeling, from shrewd and amused observation of social behaviour to analysis of character or the excitement of action. Nor did she ever lose touch with the detail of everyday life and activity.

Her upbringing provided her with a remarkably appropriate background to her talents. She was brought up as an orphan by a loving aunt in the quiet, old-fashioned little country town of Knutsford, where her uncles and their families included doctors and farmers. She was then given a better than normal education at one of the best girls' schools in the country. As a Unitarian she absorbed and firmly held to a strong tradition of tolerance and independent enquiry. Marriage to an intellectual young Unitarian minister brought her to Manchester and active contact with all levels of society in the explosive growth of the greatest of all Victorian industrial cities. Later travel and friendships abroad, as well as the custom of long holidays for rest and writing in the countryside of the North of England and North Wales, added to her store of knowledge about local custom and legend.

She became famous with a first novel in 1848, *Mary Barton*, as Charlotte Brontë had done in 1847 with *Jane Eyre*, and like Brontë she had used personal background, in this case knowledge of the lives and conditions of factory workers in Manchester, to tell the story and express her feelings. But it was Knutsford, and its old-fashioned ladies with their 'elegant economy' and ingrained customs, that were the basis for her next success, *Cranford*. She had early made the acquaintance of Charlotte Brontë, and the two women, so different in background and temperament, became friends. This friendship and Gaskell's continuing success as an author led to the request that she write the biography of her friend on Charlotte's death in 1855. For two years she devoted most of her energy to the task; the result was *The Life of Charlotte Brontë*, one of the great biographies of the language. But there was a cost to the creative writer; during the period, and for a time after it while she recovered from the effort, she could turn only occasionally to her fiction, partly to earn money for holidays and travel, partly in response to pressures from publishers and editors. When she did write, it was in the short-story form, often drawing for ideas on backgrounds or incidents she learned about on holidays or through her reading. Such holidays, in areas where old traditions and local stories still flourished, provided a strong contrast to the grimly modern bustle of Manchester, and appealed both to the local historian in her and to the lover of the countryside.

The stories in this collection, diverse as they are, have certain common elements, among which should be noted the absence of the Manchester world that had provided the social basis for her previous novels and some of the earlier short stories. Her response to the Northern countryside is apparent; a response that may have been deepened by her examination of the effect of such surroundings on the Brontës. Apparent too is her feeling for the importance of tolerance and understanding that is always present, and her sense of the disastrous consequences of hatred and revenge. Above all, perhaps, is her understanding of the emotions and beliefs, good or bad, that can drive individuals to act. She deals with people and the way they behave; she knows that individual behaviour is a matter of relationships with other individuals and with the social community, small or large, whose attitudes mould conduct. Her own life and beliefs were firmly based on Christian principles, but her Unitarian upbringing, as well as her temperament, led her to prefer explaining life through examples and incidents rather than by protestation or preaching; she sees conduct as the true gauge of the spirit. She is interested in the moral and psychological motives and reactions that control the feelings and create the tensions behind the actions in her stories. These may occur as sensational drama, such as the supernatural suggestion or manifestation in *The Doom of the Griffiths* and *The Poor Clare*. Social pressures may affect a whole community, as they do in *My Lady Ludlow*, or be narrowed within the small family circle of *The Half Brothers*. But in all of her stories the emphasis is ultimately on the integrity of character in the face of social or emotional pressure. The narratives develop as problems of conduct created by circumstances, placed within detailed settings of local life and custom. It is this concern for and sympathy with people rather than with abstract ideas of belief and behaviour that is the basis of her strength as a writer and her ability to portray character.

The final story in this collection, *Mr. Harrison's Confessions*, is an early study of the Knutsford world that predates *Cranford*, and makes an interesting link with *My Lady Ludlow*. One of the stories originally republished in *Round the Sofa* (*Half a Life-Time Ago*) appears in *Cousin Phillis and Other Tales*, a previous volume in this series.

The only comment by Gaskell on *My Lady Ludlow*, other than to note that the money she got for it was used for a holiday abroad, is the modest disclaimer that she makes in the introductory 'Round the Sofa' prologue. This passes it off as 'an old-world story which, after all, would be no story at all, neither beginning, nor middle, nor end, only a bundle of recollections', a disclaimer briefly repeated in the story's opening: 'It is no story: it has, as I said, neither beginning, middle, nor end.' We need to trust the tale as told rather than the teller as critic. What we have is a stated artlessness that conceals much art. The comment points back, and I believe is meant to point back, to the method of *Cranford*, and there is indeed a degree of episodic structure. But there is also a controlled development and purpose from the beginning; the story has a definite structure of theme as well as narration. Even the long interpolated story of the de Crequys, which takes up nearly a third of the novel, has its place in the considered scheme of things. The problem for criticism lies with the contrast in the two methods and the two narratives which were used to present two approaches to one theme. Like two sides of a coin, they are difficult to see together.

*My Lady Ludlow* is written round the problems of social change and individual response to it. The awareness of living in an age of major transition was a constant theme for Gaskell, a theme personally encountered in the transition from the gentle ways, old traditions, and settled beliefs of her early days to the challenges implicit in life in Manchester. She had used these backgrounds directly in the industrial novels and short stories and in *Cranford*. She had dealt with revolutionary types of change in England at a time when there had been, and still were, actual revolutions in Europe. In *My Lady Ludlow* she steps back from the problem in time and place, and illustrates the two types of revolution. Through the eyes of her chosen narrator, Margaret Dawson as a young girl, Gaskell looks back at the changes that were achieved by a process of individual adjustment and tolerance, peacefully and without sacrifice of humanity or human affections, though not without the natural round of pain and sorrow mixed with pleasure. In contrast we have the upheaval of violent revolution in France, with its tragic brutality and unnatural disregard of human feelings and personal merit.

For the first view she adopted the mode of comedy; the tone is the quietly humorous, shrewdly and affectionately observant viewpoint of someone who is emotionally involved in what is happening, yet is only indirectly a part of it. So we have the comedy of social behaviour and situation, presented with an acute sensitivity to and sympathy with feelings and principles, and realized through some memorable characters, of whom the finest is Lady Ludlow herself. In the social hierarchy dependent on Hanbury Court, she is a benevolent and proudly aristocratic autocrat, imposing her standards, her version of Anglican christianity, and her attitudes on the surrounding countryside. At the same time she is a widow, physically frail, growing old, isolated by her position and sense of propriety from close companionship with those around her, and aware, when her last surviving son dies, that she is the last of her line—and of her type. She is left with only the integrity of character, her faith, and the humanity of her beliefs to deal with the pressures for change. These prove to be qualities that earn her, in turn, the respect and the affection of those around her, even when they disagree with or disobey her wishes.

Individual grief and suffering at all levels of the community are mediated through the routines of normal life and the comedy of particular incidents. Like Jane Austen, one of

her favourite authors, Gaskell works with the characters in
a defined community. Her range, however, is not limited as
was Jane Austen's. From the engaging young ragamuffin
Harry Gregson to the eager and over-enthusiastic
evangelical Mr Gray, from the boorish squire, Mr Lathom,
to the gloriously eccentric Miss Galindo, we are given the
outline of a whole society and its character; each episode is
revealing not only of individual character but of the attitudes
involved. At the beginning, for example, we are shown Lady
Ludlow in church standing up to tell the clergyman, who
owes the living to her patronage, that she will do without a
sermon that day. By the end of the novel we have the scene,
comic yet sensitive, in which Lady Ludlow meekly imitates
the 'vulgarity' of the dissenter's wife, Mrs Brooke, to prevent her being ridiculed. As the various episodes follow each
other, as Margaret Dawson watches and learns while her
own increasing ill-health brings privileged closeness to Lady
Ludlow and her activities, so the gradual adjustment to new
ideas is chronicled. There is no idealization of the past; its
crudenesses and inequalities are shown, as when Mr Mountford has literally to eat crow, along with its comfortable
tranquillity and aesthetic pleasantness. Nor is the countryside idealized; 'Nature' contains the squalor of
Hareman's Common with its 'yellow pools of stagnant
water' and the wattle-and-clay cottages whose interiors
made Lady Ludlow 'hesitate before entering or even speaking to any of the children who were playing about in the
puddles'. This is a rustic version of the Manchester slums;
we are left in no doubt that there is much that needs changing, as Mr Gray insists, and that education has to come to
the aid of change. But the importance of feelings, of affection
and Christian (but not doctrinal) conduct are never forgotten. The virtues of tolerance and understanding
predominate, along with the ability to admit one's own
mistakes or weaknesses, as Miss Galindo does when con-
fronted with the pet duck named after her because of its
habit of constantly intruding. Humour and a sense of proportion control the outlook.

As with all the Knutsford-based stories there is an autobiographical element to *My Lady Ludlow*. Gaskell draws on her recollections of people and local history as well as of place. (Joan Leach has recently provided new evidence that Lady Ludlow borrows characteristics of Lady Jane Stanley, who lived in Knutsford during the time in which the story is set, while Mrs Chadwick gives a good deal of detail to connect certain aspects with Gaskell's school years with the Misses Byerley at their school 'Avonbank' near Stratford.) This personal involvement, grateful and affectionate even when the narrative is critical or judgemental of particular events and attitudes, provides some of the warmth that permeates the story; individual character values are recognized without our needing to forgo a smile at the eccentric or a laugh at the ludicrous.

Within this structure of the theme of change we should realize how deftly the sub-plots merge until, by the end, a new and strong sense of community has grown out of a series of relationships that symbolize a new social order. Mr Gray will marry Miss Galindo's adopted niece, the illegitimate Bessy, while Lady Ludlow's carefully selected new steward, Captain James, will marry the daughter of 'the dissenting baker from Birmingham'. Time reveals the union that finally ties all together, as the adult narrator turns to her present audience: 'As I dare say you know, the Reverend Henry Gregson is now vicar of Hanbury, and his wife is the daughter of Mr. Gray and Miss Bessy.' The process of education has gone far beyond the mere establishing of a school; a quiet revolution has taken place, without harm.

In marked contrast are the hatred, intolerance, and selfishness fostered by the French Revolution. Individual good intentions and affections are doomed during a period when excess and the passion of power control conduct. The story of Clément de Crequy, while it shows the persistence of love and other virtues in the conduct of individuals, also shows their tragic impotence in a world governed by revenge and jealousy. The tone and form of the narrative are matched to the violent activity of its background, the story moving strongly and tautly to its tragic conclusion. The style is direct and tinged with a Carlylean emphasis—a precursor to Dickens's powerful *A Tale of Two Cities* which appeared a year later. The emphasis is on the action rather than on the characters; it is unfolded rapidly and expertly.

The link used to connect the two stories is Lady Ludlow's desire to prove that educating the lower classes, who are assumed to lack the moral and religious discipline of their superiors, courts disaster. The problem for the reader is not only with the obviousness of the artifice but with the length of the episode, which imposes its own mood and pace, disrupting the effect built up by the preceding account of life at Hanbury Court. This could be another tale in the chain of stories. The connection that Gaskell surely wished to make, between the two ways of achieving social change, is buried in the completeness of the contrast. An unfortunate result of the failure to mesh the two stories is that the Lady Ludlow portion of the novel has been undervalued. It takes the spirit of *Cranford* a step further. The apparently loose structure of episodes, amusing or affecting in themselves, mark stages in a progressive change of attitudes and in the development of Lady Ludlow herself as one of Gaskell's most finely conceived characters. The technique of the narrative voice is also carefully chosen: the sensitive and intelligent adult reflecting on the past and re-creating the events and emotions of her own formative years, while preserving enough of the tone of detached maturity to be able to smile affectionately at them, and at the people who were involved. It is a technique that Dickens was to use a few years later for *Great Expectations*.

The remaining stories from *Round the Sofa* reveal, in one way or another, the attraction for Gaskell of local legends, local histories, and the supernatural. However, it is always individual conduct and the moral attitudes involved that spur her creative imagination. This is so equally in the short non-fiction item, *An Accursed Race*. She probably became aware of the details of the long persecution of the Gagots, as Shorter notes, on one of her French holidays. It is told something in the manner of her fiction, using episodes and characters to present her account, while the moral of the ending emphasizes the whole as an example of the quirks in human behaviour which present a puzzle to be shared with the reader, who is addressed directly in the quiet, sensible comments of the narrator.

*The Doom of the Griffiths* is a good example of Gaskell's way of taking a local story and giving it strength and depth by exploring the psychological and emotional bases for the events. Her own single direct comment on it is a typically dismissive one: 'The story per se', she wrote to Charles Eliot Norton in 1857, 'is an old rubbishy one,—begun when Marianne was a baby—the only merit whereof is that it is founded on fact.' The time reference (Marianne was born in 1834) would indicate that she heard the story while on a visit to her uncle Sam Holland at Portmadoc, and that the urge to write was present very early. But there is no evidence that the original beginning, if indeed it was ever more than a thought, had anything to do with the story as we have it, which 'at Mr. Sampson Low's earnest entreaty I promised to Messrs Harper's more than a year ago'. In fact, she turns what could have been a simple tale about a curse into a more complex study of emotions set in a solidly realized background; the love between Owen and Nest is made tragic through the jealousy and pride of his family, whose bitterness turns the curse into a self-fulfilling prophecy. The psychology and conduct of the main characters, as with everything Gaskell wrote, is given support by its setting of a countryside she knew well; our interest is attracted by the detail of local custom and domestic habits that creates a confident realism. In this story the supernatural element is kept at the level of hearsay; the tragedy depends immediately on a failure of sympathy, and so is credible in itself, if verging on the melodramatic for its climax.

Nothing is known about any direct sources or inspiration for *The Poor Clare*. It is another of the tales from a region that Gaskell knew well, in this case the unfrequented part of Lancashire known as the Trough of Boland. The matter of

Catholic loyalty to an officially Protestant country might be
indirectly relevant to the controversy stirred up in the 1850s
over the reintroduction of Catholic sees in England. A. W.
Ward points out that there was a community of Poor Clares
at Levenshulme, only a short walk from the Gaskell home
in Plymouth Grove. There is little doubt that her researches
for the *Life of Charlotte Brontë* gave an impetus to her interest
in local history and in the impression created by a wild and
isolated countryside; there was a tendency for her later work
to be based on research as well as set back in time. But
whatever sources may have been available, the characters
and the plot are Gaskell's own creation, as is the conflict of
good and evil resulting from the power of passionate feeling
opposed to the moral and religious obligations of tolerance
and forgiveness. Religion, or more accurately Christian conduct based on faith, is, from the nature of the plot and the
main character, a prominent element, but the emphasis is on
conduct and motive, not on aspects of belief. Catholics,
Anglicans, Dissenters, sincere believers, and lukewarm con-
formists reflect the religious differences of the period during
which the action takes place, but the impression left of any
one group depends on the person involved. The test of true
Christianity, as in her other stories, lies in behaviour, not in
profession. The curse that Bridget lays on Gisborne re-
bounds on to Bridget herself, nor can it be lifted until
forgiveness is felt in the heart as well as in the mind. The
supernatural materializes to serve a moral purpose and, as
Margaret Ganz noted, to create 'a progressive stress on
moral and psychological rather than merely sensational
aspects'. The sinfulness of the curse thus becomes the
fulcrum of the plot; the effectiveness of the story lies in the
sensational manner of its operation. Bridget is a commanding character, energetic and extreme in affections and
actions, a figure of fate who, like Meg Merrilies in Scott's
*Guy Mannering*, dominates the action not only by the doom
of her curse but by the intensity of the passion that produces
it. The other characters are less powerfully drawn, living
under her shadow. The narrator himself, for all his central

role as Lucy's lover whose determination and strength of affection finally tracks down Bridget and brings an end to the haunting, remains nameless. His search for help for Lucy turns necessarily into a search for Bridget's salvation.

The effectiveness of the style supports the dramatic plot. The use of dialogue and the constant change of scene reinforces the sense of activity and urgency. The final dramatic episode gives a focus to the desperate revolt of the starving Antwerpers against their Austrian oppressors. The incident has no factual base but through it the reader's attention is firmly fixed on the plight of individuals within the generalities of history. The death and salvation of Bridget, left vague in time, rises out of the historical reality to vindicate a belief in the ultimate power of human goodness.

*The Half Brothers* is the final tale in this collection from *Round the Sofa*, and appears not to have been previously published. It is slighter than the other stories, but shares a Wordsworthian tone with several of them, and is effective in its descriptions of Cumberland life and countryside. Ward notes that 'it illustrates a famous passage in Thomas à Kempis (*Imitation of Christ*, chap. xlix, section 4 and 5) which she was accustomed to cite with particular solemnity—the passage beginning, "That which pleaseth others shall go well forward; that which pleaseth thee shall not speed," etc.' There is little room for developing character or motivation, so consequently the emphasis on death and sacrifice is hardly relieved, while the pathos verges on the sentimental.

*Mr. Harrison's Confessions* is an early work, the first attempt by Gaskell to turn the impressions and memories of Knutsford into fiction. It was an attempt that also released into her writing the sense of humour and sometimes downright fun that was an essential part of her own temperament. As a child she had accompanied her uncle, Peter Holland, on his doctor's rounds; she wrote from familiarity as well as observation, and certain personalities from her childhood days who appeared for the first time in this story reappear with modifications in later stories based on the same recollections. The humour is broader, the sentiment less delicately controlled, the pathos more overt than in *Cranford*, but the delight in eccentricity of behaviour and the complications of social etiquette are already convincingly present, along with an insider's knowledge of a society dominated by women. The plot is still a simple one, a structure which can be filled with episodes; the treatment is to create humour that touches on farce at times, while the characters, with a few exceptions, have little subtlety in their presentation. But they do hint at the art that would lead to *My Lady Ludlow*; Miss Galindo would not be out of place in Duncombe. The old-fashioned customs and conventions contained virtues and values as well as promoting habits that led to ludicrous actions and misunderstandings. The pathos and the comedy in this early story are divided; the unwitting hero moves from one to the other as he moves from the society of the ladies to the family of Sophy. The comic and the painful are juxtaposed as much as unified. The successful synthesis began with *Cranford* and was to develop through *My Lady Ludlow* to the final achievements of *Cousin Phillis* and *Wives and Daughters*. Nevertheless, this early story, with its lively evocation of the little country town and its inhabitants, has its own pleasures and at least one memorable sketch in the character of Mr Morgan. When the time came for republication to be considered in 1855, Mrs Gaskell raised a query with her publisher, Chapman. She would write to *Household Words* for permission to republish other tales, she said, and added: 'Must I do the same with "Mr. Harrison's Confessions?" or should you not think them worth re-printing?' For its own sake, as well as for its importance in her development as a major writer of fiction, the republishing of *Mr. Harrison's Confessions* needs no justification.

# A NOTE ON THE TEXT

The text of all the items, with the exception of 'Mr. Harrison's Confessions', is based on the two-volume first edition of *Round the Sofa*, published by Sampson Low and Son, London, 1859, and used by Clement Shorter for the 1913 World's Classics edition. A one-volume edition, with the title changed to *My Lady Ludlow and Other Stories*, appeared in 1861 using the same text.

Details of the original periodical publication for each item, including 'Mr. Harrison's Confessions', are given separately in the notes.

There has been a small amount of silent editing to deal with a few misprints and some variations in punctuation between periodical and book forms. Any changes of substance are referred to in the detailed textual annotation.

# SELECT BIBLIOGRAPHY

There has been little critical comment on *Round the Sofa* or, more specifically, on *My Lady Ludlow*. The introductions to the volumes in the earlier collected editions are still relevant, particularly that of A. W. Ward for the Knutsford edition of *My Lady Ludlow and Other Tales* (London, John Murray, 1906). This volume also contains, and has comment on, 'Mr. Harrison's Confessions'. The other edition is that of C. Shorter for the World's Classics (OUP, London); the two volumes are *Round the Sofa* (1913), and *Cousin Phillis* (1911).

The background of *My Lady Ludlow* is discussed in detail, with bibliographical data, in J. G. Sharps's *Mrs. Gaskell's Observation and Invention* (Fontwell, 1970). E. H. Chadwick's *Mrs. Gaskell, Haunts, Homes, and Stories* (London, 1910), discusses the personal background. Joan Leach's 'Lady Jane Stanley of Knutsford', in the magazine of *The Knutsford Historical and Archaeological Association* (Autumn, 1984), details one connection.

Relevant general comment on Mrs Gaskell as a short-story writer, with incidental reference to particular items, can be found in Angus Easson, *Elizabeth Gaskell* (London, 1979), and in Easson's introduction to *Cousin Phillis and Other Tales*, (London, 1981); Margaret L. Ganz, *Elizabeth Gaskell, the Artist in Conflict* (New York, 1969); Annette B. Hopkins, *Elizabeth Gaskell, Her Life and Work* (London, 1952); Coral Lansbury, *Elizabeth Gaskell* (Boston, 1984); Arthur Pollard, *Mrs. Gaskell, Novelist and Biographer* (Manchester, 1965); Edgar Wright, *Mrs. Gaskell, The Basis for Reassessment* (London, 1965).

Winifred Gérin's *Elizabeth Gaskell, A Biography* (Oxford, 1976), and of course *The Letters of Mrs. Gaskell*, edited by J. A. V. Chapple and A. Pollard (Manchester, 1966), provide background and biographical information.

# A CHRONOLOGY OF
# ELIZABETH GASKELL

*Age*

1810    Elizabeth Cleghorn Stevenson, second child of William Stevenson and Elizabeth Holland, born in Chelsea

1811    (November) After her mother's death, Elizabeth is taken to Knutsford by her Aunt Hannah Lumb    1

1826    Attends the Avonbank School at Stratford-upon-Avon for two years    15–16

1827    Her elder brother, John Stevenson (b. 1799), disappears while a voyage to India. Elizabeth goes to Chelsea to live with her father and stepmother    16–17

1829–    (22 March) Elizabeth's father dies; she goes to
30    Newcastle upon Tyne, to the home of the Revd William Turner    18–19

1831    Spends much of this year in Edinburgh with Mr Turner's daughter    20–1

1832    (30 August) Marries the Revd William Gaskell, assistant Minister at Cross Street Chapel, Manchester, at St John's Parish Church, Knutsford    21

1833    Her first child, a daughter, born dead    22

1834    Her second daughter, Marianne, born    23

1837    A poem, 'Sketches among the Poor', by Mr and Mrs Gaskell, appears in *Blackwood's Magazine* (January). Her third daughter, Margaret Emily (Meta), born. Mrs Hannah Lumb dies    26

1840    Her description of Clopton Hall included by William Howitt in *Visits to Remarkable Places*    30

1841    Mr and Mrs Gaskell visit the Continent, touring the Rhine country    30–1

1842    Her fourth daughter, Florence Elizabeth, born. The family move to 121 Upper Rumford Street, Manchester    31–2

## AUTHOR'S PREFACE

MOST of these Stories have already appeared in *Household Words*: one, however, has never been published in England, and another has obtained only a limited circulation.

# MY LADY LUDLOW

## CHAPTER I

I AM an old woman now, and things are very different
to what they were in my youth. Then we, who
travelled, travelled in coaches, carrying six inside, and
making a two days' journey out of what people now
go over in a couple of hours with a whizz and a flash,
and a screaming whistle, enough to deafen one. Then
letters came in but three times a week: indeed, in
some places in Scotland where I have stayed when
I was a girl, the post came in but once a month;—
but letters were letters then; and we made great prizes
of them, and read them and studied them like books.
Now the post comes rattling in twice a day, bringing
short jerky notes, some without beginning or end, but
just a little sharp sentence, which well-bred folks would
think too abrupt to be spoken. Well, well! they may
all be improvements,—I dare say they are; but you
will never meet with a Lady Ludlow in these days.

I will try and tell you about her. It is no story: it
has, as I said, neither beginning, middle, nor end.

My father was a poor clergyman with a large family.
My mother was always said to have good blood in her
veins; and when she wanted to maintain her position
with the people she was thrown among,—principally
rich democratic manufacturers, all for liberty and the
French Revolution,—she would put on a pair of ruffles,
trimmed with real old English point, very much darned
to be sure,—but which could not be bought new for
love or money, as the art of making it was lost years
before. These ruffles showed, as she said, that her
ancestors had been Somebodies, when the grandfathers

of the rich folk, who now looked down upon her, had been Nobodies,—if, indeed, they had any grandfathers at all. I don't know whether any one out of our own family ever noticed these ruffles,—but we were all taught as children to feel rather proud when my mother put them on, and to hold up our heads as became the descendants of the lady who had first possessed the lace. Not but what my dear father often told us that pride was a great sin; we were never allowed to be proud of anything but my mother's ruffles: and she was so innocently happy when she put them on,—often, poor dear creature, to a very worn and thread-bare gown,—that I still think, even after all my experience of life, they were a blessing to the family. You will think that I am wandering away from my Lady Ludlow. Not at all. The lady who had owned the lace, Ursula Hanbury, was a common ancestress of both my mother and my Lady Ludlow. And so it fell out, that when my poor father died, and my mother was sorely pressed to know what to do with her nine children, and looked far and wide for signs of willingness to help, Lady Ludlow sent her a letter, proffering aid and assistance. I see that letter now: a large sheet of thick yellow paper, with a straight broad margin left on the left-hand side of the delicate Italian writing,—writing which contained far more in the same space of paper than all the sloping, or masculine hand-writings of the present day. It was sealed with a coat of arms,*—a lozenge,—for Lady Ludlow was a widow. My mother made us notice the motto, 'Foy et Loy,' and told us where to look for the quarterings of the Hanbury arms before she opened the letter. Indeed, I think she was rather afraid of what the contents might be; for, as I have said, in her anxious love for her fatherless children, she had written to many people upon whom, to tell truly, she had but little claim; and their cold, hard answers had many a time made her cry, when she thought none of us were looking. I do not even know if she had ever seen Lady Ludlow: all I knew of her was that she was a very grand lady, whose grandmother had been half-sister to my mother's great-grandmother ; but of her character and circumstances I had heard nothing, and I doubt if my mother was acquainted with them.

I looked over my mother's shoulder to read the letter ; it began, ' Dear Cousin Margaret Dawson,' and I think I felt hopeful from the moment I saw those words. She went on to say,—stay, I think I can remember the very words :—

' DEAR COUSIN MARGARET DAWSON,—I have been much grieved to hear of the loss you have sustained in the death of so good a husband, and so excellent a clergyman as I have always heard that my late cousin Richard was esteemed to be.'

' There ! ' said my mother, laying her finger on the passage, ' read that aloud to the little ones. Let them hear how their father's good report travelled far and wide, and how well he is spoken of by one whom he never saw. COUSIN Richard, how prettily her ladyship writes ! Go on, Margaret ! ' She wiped her eyes as she spoke : and laid her finger on her lips, to still my little sister, Cecily, who, not understanding anything about the important letter, was beginning to talk and make a noise.

' You say you are left with nine children. I too should have had nine, if mine had all lived. I have none left but Rudolph, the present Lord Ludlow. He is married, and lives, for the most part, in London. But I entertain six young gentlewomen at my house at Connington, who are to me as daughters—save that, perhaps, I restrict them in certain indulgences in dress and diet that might be befitting in young ladies of a higher rank, and of more probable wealth. These young persons—all of condition, though out of means —are my constant companions, and I strive to do my duty as a Christian lady towards them. One of these young gentlewomen died (at her own home, whither she had gone upon a visit) last May. Will you do me the favour to allow your eldest daughter to supply her place in my household ? She is, as I make out, about sixteen years of age. She will find companions here who are but a little older than herself. I dress my young friends myself, and make each of them a small allowance for pocket-money. They have but few opportunities for matrimony, as Connington is far removed from any town. The clergyman is a deaf old widower; my agent is married; and as for the neighbouring farmers, they are, of course, below the notice of the young gentlewomen under my protection. Still, if any young woman wishes to marry, and has conducted herself to my satisfaction, I give her a wedding dinner, her clothes, and her house-linen. And such as remain with me to my death, will find a small competency provided for them in my will. I reserve to myself the option of paying their travelling expenses, —disliking gadding women, on the one hand; on the other, not wishing by too long absence from the family home to weaken natural ties.

'If my proposal pleases you and your daughter—or rather, if it pleases you, for I trust your daughter has been too well brought up to have a will in opposition to yours—let me know, dear cousin Margaret Dawson, and I will make arrangements for meeting the young gentlewoman at Cavistock, which is the nearest point to which the coach will bring her.'

My mother dropped the letter, and sat silent.

'I shall not know what to do without you, Margaret.'

A moment before, like a young untried girl as I was, I had been pleased at the notion of seeing a new place, and leading a new life. But now,—my mother's look of sorrow, and the children's cry of remonstrance: 'Mother, I won't go,' I said.

'Nay! but you had better,' replied she, shaking her head. 'Lady Ludlow has much power. She can help your brothers. It will not do to slight her offer.'

So we accepted it, after much consultation. We were rewarded—or so we thought,—for afterwards, when I came to know Lady Ludlow, I saw that she would have done her duty by us, as helpless relations, however we might have rejected her kindness,—by a presentation to Christ's Hospital* for one of my brothers.

And this was how I came to know my Lady Ludlow.

I remember well the afternoon of my arrival at Hanbury Court. Her ladyship had sent to meet me at the nearest post-town at which the mail-coach stopped. There was an old groom inquiring for me, the ostler said, if my name was Dawson—from Hanbury Court, he believed. I felt it rather formidable ; and first began to understand what was meant by going among strangers, when I lost sight of the guard to whom my mother had entrusted me. I was perched up in a high gig with a hood to it, such as in those days was called a chair, and my companion was driving deliberately through the most pastoral country I had ever yet seen. By-and-by we ascended a long hill, and the man got out and walked at the horse's head. I should have liked to walk, too, very much indeed ; but I did not know how far I might do it ; and, in fact, I dared not speak to ask to be helped down the deep steps of the gig. We were at last at the top,—on a long, breezy, sweeping, unenclosed piece of ground, called, as I afterwards learnt, a Chase. The groom stopped, breathed, patted his horse, and then mounted again to my side.

' Are we near Hanbury Court ? ' I asked.

' Near ! Why, Miss ! we've a matter of ten mile yet to go.'

Once launched into conversation, we went on pretty glibly. I fancy he had been afraid of beginning to speak to me, just as I was to him ; but he got over his shyness with me sooner than I did mine with him. I let him choose the subjects of conversation, although very often I could not understand the points of interest in them : for instance, he talked for more than a quarter of an hour of a famous race which a certain dog-fox had given him, above thirty years before ; and spoke of all the covers and turns just as if I knew them

as well as he did ; and all the time I was wondering
what kind of an animal a dog-fox might be.

After we left the Chase, the road grew worse.  No
one in these days, who has not seen the byroads of
fifty years ago, can imagine what they were.  We had
to quarter, as Randal called it, nearly all the way along
the deep-rutted, miry lanes ; and the tremendous jolts
I occasionally met with made my seat in the gig so
unsteady that I could not look about me at all, I was
so much occupied in holding on.  The road was too
muddy for me to walk without dirtying myself more
than I liked to do, just before my first sight of my Lady
Ludlow.  But by-and-by, when we came to the fields
in which the lane ended, I begged Randal to help me
down, as I saw that I could pick my steps among the
pasture grass without making myself unfit to be seen ;
and Randal, out of pity for his steaming horse, wearied
with the hard struggle through the mud, thanked
me kindly, and helped me down with a springing
jump.

The pastures fell gradually down to the lower land,
shut in on either side by rows of high elms, as if there
had been a wide grand avenue here in former times.
Down the grassy gorge we went, seeing the sunset sky
at the end of the shadowed descent.  Suddenly we
came to a long flight of steps.

' If you'll run down there, Miss, I'll go round and
meet you, and then you'd better mount again, for my
lady will like to see you drive up to the house.'

' Are we near the house ? ' said I, suddenly checked
by the idea.

' Down there, Miss,' replied he, pointing with his
whip to certain stacks of twisted chimneys rising out
of a group of trees, in deep shadow against the crimson
light, and which lay just beyond a great square lawn
at the base of the steep slope of a hundred yards, on
the edge of which we stood.

I went down the steps quietly enough.  I met
Randal and the gig at the bottom ; and, falling into a
side road to the left, we drove sedately round, through

the gateway, and into the great court in front of the house.

The road by which we had come lay right at the back.

Hanbury Court is a vast red-brick house—at least, it is cased in part with red bricks ; and the gate-house and walls about the place are of brick,—with stone facings at every corner, and door, and window, such as you see at Hampton Court.* At the back are the gables, and arched doorways, and stone mullions, which show (so Lady Ludlow used to tell us) that it was once a priory. There was a prior's parlour, I know—only we called it Mrs. Medlicott's room ; and there was a tithe-barn as big as a church, and rows of fish-ponds, all got ready for the monks' fasting-days in old time. But all this I did not see till afterwards. I hardly noticed, this first night, the great Virginian Creeper (said to have been the first planted in England by one of my lady's ancestors) that half-covered the front of the house. As I had been unwilling to leave the guard of the coach, so did I now feel unwilling to leave Randal, a known friend of three hours. But there was no help for it ; in I must go ; past the grand-looking old gentleman holding the door open for me, on into the great hall on the right hand, into which the sun's last rays were sending in glorious red light,—the gentleman was now walking before me,— up a step on to the dais, as I afterwards learned that it was called,—then again to the left, through a series of sitting-rooms, opening one out of another, and all of them looking into a stately garden, glowing, even in the twilight, with the bloom of flowers. We went up four steps out of the last of these rooms, and then my guide lifted up a heavy silk curtain, and I was in the presence of my Lady Ludlow.

She was very small of stature, and very upright. She wore a great lace cap, nearly half her own height, I should think, that went round her head (caps which tied under the chin, and which we called 'mobs,' came in later, and my lady held them in great contempt, saying people might as well come down in their night-caps). In front of my lady's cap was a great bow of white satin ribbon; and a broad band of the same ribbon was tied tight round her head, and served to keep the cap straight. She had a fine Indian muslin shawl folded over her shoulders and across her chest, and an apron of the same; a black silk mode gown,* made with short sleeves and ruffles, and with the tail thereof pulled through the pocket-hole, so as to shorten it to a useful length: beneath it she wore, as I could plainly see, a quilted lavender satin petticoat. Her hair was snowy white, but I hardly saw it, it was so covered with her cap: her skin, even at her age, was waxen in texture and tint; her eyes were large and dark blue, and must have been her great beauty when she was young, for there was nothing particular, as far as I can remember, either in mouth or nose. She had a great gold-headed stick by her chair; but I think it was more as a mark of state and dignity than for use; for she had as light and brisk a step when she chose as any girl of fifteen, and, in her private early walk of meditation in the mornings, would go as swiftly from garden alley to garden alley as any one of us.

She was standing up when I went in. I dropped my curtsy at the door, which my mother had always taught me as a part of good manners, and went up instinctively to my lady. She did not put out her hand, but raised herself a little on tiptoe, and kissed me on both cheeks.

'You are cold, my child. You shall have a dish of tea with me.' She rang a little hand-bell on the table by her, and her waiting-maid came in from a small anteroom; and, as if all had been prepared, and was awaiting my arrival, brought with her a small china-service with tea ready made, and a plate of delicately-cut bread-and-butter, every morsel of which I could have eaten, and been none the better for it, so hungry was I after my long ride. The waiting-maid took off my cloak, and I sat down, sorely alarmed at the silence, the hushed foot-falls of the subdued maiden over the

thick carpet, and the soft voice and clear pronunciation
of my Lady Ludlow. My tea-spoon fell against my
cup with a sharp noise, that seemed so out of place
and season that I blushed deeply. My lady caught
my eye with hers,—both keen and sweet were those
dark-blue eyes of her ladyship's :—

' Your hands are very cold, my dear ; take off those
gloves ' (I wore thick serviceable doeskin, and had
been too shy to take them off unbidden), ' and let me
try and warm them—the evenings are very chilly.'
And she held my great red hands in hers,—soft, warm,
white, ring-laden. Looking at last a little wistfully
into my face, she said—' Poor child ! And you're the
eldest of nine ! I had a daughter who would have been
just your age ; but I cannot fancy her the eldest of
nine.' Then came a pause of silence ; and then she
rang her bell, and desired her waiting-maid, Adams,
to show me to my room.

It was so small that I think it must have been a cell.
The walls were whitewashed stone ; the bed was of
white dimity.* There was a small piece of red stair-
carpet on each side of the bed, and two chairs. In
a closet adjoining were my washstand and toilet-table.
There was a text of Scripture painted on the wall
right opposite to my bed ; and below hung a print,
common enough in those days, of King George and
Queen Charlotte, with all their numerous children,
down to the little Princess Amelia in a go-cart. On
each side hung a small portrait, also engraved : on
the left, it was Louis the Sixteenth, on the other,
Marie Antoinette. On the chimney-piece there was a
tinder-box and a Prayer-book. I do not remember
anything else in the room. Indeed, in those days
people did not dream of writing-tables, and inkstands,
and portfolios, and easy chairs, and what not. We
were taught to go into our bedrooms for the purposes
of dressing, and sleeping, and praying.

Presently I was summoned to supper. I followed
the young lady who had been sent to call me, down
the wide shallow stairs, into the great hall, through

which I had first passed on my way to my Lady
Ludlow's room. There were four other young gentlewomen, all standing, and all silent, who curtsied to
me when I first came in. They were dressed in a kind
of uniform : muslin caps bound round their heads with
blue ribbons, plain muslin handkerchiefs, lawn aprons,
and drab-coloured stuff gowns. They were all gathered
together at a little distance from the table, on which
were placed a couple of cold chickens, a salad, and
a fruit-tart. On the dais there was a smaller round
table, on which stood a silver jug filled with milk, and
a small roll. Near that was set a carved chair, with
a countess's coronet surmounting the back of it. I
thought that some one might have spoken to me ; but
they were shy, and I was shy ; or else there was some
other reason ; but, indeed, almost the minute after
I had come into the hall by the door at the lower end,
her ladyship entered by the door opening upon the
dais ; whereupon we all curtsied very low ; I, because
I saw the others do it. She stood, and looked at us
for a moment.

'Young gentlewomen,' said she, 'make Margaret
Dawson welcome among you ; ' and they treated me
with the kind politeness due to a stranger, but still
without any talking beyond what was required for the
purposes of the meal. After it was over, and grace
was said by one of our party, my lady rang her hand-
bell, and the servants came in and cleared away the
supper things : then they brought in a portable reading-
desk, which was placed on the dais, and, the whole
household trooping in, my lady called to one of my
companions to come up and read the Psalms and
Lessons for the day. I remember thinking how afraid
I should have been had I been in her place. There
were no prayers. My lady thought it schismatic to
have any prayers excepting those in the Prayer-book ;
and would as soon have preached a sermon herself in
the parish church, as have allowed any one not a
deacon at the least to read prayers in a private dwelling-
house. I am not sure that even then she would have

approved of his reading them in an unconsecrated place.

She had been maid of honour to Queen Charlotte : a Hanbury of that old stock that flourished in the days of the Plantagenets, and heiress of all the land that remained to the family, of the great estates which had once stretched into four separate counties. Hanbury Court was hers by right. She had married Lord Ludlow, and had lived for many years at his various seats, and away from her ancestral home. She had lost all her children but one, and most of them had died at these houses of Lord Ludlow's ; and, I dare say, that gave my lady a distaste to the places, and a longing to come back to Hanbury Court, where she had been so happy as a girl. I imagine her girlhood had been the happiest time of her life ; for, now I think of it, most of her opinions, when I knew her in later life, were singular enough then, but had been universally prevalent fifty years before. For instance, while I lived at Hanbury Court, the cry for education was beginning to come up : Mr. Raikes* had set up his Sunday Schools ; and some clergymen were all for teaching writing and arithmetic, as well as reading. My lady would have none of this ; it was levelling and revolutionary, she said. When a young woman came to be hired, my lady would have her in, and see if she liked her looks and her dress, and question her about her family. Her ladyship laid great stress upon this latter point, saying that a girl who did not warm up when any interest or curiosity was expressed about her mother, or the 'baby' (if there was one), was not likely to make a good servant. Then she would make her put out her feet, to see if they were well and neatly shod. Then she would bid her say the Lord's Prayer and the Creed. Then she inquired if she could write. If she could, and she had liked all that had gone before, her face sank—it was a great disappointment, for it was an all but inviolable rule with her never to engage a servant who could write. But I have known her ladyship break through it, although in both

cases in which she did so she put the girl's principles
to a further and unusual test in asking her to repeat
the Ten Commandments. One pert young woman—
and yet I was sorry for her too, only she afterwards
married a rich draper in Shrewsbury—who had got
through her trials pretty tolerably, considering she
could write, spoilt all, by saying glibly, at the end of
the last Commandment, ' An't please your ladyship,
I can cast accounts.'

' Go away, wench,' said my lady in a hurry, ' you're
only fit for trade ; you will not suit me for a servant.'
The girl went away crestfallen : in a minute, however,
my lady sent me after her to see that she had something to eat before leaving the house ; and, indeed,
she sent for her once again, but it was only to give
her a Bible, and to bid her beware of French principles,
which had led the French to cut off their king's and
queen's heads.

The poor, blubbering girl said, ' Indeed, my lady,
I wouldn't hurt a fly, much less a king, and I cannot
abide the French, nor frogs neither, for that matter.'

But my lady was inexorable, and took a girl who
could neither read nor write, to make up for her alarm
about the progress of education towards addition and
subtraction ; and, afterwards, when the clergyman who
was at Hanbury parish when I came there, had died,
and the bishop had appointed another, and a younger
man, in his stead, this was one of the points on which
he and my lady did not agree. While good old deaf
Mr. Mountford lived, it was my lady's custom, when
indisposed for a sermon, to stand up at the door of her
large square pew,—just opposite to the reading-desk,—
and to say (at that part of the morning service where
it is decreed that, in quires and places where they sing,
here followeth the Anthem) : ' Mr. Mountford, I will
not trouble you for a discourse this morning.' And
we all knelt down to the Litany with great satisfaction ; for Mr. Mountford, though he could not hear,
had always his eyes open about this part of the service,
for any of my lady's movements. But the new clergy-

man, Mr. Gray, was of a different stamp. He was
very zealous in all his parish work ; and my lady, who
was just as good as she could be to the poor, was often
crying him up as a godsend to the parish, and he never
could send amiss to the Court when he wanted broth,
or wine, or jelly, or sago for a sick person. But he
needs must take up the new hobby of education ; and
I could see that this put my lady sadly about one
Sunday, when she suspected, I know not how, that
there was something to be said in his sermon about
a Sunday-school which he was planning. She stood
up, as she had not done since Mr. Mountford's death,
two years and better before this time, and said,—

'Mr. Gray, I will not trouble you for a discourse
this morning.'

But her voice was not well-assured and steady ; and
we knelt down with more of curiosity than satisfaction
in our minds. Mr. Gray preached a very rousing
sermon, on the necessity of establishing a Sabbath-
school in the village. My lady shut her eyes, and
seemed to go to sleep ; but I don't believe she lost
a word of it, though she said nothing about it that
I heard until the next Saturday, when two of us, as was
the custom, were riding out with her in her carriage,
and we went to see a poor bed-ridden woman, who
lived some miles away at the other end of the estate
and of the parish : and as we came out of the cottage
we met Mr. Gray walking up to it, in a great heat,
and looking very tired. My lady beckoned him to her,
and told him she should wait and take him home with
her, adding that she wondered to see him there, so far
from his home, for that it was beyond a Sabbath-day's
journey, and, from what she had gathered from his
sermon the last Sunday, he was all for Judaism against
Christianity. He looked as if he did not understand
what she meant ; but the truth was that, besides the
way in which he had spoken up for schools and schooling, he had kept calling Sunday the Sabbath : and, as
her ladyship said, 'The Sabbath is the Sabbath, and
that 's one thing—it is Saturday ; and if I keep it,

I'm a Jew, which I'm not. And Sunday is Sunday;
and that's another thing; and if I keep it, I'm a
Christian, which I humbly trust I am.'

But when Mr. Gray got an inkling of her meaning
in talking about a Sabbath-day's journey, he only took
notice of a part of it: he smiled and bowed, and said
no one knew better than her ladyship what were the
duties that abrogated all inferior laws regarding the
Sabbath; and that he must go in and read to old
Betty Brown, so that he would not detain her ladyship.

'But I shall wait for you, Mr. Gray,' said she. 'Or
I will take a drive round by Oakfield, and be back in
an hour's time.' For, you see, she would not have
him feel hurried or troubled with a thought that he
was keeping her waiting, while he ought to be comforting and praying with old Betty.

'A very pretty young man, my dears,' said she, as
we drove away. 'But I shall have my pew glazed all
the same.'

We did not know what she meant at the time; but
the next Sunday but one we did. She had the curtains
all round the grand old Hanbury family seat taken
down, and, instead of them, there was glass up to the
height of six or seven feet. We entered by a door,
with a window in it that drew up or down just like
what you see in carriages. This window was generally
down, and then we could hear perfectly; but if Mr.
Gray used the word 'Sabbath,' or spoke in favour of
schooling and education, my lady stepped out of her
corner, and drew up the window with a decided clang
and clash.

I must tell you something more about Mr. Gray.
The presentation to the living of Hanbury was vested
in two trustees, of whom Lady Ludlow was one: Lord
Ludlow had exercised this right in the appointment of
Mr. Mountford, who had won his lordship's favour by
his excellent horsemanship. Nor was Mr. Mountford
a bad clergyman, as clergymen went in those days.
He did not drink, though he liked good eating as much

as any one. And if any poor person was ill, and he heard of it, he would send them plates from his own dinner of what he himself liked best; sometimes of dishes which were almost as bad as poison to sick people. He meant kindly to everybody except dissenters, whom Lady Ludlow and he united in trying to drive out of the parish; and among dissenters he particularly abhorred Methodists—some one said, because John Wesley* had objected to his hunting. But that must have been long ago, for when I knew him he was far too stout and too heavy to hunt; besides, the bishop of the diocese disapproved of hunting, and had intimated his disapprobation to the clergy. For my own part, I think a good run would not have come amiss, even in a moral point of view, to Mr. Mountford. He ate so much, and took so little exercise, that we young women often heard of his being in terrible passions with his servants, and the sexton and clerk. But they none of them minded him much, for he soon came to himself, and was sure to make them some present or other—some said in proportion to his anger; so that the sexton, who was a bit of a wag (as all sextons are, I think), said that the vicar's saying, ' the Devil take you,' was worth a shilling any day, whereas ' the Deuce ' was a shabby sixpenny speech, only fit for a curate.

There was a great deal of good in Mr. Mountford, too. He could not bear to see pain, or sorrow, or misery of any kind; and, if it came under his notice, he was never easy till he had relieved it, for the time, at any rate. But he was afraid of being made uncomfortable; so, if he possibly could, he would avoid seeing any one who was ill or unhappy; and he did not thank any one for telling him about them.

' What would your ladyship have me to do ? ' he once said to my Lady Ludlow, when she wished him to go and see a poor man who had broken his leg. ' I cannot piece the leg as the doctor can; I cannot nurse him as well as his wife does; I may talk to him, but he no more understands me than I do the language of the alchemists. My coming puts him out ; he stiffens himself into an uncomfortable posture, out of respect to the cloth, and dare not take the comfort of kicking, and swearing, and scolding his wife, while I am there. I hear him, with my figurative ears, my lady, heave a sigh of relief when my back is turned, and the sermon that he thinks I ought to have kept for the pulpit, and have delivered to his neighbours (whose case, as he fancies, it would just have fitted, as it seemed to him to be addressed to the sinful), is all ended, and done for the day. I judge others as myself ; I do to them as I would be done to. That's Christianity, at any rate. I should hate—saving your ladyship's presence—to have my Lord Ludlow coming and seeing me, if I were ill. 'Twould be a great honour, no doubt ; but I should have to put on a clean nightcap for the occasion ; and sham patience, in order to be polite, and not weary his lordship with my complaints. I should be twice as thankful to him if he would send me game, or a good fat haunch, to bring me up to that pitch of health and strength one ought to be in, to appreciate the honour of a visit from a nobleman. So I shall send Jerry Butler a good dinner every day till he is strong again ; and spare the poor old fellow my presence and advice.'

My lady would be puzzled by this, and by many other of Mr. Mountford's speeches. But he had been appointed by my lord, and she could not question her dead husband's wisdom ; and she knew that the dinners were always sent, and often a guinea or two to help to pay the doctor's bills ; and Mr. Mountford was true blue, as we call it, to the backbone ; hated the dissenters and the French ; and could hardly drink a dish of tea without giving out the toast of 'Church and King, and down with the Rump.'* Moreover, he had once had the honour of preaching before the King and Queen, and two of the Princesses, at Weymouth ; and the King had applauded his sermon audibly with, —'Very good ; very good ; ' and that was a seal put upon his merit in my lady's eyes.

Besides, in the long winter Sunday evenings, he would come up to the Court, and read a sermon to us girls, and play a game of picquet with my lady afterwards ; which served to shorten the tedium of the time. My lady would, on those occasions, invite him to sup with her on the dais ; but as her meal was invariably bread and milk only, Mr. Mountford preferred sitting down amongst us, and made a joke about its being wicked and heterodox to eat meagre on Sunday, a festival of the Church. We smiled at this joke just as much the twentieth time we heard it as we did at the first ; for we knew it was coming, because he always coughed a little nervously before he made a joke, for fear my lady should not approve : and neither she nor he seemed to remember that he had ever hit upon the idea before.

Mr. Mountford died quite suddenly at last. We were all very sorry to lose him. He left some of his property (for he had a private estate) to the poor of the parish, to furnish them with an annual Christmas dinner of roast-beef and plum-pudding, for which he wrote out a very good receipt in the codicil to his will.

Moreover, he desired his executors to see that the vault, in which the vicars of Hanbury were interred, was well aired, before his coffin was taken in ; for, all his life long, he had had a dread of damp, and latterly he kept his rooms to such a pitch of warmth that some thought it hastened his end.

Then the other trustee, as I have said, presented the living to Mr. Gray, Fellow of Lincoln College, Oxford. It was quite natural for us all, as belonging in some sort to the Hanbury family, to disapprove of the other trustee's choice. But when some ill-natured person circulated the report that Mr. Gray was a Moravian Methodist,* I remember my lady said, ' She could not believe anything so bad, without a great deal of evidence.'

## CHAPTER II

BEFORE I tell you about Mr. Gray, I think I ought
to make you understand something more of what we
did all day long at Hanbury Court. There were five
of us at the time of which I am speaking, all young
women of good descent, and allied (however distantly)
to people of rank. When we were not with my lady,
Mrs. Medlicott looked after us ; a gentle little woman,
who had been companion to my lady for many years,
and was indeed, I have been told, some kind of relation
to her. Mrs. Medlicott's parents had lived in Germany,
and the consequence was, she spoke English with a very
foreign accent. Another consequence was, that she
excelled in all manner of needlework, such as is not
known even by name in these days. She could darn
either lace, table-linen, India muslin, or stockings, so
that no one could tell where the hole or rent had been.
Though a good Protestant, and never missing Guy
Faux' day*at church, she was as skilful at fine work as
any nun in a Papist convent. She would take a piece
of French cambric, and by drawing out some threads,
and working in others, it became delicate lace in a very
few hours. She did the same by Hollands cloth, and
made coarse strong lace, with which all my lady's
napkins and table-linen were trimmed. We worked
under her during a great part of the day, either in the
still-room, or at our sewing in a chamber that opened
out of the great hall. My lady despised every kind of
work that would now be called Fancy-work. She considered that the use of coloured threads or worsted
was only fit to amuse children ; but that grown women
ought not to be taken with mere blues and reds, but
to restrict their pleasure in sewing to making small and
delicate stitches. She would speak of the old tapestry
in the hall as the work of her ancestresses, who lived
before the Reformation, and were consequently unacquainted with pure and simple tastes in work, as
well as in religion. Nor would my lady sanction the

fashion of the day, which, at the beginning of this
century, made all the fine ladies take to making shoes.
She said that such work was a consequence of the
French Revolution, which had done much to annihilate
all distinctions of rank and class, and hence it was,
that she saw young ladies of birth and breeding
handling lasts, and awls, and dirty cobblers'-wax, like
shoemakers' daughters.

Very frequently one of us would be summoned to
my lady to read aloud to her, as she sat in her
small withdrawing-room, some improving book. It
was generally Mr. Addison's 'Spectator';*but one year,
I remember, we had to read 'Sturm's Reflections',*
translated from a German book Mrs. Medlicott recommended. Mr. Sturm told us what to think about for
every day in the year; and very dull it was. But
I believe Queen Charlotte had liked the book very
much, and the thought of her royal approbation kept
my lady awake during the reading. 'Mrs. Chapone's
Letters' and 'Dr. Gregory's Advice to Young Ladies'
composed the rest of our library for week-day reading.
I, for one, was glad to leave my fine sewing, and even
my reading aloud (though this last did keep me with
my dear lady), to go to the still-room and potter about
among the preserves and the medicated waters. There
was no doctor for many miles round, and with Mrs.
Medlicott to direct us, and Dr. Buchan to go by for
recipes, we sent out many a bottle of physic, which,
I dare say, was as good as what comes out of the
druggist's shop. At any rate, I do not think we did
much harm; for if any of our physics tasted stronger
than usual, Mrs. Medlicott would bid us let it down
with cochineal and water, to make all safe, as she said.
So our bottles of medicine had very little real physic
in them at last; but we were careful in putting labels
on them, which looked very mysterious to those who
could not read, and helped the medicine to do its work.
I have sent off many a bottle of salt-and-water coloured
red; and whenever we had nothing else to do in the
still-room, Mrs. Medlicott would set us to making bread-

pills by way of practice, and, as far as I can say, they were very efficacious, as before we gave out a box Mrs. Medlicott always told the patient what symptoms to expect ; and I hardly ever inquired without hearing that they had produced their effect. There was one old man, who took six pills a-night, of any kind we liked to give him, to make him sleep ; and if, by any chance, his daughter had forgotten to let us know that he was out of his medicine, he was so restless and miserable that, as he said, he thought he was like to die. I think ours was what would be called homœopathic practice now-a-days. Then we learnt to make all the cakes and dishes of the season in the still-room. We had plum-porridge and mince-pies at Christmas, fritters and pancakes on Shrove Tuesday, furmenty on Mothering Sunday, violet-cakes in Passion Week, tansy-pudding on Easter Sunday, three-cornered cakes on Trinity Sunday, and so on through the year : all made from good old Church receipts, handed down from one of my lady's earliest Protestant ancestresses. Every one of us passed a portion of the day with Lady Ludlow ; and now and then we rode out with her in her coach-and-four. She did not like to go out with a pair of horses, considering this rather beneath her rank ; and, indeed, four horses were very often needed to pull her heavy coach through the stiff mud. But it was rather a cumbersome equipage through the narrow Warwickshire lanes ; and I used often to think it was well that countesses were not plentiful, or else we might have met another lady of quality in another coach-and-four where there would have been no possibility of turning, or passing each other, and very little chance of backing. Once when the idea of this danger of meeting another countess in a narrow deep-rutted lane was very prominent in my mind, I ventured to ask Mrs. Medlicott what would have to be done on such an occasion ; and she told me that ' de latest creation must back, for sure,' which puzzled me a good deal at the time, although I understand it now. I began to find out the use of the ' Peerage,' a book which had

seemed to me rather dull before ; but, as I was always
a coward in a coach, I made myself well acquainted
with the dates of creation of our three Warwickshire
earls, and was happy to find that Earl Ludlow ranked
second, the oldest earl being a hunting widower, and
not likely to drive out in a carriage.

All this time I have wandered from Mr. Gray. Of
course, we first saw him in church when he read himself in. He was very red-faced, the kind of redness
which goes with light hair, and a blushing complexion ;
he looked slight and short, and his bright light frizzy
hair had hardly a dash of powder in it. I remember
my lady making this observation, and sighing over it ;
for, though since the famine in seventeen hundred and
ninety-nine and eighteen hundred, there had been a
tax on hair-powder, yet it was reckoned very revolutionary and Jacobin not to wear a good deal of it.
My lady hardly liked the opinions of any man who
wore his own hair ; but this she would say was rather
a prejudice : only in her youth none but the mob had
gone wigless, and she could not get over the association
of wigs with birth and breeding ; a man's own hair
with that class of people who had formed the rioters
in seventeen hundred and eighty, when Lord George
Gordon* had been one of the bugbears of my lady's
life. Her husband and his brothers, she told us, had
been put into breeches, and had their heads shaved
on their seventh birthday, each of them ; a handsome
little wig of the newest fashion forming the old Lady
Ludlow's invariable birthday present to her sons as
they each arrived at that age ; and afterwards, to the
day of their death, they never saw their own hair. To
be without powder, as some underbred people were
talking of being now, was in fact to insult the pro-
prieties of life, by being undressed. It was English
sans-culottism.* But Mr. Gray did wear a little powder,
enough to save him in my lady's good opinion ; but
not enough to make her approve of him decidedly.

The next time I saw him was in the great hall.
Mary Mason and I were going to drive out with my

lady in her coach, and when we went downstairs with
our best hats and cloaks on, we found Mr. Gray
awaiting my lady's coming. I believe he had paid his
respects to her before, but we had never seen him;
and he had declined her invitation to spend Sunday
evening at the Court (as Mr. Mountford used to do
pretty regularly,—and play a game of picquet too—),
which, Mrs. Medlicott told us, had caused my lady to
be not over well pleased with him.

He blushed redder than ever at the sight of us, as
we entered the hall, and dropped him our curtsies.
He coughed two or three times, as if he would have
liked to speak to us, if he could but have found something to say; and every time he coughed, he became
hotter-looking than ever. I am ashamed to say, we
were nearly laughing at him; half because we, too, were
so shy that we understood what his awkwardness meant.

My lady came in, with her quick active step—she
always walked quickly when she did not bethink herself of her cane,—as if she were sorry to have kept us
waiting,—and, as she entered, she gave us all round
one of those graceful sweeping curtsies, of which I
think the art must have died out with her,—it implied
so much courtesy;—this time it said, as well as words
could do, ' I am sorry to have kept you all waiting,—
forgive me.'

She went up to the mantelpiece, near which Mr. Gray
had been standing until her entrance, and curtsying
afresh to him, and pretty deeply this time, because of
his cloth, and her being hostess, and he, a new guest.
She asked him if he would not prefer speaking to her
in her own private parlour, and looked as though she
would have conducted him there. But he burst out
with his errand, of which he was full even to choking,
and which sent the glistening tears into his large blue
eyes, which stood farther and farther out with his
excitement.

' My lady, I want to speak to you, and to persuade
you to exert your kind interest with Mr. Lathom—
Justice Lathom of Hathaway Manor '—

'Harry Lathom?' inquired my lady,—as Mr. Gray stopped to take the breath he had lost in his hurry,— 'I did not know he was in the commission.'

'He is only just appointed; he took the oaths not a month ago,—more's the pity!'

'I do not understand why you should regret it. The Lathoms have held Hathaway since Edward the First, and Mr. Lathom bears a good character, although his temper is hasty—'

'My lady! he has committed Job Gregson for stealing—a fault of which he is as innocent as I—and all the evidence goes to prove it, now that the case is brought before the Bench; only the Squires hang so together that they can't be brought to see justice, and are all for sending Job to gaol, out of compliment to Mr. Lathom, saying it is his first committal, and it won't be civil to tell him there is no evidence against his man. For God's sake, my lady, speak to the gentlemen; they will attend to you, while they only tell me to mind my own business.'

Now my lady was always inclined to stand by her order, and the Lathoms of Hathaway Court were cousins to the Hanburys. Besides, it was rather a point of honour in those days to encourage a young magistrate, by passing a pretty sharp sentence on his first committals; and Job Gregson was the father of a girl who had been lately turned away from her place as scullery-maid for sauciness to Mrs. Adams, her ladyship's own maid; and Mr. Gray had not said a word of the reasons why he believed the man innocent,— for he was in such a hurry, I believe he would have had my lady drive off to the Henley Court-house then and there;—so there seemed a good deal against the man, and nothing but Mr. Gray's bare word for him; and my lady drew herself a little up, and said:

'Mr. Gray! I do not see what reason either you or I have to interfere. Mr. Harry Lathom is a sensible kind of young man, well capable of ascertaining the truth without our help—'

'But more evidence has come out since,' broke in Mr. Gray.

My lady went a little stiffer, and spoke a little more coldly :

'I suppose this additional evidence is before the justices ; men of good family, and of honour and credit, well known in the county. They naturally feel that the opinion of one of themselves must have more weight than the words of a man like Job Gregson, who bears a very indifferent character,—has been strongly suspected of poaching, coming from no one knows where, squatting on Hareman's Common—which, by the way, is extra-parochial, I believe ; consequently you, as a clergyman, are not responsible for what goes on there ; and, although impolitic, there might be some truth in what the magistrates said, in advising you to mind your own business,'—said her ladyship, smiling,—' and they might be tempted to bid me mind mine, if I interfered, Mr. Gray ; might they not ? '

He looked extremely uncomfortable, half angry. Once or twice he began to speak, but checked himself, as if his words would not have been wise or prudent. At last he said :

'It may seem presumptuous in me,—a stranger of only a few weeks' standing—to set up my judgement as to men's character against that of residents'—' Lady Ludlow gave a little bow of acquiescence, which was, I think, involuntary on her part, and which I don't think he perceived,—' but I am convinced that the man is innocent of this offence,—and besides, the justices themselves allege this ridiculous custom of paying a compliment to a newly-appointed magistrate as their only reason.'

That unlucky word ' ridiculous ! ' It undid all the good his modest beginning had done him with my lady. I knew, as well as words could have told me, that she was affronted at the expression being used by a man inferior in rank to those whose actions he applied it to,—and, truly, it was a great want of tact, considering to whom he was speaking.

Lady Ludlow spoke very gently and slowly; she always did so when she was annoyed; it was a certain sign, the meaning of which we had all learnt.

'I think, Mr. Gray, we will drop the subject. It is one on which we are not likely to agree.'

Mr. Gray's ruddy colour grew purple, and then faded away, and his face became pale. I think both my lady and he had forgotten our presence; and we were beginning to feel too awkward to wish to remind them of it. And yet we could not help watching and listening with the greatest interest.

Mr. Gray drew himself up to his full height, with an unconscious feeling of dignity. Little as was his stature, and awkward and embarrassed as he had been only a few minutes before, I remember thinking he looked almost as grand as my lady when he spoke.

'Your ladyship must remember that it may be my duty to speak to my parishioners on many subjects on which they do not agree with me. I am not at liberty to be silent, because they differ in opinion from me.'

Lady Ludlow's great blue eyes dilated with surprise, and—I do think—anger, at being thus spoken to. I am not sure whether it was very wise in Mr. Gray. He himself looked afraid of the consequences, but as if he was determined to bear them without flinching. For a minute there was silence. Then my lady replied:

'Mr. Gray, I respect your plain speaking, although I may wonder whether a young man of your age and position has any right to assume that he is a better judge than one with the experience which I have naturally gained at my time of life, and in the station I hold.'

'If I, madam, as the clergyman of this parish, am not to shrink from telling what I believe to be the truth to the poor and lowly, no more am I to hold my peace in the presence of the rich and titled.'

Mr. Gray's face showed that he was in that state of excitement which in a child would have ended in a good fit of crying. He looked as if he had nerved himself up to doing and saying things, which he disliked above everything, and which nothing short of serious duty

could have compelled him to do and say. And at such
times every minute circumstance which could add to
pain comes vividly before one. I saw that he became
aware of our presence, and that it added to his discomfiture.

My lady flushed up. ' Are you aware, sir,' asked
she, ' that you have gone far astray from the original
subject of conversation ? But as you talk of your
parish, allow me to remind you that Hareman's Common is beyond the bounds, and that you are really not
responsible for the characters and lives of the squatters
on that unlucky piece of ground.'

' Madam, I see I have only done harm in speaking
to you about the affair at all. I beg your pardon, and
take my leave.'

He bowed, and looked very sad. Lady Ludlow
caught the expression of his face.

' Good morning ! ' she cried, in rather a louder and
quicker way than that in which she had been speaking.
' Remember Job Gregson is a notorious poacher and
evildoer, and you really are not responsible for what
goes on at Hareman's Common.'

He was near the hall-door, and said something—
half to himself, which we heard (being nearer to him),
but my lady did not ; although she saw that he spoke.
' What did he say ? ' she asked, in a somewhat hurried
manner, as soon as the door was closed—' I did not
hear.' We looked at each other, and then I spoke :

' He said, my lady, that " God help him ! he was
responsible for all the evil he did not strive to overcome." '

My lady turned sharp round away from us, and
Mary Mason said afterwards she thought her ladyship
was much vexed with both of us, for having been
present, and with me for having repeated what Mr. Gray
had said. But it was not our fault that we were in the
hall, and when my lady asked what Mr. Gray had said,
I thought it right to tell her.

In a few minutes she bade us accompany her in her
ride in the coach.

Lady Ludlow always sat forwards by herself, and we girls backwards. Somehow this was a rule, which we never thought of questioning. It was true that riding backwards made some of us feel very uncomfortable and faint ; and to remedy this my lady always drove with both windows open, which occasionally gave her the rheumatism ; but we always went on in the old way. This day she did not pay any great attention to the road by which we were going, and Coachman took his own way. We were very silent, as my lady did not speak, and looked very serious. Or else, in general, she made these rides very pleasant (to those who were not qualmish with riding backwards), by talking to us in a very agreeable manner, and telling us of the different things which had happened to her at various places,—at Paris and Versailles, where she had been in her youth,—at Windsor and Kew and Weymouth, where she had been with the Queen, when maid-of-honour—and so on. But this day she did not talk at all. All at once she put her head out of the window.

' John Footman,' said she, ' where are we ? Surely this is Hareman's Common.'

' Yes, an't please my lady,' said John Footman, and waited for further speech or orders. My lady thought awhile, and then said she would have the steps put down and get out.

As soon as she was gone, we looked at each other, and then without a word began to gaze after her. We saw her pick her dainty way, in the little high-heeled shoes she always wore (because they had been in fashion in her youth), among the yellow pools of stagnant water that had gathered in the clayey soil. John Footman followed, stately, after ; afraid too, for all his stateliness, of splashing his pure white stockings. Suddenly my lady turned round, and said something to him, and he returned to the carriage with a half-pleased, half-puzzled air.

My lady went on to a cluster of rude mud houses at the higher end of the Common ; cottages built, as they were occasionally at that day, of wattles and clay, and

thatched with sods. As far as we could make out from
dumb show, Lady Ludlow saw enough of the interiors
of these places to make her hesitate before entering
or even speaking to any of the children who were
playing about in the puddles. After a pause, she
disappeared into one of the cottages. It seemed to us
a long time before she came out; but I dare say it
was not more than eight or ten minutes. She came
back with her head hanging down, as if to choose
her way,—but we saw it was more in thought and
bewilderment than for any such purpose.

She had not made up her mind where we should
drive to when she got into the carriage again. John
Footman stood, bare-headed, waiting for orders.

'To Hathaway. My dears, if you are tired, or if
you have anything to do for Mrs. Medlicott, I can
drop you at Barford Corner, and it is but a quarter
of an hour's brisk walk home.'

But luckily we could safely say that Mrs. Medlicott
did not want us; and as we had whispered to each
other, as we sat alone in the coach, that surely my
lady must have gone to Job Gregson's, we were far
too anxious to know the end of it all to say that we
were tired. So we all set off to Hathaway. Mr. Harry
Lathom was a bachelor squire, thirty or thirty-five
years of age, more at home in the field than in the
drawing-room, and with sporting men than with ladies.

My lady did not alight, of course; it was Mr.
Lathom's place to wait upon her, and she bade the
butler,—who had a smack of the gamekeeper in him,
very unlike our own powdered venerable fine gentleman
at Hanbury,—tell his master, with her compliments,
that she wished to speak to him. You may think how
pleased we were to find that we should hear all that
was said; though, I think, afterwards we were half
sorry when we saw how our presence confused the
squire, who would have found it bad enough to answer
my lady's questions, even without two eager girls for
audience.

'Pray, Mr. Lathom,' began my lady, something

abruptly for her,—but she was very full of her subject,
—' what is this I hear about Job Gregson ? '

Mr. Lathom looked annoyed and vexed, but dared
not show it in his words.

' I gave out a warrant against him, my lady, for
theft, that is all. You are doubtless aware of his
character ; a man who sets nets and springes in long
cover, and fishes wherever he takes a fancy. It is but
a short step from poaching to thieving.'

' That is quite true,' replied Lady Ludlow (who had
a horror of poaching for this very reason) : ' but I
imagine you do not send a man to gaol on account of
his bad character.'

Rogues and vagabonds,' said Mr. Lathom. ' A man
may be sent to prison for being a vagabond ; for no
specific act, but for his general mode of life.'

He had the better of her ladyship for one moment ;
but then she answered :

' But in this case, the charge on which you committed him was theft ; now his wife tells me he can
prove he was some miles distant from Holmwood,
where the robbery took place, all that afternoon ; she
says you had the evidence before you.'

Mr. Lathom here interrupted my lady, by saying, in
a somewhat sulky manner,—

' No such evidence was brought before me when I
gave the warrant. I am not answerable for the other
magistrates' decision, when they had more evidence
before them. It was they who committed him to gaol.
I am not responsible for that.'

My lady did not often show signs of impatience ;
but we knew she was feeling irritated by the little
perpetual tapping of her high-heeled shoe against the
bottom of the carriage. About the same time we,
sitting backwards, caught a glimpse of Mr. Gray
through the open door, standing in the shadow of the
hall. Doubtless Lady Ludlow's arrival had interrupted
a conversation between Mr. Lathom and Mr. Gray.
The latter must have heard every word of what she
was saying ; but of this she was not aware, and caught

at Mr. Lathom's disclaimer of responsibility with pretty much the same argument which she had heard (through our repetition) that Mr. Gray had used not two hours before.

'And do you mean to say, Mr. Lathom, that you don't consider yourself responsible for all injustice or wrong-doing that you might have prevented, and have not ? Nay, in this case the first germ of injustice was your own mistake. I wish you had been with me a little while ago, and seen the misery in that poor fellow's cottage.' She spoke lower, and Mr. Gray drew near, in a sort of involuntary manner ; as if to hear all she was saying. We saw him, and doubtless Mr. Lathom heard his footstep, and knew who it was that was listening behind him, and approving of every word that was said. He grew yet more sullen in manner ; but still my lady was my lady, and he dared not speak out before her, as he would have done to Mr. Gray. Lady Ludlow, however, caught the look of stubbornness in his face, and it roused her as I had never seen her roused.

'I am sure you will not refuse, sir, to accept my bail. I offer to bail the fellow out, and to be responsible for his appearance at the sessions. What say you to that, Mr. Lathom ?'

'The offence of theft is not bailable, my lady.'

'Not in ordinary cases, I dare say. But I imagine this is an extraordinary case. The man is sent to prison out of compliment to you, and against all evidence, as far as I can learn. He will have to rot in gaol for two months, and his wife and children to starve. I, Lady Ludlow, offer to bail him out, and pledge myself for his appearance at next quarter-sessions.'

'It is against the law, my lady.'

'Bah ! Bah ! Bah ! Who makes laws ? Such as I, in the House of Lords—such as you, in the House of Commons. We, who make the laws in St. Stephen's,* may break the mere forms of them, when we have right on our sides, on our own land, and amongst our own people.'

'The lord-lieutenant may take away my commission, if he heard of it.'

'And a very good thing for the county, Harry Lathom; and for you too, if he did,—if you don't go on more wisely than you have begun. A pretty set you and your brother magistrates are to administer justice through the land! I always said a good despotism was the best form of government; and I am twice as much in favour of it now I see what a quorum is! My dears!' suddenly turning round to us, 'if it would not tire you to walk home, I would beg Mr. Lathom to take a seat in my coach, and we would drive to Henley Gaol, and have the poor man out at once.

'A walk over the fields at this time of day is hardly fitting for young ladies to take alone,' said Mr. Lathom, anxious no doubt to escape from his tête-à-tête drive with my lady, and possibly not quite prepared to go to the illegal length of prompt measures, which she had in contemplation.

But Mr. Gray now stepped forward, too anxious for the release of the prisoner to allow any obstacle to intervene which he could do away with. To see Lady Ludlow's face when she first perceived whom she had had for auditor and spectator of her interview with Mr. Lathom, was as good as a play. She had been doing and saying the very things she had been so much annoyed at Mr. Gray's saying and proposing only an hour or two ago. She had been setting down Mr. Lathom pretty smartly, in the presence of the very man to whom she had spoken of that gentleman as so sensible, and of such a standing in the county, that it was presumption to question his doings. But before Mr. Gray had finished his offer of escorting us back to Hanbury Court, my lady had recovered herself. There was neither surprise nor displeasure in her manner, as she answered:

'I thank you, Mr. Gray. I was not aware that you were here, but I think I can understand on what errand you came. And seeing you here, recalls me

to a duty I owe Mr. Lathom. Mr. Lathom, I have
spoken to you pretty plainly,—forgetting, until I saw
Mr. Gray, that only this very afternoon I differed from
him on this very question ; taking completely, at that
time, the same view of the whole subject which you
have done ; thinking that the county would be well
rid of such a man as Job Gregson, whether he had
committed this theft or not. Mr. Gray and I did not
part quite friends,' she continued, bowing towards
him ; ' but it so happened that I saw Job Gregson's
wife and home,—I felt that Mr. Gray had been right
and I had been wrong, so, with the famous incon-
sistency of my sex, I came hither to scold you,' smiling
towards Mr. Lathom, who looked half-sulky yet, and
did not relax a bit of his gravity at her smile, ' for
holding the same opinions that I had done an hour
before. Mr. Gray,' (again bowing towards him) ' these
young ladies will be very much obliged to you for your
escort, and so shall I. Mr. Lathom, may I beg of you
to accompany me to Henley ? '

Mr. Gray bowed very low, and went very red ;
Mr. Lathom said something which we none of us heard,
but which was, I think, some remonstrance against the
course he was, as it were, compelled to take. Lady
Ludlow, however, took no notice of his murmur, but
sat in an attitude of polite expectancy ; and as we
turned off on our walk, I saw Mr. Lathom getting into
the coach with the air of a whipped hound. I must
say, considering my lady's feeling, I did not envy him
his ride,—though, I believe, he was quite in the right
as to the object of the ride being illegal.

Our walk home was very dull. We had no fears ;
and would far rather have been without the awkward,
blushing young man, into which Mr. Gray had sunk.
At every stile he hesitated,—sometimes he half got
over it, thinking that he could assist us better in that
way ; then he would turn back, unwilling to go before
ladies. He had no ease of manner, as my lady once
said of him, though on any occasion of duty, he had
an immense deal of dignity.

## CHAPTER III

As far as I can remember, it was very soon after this that I first began to have the pain in my hip, which has ended in making me a cripple for life. I hardly recollect more than one walk after our return under Mr. Gray's escort from Mr. Lathom's. Indeed, at the time, I was not without suspicions (which I never named) that the beginning of all the mischief was a great jump I had taken from the top of one of the stiles on that very occasion.

Well, it is a long while ago, and God disposes of us all, and I am not going to tire you out with telling you how I thought and felt, and how, when I saw what my life was to be, I could hardly bring myself to be patient, but rather wished to die at once. You can every one of you think for yourselves what becoming all at once useless and unable to move, and by-and-by growing hopeless of cure, and feeling that one must be a burden to some one all one's life long, would be to an active, wilful, strong girl of seventeen, anxious to get on in the world, so as, if possible, to help her brothers and sisters. So I shall only say, that one among the blessings which arose out of what seemed at the time a great, black sorrow was, that Lady Ludlow for many years took me, as it were, into her own especial charge ; and now, as I lie still and alone in my old age, it is such a pleasure to think of her !

Mrs. Medlicott was great as a nurse, and I am sure I can never be grateful enough to her memory for all her kindness. But she was puzzled to know how to manage me in other ways. I used to have long, hard fits of crying ; and, thinking that I ought to go home— and yet what could they do with me there ?—and a hundred and fifty other anxious thoughts, some of which I could tell to Mrs. Medlicott, and others I could not. Her way of comforting me was hurrying away for some kind of tempting or strengthening food—a

basin of melted calves'-foot jelly was, I am sure she
thought, a cure for every woe.

'There! take it, dear, take it!' she would say;
'and don't go on fretting for what can't be helped.'

But, I think, she got puzzled at length at the non-
efficacy of good things to eat; and one day, after I had
limped down to see the doctor, in Mrs. Medlicott's
sitting room—a room lined with cupboards, containing
preserves and dainties of all kinds, which she perpetually made, and never touched herself—when I was
returning to my bed-room to cry away the afternoon,
under pretence of arranging my clothes, John Footman
brought me a message from my lady (with whom the
doctor had been having a conversation) to bid me go
to her in that private sitting-room at the end of the
suite of apartments, about which I spoke in describing
the day of my first arrival at Hanbury. I had hardly
been in it since; as, when we read to my lady, she
generally sat in the small withdrawing-room out of
which this private room of hers opened. I suppose
great people do not require what we smaller people
value so much,—I mean privacy. I do not think that
there was a room which my lady occupied that had not
two doors, and some of them had three or four. Then
my lady had always Adams waiting upon her in her
bed-chamber; and it was Mrs. Medlicott's duty to sit
within call, as it were, in a sort of anteroom that led
out of my lady's own sitting-room, on the opposite side
to the drawing-room door. To fancy the house, you
must take a great square, and halve it by a line; at
one end of this line was the hall-door, or public-
entrance; at the opposite the private entrance from
a terrace, which was terminated at one end by a sort
of postern door in an old gray stone wall, beyond which
lay the farm buildings and offices; so that people could
come in this way to my lady on business, while, if she
were going into the garden from her own room, she had
nothing to do but to pass through Mrs. Medlicott's
apartment, out into the lesser hall, and then turning
to the right as she passed on to the terrace, she could

go down the flight of broad, shallow steps at the corner
of the house into the lovely garden, with stretching,
sweeping lawns, and gay flower-beds, and beautiful,
bossy laurels, and other blooming or massy shrubs,
with full-grown beeches, or larches feathering down to
the ground a little farther off. The whole was set in
a frame, as it were, by the more distant woodlands.
The house had been modernized in the days of Queen
Anne, I think ; but the money had fallen short that
was requisite to carry out all the improvements, so
it was only the suite of withdrawing-rooms and the
terrace-rooms, as far as the private entrance, that had
the new, long, high windows put in, and these were
old enough by this time to be draped with roses, and
honeysuckles, and pyracanthus, winter and summer
long.

Well, to go back to that day when I limped into my
lady's sitting-room, trying hard to look as if I had not
been crying, and not to walk as if I was in much pain.
I do not know whether my lady saw how near my
tears were to my eyes, but she told me she had sent
for me, because she wanted some help in arranging the
drawers of her bureau, and asked me—just as if it
was a favour I was to do her—if I could sit down in
the easy chair near the window—(all quietly arranged
before I came in, with a footstool, and a table quite
near)—and assist her. You will wonder, perhaps, why
I was not bidden to sit or lie on the sofa ; but (although
I found one there a morning or two afterwards, when
I came down) the fact was, that there was none in
the room at this time. I have even fancied that the
easy-chair was brought in on purpose for me, for it
was not the chair in which I remembered my lady
sitting the first time I saw her. That chair was very
much carved and gilded, with a countess's coronet at
the top. I tried it one day, some time afterwards,
when my lady was out of the room, and I had a fancy
for seeing how I could move about, and very uncomfortable it was. Now my chair (as I learnt to call it,
and to think it) was soft and luxurious, and seemed

somehow to give one's body rest just in that part where one most needed it.

I was not at my ease that first day, nor indeed for many days afterwards, notwithstanding my chair was so comfortable. Yet I forgot my sad pain in silently wondering over the meaning of many of the things we turned out of those curious old drawers. I was puzzled to know why some were kept at all; a scrap of writing maybe, with only half-a-dozen commonplace words written on it, or a bit of broken riding-whip, and here and there a stone, of which I thought I could have picked up twenty just as good in the first walk I took. But it seems that was just my ignorance; for my lady told me they were pieces of valuable marble, used to make the floors of the great Roman emperors' palaces long ago; and that when she had been a girl, and made the grand tour long ago, her cousin, Sir Horace Mann, the Ambassador or Envoy at Florence, had told her to be sure to go into the fields inside the walls of ancient Rome, when the farmers were preparing the ground for the onion-sowing, and had to make the soil fine, and pick up what bits of marble she could find. She had done so, and meant to have had them made into a table; but somehow that plan fell through, and there they were with all the dirt out of the onion-field upon them; but once when I thought of cleaning them with soap and water, at any rate, she bade me not to do so, for it was Roman dirt—earth, I think, she called it—but it was dirt all the same.

Then, in this bureau, were many other things, the value of which I could understand—locks of hair carefully ticketed, which my lady looked at very sadly; and lockets and bracelets with miniatures in them,— very small pictures to what they make now-a-days, and call miniatures; some of them had even to be looked at through a microscope before you could see the individual expression of the faces, or how beautifully they were painted. I don't think that looking at these made my lady seem so melancholy, as the seeing and touching of the hair did. But, to be sure, the hair was, as it were, a part of some beloved body which she might never touch and caress again, but which lay beneath the turf, all faded and disfigured, except perhaps the very hair, from which the lock she held had been dissevered ; whereas the pictures were but pictures after all—likenesses, but not the very things themselves. This is only my own conjecture, mind. My lady rarely spoke out her feelings. For, to begin with, she was of rank : and I have heard her say that people of rank do not talk about their feelings except to their equals, and even to them they conceal them, except upon rare occasions. Secondly,—and this is my own reflection,—she was an only child and an heiress ; and as such was more apt to think than to talk, as all well-brought-up heiresses must be, I think. Thirdly, she had long been a widow, without any companion of her own age with whom it would have been natural for her to refer to old associations, past pleasures, or mutual sorrows. Mrs. Medlicott came nearest to her as a companion of this sort ; and her ladyship talked more to Mrs. Medlicott, in a kind of familiar way, than she did to all the rest of the household put together. But Mrs. Medlicott was silent by nature, and did not reply at any great length. Adams, indeed, was the only one who spoke much to Lady Ludlow.

After we had worked away about an hour at the bureau, her ladyship said we had done enough for one day ; and as the time was come for her afternoon ride, she left me, with a volume of engravings from Mr. Hogarth's*pictures on one side of me (I don't like to write down the names of them, though my lady thought nothing of it, I am sure), and upon a stand her great prayer-book open at the evening-psalms for the day, on the other. But as soon as she was gone, I troubled myself little with either, but amused myself with looking round the room at my leisure. The side on which the fire-place stood, was all panelled,—part of the old ornaments of the house, for there was an Indian paper with birds and beasts and insects on it,

on all the other sides. There were coats of arms, of
the various families with whom the Hanburys had
intermarried, all over these panels, and up and down
the ceiling as well. There was very little looking-glass
in the room, though one of the great drawing-rooms
was called the 'Mirror Room,' because it was lined
with glass, which my lady's great-grandfather had
brought from Venice when he was ambassador there.
There were china jars of all shapes and sizes round
and about the room, and some china monsters, or
idols, of which I could never bear the sight, they were
so ugly, though I think my lady valued them more
than all. There was a thick carpet on the middle of
the floor, which was made of small pieces of rare wood
fitted into a pattern ; the doors were opposite to each
other, and were composed of two heavy tall wings, and
opened in the middle, moving on brass grooves inserted
into the floor—they would not have opened over a
carpet. There were two windows reaching up nearly
to the ceiling, but very narrow, and with deep window-
seats in the thickness of the wall. The room was full
of scent, partly from the flowers outside, and partly
from the great jars of pot-pourri inside. The choice of
odours was what my lady piqued herself upon, saying
nothing showed birth like a keen susceptibility of smell.
We never named musk in her presence, her antipathy
to it was so well understood through the household :
her opinion on the subject was believed to be, that no
scent derived from an animal could ever be of a sufficiently pure nature to give pleasure to any person of
good family, where, of course, the delicate perception
of the senses had been cultivated for generations. She
would instance the way in which sportsmen preserve
the breed of dogs who have shown keen scent ; and
how such gifts descend for generations amongst animals,
who cannot be supposed to have anything of ancestral
pride, or hereditary fancies about them. Musk, then,
was never mentioned at Hanbury Court. No more
were bergamot or southernwood, although vegetable
in their nature. She considered these two latter as

betraying a vulgar taste in the person who chose to gather or wear them. She was sorry to notice sprigs of them in the button-hole of any young man in whom she took an interest, either because he was engaged to a servant of hers or otherwise, as he came out of church on a Sunday afternoon. She was afraid that he liked coarse pleasures; and I am not sure if she did not think that his preference for these coarse sweetnesses did not imply a probability that he would take to drinking. But she distinguished between vulgar and common. Violets, pinks, and sweetbriar were common enough; roses and mignonette, for those who had gardens, honeysuckle for those who walked along the bowery lanes; but wearing them betrayed no vulgarity of taste: the queen upon her throne might be glad to smell at a nosegay of these flowers. A beau-pot (as we called it) of pinks and roses freshly gathered was placed every morning that they were in bloom on my lady's own particular table. For lasting vegetable odours she preferred lavender and sweet-woodroof to any extract whatever. Lavender reminded her of old customs, she said, and of homely cottage-gardens, and many a cottager made his offering to her of a bundle of lavender. Sweet woodroof, again, grew in wild, woodland places, where the soil was fine and the air delicate: the poor children used to go and gather it for her up in the woods on the higher lands; and for this service she always rewarded them with bright new pennies, of which my lord, her son, used to send her down a bagful fresh from the Mint in London every February.

Attar-of-roses, again, she disliked. She said it re-minded her of the city and of merchants' wives, over-rich, over-heavy in its perfume. And lilies-of-the-valley somehow fell under the same condemnation. They were most graceful and elegant to look at (my lady was quite candid about this), flower, leaf, colour—everything was refined about them but the smell. That was too strong. But the great hereditary faculty on which my lady piqued herself, and with reason, for I never met with any other person who possessed it,

was the power she had of perceiving the delicious odour
arising from a bed of strawberries in the late autumn,
when the leaves were all fading and dying. 'Bacon's
Essays'* was one of the few books that lay about in
my lady's room ; and if you took it up and opened it
carelessly, it was sure to fall apart at his 'Essay on
Gardens.' 'Listen,' her ladyship would say, 'to what
that great philosopher and statesman says, "Next to
that,"—he is speaking of violets, my dear,—" is the
musk-rose,"—of which you remember the great bush
at the corner of the south wall just by the Blue
Drawing-room windows ; that is the old musk-rose,
Shakespeare's musk-rose, which is dying out through
the kingdom now. But to return to my Lord Bacon :
" Then the strawberry leaves, dying with a most excellent cordial smell." Now the Hanburys can always
smell this excellent cordial odour, and very delicious
and refreshing it is. You see, in Lord Bacon's time,
there had not been so many intermarriages between
the court and the city as there have been since the
needy days of his Majesty Charles the Second ; and
altogether in the time of Queen Elizabeth, the great
old families of England were a distinct race, just as
a cart-horse is one creature, and very useful in its
place, and Childers or Eclipse* is another creature,
though both are of the same species. So the old
families have gifts and powers of a different and higher
class to what the other orders have. My dear, remember that you try if you can smell the scent of dying
strawberry-leaves in this next autumn. You have
some of Ursula Hanbury's blood in you, and that gives
you a chance.'

But when October came, I sniffed and sniffed, and
all to no purpose ; and my lady—who had watched the
little experiment rather anxiously—had to give me up
as a hybrid. I was mortified, I confess, and thought
that it was in some ostentation of her own powers that
she ordered the gardener to plant a border of strawberries on that side the terrace that lay under her
windows.

I have wandered away from time and place. I tell you all the remembrances I have of those years just as they come up, and I hope that, in my old age, I am not getting too like a certain Mrs. Nickleby,* whose speeches were once read out aloud to me.

I came by degrees to be all day long in this room which I have been describing; sometimes sitting in the easy chair, doing some little piece of dainty work for my lady, or sometimes arranging flowers, or sorting letters according to their handwriting, so that she could arrange them afterwards, and destroy or keep, as she planned, looking ever onward to her death. Then, after the sofa was brought in, she would watch my face, and if she saw my colour change, she would bid me lie down and rest. And I used to try to walk upon the terrace every day for a short time : it hurt me very much, it is true, but the doctor had ordered it, and I knew her ladyship wished me to obey.

Before I had seen the background of a great lady's life, I had thought it all play and fine doings. But whatever other grand people are, my lady was never idle. For one thing, she had to superintend the agent for the large Hanbury estate. I believe it was mort-gaged for a sum of money which had gone to improve the late lord's Scotch lands ; but she was anxious to pay off this before her death, and so to leave her own inheritance free of encumbrance to her son, the present Earl ; whom, I secretly think, she considered a greater person, as being the heir of the Hanburys (though through a female line), than as being my Lord Ludlow with half-a-dozen other minor titles.

With this wish of releasing her property from the mortgage, skilful care was much needed in the manage-ment of it : and as far as my lady could go, she took every pains. She had a great book, in which every page was ruled into three divisions ; on the first column was written the date and the name of the tenant who addressed any letter on business to her ; on the second was briefly stated the subject of the letter, which generally contained a request of some kind. This

request would be surrounded and enveloped in so many
words, and often inserted amidst so many odd reasons
and excuses, that Mr. Horner (the steward) would
sometimes say it was like hunting through a bushel of
chaff to find a grain of wheat. Now, in the second
column of this book, the grain of meaning was placed,
clean and dry, before her ladyship every morning. She
sometimes would ask to see the original letter; sometimes she simply answered the request by a 'Yes,' or
a 'No;' and often she would send for leases and
papers, and examine them well, with Mr. Horner at
her elbow, to see if such petitions, as to be allowed to
plough up pasture fields, &c., were provided for in the
terms of the original agreement. On every Thursday
she made herself at liberty to see her tenants, from
four to six in the afternoon. Mornings would have
suited my lady better, as far as convenience went, and
I believe the old custom had been to have these levées
(as her ladyship used to call them) held before twelve.
But, as she said to Mr. Horner, when he urged returning
to the former hours, it spoilt a whole day for a farmer,
if he had to dress himself in his best and leave his
work in the forenoon (and my lady liked to see her
tenants come in their Sunday-clothes; she would not
say a word, maybe, but she would take her spectacles
slowly out, and put them on with silent gravity, and
look at a dirty or raggedly-dressed man so solemnly
and earnestly, that his nerves must have been pretty
strong if he did not wince, and resolve that, however
poor he might be, soap and water, and needle and
thread should be used before he again appeared in her
ladyship's anteroom). The outlying tenants had always
a supper provided for them in the servants'-hall on
Thursdays, to which, indeed, all comers were welcome
to sit down. For my lady said, though there were not
many hours left of a working-man's day when their
business with her was ended, yet that they needed
food and rest, and that she should be ashamed if they
sought either at the 'Fighting Lion' (called at this day
the 'Hanbury Arms'). They had as much beer as they

could drink while they were eating; and when the food was cleared away, they had a cup a-piece of good ale, in which the oldest tenant present, standing up, gave Madam's health; and after that was drunk, they were expected to set off homewards; at any rate, no more liquor was given them. The tenants one and all called her 'Madam;' for they recognised in her the married heiress of the Hanburys, not the widow of a Lord Ludlow, of whom they and their forefathers knew nothing; and against whose memory, indeed, there rankled a dim unspoken grudge, the cause of which was accurately known to the very few who understood the nature of a mortgage, and were there-fore aware that Madam's money had been taken to enrich my lord's poor land in Scotland. I am sure— for you can understand I was behind the scenes, as it were, and had many an opportunity of seeing and hearing, as I lay or sat motionless in my lady's room, with the double doors open between it and the ante-room beyond, where Lady Ludlow saw her steward, and gave audience to her tenants,—I am certain, I say, that Mr. Horner was silently as much annoyed at the money that was swallowed up by this mortgage as any one; and, some time or other, he had probably spoken his mind out to my lady; for there was a sort of offended reference on her part, and respectful sub-mission to blame on his, while every now and then there was an implied protest,—whenever the payments of the interest became due, or whenever my lady stinted herself of any personal expense, such as Mr. Horner thought was only decorous and becoming in the heiress of the Hanburys. Her carriages were old and cum-brous, wanting all the improvements which had been adopted by those of her rank throughout the county. Mr. Horner would fain have had the ordering of a new coach. The carriage-horses, too, were getting past their work; yet all the promising colts bred on the estate were sold for ready money; and so on. My lord, her son, was ambassador at some foreign place; and very proud we all were of his glory and dignity;

but I fancy it cost money, and my lady would have lived on bread and water sooner than have called upon him to help her in paying off the mortgage, although he was the one who was to benefit by it in the end.

Mr. Horner was a very faithful steward, and very respectful to my lady ; although, sometimes, I thought she was sharper to him than to any one else ; perhaps because she knew that, although he never said anything, he disapproved of the Hanburys being made to pay for the Earl Ludlow's estates and state.

The late lord had been a sailor, and had been as extravagant in his habits as most sailors are, I am told, —for I never saw the sea ; and yet he had a long sight to his own interests ; but whatever he was, my lady loved him and his memory, with about as fond and proud a love as ever wife gave husband, I should think.

For a part of his life Mr. Horner, who was born on the Hanbury property, had been a clerk to an attorney in Birmingham ; and these few years had given him a kind of worldly wisdom, which, though always exerted for her benefit, was antipathetic to her ladyship, who thought that some of her steward's maxims savoured of trade and commerce. I fancy that if it had been possible, she would have preferred a return to the primitive system of living on the produce of the land, and exchanging the surplus for such articles as were needed, without the intervention of money.

But Mr. Horner was bitten with new-fangled notions, as she would say, though his new-fangled notions were what folk at the present day would think sadly behindhand ; and some of Mr. Gray's ideas fell on Mr. Horner's mind like sparks on tow, though they started from two different points. Mr. Horner wanted to make every man useful and active in this world, and to direct as much activity and usefulness as possible to the improvement of the Hanbury estates, and the aggrandisement of the Hanbury family, and therefore he fell into the new cry for education.

Mr. Gray did not care much—Mr. Horner thought

not enough,—for this world, and where any man or family stood in their earthly position ; but he would have every one prepared for the world to come, and capable of understanding and receiving certain doctrines, for which latter purpose, it stands to reason, he must have heard of these doctrines ; and therefore Mr. Gray wanted education. The answer in the catechism* that Mr. Horner was most fond of calling upon a child to repeat, was that to, ' What is thy duty towards thy neighbour ? ' The answer Mr. Gray liked best to hear repeated with unction, was that to the question, ' What is the inward and spiritual grace ? ' The reply to which Lady Ludlow bent her head the lowest, as we said our Catechism to her on Sundays, was to, ' What is thy duty towards God ? ' But neither Mr. Horner nor Mr. Gray had heard many answers to the Catechism as yet.

Up to this time there was no Sunday-school in Hanbury. Mr. Gray's desires were bounded by that object. Mr. Horner looked farther on : he hoped for a day-school at some future time, to train up intelligent labourers for working on the estate. My lady would hear of neither one nor the other : indeed, not the boldest man whom she ever saw would have dared to name the project of a day-school within her hearing.

So Mr. Horner contented himself with quietly teaching a sharp, clever lad to read and write, with a view to making use of him as a kind of foreman in process of time. He had his pick of the farm-lads for this purpose ; and, as the brightest and sharpest, although by far the raggedest and dirtiest, singled out Job Gregson's son. But all this—as my lady never listened to gossip, or indeed, was spoken to unless she spoke first—was quite unknown to her, until the unlucky incident took place which I am going to relate.

## CHAPTER IV

I THINK my lady was not aware of Mr. Horner's
views on education (as making men into more useful
members of society) or the practice to which he was
putting his precepts in taking Harry Gregson as pupil
and protégé ; if, indeed, she were aware of Harry's
distinct existence at all, until the following unfortunate
occasion. The anteroom, which was a kind of business-
place for my lady to receive her steward and tenants
in, was surrounded by shelves. I cannot call them
book-shelves, though there were many books on them ;
but the contents of the volumes were principally manuscript, and relating to details connected with the
Hanbury property. There were also one or two
dictionaries, gazetteers, works of reference on the
management of property ; all of a very old date (the
dictionary*was Bailey's, I remember ; we had a great
Johnson in my lady's room, but where lexicographers
differed, she generally preferred Bailey).

In this antechamber a footman generally sat, awaiting orders from my lady ; for she clung to the grand
old customs, and despised any bells, except her own
little hand-bell, as modern inventions ; she would have
her people always within summons of this silvery bell,
or her scarce less silvery voice. This man had not the
sinecure you might imagine. He had to reply to the
private entrance ; what we should call the back door
in a smaller house. As none came to the front door
but my lady, and those of the county whom she
honoured by visiting, and her nearest acquaintance of
this kind lived eight miles (of bad road) off, the majority
of comers knocked at the nail-studded terrace-door ;
not to have it opened (for open it stood, by my lady's
orders, winter and summer, so that the snow often
drifted into the back-hall, and lay there in heaps when
the weather was severe), but to summon some one to
receive their message, or carry their request to be
allowed to speak to my lady. I remember it was long

before Mr. Gray could be made to understand that the great door was only opened on state occasions, and even to the last he would as soon come in by that as the terrace entrance. I had been received there on my first setting foot over my lady's threshold; every stranger was led in by that way the first time they came; but after that (with the exceptions I have named) they went round by the terrace, as it were by instinct. It was an assistance to this instinct to be aware that from time immemorial, the magnificent and fierce Hanbury wolf-hounds, which were extinct in every other part of the island, had been and still were kept chained in the front quadrangle, where they bayed through a great part of the day and night, and were always ready with their deep, savage growl at the sight of every person and thing, excepting the man who fed them, my lady's carriage-and-four, and my lady herself. It was pretty to see her small figure go up to the great, crouching brutes, thumping the flags with their heavy, wagging tails, and slobbering in an ecstacy of delight, at her light approach and soft caress. She had no fear of them; but she was a Hanbury born, and the tale went, that they and their kind knew all Hanburys instantly, and acknowledged their supremacy, ever since the ancestors of the breed had been brought from the East by the great Sir Urian Hanbury, who lay with his legs crossed on the altar-tomb in the church. Moreover, it was reported that, not fifty years before, one of these dogs had eaten up a child, which had inadvertently strayed within reach of its chain. So you may imagine how most people preferred the terrace-door. Mr. Gray did not seem to care for the dogs. It might be absence of mind, for I have heard of his starting away from their sudden spring when he had unwittingly walked within reach of their chains; but it could hardly have been absence of mind when one day he went right up to one of them, and patted him in the most friendly manner, the dog meanwhile looking pleased, and affably wagging his tail, just as if Mr. Gray had been a Hanbury. We were all very much puzzled by this, and to this day I have not been able to account for it.

But now let us go back to the terrace-door, and the footman sitting in the antechamber.

One morning we heard a parleying which rose to such a vehemence, and lasted for so long, that my lady had to ring her hand-bell twice before the footman heard it.

'What is the matter, John ?' asked she, when he entered.

'A little boy, my lady, who says he comes from Mr. Horner, and must see your ladyship. Impudent little lad !' (this last to himself).

'What does he want ?'

'That's just what I have asked him, my lady, but he won't tell me, please your ladyship.'

'It is, probably, some message from Mr. Horner,' said Lady Ludlow, with just a shade of annoyance in her manner ; for it was against all etiquette to send a message to her, and by such a messenger too !

'No ! please your ladyship, I asked him if he had any message, and he said no, he had none ; but he must see your ladyship for all that.'

'You had better show him in then, without more words,' said her ladyship, quietly, but still, as I have said, rather annoyed.

As if in mockery of the humble visitor, the footman threw open both battants*of the door, and in the opening there stood a lithe, wiry lad, with a thick head of hair, standing out in every direction, as if stirred by some electrical current, a short, brown face, red now from affright and excitement, wide, resolute mouth, and bright, deep-set eyes ; which glanced keenly and rapidly round the room, as if taking in everything (and all was new and strange) to be thought and puzzled over at some future time. He knew enough of manners not to speak first to one above him in rank, or else he was afraid.

'What do you want with me ?' asked my lady, in so gentle a tone that it seemed to surprise and stun him.

'An't please your ladyship?' said he, as if he had been deaf.

'You come from Mr. Horner's: why do you want to see me?' again asked she, a little more loudly.

'An't please your ladyship, Mr. Horner was sent for all on a sudden to Warwick this morning.'

His face began to work; but he felt it, and closed his lips into a resolute form.

'Well?'

'And he went off all on a sudden-like.'

'Well?'

'And he left a note for your ladyship with me, your ladyship.'

'Is that all? You might have given it to the footman.'

'Please your ladyship, I've clean gone and lost it.'

He never took his eyes off her face. If he had not kept his look fixed, he would have burst out crying.

'That was very careless,' said my lady, gently. 'But I am sure you are very sorry for it. You had better try and find it. It may have been of consequence.'

'Please, Mum—please your ladyship—I can say it off by heart.'

'You! What do you mean?' I was really afraid now. My lady's blue eyes absolutely gave out light, she was so much displeased, and, moreover, perplexed. The more reason he had for affright, the more his courage rose. He must have seen,—so sharp a lad must have perceived her displeasure, but he went on quickly and steadily.

'Mr. Horner, my lady, has taught me to read, write, and cast accounts, my lady. And he was in a hurry, and he folded his paper up, but he did not seal it; and I read it, my lady; and now, my lady, it seems like as if I had got it off by heart;' and he went on with a high pitched voice, saying out very loud what, I have no doubt, were the identical words of the letter, date, signature and all: it was merely something about a deed, which required my lady's signature.

When he had done, he stood almost as if he expected commendation for his accurate memory.

My lady's eyes contracted till the pupils were as needle-points ; it was a way she had when much disturbed. She looked at me, and said :

' Margaret Dawson, what will this world come to ? ' And then she was silent.

The lad, beginning to perceive he had given deep offence, stood stock still—as if his brave will had brought him into this presence, and impelled him to confession, and the best amends he could make, but had now deserted him, or was extinct, and left his body motionless, until some one else with word or deed made him quit the room. My lady looked again at him, and saw the frowning, dumb-foundering terror at his misdeed, and the manner in which his confession had been received.

' My poor lad ! ' said she, the angry look leaving her face, ' into whose hands have you fallen ? '

The boy's lips began to quiver.

' Don't you know what tree we read of in Genesis ?*— No ! I hope you have not got to read so easily as that.' A pause. ' Who has taught you to read and write ? '

' Please, my lady, I meant no harm, my lady.' He was fairly blubbering, overcome by her evident feeling of dismay and regret, the soft repression of which was more frightening to him than any strong or violent words would have been.

' Who taught you, I ask ? '

' It were Mr. Horner's clerk who learned me, my lady.'

' And did Mr. Horner know of it ? '

' Yes, my lady. And I am sure I thought for to please him.'

' Well ! perhaps you were not to blame for that. But I wonder at Mr. Horner. However, my boy, as you have got possession of edge-tools, you must have some rules how to use them. Did you never hear that you were not to open letters ? '

' Please, my lady, it were open.  Mr. Horner forgot for to seal it, in his hurry to be off.'

' But you must not read letters that are not intended for you.  You must never try to read any letters that are not directed to you, even if they be open before you.'

' Please, my lady, I thought it were good for practice, all as one as a book.'

My lady looked bewildered as to what way she could farther explain to him the laws of honour as regarded letters.

' You would not listen, I am sure,' said she, ' to anything you were not intended to hear ? '

He hesitated for a moment, partly because he did not fully comprehend the question.  My lady repeated it.  The light of intelligence came into his eager eyes, and I could see that he was not certain if he could tell the truth.

' Please, my lady, I always hearken when I hear folk talking secrets ;  but I mean no harm.'

My poor lady sighed :  she was not prepared to begin a long way off in morals.  Honour was, to her, second nature, and she had never tried to find out on what principle its laws were based.  So, telling the lad that she wished to see Mr. Horner when he returned from Warwick, she dismissed him with a despondent look ; he, meanwhile, right glad to be out of the awful gentleness of her presence.

' What is to be done ? ' said she, half to herself and half to me.  I could not answer, for I was puzzled myself.

' It was a right word,' she continued, ' that I used, when I called reading and writing " edge-tools."  If our lower orders have these edge-tools given to them, we shall have the terrible scenes of the French Revolution acted over again in England.  When I was a girl, one never heard of the rights of men, one only heard of the duties.  Now, here was Mr. Gray, only last night, talking of the right every child had to instruction.  I could hardly keep my patience with him, and

at length we fairly came to words; and I told him
I would have no such thing as a Sunday-school (or
a Sabbath-school, as he calls it, just like a Jew) in my
village.'

'And what did he say, my lady?' I asked; for
the struggle that seemed now to have come to a crisis,
had been going on for some time in a quiet way.

'Why, he gave way to temper, and said he was bound
to remember he was under the bishop's authority, not
under mine; and implied that he should persevere in
his designs, notwithstanding my expressed opinion.'

'And your ladyship—' I half inquired.

'I could only rise and curtsy, and civilly dismiss
him. When two persons have arrived at a certain
point of expression on a subject, about which they
differ as materially as I do from Mr. Gray, the wisest
course, if they wish to remain friends, is to drop the
conversation entirely and suddenly. It is one of the
few cases where abruptness is desirable.'

I was sorry for Mr. Gray. He had been to see me
several times, and had helped me to bear my illness
in a better spirit than I should have done without his
good advice and prayers. And I had gathered, from
little things he said, how much his heart was set upon
this new scheme. I liked him so much, and I loved
and respected my lady so well, that I could not bear
them to be on the cool terms to which they were
constantly getting. Yet I could do nothing but keep
silence.

I suppose my lady understood something of what
was passing in my mind; for, after a minute or two,
she went on :—

'If Mr. Gray knew all I know,—if he had my
experience, he would not be so ready to speak of
setting up his new plans in opposition to my judgement. Indeed,' she continued, lashing herself up with
her own recollections, 'times are changed when the
parson of a village comes to beard the liege lady in
her own house. Why, in my grandfather's days, the
parson was family chaplain too, and dined at the Hall

every Sunday. He was helped last, and expected to
have done first. I remember seeing him take up his
plate and knife and fork, and say, with his mouth full
all the time he was speaking : " If you please, Sir
Urian, and my Lady, I'll follow the beef into the
housekeeper's room ; " for, you see, unless he did so,
he stood no chance of a second helping. A greedy
man, that parson was, to be sure ! I recollect his
once eating up the whole of some little bird at dinner,
and by way of diverting attention from his greediness,
he told how he had heard that a rook soaked in vinegar
and then dressed in a particular way, could not be
distinguished from the bird he was then eating. I saw
by the grim look of my grandfather's face that the
parson's doing and saying displeased him ; and, child
as I was, I had some notion what was coming, when,
as I was riding out on my little, white pony, by my
grandfather's side, the next Friday, he stopped one of
the gamekeepers, and bade him shoot one of the oldest
rooks he could find. I knew no more about it till
Sunday, when a dish was set right before the parson,
and Sir Urian said : " Now, Parson Hemming, I have
had a rook shot, and soaked in vinegar, and dressed
as you described last Sunday. Fall to, man, and eat
it with as good an appetite as you had last Sunday.
Pick the bones clean, or by ——, no more Sunday
dinners shall you eat at my table ! " I gave one look
at poor Mr. Hemming's face, as he tried to swallow
the first morsel, and make believe as though he thought
it very good ; but I could not look again, for shame,
although my grandfather laughed, and kept asking us
all round if we knew what could have become of the
parson's appetite.'

'And did he finish it ? ' I asked.

'O yes, my dear. What my grandfather said was
to be done, was done always. He was a terrible man
in his anger ! But to think of the difference between
Parson Hemming and Mr. Gray ! or even of poor,
dear Mr. Mountford and Mr. Gray. Mr. Mountford
would never have withstood me as Mr. Gray did ! '

'And your ladyship really thinks that it would not be right to have a Sunday-school?' I asked, feeling very timid as I put the question.

'Certainly not. As I told Mr. Gray, I consider a knowledge of the Creed, and of the Lord's Prayer, as essential to salvation; and that any child may have, whose parents bring it regularly to church. Then there are the Ten Commandments, which teach simple duties in the plainest language. Of course, if a lad is taught to read and write (as that unfortunate boy has been who was here this morning) his duties become complicated, and his temptations much greater, while, at the same time, he has no hereditary principles and honourable training to serve as safeguards. I might take up my old simile of the race-horse and cart-horse. I am distressed,' continued she, with a break in her ideas, 'about that boy. The whole thing reminds me so much of a story of what happened to a friend of mine—Clément de Créquy. Did I ever tell you about him?'

'No, your ladyship,' I replied.

'Poor Clément! More than twenty years ago, Lord Ludlow and I spent a winter in Paris. He had many friends there; perhaps not very good or very wise men, but he was so kind that he liked every one, and every one liked him. We had an apartment, as they call it there, in the Rue de Lille; we had the first-floor of a grand hôtel, with the basement for our servants. On the floor above us the owner of the house lived, a Marquise de Créquy, a widow. They tell me that the Créquy coat-of-arms is still emblazoned, after all these terrible years, on a shield above the arched porte-cochère, just as it was then, though the family is quite extinct. Madam de Créquy had only one son, Clément, who was just the same age as my Urian—you may see his portrait in the great hall—Urian's, I mean.' I knew that Master Urian had been drowned at sea; and often had I looked at the presentment of his bonny hopeful face, in his sailor's dress, with right hand outstretched to a ship on the sea in the distance,

as if he had just said, 'Look at her! all her sails are
set, and I'm just off.' Poor Master Urian! he went
down in this very ship not a year after the picture was
taken! But now I will go back to my lady's story.
'I can see those two boys playing now,' continued
she, softly, shutting her eyes, as if the better to call up
the vision, 'as they used to do five-and-twenty years
ago in those old-fashioned French gardens behind our
hôtel. Many a time have I watched them from my
windows. It was, perhaps, a better play-place than an
English garden would have been, for there were but
few flower-beds, and no lawn at all to speak about;
but instead, terraces and balustrades and vases and
flights of stone steps more in the Italian style; and
there were jets-d'eau, and little fountains that could be
set playing by turning water-cocks that were hidden
here and there. How Clément delighted in turning
the water on to surprise Urian, and how gracefully he
did the honours, as it were, to my dear, rough, sailor
lad! Urian was as dark as a gypsy boy, and cared
little for his appearance, and resisted all my efforts at
setting off his black eyes and tangled curls; but
Clément, without ever showing that he thought about
himself and his dress, was always dainty and elegant,
even though his clothes were sometimes but thread-
bare. He used to be dressed in a kind of hunter's
green suit, open at the neck and half-way down the
chest to beautiful old lace frills; his long golden curls
fell behind just like a girl's, and his hair in front was
cut over his straight dark eyebrows in a line almost
as straight. Urian learnt more of a gentleman's care-
fulness and propriety of appearance from that lad in
two months than he had done in years from all my
lectures. I recollect one day, when the two boys were
in full romp—and, my window being open, I could
hear them perfectly—and Urian was daring Clément
to some scrambling or climbing, which Clément refused
to undertake, but in a hesitating way, as though he
longed to do it if some reason had not stood in the
way; and at times, Urian, who was hasty and thought-

less, poor fellow, told Clément that he was afraid.
"Fear!" said the French boy, drawing himself up;
"you do not know what you say. If you will be here
at six to-morrow morning, when it is only just light,
I will take that starling's nest on the top of yonder
chimney." "But why not now, Clément?" said
Urian, putting his arm round Clément's neck. "Why
then, and not now, just when we are in the humour
for it?" "Because we De Créquys are poor, and my
mother cannot afford me another suit of clothes this
year, and yonder stone carving is all jagged, and would
tear my coat and breeches. Now, to-morrow morning
I could go up with nothing on but an old shirt."

' " But you would tear your legs."

' " My race do not care for pain," said the boy,
drawing himself from Urian's arm, and walking a few
steps away, with a becoming pride and reserve; for
he was hurt at being spoken to as if he were afraid,
and annoyed at having to confess the true reason for
declining the feat. But Urian was not to be thus
baffled. He went up to Clément, and put his arm
once more about his neck, and I could see the two
lads as they walked down the terrace away from the
hôtel windows: first Urian spoke eagerly, looking with
imploring fondness into Clément's face, which sought
the ground, till at last the French boy spoke, and by-
and-by his arm was round Urian too, and they paced
backwards and forwards in deep talk, but gravely, as
became men, rather than boys.

' All at once, from the little chapel at the corner of
the large garden belonging to the Missions Etrangères,
I heard the tinkle of the little bell, announcing the
elevation of the host. Down on his knees went Clément,
hands crossed, eyes bent down: while Urian stood
looking on in respectful thought.

' What a friendship that might have been! I never
dream of Urian without seeing Clément too,—Urian
speaks to me, or does something,—but Clément only
flits round Urian, and never seems to see any one
else!

'But I must not forget to tell you, that the next morning, before he was out of his room, a footman of Madame de Créquy's brought Urian the starling's nest.

'Well! we came back to England, and the boys were to correspond; and Madame de Créquy and I exchanged civilities; and Urian went to sea.

'After that, all seemed to drop away. I cannot tell you all. However, to confine myself to the De Créquys. I had a letter from Clément; I knew he felt his friend's death deeply; but I should never have learnt it from the letter he sent. It was formal, and seemed like chaff to my hungering heart. Poor fellow! I dare say he had found it hard to write. What could he—or any one—say to a mother who has lost her child? The world does not think so, and, in general, one must conform to the customs of the world; but, judging from my own experience, I should say that reverent silence at such times is the tenderest balm. Madame de Créquy wrote too. But I knew she could not feel my loss so much as Clément, and therefore her letter was not such a disappointment. She and I went on being civil and polite in the way of commissions, and occasionally introducing friends to each other, for a year or two, and then we ceased to have any intercourse. Then the terrible Revolution came. No one who did not live at those times can imagine the daily expectation of news,—the hourly terror of rumours affecting the fortunes and lives of those whom most of us had known as pleasant hosts, receiving us with peaceful welcome in their magnificent houses. Of course, there was sin enough and suffering enough behind the scenes; but we English visitors to Paris had seen little or nothing of that,—and I had sometimes thought, indeed, how even Death seemed loth to choose his victims out of that brilliant throng whom I had known. Madame de Créquy's one boy lived; while three out of my six were gone since we had met! I do not think all lots are equal, even now that I know the end of her hopes; but I do say, that whatever our individual lot is, it is our duty to accept it, without comparing it with that of others.

'The times were thick with gloom and terror. "What next?" was the question we asked of every one who brought us news from Paris. Where were these demons hidden when, so few years ago, we danced and feasted, and enjoyed the brilliant salons and the charming friendships of Paris?

'One evening, I was sitting alone in Saint James's Square; my lord off at the club with Mr. Fox* and others: he had left me, thinking that I should go to one of the many places to which I had been invited for that evening; but I had no heart to go anywhere, for it was poor Urian's birthday, and I had not even rung for lights, though the day was fast closing in, but was thinking over all his pretty ways, and on his warm affectionate nature, and how often I had been too hasty in speaking to him, for all I loved him so dearly; and how I seemed to have neglected and dropped his dear friend Clément, who might even now be in need of help in that cruel, bloody Paris. I say I was thinking reproachfully of all this, and particularly of Clément de Créquy in connection with Urian, when Fenwick brought me a note, sealed with a coat-of-arms I knew well, though I could not remember at the moment where I had seen it. I puzzled over it, as one does sometimes, for a minute or more, before I opened the letter. In a moment I saw it was from Clément de Créquy. "My mother is here," he said: "she is very ill, and I am bewildered in this strange country. May I entreat you to receive me for a few minutes?" The bearer of the note was the woman of the house where they lodged. I had her brought up into the anteroom, and questioned her myself, while my carriage was being brought round. They had arrived in London a fortnight or so before: she had not known their quality, judging them (according to her kind) by their dress and their luggage; poor enough, no doubt. The lady had never left her bedroom since her arrival; the young man waited upon her, did everything for her, never left her, in fact; only she (the messenger) had promised to stay within call, as soon as she returned, while he went out somewhere. She could hardly understand him, he spoke English so badly. He had never spoken it, I dare say, since he had talked to my Urian.

## CHAPTER V

'In the hurry of the moment I scarce knew what I did. I bade the housekeeper put up every delicacy she had, in order to tempt the invalid, whom yet I hoped to bring back with me to our house. When the carriage was ready, I took the good woman with me to show us the exact way, which my coachman professed not to know; for, indeed, they were staying at but a poor kind of place at the back of Leicester Square, of which they had heard, as Clément told me afterwards, from one of the fishermen who had carried them across from the Dutch coast in their disguises as a Friesland peasant and his mother. They had some jewels of value concealed round their persons; but their ready money was all spent before I saw them, and Clément had been unwilling to leave his mother, even for the time necessary to ascertain the best mode of disposing of the diamonds. For, overcome with distress of mind and bodily fatigue, she had reached London only to take to her bed in a sort of low, nervous fever, in which her chief and only idea seemed to be, that Clément was about to be taken from her to some prison or other; and if he were out of her sight, though but for a minute, she cried like a child, and could not be pacified or comforted. The landlady was a kind, good woman, and though she but half understood the case, she was truly sorry for them, as foreigners, and the mother sick in a strange land.

'I sent her forwards to request permission for my entrance. In a moment I saw Clément—a tall, elegant young man, in a curious dress of coarse cloth, standing at the open door of a room, and evidently—even before he accosted me—striving to soothe the terrors of his mother inside. I went towards him, and would have taken his hand, but he bent down and kissed mine.

' " May I come in, madame ? " I asked, looking at the poor sick lady, lying in the dark, dingy bed, her head propped up on coarse and dirty pillows, and gazing with affrighted eyes at all that was going on.

' " Clément ! Clément ! come to me ! " she cried ; and when he went to the bedside she turned on one side, and took his hand in both of hers, and began stroking it, and looking up in his face. I could scarce keep back my tears.

' He stood there quite still, except that from time to time he spoke to her in a low tone. At last I advanced into the room, so that I could talk to him, without renewing her alarm. I asked for the doctor's address ; for I had heard that they had called in some one, at their landlady's recommendation : but I could hardly understand Clément's broken English, and mispronunciation of our proper names, and was obliged to apply to the woman herself. I could not say much to Clément, for his attention was perpetually needed by his mother, who never seemed to perceive that I was there. But I told him not to fear, however long I might be away, for that I would return before night ; and, bidding the woman take charge of all the heterogeneous things the housekeeper had put up, and leaving one of my men in the house, who could understand a few words of French, with directions that he was to hold himself at Madame de Créquy's orders until I sent or gave him fresh commands, I drove off to the doctor's. What I wanted was his permission to remove Madame de Créquy to my own house, and to learn how it best could be done ; for I saw that every movement in the room, every sound, except Clément's voice, brought on a fresh access of trembling and nervous agitation.

' The doctor was, I should think, a clever man ; but he had that kind of abrupt manner which people get who have much to do with the lower orders.

'I told him the story of his patient, the interest I had in her, and the wish I entertained of removing her to my own house.

'"It can't be done," said he. "Any change will kill her."

'"But it must be done," I replied. "And it shall not kill her."

'"Then I have nothing more to say," said he, turning away from the carriage-door, and making as though he would go back into the house.

'"Stop a moment. You must help me; and, if you do, you shall have reason to be glad, for I will give you fifty pounds down with pleasure. If you won't do it, another shall."

'He looked at me, then (furtively) at the carriage, hesitated, and then said: "You do not mind expense, apparently. I suppose you are a rich lady of quality. Such folks will not stick at such trifles as the life or death of a sick woman to get their own way. I suppose I must e'en help you, for if I don't, another will."

'I did not mind what he said, so that he would assist me. I was pretty sure that she was in a state to require opiates; and I had not forgotten Christopher Sly,* you may be sure, so I told him what I had in my head. That in the dead of night,—the quiet time in the streets,—she should be carried in a hospital litter, softly and warmly covered over, from the Leicester Square lodging-house to rooms that I would have in perfect readiness for her. As I planned, so it was done. I let Clément know, by a note, of my design. I had all prepared at home, and we walked about my house as though shod with velvet, while the porter watched at the open door. At last, through the darkness, I saw the lanterns carried by my men, who were leading the little procession. The litter looked like a hearse; on one side walked the doctor, on the other Clément: they came softly and swiftly along. I could not try any farther experiment; we dared not change her clothes; she was laid in the bed in the landlady's coarse night-gear, and covered over warmly, and left in the shaded, scented room, with a nurse and the doctor watching by her, while I led Clément to the dressing-room adjoining, in which I had had a bed placed for him. Farther than that he would not go ; and there I had refreshments brought. Meanwhile, he had shown his gratitude by every possible action (for we none of us dared to speak) : he had kneeled at my feet, and kissed my hand, and left it wet with his tears. He had thrown up his arms to Heaven, and prayed earnestly, as I could see by the movement of his lips. I allowed him to relieve himself by these dumb expressions, if I may so call them,—and then I left him, and went to my own rooms to sit up for my lord, and tell him what I had done.

' Of course, it was all right ; and neither my lord nor I could sleep for wondering how Madame de Créquy would bear her awakening. I had engaged the doctor, to whose face and voice she was accustomed, to remain with her all night : the nurse was experienced, and Clément was within call. But it was with the greatest relief that I heard from my own woman, when she brought me my chocolate, that Madame de Créquy (Monsieur had said) had awakened more tranquil than she had been for many days. To be sure, the whole aspect of the bed-chamber must have been more familiar to her than the miserable place where I had found her, and she must have intuitively felt herself among friends.

' My lord was scandalized at Clément's dress, which, after the first moment of seeing him, I had forgotten, in thinking of other things, and for which I had not prepared Lord Ludlow. He sent for his own tailor, and bade him bring patterns of stuffs, and engage his men to work night and day till Clément could appear as became his rank. In short, in a few days so much of the traces of their flight were removed, that we had almost forgotten the terrible causes of it, and rather felt as if they had come on a visit to us than that they had been compelled to fly their country. Their diamonds, too, were sold well by my lord's agents, though the London shops were stocked with jewellery, and such portable valuables, some of rare and curious fashion, which were sold for half their real value by emigrants who could not afford to wait. Madame de Créquy was recovering her health, although her strength was sadly gone, and she would never be equal to such another flight as the perilous one which she had gone through, and to which she could not bear the slightest reference. For some time things continued in this state ;—the De Créquys still our honoured visitors,— many houses besides our own, even among our own friends, open to receive the poor flying nobility of France, driven from their country by the brutal republicans, and every freshly-arrived emigrant bringing new tales of horror, as if these revolutionists were drunk with blood, and mad to devise new atrocities. One day Clément—I should tell you he had been presented to our good King George and the sweet Queen, and they had accosted him most graciously, and his beauty and elegance, and some of the circumstances attendant on his flight, made him be received in the world quite like a hero of romance : he might have been on intimate terms in many a distinguished house, had he cared to visit much ; but he accompanied my lord and me with an air of indifference and languor, which I sometimes fancied, made him be all the more sought after : Monkshaven (that was the title my eldest son bore) tried in vain to interest him in all young men's sports. But no ! it was the same through all. His mother took far more interest in the *on-dits* of the London world, into which she was far too great an invalid to venture, than he did in the absolute events themselves, in which he might have been an actor. One day, as I was saying, an old Frenchman of a humble class presented himself to our servants, several of whom understood French ; and, through Medlicott, I learnt that he was in some way connected with the De Créquys ; not with their Paris life ; but I fancy he had been intendant of their estates in the country ; estates which were more useful as hunting-grounds than as adding to their income. However, there was the old man ; and with him, wrapped round his person, he had brought the long parchment rolls, and deeds relating to their property. These he would deliver up to none but Monsieur de Créquy, the rightful owner ; and Clément was out with Monkshaven, so the old man waited ; and when Clément came in, I told him of the steward's arrival, and how he had been cared for by my people. Clément went directly to see him. He was a long time away, and I was waiting for him to drive out with me, for some purpose or another, I scarce know what, but I remember I was tired of waiting, and was just in the act of ringing the bell to desire that he might be reminded of his engagement with me, when he came in, his face as white as the powder in his hair, his beautiful eyes dilated with horror. I saw that he had heard something that touched him even more closely than the usual tales which every fresh emigrant brought.

' " What is it, Clément ? " I asked.

' He clasped his hands, and looked as though he tried to speak, but could not bring out the words.

' " They have guillotined my uncle ! " said he at last. Now, I knew that there was a Count de Créquy ; but I had always understood that the elder branch held very little communication with him ; in fact, that he was a vaurien of some kind, and rather a disgrace than otherwise to the family. So, perhaps, I was hard-hearted ; but I was a little surprised at this excess of emotion, till I saw that peculiar look in his eyes that many people have when there is more terror in their hearts than they dare put into words. He wanted me to understand something without his saying it ; but how could I ? I had never heard of a Mademoiselle de Créquy.

' " Virginie ! " at last he uttered. In an instant I understood it all, and remembered that, if Urian had lived, he too might have been in love.

' " Your uncle's daughter ? " I inquired.

' "My cousin," he replied.

' I did not say, "your betrothed," but I had no doubt of it. I was mistaken, however.

' " O madame ! " he continued, " her mother died long ago—her father now—and she is in daily fear,— alone, deserted——'

' " Is she in the Abbaye ? " asked I.

' " No ! She is in hiding with the widow of her father's old concierge. Any day they may search the house for aristocrats. They are seeking them everywhere. Then, not her life alone, but that of the old woman, her hostess, is sacrificed. The old woman knows this, and trembles with fear. Even if she is brave enough to be faithful, her fears would betray her, should the house be searched. Yet there is no one to help Virginie to escape. She is alone in Paris."

' I saw what was in his mind. He was fretting and chafing to go to his cousin's assistance; but the thought of his mother restrained him. I would not have kept back Urian from such an errand at such a time. How should I restrain him ? And yet, perhaps, I did wrong in not urging the chances of danger more. Still, if it was danger to him, was it not the same or even greater danger to her ?—for the French spared neither age nor sex in those wicked days of terror. So I rather fell in with his wish, and encouraged him to think how best and most prudently it might be fulfilled ; never doubting, as I have said, that he and his cousin were troth-plighted.

' But when I went to Madame de Créquy—after he had imparted his, or rather our plan to her—I found out my mistake. She, who was in general too feeble to walk across the room save slowly, and with a stick, was going from end to end with quick, tottering steps ; and, if now and then she sank upon a chair, it seemed as if she could not rest, for she was up again in a moment, pacing along, wringing her hands, and speaking rapidly to herself. When she saw me, she stopped : "Madame," she said, " you have lost your own boy. You might have left me mine."

'I was so astonished—I hardly knew what to say. I had spoken to Clément as if his mother's consent were secure (as I had felt my own would have been if Urian had been alive to ask it). Of course, both he and I knew that his mother's consent must be asked and obtained, before he could leave her to go on such an undertaking; but, somehow, my blood always rose at the sight or sound of danger; perhaps, because my life had been so peaceful. Poor Madame de Créquy! it was otherwise with her; she despaired while I hoped, and Clément trusted.

'"Dear Madame de Créquy," said I, "he will return safely to us; every precaution shall be taken, that either he or you, or my lord, or Monkshaven can think of; but he cannot leave a girl—his nearest relation save you—his betrothed, is she not?"

'"His betrothed!" cried she, now at the utmost pitch of her excitement. "Virginie betrothed to Clément?—no! thank heaven, not so bad as that! Yet it might have been. But Mademoiselle scorned my son! She would have nothing to do with him. Now is the time for him to have nothing to do with her!"

'Clément had entered at the door behind his mother as she thus spoke. His face was set and pale, till it looked as gray and immovable as if it had been carved in stone. He came forward and stood before his mother. She stopped her walk, threw back her haughty head, and the two looked each other steadily in the face. After a minute or two in this attitude, her proud and resolute gaze never flinching or wavering, he went down upon one knee, and, taking her hand—her hard, stony hand, which never closed on his, but remained straight and stiff:

'"Mother," he pleaded, "withdraw your prohibition. Let me go!"

'"What were her words?" Madame de Créquy replied, slowly, as if forcing her memory to the extreme of accuracy. "'My cousin,' she said, 'when I marry, I marry a man, not a petit-maître. I marry a man who, whatever his rank may be, will add dignity to the human race by his virtues, and not be content to live in an effeminate court on the traditions of past grandeur.' She borrowed her words from the infamous Jean-Jacques Rousseau, the friend of her scarce less infamous father,—nay ! I will say it,—if not her words, she borrowed her principles. And my son to request her to marry him ! "

' "It was my father's written wish," said Clément.

' "But did you not love her ? You plead your father's words,—words written twelve years before,—and as if that were your reason for being indifferent to my dislike to the alliance. But you requested her to marry you,—and she refused you with insolent contempt ; and now you are ready to leave me,—leave me desolate in a foreign land—"

' "Desolate ! my mother ! and the Countess Ludlow stands there ! "

' "Pardon, madame ! But all the earth, though it were full of kind hearts, is but a desolation and a desert place to a mother when her only child is absent. And you, Clément, would leave me for this Virginie,—this degenerate De Créquy, tainted with the atheism of the Encyclopédistes !* She is only reaping some of the fruit of the harvest whereof her friends have sown the seed. Let her alone ! Doubtless she has friends—it may be lovers—among these demons, who, under the cry of liberty, commit every licence. Let her alone, Clément ! She refused you with scorn : be too proud to notice her now."

' "Mother, I cannot think of myself ; only of her."

' "Think of me, then ! I, your mother, forbid you to go."

'Clément bowed low, and went out of the room instantly, as one blinded. She saw his groping movement, and, for an instant, I think her heart was touched. But she turned to me, and tried to exculpate her past violence by dilating upon her wrongs, and they certainly were many. The Count, her husband's younger

brother, had invariably tried to make mischief between
husband and wife. He had been the cleverer man of
the two, and had possessed extraordinary influence
over her husband. She suspected him of having
instigated that clause in her husband's will, by which
the Marquis expressed his wish for the marriage of the
cousins. The Count had had some interest in the
management of the De Créquy property during her
son's minority. Indeed, I remembered then that it
was through Count de Créquy that Lord Ludlow had
first heard of the apartment which we afterwards took
in the Hôtel de Créquy; and then the recollection of
a past feeling came distinctly out of the mist, as it
were; and I called to mind how, when we first took
up our abode in the Hôtel de Créquy, both Lord
Ludlow and I imagined that the arrangement was
displeasing to our hostess; and how it had taken us
a considerable time before we had been able to establish
relations of friendship with her. Years after our visit,
she began to suspect that Clément (whom she could
not forbid to visit at his uncle's house, considering the
terms on which his father had been with his brother;
though she herself never set foot over the Count de
Créquy's threshold) was attaching himself to Mademoiselle, his cousin; and she made cautious inquiries
as to the appearance, character, and disposition of the
young lady. Mademoiselle was not handsome, they
said; but of a fine figure, and generally considered as
having a very noble and attractive presence. In
character she was daring and wilful (said one set);
original and independent (said another). She was
much indulged by her father, who had given her
something of a man's education, and selected for her
intimate friend a young lady below her in rank, one
of the Bureaucracie, a Mademoiselle Necker,* daughter
of the Minister of Finance. Mademoiselle de Créquy
was thus introduced into all the free-thinking salons of
Paris; among people who were always full of plans
for subverting society. "And did Clément affect such
people?" Madame de Créquy had asked, with some

anxiety. No! Monsieur de Créquy had neither eyes nor ears nor thought for anything but his cousin, while she was by. And she? She hardly took notice of his devotion, so evident to every one else. The proud creature! But perhaps that was her haughty way of concealing what she felt. And so Madame de Créquy listened, and questioned, and learnt nothing decided, until one day she surprised Clément with the note in his hand, of which she remembered the stinging words so well, in which Virginie had said, in reply to a proposal Clément had sent her through her father, that "When she married she married a man, not a petit-maître."

' Clément was justly indignant at the insulting nature of the answer Virginie had sent to a proposal, respectful in its tone, and which was, after all, but the cool, hardened lava over a burning heart. He acquiesced in his mother's desire, that he should not again present himself in his uncle's salons; but he did not forget Virginie, though he never mentioned her name.

' Madame de Créquy and her son were among the earliest proscrits, as they were of the strongest possible royalists, and aristocrats, as it was the custom of the horrid Sansculottes to term those who adhered to the habits of expression and action in which it was their pride to have been educated. They had left Paris some weeks before they had arrived in England, and Clément's belief at the time of quitting the Hôtel de Créquy had certainly been that his uncle was not merely safe, but rather a popular man with the party in power. And, as all communication having relation to private individuals of a reliable kind was intercepted, Monsieur de Créquy had felt but little anxiety for his uncle and cousin, in comparison with what he did for many other friends of very different opinions in politics, until the day when he was stunned by the fatal information that even his progressive uncle was guillotined, and learnt that his cousin was imprisoned by the licence of the mob, whose rights (as she called them) she was always advocating.

'When I had heard all this story, I confess I lost in sympathy for Clément what I gained for his mother. Virginie's life did not seem to me worth the risk that Clément's would run. But when I saw him—sad, depressed, nay, hopeless—going about like one oppressed by a heavy dream which he cannot shake off ; caring neither to eat, drink, nor sleep, yet bearing all with silent dignity, and even trying to force a poor, faint smile when he caught my anxious eyes ; I turned round again, and wondered how Madame de Créquy could resist this mute pleading of her son's altered appearance. As for my Lord Ludlow and Monkshaven, as soon as they understood the case, they were indignant that any mother should attempt to keep a son out of honourable danger ; and it was honourable, and a clear duty (according to them), to try to save the life of a helpless orphan girl, his next of kin. None but a Frenchman, said my lord, would hold himself bound by an old woman's whimsies and fears, even though she were his mother. As it was, he was chafing himself to death under the restraint. If he went, to be sure, the —— wretches might make an end of him, as they had done of many a fine fellow ; but my lord would take heavy odds that, instead of being guillotined, he would save the girl, and bring her safe to England, just desperately in love with her preserver, and then we would have a jolly wedding down at Monkshaven. My lord repeated his opinion so often, that it became a certain prophecy in his mind of what was to take place ; and, one day seeing Clément look even paler and thinner than he had ever done before, he sent a message to Madame de Créquy, requesting permission to speak to her in private.

' "For, by George !" said he, " she shall hear my opinion, and not let that lad of hers kill himself by fretting. He's too good for that. If he had been an English lad, he would have been off to his sweetheart long before this, without saying with your leave or by your leave ; but being a Frenchman, he is all for Æneas* and filial piety,—filial fiddle-sticks !" (My lord had run away to sea, when a boy, against his father's consent, I am sorry to say; and, as all had ended well, and he had come back to find both his parents alive, I do not think he was ever as much aware of his fault as he might have been under other circumstances.) "No, my lady," he went on, "don't come with me. A woman can manage a man best when he has a fit of obstinacy, and a man can persuade a woman out of her tantrums, when all her own sex, the whole army of them, would fail. Allow me to go alone to my tête-à-tête with madame."

'What he said, what passed, he never could repeat; but he came back graver than he went. However, the point was gained; Madame de Créquy withdrew her prohibition, and had given him leave to tell Clément as much.

'"But she is an old Cassandra,"*said he. "Don't let the lad be much with her; her talk would destroy the courage of the bravest man; she is so given over to superstition." Something that she had said had touched a chord in my lord's nature which he inherited from his Scotch ancestors. Long afterwards, I heard what this was. Medlicott told me.

'However, my lord shook off all fancies that told against the fulfilment of Clément's wishes. All that afternoon we three sat together, planning; and Monkshaven passed in and out, executing our commissions, and preparing everything. Towards nightfall all was ready for Clément's start on his journey towards the coast.

'Madame had declined seeing any of us since my lord's stormy interview with her. She sent word that she was fatigued, and desired repose. But, of course, before Clément set off, he was bound to wish her farewell, and to ask for her blessing. In order to avoid an agitating conversation between mother and son, my lord and I resolved to be present at the interview. Clément was already in his travelling-dress, that of a Norman fisherman, which Monkshaven had, with infinite trouble, discovered in the possession of one of the émigrés who thronged London, and who had made his escape from the shores of France in this disguise. Clément's plan was to go down to the coast of Sussex, and get some of the fishing or smuggling boats to take him across to the French Coast near Dieppe. There again he would have to change his dress. O, it was so well planned! His mother was startled by his disguise (of which we had not thought to forewarn her) as he entered her apartment. And either that, or the being suddenly roused from the heavy slumber into which she was apt to fall when she was left alone, gave her manner an air of wildness that was almost like insanity.

' "Go, go!" she said to him, almost pushing him away as he knelt to kiss her hand. "Virginie is beckoning to you, but you don't see what kind of a bed it is——"

' "Clément, make haste!" said my lord, in a hurried manner, as if to interrupt madame. "The time is late than I thought, and you must not miss the morning's tide. Bid your mother good-bye at once, and let us be off." For my lord and Monkshaven were to ride with him to an inn near the shore, from whence he was to walk to his destination. My lord almost took him by the arm to pull him away; and they were gone, and I was left alone with Madame de Créquy. When she heard the horses' feet, she seemed to find out the truth, as if for the first time. She set her teeth together. "He has left me for her!" she almost screamed. "Left me for her!" she kept muttering; and then, as the wild look came back into her eyes, she said, almost with exultation, "But I did not give him my blessing!" '

## CHAPTER VI

' ALL night Madame de Créquy raved in delirium.
If I could, I would have sent for Clément back again.
I did send off one man, but I suppose my directions
were confused, or they were wrong, for he came back
after my lord's return, on the following afternoon.  By
this time Madame de Créquy was quieter : she was,
indeed, asleep from exhaustion when Lord Ludlow and
Monkshaven came in.  They were in high spirits, and
their hopefulness brought me round to a less dispirited
state.   All had gone well : they had accompanied
Clément on foot along the shore, until they had met
with a lugger, which my lord had hailed in good
nautical language.  The captain had responded to these
freemason terms by sending a boat to pick up his
passenger, and by an invitation to breakfast sent
through a speaking-trumpet.  Monkshaven did not
approve of either the meal or the company, and had
returned to the inn, but my lord had gone with Clément,
and breakfasted on board, upon grog, biscuit, fresh-
caught fish—" the best breakfast he ever ate," he said,
but that was probably owing to the appetite his night's
ride had given him.  However, his good fellowship had
evidently won the captain's heart, and Clément had
set sail under the best auspices.  It was agreed that
I should tell all this to Madame de Créquy, if she
inquired ; otherwise, it would be wiser not to renew
her agitation by alluding to her son's journey.

' I sat with her constantly for many days ; but she
never spoke of Clément.  She forced herself to talk
of the little occurrences of Parisian society in former
days : she tried to be conversational and agreeable,
and to betray no anxiety or even interest in the object
of Clément's journey ; and, as far as unremitting efforts
could go, she succeeded.  But the tones of her voice
were sharp and yet piteous, as if she were in constant
pain ; and the glance of her eye hurried and fearful,
as if she dared not let it rest on any object.

'In a week we heard of Clément's safe arrival on the French coast. He sent a letter to this effect by the captain of the smuggler, when the latter returned. We hoped to hear again; but week after week elapsed, and there was no news of Clément. I had told Lord Ludlow, in Madame de Créquy's presence, as he and I had arranged, of the note I had received from her son, informing us of his landing in France. She heard, but she took no notice. Yet now, evidently, she began to wonder that we did not mention any further intelligence of him in the same manner before her; and daily I began to fear that her pride would give way, and that she would supplicate for news before I had any to give her.

'One morning, on my awakening, my maid told me that Madame de Créquy had passed a wretched night, and had bidden Medlicott (whom, as understanding French, and speaking it pretty well, though with that horrid German accent, I had put about her) request that I would go to Madame's room as soon as I was dressed.

'I knew what was coming, and I trembled all the time they were doing my hair, and otherwise arranging me. I was not encouraged by my lord's speeches. He had heard the message, and kept declaring that he would rather be shot than have to tell her that there was no news of her son; and yet he said, every now and then, when I was at the lowest pitch of uneasiness, that he never expected to hear again : that some day soon we should see him walking in, and introducing Mademoiselle de Créquy to us.

'However, at last I was ready, and go I must.

'Her eyes were fixed on the door by which I entered. I went up to the bedside. She was not rouged,—she had left it off now for several days,—she no longer attempted to keep up the vain show of not feeling and loving and fearing.

'For a moment or two she did not speak, and I was glad of the respite.

'"Clément?" she said at length, covering her mouth

with a handkerchief the minute she had spoken, that I might not see it quiver.

' "There has been no news since the first letter, saying how well the voyage was performed, and how safely he had landed,—near Dieppe, you know," I replied as cheerfully as possible. "My lord does not expect that we shall have another letter; he thinks that we shall see him soon."

' There was no answer. As I looked, uncertain whether to do or say more, she slowly turned herself in bed, and lay with her face to the wall; and, as if that did not shut out the light of day and the busy, happy world enough, she put out her trembling hands, and covered her face with her handkerchief. There was no violence : hardly any sound.

' I told her what my lord had said about Clément's coming in some day, and taking us all by surprise. I did not believe it myself, but it was just possible,— and I had nothing else to say. Pity, to one who was striving so hard to conceal her feelings, would have been impertinent. She let me talk ; but she did not reply. She knew that my words were vain and idle, and had no root in my belief, as well as I did myself.

' I was very thankful when Medlicott came in with Madame's breakfast, and gave me an excuse for leaving.

' But I think that conversation made me feel more anxious and impatient than ever. I felt almost pledged to Madame de Créquy for the fulfilment of the vision I had held out. She had taken entirely to her bed by this time ; not from illness, but because she had no hope within her to stir her up to the effort of dressing. In the same way she hardly cared for food. She had no appetite,—why eat to prolong a life of despair ? But she let Medlicott feed her, sooner than take the trouble of resisting.

' And so it went on,—for weeks, months,—I could hardly count the time, it seemed so long. Medlicott told me she noticed a preternatural sensitiveness of ear in Madame de Créquy, induced by the habit of

listening silently for the slightest unusual sound in the
house. Medlicott was always a minute watcher of any
one whom she cared about ; and, one day, she made
me notice by a sign madame's acuteness of hearing,
although the quick expectation was but evinced for
a moment in the turn of the eye, the hushed breath—
and then, when the unusual footstep turned into my
lord's apartments, the soft quivering sigh, and the
closed eyelids.

' At length the intendant of the De Créquy estates,—
the old man, you will remember, whose information
respecting Virginie de Créquy first gave Clément the
desire to return to Paris,—came to St. James's Square,
and begged to speak to me. I made haste to go down
to him in the housekeeper's room, sooner than that
he should be ushered into mine, for fear of Madame
hearing any sound.

' The old man stood—I see him now—with his hat
held before him in both his hands ; he slowly bowed
till his face touched it when I came in. Such long
excess of courtesy augured ill. He waited for me to
speak.

' " Have you any intelligence ? " I inquired. He
had been often to the house before, to ask if we had
received any news ; and once or twice I had seen him,
but this was the first time he had begged to see me.

' " Yes, madame," he replied, still standing with his
head bent down, like a child in disgrace.

' " And it is bad ! " I exclaimed.

' " It is bad." For a moment I was angry at the
cold tone in which my words were echoed ; but directly
afterwards I saw the large, slow, heavy tears of age
falling down the old man's cheeks, and on to the sleeves
of his poor, thread-bare coat.

' I asked him how he had heard it : it seemed as
though I could not all at once bear to hear what it
was. He told me that the night before, in crossing
Long Acre, he had stumbled upon an old acquaintance
of his ; one who, like himself, had been a dependant
upon the De Créquy family, but had managed their

Paris affairs, while Fléchier had taken charge of their estates in the country. Both were now emigrants, and living on the proceeds of such small available talents as they possessed. Fléchier, as I knew, earned a very fair livelihood by going about to dress salads for dinner parties. His compatriot, Le Fèbvre, had begun to give a few lessons as a dancing-master. One of them took the other home to his lodgings; and there, when their most immediate personal adventures had been hastily talked over, came the inquiry from Fléchier as to Monsieur de Créquy.

' " Clément was dead—guillotined. Virginie was dead—guillotined."

' When Fléchier had told me thus much, he could not speak for sobbing; and I, myself, could hardly tell how to restrain my tears sufficiently, until I could go to my own room and be at liberty to give way. He asked my leave to bring in his friend Le Fèbvre, who was walking in the square, awaiting a possible summons to tell his story. I heard afterwards a good many details, which filled up the account, and made me feel—which brings me back to the point I started from—how unfit the lower orders are for being trusted indiscriminately with the dangerous powers of education. I have made a long preamble, but now I am coming to the moral of my story.'

My lady was trying to shake off the emotion which she evidently felt in recurring to this sad history of Monsieur de Créquy's death. She came behind me, and arranged my pillows, and then, seeing I had been crying—for, indeed, I was weak-spirited at the time, and a little served to unloose my tears—she stooped down, and kissed my forehead, and said ' Poor child ! ' almost as if she thanked me for feeling that old grief of hers.

' Being once in France, it was no difficult thing for Clément to get into Paris. The difficulty in those days was to leave, not to enter. He came in dressed as a Norman peasant, in charge of a load of fruit and vegetables, with which one of the Seine barges was freighted. He worked hard with his companions in landing and arranging their produce on the quays; and then, when they dispersed to get their breakfasts at some of the estaminets near the old Marché aux Fleurs, he sauntered up a street which conducted him, by many an odd turn, through the Quartier Latin to a horrid back alley, leading out of the Rue l'Ecole de Médécine; some atrocious place, as I have heard, not far from the shadow of that terrible Abbaye, where so many of the best blood of France awaited their deaths. But here some old man lived on whose fidelity Clément thought that he might rely. I am not sure if he had not been gardener in those very gardens behind the Hôtel Créquy where Clément and Urian used to play together years before. But, whatever the old man's dwelling might be, Clément was only too glad to reach it, you may be sure. He had been kept in Normandy, in all sorts of disguises, for many days after landing in Dieppe, through the difficulty of entering Paris unsuspected by the many ruffians who were always on the look-out for aristocrats.

'The old gardener was, I believe, both faithful and tried, and sheltered Clément in his garret as well as might be. Before he could stir out, it was necessary to procure a fresh disguise; and one more in character with an inhabitant of Paris than that of a Norman carter was procured; and, after waiting in-doors for one or two days, to see if any suspicion was excited, Clément set off to discover Virginie.

'He found her at the old concièrge's dwelling. Madame Babette was the name of this woman, who must have been a less faithful—or rather, perhaps I should say, a more interested—friend to her guest than the old gardener Jacques was to Clément.

'I have seen a miniature of Virginie, which a French lady of quality happened to have in her possession at the time of her flight from Paris, and which she brought with her to England unwittingly; for it belonged to the Count de Créquy, with whom she was slightly acquainted. I should fancy from it, that Virginie was

taller and of a more powerful figure for a woman than
her cousin Clément was for a man.  Her dark-brown
hair was arranged in short curls—the way of dressing
the hair announced the politics of the individual, in
those days, just as patches did in my grandmother's
time ;  and Virginie's hair was not to my taste, or
according to my principles ; it was too classical.  Her
large, black eyes looked out at you steadily.  One
cannot judge of the shape of a nose from a full-face
miniature, but the nostrils were clearly cut and largely
opened.  I do not fancy her nose could have been
pretty ; but her mouth had a character all its own, and
which would, I think, have redeemed a plainer face.
It was wide and deep set into the cheeks at the corners ;
the upper lip was very much arched, and hardly closed
over the teeth ; so that the whole face looked (from
the serious, intent look in the eyes, and the sweet
intelligence of the mouth) as if she were listening
eagerly to something to which her answer was quite
ready, and would come out of those red, opening lips
as soon as ever you had done speaking, and you longed
to know what she would say.

'Well ; this Virginie de Créquy was living with
Madame Babette in the concièrgerie of an old French
inn, somewhere to the north of Paris, so, far enough
from Clément's refuge.  The inn had been frequented
by farmers from Brittany and such kind of people, in
the days when that sort of intercourse went on between
Paris and the provinces which had nearly stopped now.
Few Bretons came near it now, and the inn had fallen
into the hands of Madame Babette's brother, as payment for a bad wine debt of the last proprietor.  He
put his sister and her child in, to keep it open, as it
were, and sent all the people he could to occupy the
half-furnished rooms of the house.  They paid Babette
for their lodging every morning as they went out to
breakfast, and returned or not as they chose, at night.
Every three days, the wine-merchant or his son came
to Madame Babette, and she accounted to them for the
money she had received.  She and her child occupied

the porter's office (in which the lad slept at nights) and
a little, miserable bed-room which opened out of it,
and received all the light and air that was admitted
through the door of communication, which was half
glass. Madame Babette must have had a kind of
attachment for the De Créquys—her De Créquys, you
understand—Virginie's father, the Count; for, at
some risk to herself, she had warned both him and his
daughter of the danger impending over them. But he,
infatuated, would not believe that his dear Human
Race could ever do him harm; and, as long as he did
not fear, Virginie was not afraid. It was by some
ruse, the nature of which I never heard, that Madame
Babette induced Virginie to come to her abode at the
very hour in which the Count had been recognized in
the streets, and hurried off to the Lanterne.* It was
after Babette had got her there, safe shut up in the
little back den, that she told her what had befallen her
father. From that day, Virginie had never stirred out
of the gates, or crossed the threshold of the porter's
lodge. I do not say that Madame Babette was tired
of her continual presence, or regretted the impulse
which had made her rush to the De Créquy's well-
known house—after being compelled to form one of
the mad crowds that saw the Count de Créquy seized
and hung—and hurry his daughter out, through alleys
and back-ways, until at length she had the orphan
safe in her own dark sleeping-room, and could tell her
tale of horror: but Madame Babette was poorly paid
for her porter's work by her avaricious brother; and
it was hard enough to find food for herself and her
growing boy; and, though the poor girl ate little
enough, I dare say, yet there seemed no end to the
burthen that Madame Babette had imposed upon herself: the De Créquys were plundered, ruined, had
become an extinct race, all but a lonely, friendless
girl, in broken health and spirits; and, though she
lent no positive encouragement to his suit, yet, at the
time, when Clément reappeared in Paris, Madame
Babette was beginning to think that Virginie might

do worse than encourage the attentions of Monsieur
Morin Fils, her nephew, and the wine-merchant's son.
Of course, he and his father had the entrée into the
concièrgerie of the hotel that belonged to them, in
right of being both proprietors and relations. The son,
Morin, had seen Virginie in this manner. He was fully
aware that she was far above him in rank, and guessed
from her whole aspect that she had lost her natural
protectors by the terrible guillotine ; but he did not
know her exact name or station, nor could he persuade
his aunt to tell him. However, he fell head over ears
in love with her, whether she were princess or peasant ;
and, though at first there was something about her
which made his passionate love conceal itself with shy,
awkward reserve, and then, made it only appear in the
guise of deep, respectful devotion ; yet, by-and-by,—
by the same process of reasoning I suppose that his
aunt had gone through even before him—Jean Morin
began to let Hope oust Despair from his heart. Sometimes he thought—perhaps years hence—that solitary,
friendless lady, pent up in squalor, might turn to him
as to a friend and comforter—and then—and then——.
Meanwhile Jean Morin was most attentive to his aunt ;
whom he had rather slighted before. He would linger
over the accounts ; would bring her little presents ;
and, above all, he made a pet and favourite of Pierre,
the little cousin who could tell him about all the ways
of going on of Mam'selle Cannes, as Virginie was called.
Pierre was thoroughly aware of the drift and cause of
his cousin's inquiries ; and was his ardent partisan,
as I have heard, even before Jean Morin had exactly
acknowledged his wishes to himself.

'It must have required some patience and much
diplomacy, before Clément de Créquy found out the
exact place where his cousin was hidden. The old
gardener took the cause very much to heart ; as,
judging from my recollections, I imagine he would
have forwarded any fancy, however wild, of Monsieur
Clément's. (I will tell you afterwards how I came to
know all these particulars so well.)

'After Clément's return, on two succeeding days, from his dangerous search without meeting with any good result, Jacques entreated Monsieur de Créquy to let him take it in hand. He represented that he, as gardener for the space of twenty years and more at the Hôtel de Créquy, had a right to be acquainted with all the successive concièrges at the Count's house ; that he should not go among them as a stranger, but as an old friend, anxious to renew pleasant intercourse ; and that if the Intendant's story, which he had told Monsieur de Créquy in England, was true, that Mademoiselle was in hiding at the house of a former concièrge, why, something relating to her would surely drop out in the course of conversation. So he persuaded Clément to remain in-doors, while he set off on his round, with no apparent object but to gossip.

'At night he came home,—having seen Mademoiselle. He told Clément much of the story relating to Madame Babette that I have told to you. Of course, he had heard nothing of the ambitious hopes of Morin Fils,—hardly of his existence, I should think. Madame Babette had received him kindly ; although, for some time, she had kept him standing in the carriage gateway outside her door. But, on his complaining of the draught and his rheumatism, she had asked him in : first looking round with some anxiety, to see who was in the room behind her. No one was there when he entered and sat down. But, in a minute or two, a tall, thin young lady, with great, sad eyes, and pale cheeks, came from the inner room, and, seeing him, retired. "It is Mademoiselle Cannes," said Madame Babette, rather unnecessarily ; for, if he had not been on the watch for some sign of Mademoiselle de Créquy, he would hardly have noticed the entrance and withdrawal.

'Clément and the good old gardener were always rather perplexed by Madame Babette's evident avoidance of all mention of the De Créquy family. If she were so much interested in one member as to be willing to undergo the pains and penalties of a domiciliary

visit, it was strange that she never inquired after the
existence of her charge's friends and relations from
one who might very probably have heard something
of them.  They settled that Madame Babette must
believe that the Marquise and Clément were dead ;
and admired her for her reticence in never speaking
of Virginie.  The truth was, I suspect, that she was
so desirous of her nephew's success by this time, that
she did not like letting any one into the secret of
Virginie's whereabouts who might interfere with their
plan.  However, it was arranged between Clément and
his humble friend, that the former, dressed in the
peasant's clothes in which he had entered Paris, but
smartened up in one or two particulars, as if, although
a countryman, he had money to spare, should go and
engage a sleeping-room in the old Bréton Inn ; where,
as I told you, accommodation for the night was to be
had.  This was accordingly done, without exciting
Madame Babette's suspicions, for she was unacquainted
with the Normandy accent, and consequently did not
perceive the exaggeration of it which Monsieur de
Créquy adopted in order to disguise his pure Parisian.
But after he had for two nights slept in a queer, dark
closet, at the end of one of the numerous short galleries
in the Hôtel Duguesclin, and paid his money for such
accommodation each morning at the little bureau under
the window of the concièrgerie, he found himself no
nearer to his object.  He stood outside in the gateway :
Madame Babette opened a pane in her window, counted
out the change, gave polite thanks, and shut to the
pane with a clack, before he could ever find out what
to say that might be the means of opening a conversation.  Once in the streets, he was in danger from the
bloodthirsty mob, who were ready in those days to
hunt to death every one who looked like a gentleman,
as an aristocrat : and Clément, depend upon it, looked
a gentleman, whatever dress he wore.  Yet it was
unwise to traverse Paris to his old friend the gardener's
grénier, so he had to loiter about, where I hardly know.
Only he did leave the Hôtel Duguesclin, and he did

not go to old Jacques, and there was not another
house in Paris open to him. At the end of two days,
he had made out Pierre's existence ; and he began to
try to make friends with the lad. Pierre was too sharp
and shrewd not to suspect something from the confused attempts at friendliness. It was not for nothing
that the Norman farmer lounged in the court and
doorway, and brought home presents of galette.* Pierre
accepted the galette, reciprocated the civil speeches,
but kept his eyes open. Once, returning home pretty
late at night, he surprised the Norman studying
the shadows on the blind, which was drawn down
when Madame Babette's lamp was lighted. On going
in, he found Mademoiselle Cannes with his mother,
sitting by the table, and helping in the family
mending.

' Pierre was afraid that the Norman had some view
upon the money which his mother, as concièrge, collected for her brother. But the money was all safe
next evening when his cousin, Monsieur Morin Fils,
came to collect it. Madame Babette asked her nephew
to sit down, and skilfully barred the passage to the
inner door, so that Virginie, had she been ever so
much disposed, could not have retreated. She sat
silently sewing. All at once the little party were
startled by a very sweet tenor voice, just close to the
street window, singing one of the airs out of Beaumarchais'*operas, which, a few years before, had been
popular all over Paris. But after a few moments of
silence, and one or two remarks, the talking went on
again. Pierre, however, noticed an increased air of
abstraction in Virginie, who, I suppose, was recurring
to the last time that she had heard the song, and did
not consider, as her cousin had hoped she would have
done, what were the words set to the air, which he
imagined she would remember, and which would have
told her so much. For, only a few years before, Adam`s*
opera of *Richard le Roi* had made the story of the
Minstrel Blondel and our English Cœur de Lion familiar
to all the opera-going part of the Parisian public, and

Clément had bethought him of establishing a communication with Virginie by some such means.

'The next night, about the same hour, the same voice was singing outside the window again. Pierre, who had been irritated by the proceeding the evening before, as it had diverted Virginie's attention from his cousin, who had been doing his utmost to make himself agreeable, rushed out to the door, just as the Norman was ringing the bell to be admitted for the night. Pierre looked up and down the street; no one else was to be seen. The next day, the Norman mollified him somewhat by knocking at the door of the concièrgerie, and begging Monsieur Pierre's acceptance of some knee-buckles, which had taken the country farmer's fancy the day before, as he had been gazing into the shops, but which, being too small for his purpose, he took the liberty of offering to Monsieur Pierre. Pierre, a French boy, inclined to foppery, was charmed, ravished by the beauty of the present and with Monsieur's goodness, and he began to adjust them to his breeches immediately, as well as he could, at least, in his mother's absence. The Norman, whom Pierre kept carefully on the outside of the threshold, stood by, as if amused at the boy's eagerness.

' " Take care," said he, clearly and distinctly; " take care, my little friend, lest you become a fop; and, in that case, some day, years hence, when your heart is devoted to some young lady, she may be inclined to say to you "—here he raised his voice—" No, thank you; when I marry, I marry a man, not a petit-maître; I marry a man, who, whatever his position may be, will add dignity to the human race by his virtues." Farther than that in his quotation Clément dared not go. His sentiments (so much above the apparent occasion) met with applause from Pierre, who liked to contemplate himself in the light of a lover, even though it should be a rejected one, and who hailed the mention of the words " virtues " and " dignity of the human race " as belonging to the cant of a good citizen.

'But Clément was more anxious to know how the invisible lady took his speech. There was no sign at the time. But when he returned at night, he heard a voice, low singing, behind Madame Babette, as she handed him his candle, the very air he had sung without effect for two nights past. As if he had caught it up from her murmuring voice, he sang it loudly and clearly as he crossed the court.

'"Here is our opera-singer!" exclaimed Madame Babette. "Why, the Norman grazier sings like Boupré," naming a favourite singer at the neighbouring theatre.

'Pierre was struck by the remark, and quietly resolved to look after the Norman; but again, I believe, it was more because of his mother's deposit of money than with any thought of Virginie.

'However, the next morning, to the wonder of both mother and son, Mademoiselle Cannes proposed, with much hesitation, to go out and make some little purchase for herself. A month or two ago, this was what Madame Babette had been never weary of urging. But now she was as much surprised as if she had expected Virginie to remain a prisoner in her rooms all the rest of her life. I suppose she had hoped that her first time of quitting it would be when she left it for Monsieur Morin's house as his wife.

'A quick look from Madame Babette towards Pierre was all that was needed to encourage the boy to follow her. He went out cautiously. She was at the end of the street. She looked up and down, as if waiting for some one. No one was there. Back she came, so swiftly that she nearly caught Pierre before he could retreat through the porte-cochère. There he looked out again. The neighbourhood was low and wild, and strange; and some one spoke to Virginie,—nay, laid his hand upon her arm,—whose dress and aspect (he had emerged out of a side-street) Pierre did not know; but, after a start, and (Pierre could fancy) a little scream, Virginie recognised the stranger, and the two turned up the side street whence the man had come.

Pierre stole swiftly to the corner of this street; no one was there: they had disappeared up some of the alleys. Pierre returned home to excite his mother's infinite surprise. But they had hardly done talking, when Virginie returned, with a colour and a radiance in her face, which they had never seen there since her father's death.

## CHAPTER VII

'I HAVE told you that I heard much of this story from a friend of the Intendant of the De Créquys, whom he met with in London. Some years afterwards—the summer before my lord's death—I was travelling with him in Devonshire, and we went to see the French prisoners of war on Dartmoor. We fell into conversation with one of them, whom I found out to be the very Pierre of whom I had heard before, as having been involved in the fatal story of Clément and Virginie, and by him I was told much of their last days, and thus I learnt how to have some sympathy with all those who were concerned in those terrible events; yes, even with the younger Morin himself, on whose behalf Pierre spoke warmly, even after so long a time had elapsed.

'For when the younger Morin called at the porter's lodge, on the evening of the day when Virginie had gone out for the first time after so many months' confinement to the concièrgerie, he was struck with the improvement in her appearance. It seems to have hardly been that he thought her beauty greater; for, in addition to the fact that she was not beautiful, Morin had arrived at that point of being enamoured when it does not signify whether the beloved one is plain or handsome—she has enchanted one pair of eyes, which henceforward see her through their own medium. But Morin noticed the faint increase of colour and light in her countenance. It was as though she had broken through her thick cloud of hopeless sorrow, and was dawning forth into a happier life. And so, whereas during her grief, he had revered and respected it even to a point of silent sympathy, now that she was gladdened, his heart rose on the wings of strengthened hopes. Even in the dreary monotony of this existence in his Aunt Babette's concièrgerie, Time had not failed in his work, and now, perhaps, soon he might humbly strive to help Time. The very next day he returned— on some pretence of business—to the Hôtel Duguesclin, and made his aunt's room, rather than his aunt herself, a present of roses and geraniums tied up in a bouquet with a tricolour ribbon. Virginie was in the room, sitting at the coarse sewing she liked to do for Madame Babette. He saw her eyes brighten at the sight of the flowers : she asked his aunt to let her arrange them ; he saw her untie the ribbon, and with a gesture of dislike, throw it on the ground, and give it a kick with her little foot, and even in this girlish manner of insulting his dearest prejudices, he found something to admire.

'As he was coming out, Pierre stopped him. The lad had been trying to arrest his cousin's attention by futile grimaces and signs played off behind Virginie's back ; but Monsieur Morin saw nothing but Mademoiselle Cannes. However, Pierre was not to be baffled, and Monsieur Morin found him in waiting just outside the threshold. With his finger on his lips, Pierre walked on tiptoe by his companion's side till they would have been long past sight or hearing of the concièrgerie, even had the inhabitants devoted themselves to the purposes of spying or listening.

' " Chut ! " said Pierre, at last. " She goes out walking."

' " Well ? " said Monsieur Morin, half curious, half annoyed at being disturbed in the delicious reverie of the future into which he longed to fall.

' " Well ! It is not well. It is bad."

' " Why ? I do not ask who she is, but I have my ideas. She is an aristocrat. Do the people about here begin to suspect her ? "

' " No, no ! " said Pierre. " But she goes out walking.

She has gone these two mornings. I have watched her. She meets a man—she is friends with him, for she talks to him as eagerly as he does to her—mamma cannot tell who he is."

' " Has my aunt seen him ? "

' " No, not so much as a fly's wing of him. I myself have only seen his back. It strikes me like a familiar back, and yet I cannot think who it is. But they separate with sudden darts, like two birds who have been together to feed their young ones. One moment they are in close talk, their heads together chuckotting, the next he has turned up some by-street, and Mademoiselle Cannes is close upon me—has almost caught me."

' " But she did not see you ? " inquired Monsieur Morin, in so altered a voice that Pierre gave him one of his quick penetrating looks. He was struck by the way in which his cousin's features—always coarse and commonplace—had become contracted and pinched ; struck, too, by the livid look on his sallow complexion. But as if Morin was conscious of the manner in which his face belied his feelings, he made an effort, and smiled, and patted Pierre's head, and thanked him for his intelligence, and gave him a five-franc piece, and bade him go on with his observations of Mademoiselle Cannes' movements, and report all to him.

' Pierre returned home with a light heart, tossing up his five-franc piece as he ran. Just as he was at the concièrgerie door, a great tall man bustled past him, and snatched his money away from him, looking back with a laugh, which added insult to injury. Pierre had no redress ; no one had witnessed the impudent theft, and if they had, no one to be seen in the street was strong enough to give him redress. Besides, Pierre had seen enough of the state of the streets of Paris at that time to know that friends, not enemies, were required, and the man had a bad air about him. But all these considerations did not keep Pierre from bursting out into a fit of crying when he was once more under his mother's roof ; and Virginie, who was alone there (Madame Babette having gone out to make her daily purchases), might have imagined him pommelled to death by the loudness of his sobs.

' "What is the matter ? " asked she. "Speak, my child. What hast thou done ? "

' "He has robbed me !. he has robbed me ! " was all Pierre could gulp out.

' "Robbed thee ! and of what, my poor boy ? " said Virginie, stroking his hair gently.

' "Of my five-franc piece—of a five-franc piece," said Pierre, correcting himself, and leaving out the word 'my', half fearful lest Virginie should inquire how he became possessed of such a sum, and for what services it had been given him. But, of course, no such idea came into her head, for it would have been impertinent, and she was gentle-born.

' "Wait a moment, my lad," and, going to the one small drawer in the inner apartment, which held all her few possessions, she brought back a little ring— a ring just with one ruby in it—which she had worn in the days when she cared to wear jewels. "Take this," said she, "and run with it to a jeweller's. It is but a poor, valueless thing, but it will bring you in your five francs at any rate. Go ! I desire you."

' "But I cannot," said the boy, hesitating ; some dim sense of honour flitting through his misty morals.

' "Yes ; you must ! " she continued, urging him with her hand to the door. "Run ! if it brings in more than five francs, you shall return the surplus to me."

' Thus tempted by her urgency, and, I suppose, reasoning with himself to the effect that he might as well have the money, and then see whether he thought it right to act as a spy upon her or not—the one action did not pledge him to the other, nor yet did she make any conditions with her gift—Pierre went off with her ring ; and, after repaying himself his five francs, he was enabled to bring Virginie back two more, so well had he managed his affairs. But, although the whole transaction did not leave him bound, in any way, to discover or forward Virginie's wishes, it did leave him

pledged, according to his code, to act according to her
advantage, and he considered himself the judge of the
best course to be pursued to this end. And, moreover,
this little kindness attached him to her personally.
He began to think how pleasant it would be to have
so kind and generous a person for a relation; how
easily his troubles might be borne if he had always
such a ready helper at hand; how much he should
like to make her like him, and come to him for the
protection of his masculine power! First of all his
duties, as her self-appointed squire, came the necessity
of finding out who her strange new acquaintance was.
Thus, you see, he arrived at the same end, viâ supposed duty, that he was previously pledged to viâ
interest. I fancy a good number of us, when any line
of action will promote our own interest, can make
ourselves believe that reasons exist which compel us
to it as a duty.

'In the course of a very few days, Pierre had so
circumvented Virginie as to have discovered that her
new friend was no other than the Norman farmer in
a different dress. This was a great piece of knowledge
to impart to Morin. But Pierre was not prepared for
the immediate physical effect it had on his cousin.
Morin sat suddenly down on one of the seats in the
Boulevards—it was there Pierre had met with him
accidentally—when he heard who it was that Virginie
met. I do not suppose the man had the faintest idea
of any relationship or even previous acquaintanceship
between Clément and Virginie. If he thought of anything beyond the mere fact presented to him, that his
idol was in communication with another, younger,
handsomer man than himself, it must have been that
the Norman farmer had seen her at the concièrgerie,
and had been attracted by her, and, as was but natural,
had tried to make her acquaintance, and had succeeded.
But, from what Pierre told me, I should not think
that even this much thought passed through Morin's
mind. He seems to have been a man of rare and
concentrated attachments; violent, though restrained

and undemonstrative passions; and, above all, a capability of jealousy, of which his dark oriental complexion must have been a type. I could fancy that if he had married Virginie, he would have coined his life-blood for luxuries to make her happy; would have watched over and petted her, at every sacrifice to himself, as long as she would have been content to live for him alone. But, as Pierre expressed it to me: "When I saw what my cousin was, when I learned his nature too late, I perceived that he would have strangled a bird if she whom he loved was attracted by it from him."

'When Pierre had told Morin of his discovery, Morin sat down, as I have said, quite suddenly, as if he had been shot. He found out that the first meeting between the Norman and Virginie was no accidental, isolated circumstance. Pierre was torturing him with his accounts of daily rendezvous: if but for a moment, they were seeing each other every day, sometimes twice a day. And Virginie could speak to this man, though to himself she was so coy and reserved as hardly to utter a sentence. Pierre caught these broken words while his cousin's complexion grew more and more livid, and then purple, as if some great effect were produced on his circulation by the news he had just heard. Pierre was so startled by his cousin's wandering senseless eyes, and otherwise disordered looks, that he rushed into a neighbouring cabaret for a glass of absinthe, which he paid for, as he recollected afterwards, with a portion of Virginie's five francs. By-and-by Morin recovered his natural appearance; but he was gloomy and silent; and all that Pierre could get out of him was, that the Norman farmer should not sleep another night at the Hôtel Duguesclin, giving him such opportunities of passing and repassing by the concièrgerie door. He was too much absorbed in his own thoughts to repay Pierre the half-franc he had spent on the absinthe, which Pierre perceived, and seems to have noted down in the ledger of his mind as on Virginie's balance of favour.

Altogether, he was so much disappointed at his

cousin's mode of receiving intelligence, which the lad thought worth another five-franc piece at least; or, if not paid for in money, to be paid for in open-mouthed confidence and expression of feeling, that he was for a time, so far a partisan of Virginie's—unconscious Virginie—against his cousin, as to feel regret when the Norman returned no more to his night's lodging, and when Virginie's eager watch at the crevice of the closely-drawn blind ended only with a sigh of disappointment. If it had not been for his mother's presence at the time, Pierre thought he should have told her all. But how far was his mother in his cousin's confidence as regarded the dismissal of the Norman?

'In a few days, however, Pierre felt almost sure that they had established some new means of communication. Virginie went out for a short time every day; but, though Pierre followed her as closely as he could without exciting her observation, he was unable to discover what kind of intercourse she held with the Norman. She went, in general, the same short round among the little shops in the neighbourhood; not entering any, but stopping at two or three. Pierre afterwards remembered that she had invariably paused at the nosegays displayed in a certain window, and studied them long; but, then, she stopped and looked at caps, hats, fashions, confectionery (all of the humble kind common in that quarter), so how should he have known that any particular attraction existed among the flowers? Morin came more regularly than ever to his aunt's; but Virginie was apparently unconscious that she was the attraction. She looked healthier and more hopeful than she had done for months, and her manners to all were gentler and not so reserved. Almost as if she wished to manifest her gratitude to Madame Babette for her long continuance of a kindness, the necessity for which was nearly ended, Virginie showed an unusual alacrity in rendering the old woman any little service in her power, and evidently tried to respond to Monsieur Morin's civilities, he being Madame Babette's nephew, with the soft graciousness which must have made one of her principal charms; for all who knew her speak of the fascination of her manners, so winning and attentive to others, while yet her opinions, and often her actions, were of so decided a character. For, as I have said, her beauty was by no means great; yet every man who came near her seems to have fallen into the sphere of her influence. Monsieur Morin was deeper than ever in love with her during these last few days: he was worked up into a state capable of any sacrifice, either of himself or others, so that he might obtain her at last. He sat "devouring her with his eyes" (to use Pierre's expression) whenever she could not see him; but, if she looked towards him, he looked to the ground—anywhere—away from her, and almost stammered in his replies if she addressed any question to him.

' He had been, I should think, ashamed of his extreme agitation on the Boulevards, for Pierre thought that he absolutely shunned him for these few succeeding days. He must have believed that he had driven the Norman (my poor Clément!) off the field, by banishing him from his inn; and thought that the intercourse between him and Virginie, which he had thus interrupted, was of so slight and transient a character as to be quenched by a little difficulty.

' But he appears to have felt that he made but little way, and he awkwardly turned to Pierre for help—not yet confessing his love, though; he only tried to make friends again with the lad after their silent estrangement. And Pierre for some time did not choose to perceive his cousin's advances. He would reply to all the roundabout questions Morin put to him respecting household conversations when he was not present, or household occupations and tone of thought, without mentioning Virginie's name any more than his quesioner did. The lad would seem to suppose, that his cousin's strong interest in their domestic ways of going on was all on account of Madame Babette. At last he worked his cousin up to the point of making him a confidant; and then the boy was half frightened at

the torrent of vehement words he had unloosed. The
lava came down with a greater rush for having been
pent up so long. Morin cried out his words in a hoarse,
passionate voice, clenched his teeth, his fingers, and
seemed almost convulsed, as he spoke out his terrible
love for Virginie, which would lead him to kill her
sooner than see her another's ; and if another stepped
in between him and her !—and then he smiled a fierce,
triumphant smile, but did not say any more.

' Pierre was, as I said, half-frightened ; but also
half-admiring. This was really love—a "grande passion,"—a really fine, dramatic thing,—like the plays
they acted at the little theatre yonder. He had a dozen
times the sympathy with his cousin now that he had
had before, and readily swore by the infernal gods, for
they were far too enlightened to believe in one God,
or Christianity, or anything of the kind,—that he
would devote himself, body and soul, to forwarding
his cousin's views. Then his cousin took him to a shop,
and bought him a smart second-hand watch, on which
they scratched the word Fidélité, and thus was the
compact sealed. Pierre settled in his own mind, that
if he were a woman, he should like to be beloved as
Virginie was by his cousin, and that it would be an
extremely good thing for her to be the wife of so rich
a citizen as Morin Fils,—and for Pierre himself, too,
for doubtless their gratitude would lead them to give
him rings and watches *ad infinitum*.

' A day or two afterwards, Virginie was taken ill.
Madame Babette said it was because she had persevered
in going out in all weathers, after confining herself to
two warm rooms for so long ; and very probably this
was really the cause, for, from Pierre's account, she
must have been suffering from a feverish cold, aggra-
vated, no doubt, by her impatience at Madame
Babette's familiar prohibitions of any more walks until
she was better. Every day, in spite of her trembling
aching limbs, she would fain have arranged her dress
for her walk at the usual time ; but Madame Babette
was fully prepared to put physical obstacles in her

way, if she was not obedient in remaining tranquil on
the little sofa by the side of the fire. The third day,
she called Pierre to her, when his mother was not
attending (having, in fact, locked up Mademoiselle
Cannes' out-of-door things).

' "See, my child," said Virginie. "Thou must do
me a great favour. Go to the gardener's shop in the
Rue des Bons-Enfans, and look at the nosegays in
the window. I long for pinks; they are my favourite
flower. Here are two francs. If thou seest a nosegay
of pinks displayed in the window, if it be ever so
faded,—nay, if thou seest two or three nosegays of
pinks, remember, buy them all, and bring them to me,
I have so great a desire for the smell." She fell back
weak and exhausted. Pierre hurried out. Now was
the time; here was the clue to the long inspection of
the nosegay in this very shop.

' Sure enough, there was a drooping nosegay of pinks
in the window. Pierre went in, and, with all his impatience, he made as good a bargain as he could,
urging that the flowers were faded, and good for
nothing. At last he purchased them at a very moderate
price. And now you will learn the bad consequences
of teaching the lower orders anything beyond what is
immediately necessary to enable them to earn their
daily bread! The silly Count de Créquy,—he who had
been sent to his bloody rest, by the very canaille of
whom he thought so much,—he who had made Virginie
(indirectly, it is true) reject such a man as her cousin
Clément, by inflating her mind with his bubbles of
theories,—this Count de Créquy had long ago taken
a fancy to Pierre, as he saw the bright sharp child
playing about his courtyard. Monsieur de Créquy
had even begun to educate the boy himself, to try to
work out certain opinions of his into practice,—but
the drudgery of the affair wearied him, and, beside,
Babette had left his employment. Still the Count took
a kind of interest in his former pupil; and made some
sort of arrangement by which Pierre was to be taught
reading and writing, and accounts, and Heaven knows

what besides,—Latin, I dare say. So Pierre, instead
of being an innocent messenger, as he ought to have
been—(as Mr. Horner's little lad Gregson ought to
have been this morning)—could read writing as well as
either you or I. So what does he do, on obtaining the
nosegay, but examine it well. The stalks of the flowers
were tied up with slips of matting in wet moss. Pierre
undid the strings, unwrapped the moss, and out fell
a piece of wet paper, with the writing all blurred with
moisture. It was but a torn piece of writing-paper,
apparently, but Pierre's wicked mischievous eyes read
what was written on it,—written so as to look like
a fragment.—" Ready, every and any night at nine.
All is prepared. Have no fright. Trust one who,
whatever hopes he might once have had, is content
now to serve you as a faithful cousin;" and a place
was named, which I forget, but which Pierre did not,
as it was evidently the rendezvous. After the lad had
studied every word, till he could say it off by heart,
he placed the paper where he had found it, enveloped
it in moss, and tied the whole up again carefully.
Virginie's face coloured scarlet as she received it. She
kept smelling at it, and trembling : but she did not
untie it, although Pierre suggested how much fresher
it would be if the stalks were immediately put into
water. But once, after his back had been turned for
a minute, he saw it untied when he looked round again,
and Virginie was blushing, and hiding something in her
bosom.

' Pierre was now all impatience to set off and find
his cousin. But his mother seemed to want him for
small domestic purposes even more than usual; and
he had chafed over a multitude of errands connected
with the Hôtel before he could set off and search for
his cousin at his usual haunts. At last the two met ;
and Pierre related all the events of the morning to
Morin. He said the note off word by word. (That
lad this morning had something of the magpie look of
Pierre—it made me shudder to see him, and hear him
repeat the note by heart.) Then Morin asked him to

tell him all over again. Pierre was struck by Morin's
heavy sighs as he repeated the story. When he came
the second time to the note, Morin tried to write the
words down; but either he was not a good, ready
scholar, or his fingers trembled too much. Pierre
hardly remembered, but, at any rate, the lad had to
do it, with his wicked reading and writing. When this
was done, Morin sat heavily silent. Pierre would have
preferred the expected outburst, for this impenetrable
gloom perplexed and baffled him. He had even to
speak to his cousin to rouse him; and when he replied,
what he said had so little apparent connexion with the
subject which Pierre had expected to find uppermost
in his mind, that he was half-afraid that his cousin
had lost his wits.

'"My Aunt Babette is out of coffee."

'"I am sure I do not know," said Pierre.

'"Yes, she is. I heard her say so. Tell her that
a friend of mine has just opened a shop in the Rue
Saint Antoine, and that if she will join me there in an
hour, I will supply her with a good stock of coffee,
just to give my friend encouragement. His name is
Antoine Meyer, Number One hundred and Fifty, at
the sign of the Cap of Liberty."

'"I could go with you now. I can carry a few
pounds of coffee better than my mother," said Pierre,
all in good faith. He told me he should never forget
the look on his cousin's face, as he turned round, and
bade him begone, and give his mother the message
without another word. It had evidently sent him
home promptly to obey his cousin's command. Morin's
message perplexed Madame Babette.

'"How could he know I was out of coffee?" said
she. "I am; but I only used the last up this morning.
How could Victor know about it?"

'"I am sure I can't tell," said Pierre, who by this
time had recovered his usual self-possession. "All I
know is, that Monsieur is in a pretty temper, and that
if you are not sharp to your time at this Antoine Meyer's
you are likely to come in for some of his black looks."

' "Well, it is very kind of him to offer to give me some coffee, to be sure! But how could he know I was out?"

'Pierre hurried his mother off impatiently, for he was certain that the offer of the coffee was only a blind to some hidden purpose on his cousin's part; and he made no doubt that when his mother had been informed of what his cousin's real intention was, he, Pierre, could extract it from her by coaxing or bullying. But he was mistaken. Madame Babette returned home, grave, depressed, silent, and loaded with the best coffee. Some time afterwards he learnt why his cousin had sought for this interview. It was to extract from her, by promises and threats, the real name of Mam'selle Cannes, which would give him a clue to the true appellation of The Faithful Cousin. He concealed this second purpose from his aunt, who had been quite unaware of his jealousy of the Norman farmer, or of his identification of him with any relation of Virginie's. But Madame Babette instinctively shrank from giving him any information: she must have felt that, in the lowering mood in which she found him, his desire for greater knowledge of Virginie's antecedents boded her no good. And yet he made his aunt his confidante— told her what she had only suspected before that he was deeply enamoured of Mam'selle Cannes, and would gladly marry her. He spoke to Madame Babette of his father's hoarded riches; and of the share which he, as partner, had in them at the present time; and of the prospect of the succession to the whole, which he had, as an only child. He told his aunt of the provision for her (Madame Babette's) life, which he would make on the day when he married Mam'selle Cannes. And yet—and yet—Babette saw that in his eye and look which made her more and more reluctant to confide in him. By and by he tried threats. She should leave the concièrgerie, and find employment where she liked. Still silence. Then he grew angry, and swore that he would inform against her at the bureau of the Directory, for harbouring an aristocrat;

an aristocrat he knew Mademoiselle was, whatever her
real name might be. His aunt should have a domiciliary visit, and see how she liked that. The officers
of the Government were the people for finding out
secrets. In vain she reminded him that, by so doing,
he would expose to imminent danger the lady whom
he had professed to love. He told her, with a sullen
relapse into silence after his vehement outpouring of
passion, never to trouble herself about that. At last
he wearied out the old woman, and, frightened alike of
herself, and of him, she told him all,—that Mam'selle
Cannes was Mademoiselle Virginie de Créquy, daughter
of the Count of that name. Who was the Count?
Younger brother of the Marquis. Where was the
Marquis? Dead long ago, leaving a widow and child.
A son? (eagerly). Yes, a son. Where was he? Par-
bleu! how should she know?—for her courage returned
a little as the talk went away from the only person of
the De Créquy family that she cared about. But, by
dint of some small glasses out of a bottle of Antoine
Meyer's, she told him more about the De Créquys than
she liked afterwards to remember. For the exhilara-
tion of the brandy lasted but a very short time, and
she came home, as I have said, depressed, with a pre-
sentiment of coming evil. She would not answer
Pierre, but cuffed him about in a manner to which
the spoilt boy was quite unaccustomed. His cousin's
short, angry words, and sudden withdrawal of confidence,—his mother's unwonted crossness and fault-
finding, all made Virginie's kind, gentle treatment more
than ever charming to the lad. He half resolved to
tell her how he had been acting as a spy upon her
actions, and at whose desire he had done it. But he
was afraid of Morin, and of the vengeance which he
was sure would fall upon him for any breach of confidence. Towards half-past eight that evening—Pierre,
watching, saw Virginie arrange several little things—
she was in the inner room, but he sat where he could
see her through the glazed partition. His mother sat—
apparently sleeping—in the great easy-chair; Virginie

moved about softly, for fear of disturbing her. She made up one or two little parcels of the few things she could call her own : one packet she concealed about herself,—the others she directed, and left on the shelf. "She is going," thought Pierre, and (as he said in giving me the account) his heart gave a spring, to think that he should never see her again. If either his mother or his cousin had been more kind to him, he might have endeavoured to intercept her ; but as it was, he held his breath, and when she came out he pretended to read, scarcely knowing whether he wished her to succeed in the purpose which he was almost sure she entertained, or not. She stopped by him, and passed her hand over his hair. He told me that his eyes filled with tears at this caress. Then she stood for a moment, looking at the sleeping Madame Babette, and stooped down and softly kissed her on the forehead. Pierre dreaded lest his mother should awake (for by this time the wayward, vacillating boy must have been quite on Virginie's side), but the brandy she had drunk made her slumber heavily. Virginie went. Pierre's heart beat fast. He was sure his cousin would try to intercept her ; but how, he could not imagine. He longed to run out and see the catastrophe,—but he had let the moment slip ; he was also afraid of reawakening his mother to her unusual state of anger and violence.'

## CHAPTER VIII

' PIERRE went on pretending to read, but in reality listening with acute tension of ear to every little sound. His perceptions became so sensitive in this respect that he was incapable of measuring time, every moment had seemed so full of noises, from the beating of his heart up to the roll of the heavy carts in the distance. He wondered whether Virginie would have reached the place of rendezvous, and yet he was unable to compute the passage of minutes. His mother slept soundly :

that was well. By this time Virginie must have met the "faithful cousin" : if, indeed, Morin had not made his appearance.

'At length, he felt as if he could no longer sit still, awaiting the issue, but must run out and see what course events had taken. In vain his mother, half rousing herself, called after him to ask whither he was going : he was already out of hearing before she had ended her sentence, and he ran on until stopped by the sight of Mademoiselle Cannes walking along at so swift a pace that it was almost a run ; while at her side, resolutely keeping by her, Morin was striding abreast. Pierre had just turned the corner of the street when he came upon them. Virginie would have passed him without recognizing him, she was in such passionate agitation, but for Morin's gesture, by which he would fain have kept Pierre from interrupting them. Then, when Virginie saw the lad, she caught at his arm, and thanked God, as if in that boy of twelve or fourteen she held a protector. Pierre felt her tremble from head to foot, and was afraid lest she would fall, there where she stood, in the hard rough street.

' " Begone, Pierre ! " said Morin.

' " I cannot," replied Pierre, who indeed was held firmly by Virginie. " Besides, I won't," he added. " Who has been frightening Mademoiselle in this way ? " asked he, very much inclined to brave his cousin at all hazards.

' " Mademoiselle is not accustomed to walk in the streets alone," said Morin, sulkily. " She came upon a crowd attracted by the arrest of an aristocrat, and their cries alarmed her. I offered to take charge of her home. Mademoiselle should not walk in these streets alone. We are not like the cold-blooded people of the Faubourg Saint Germain."

' Virginie did not speak. Pierre doubted if she heard a word of what they were saying. She leant upon him more and more heavily.

' " Will Mademoiselle condescend to take my arm ? " said Morin, with sulky, and yet humble, uncouthness.

I dare say he would have given worlds if he might have
had that little hand within his arm ; but, though she
still kept silence, she shuddered up away from him, as
you shrink from touching a toad.  He had said something to her during that walk, you may be sure, which
had made her loathe him.  He marked and understood
the gesture.  He held himself aloof while Pierre gave
her all the assistance he could in their slow progress
homewards.  But Morin accompanied her all the same.
He had played too desperate a game to be balked
now.  He had given information against the çi-devant
Marquis de Créquy, as a returned émigré, to be met
with at such a time, in such a place.  Morin had hoped
that all sign of the arrest would have been cleared
away before Virginie reached the spot—so swiftly
were terrible deeds done in those days.  But Clément
defended himself desperately : Virginie was punctual
to a second ; and, though the wounded man was borne
off to the Abbaye, amid a crowd of the unsympathizing
jeerers who mingled with the armed officials of the
Directory, Morin feared lest Virginie had recognized
him ; and he would have preferred that she should
have thought that the " faithful cousin " was faithless,
than that she should have seen him in bloody danger
on her account.  I suppose he fancied that, if Virginie
never saw or heard more of him, her imagination would
not dwell on his simple disappearance, as it would do
if she knew what he was suffering for her sake.

' At any rate, Pierre saw that his cousin was deeply
mortified by the whole tenor of his behaviour during
their walk home.  When they arrived at Madame
Babette's, Virginie fell fainting on the floor ; her
strength had but just sufficed for this exertion of
reaching the shelter of the house.  Her first sign of
restoring consciousness consisted in avoidance of Morin.
He had been most assiduous in his efforts to bring her
round ; quite tender in his way, Pierre said ; and this
marked, instinctive repugnance to him evidently gave
him extreme pain.  I suppose Frenchmen are more
demonstrative than we are ; for Pierre declared that

he saw his cousin's eyes fill with tears, as she shrank
away from his touch, if he tried to arrange the shawl
they had laid under her head like a pillow, or as she
shut her eyes when he passed before her. Madame
Babette was urgent with her to go and lie down on
the bed in the inner room ; but it was some time
before she was strong enough to rise and do this.

'When Madame Babette returned from arranging
the girl comfortably, the three relations sat down in
silence ; a silence which Pierre thought would never
be broken. He wanted his mother to ask his cousin
what had happened. But Madame Babette was afraid
of her nephew, and thought it more discreet to wait
for such crumbs of intelligence as he might think fit
to throw to her. But, after she had twice reported
Virginie to be asleep, without a word being uttered
in reply to her whispers by either of her companions,
Morin's powers of self-containment gave way.

' "It is hard !" he said.

' "What is hard ?" asked Madame Babette, after
she had paused for a time, to enable him to add to,
or to finish, his sentence, if he pleased.

' "It is hard for a man to love a woman as I do,"
he went on. "I did not seek to love her, it came upon
me before I was aware—before I had ever thought
about it at all, I loved her better than all the world
beside. All my life, before I knew her, seems a dull
blank. I neither know nor care for what I did before
then. And now there are just two lives before me.
Either I have her, or I have not. That is all : but
that is everything. And what can I do to make her
have me ? Tell me, aunt," and he caught at Madame
Babette's arm, and gave it so sharp a shake, that she
half screamed out, Pierre said, and evidently grew
alarmed at her nephew's excitement.

' "Hush, Victor !" said she. "There are other
women in the world, if this one will not have you."

' "None other for me," he said, sinking back as if
hopeless. "I am plain and coarse, not one of the
scented darlings of the aristocrats. Say that I am

ugly, brutish; I did not make myself so, any more
than I made myself love her. It is my fate. But am
I to submit to the consequences of my fate without
a struggle ? Not I. As strong as my love is, so strong
is my will. It can be no stronger," continued he,
gloomily. "Aunt Babette, you must help me—you
must make her love me." He was so fierce here, that
Pierre said he did not wonder that his mother was
frightened.

' "I, Victor!" she exclaimed. "I make her love
you ? How can I ? Ask me to speak for you to
Mademoiselle Didot, or to Mademoiselle Cauchois even,
or to such as they, and I'll do it, and welcome. But
to Mademoiselle de Créquy, why, you don't know the
difference ! Those people—the old nobility I mean—
why, they don't know a man from a dog, out of their
own rank ! And no wonder, for the young gentlemen
of quality are treated differently to us from their very
birth. If she had you to-morrow, you would be
miserable. Let me alone for knowing the aristocracy.
I have not been a concièrge to a duke and three counts
for nothing. I tell you, all your ways are different to
her ways."

' "I would change ' my ways,' as you call them."

' "Be reasonable, Victor."

' "No, I will not be reasonable, if by that you mean
giving her up. I tell you two lives are before me ;
one with her, one without her. But the latter will be
but a short career for both of us. You said, aunt, that
the talk went in the concièrgerie of her father's hôtel,
that she would have nothing to do with this cousin
whom I put out of the way to-day ? "

' "So the servants said. How could I know ? All
I know is, that he left off coming to our hôtel, and
that at one time before then he had never been two
days absent."

' "So much the better for him. He suffers now for
having come between me and my object—in trying to
snatch her away out of my sight. Take you warning,
Pierre ! I did not like your meddling to-night." And

so he went off, leaving Madame Babette rocking herself backwards and forwards, in all the depression of spirits consequent upon the reaction after the brandy, and upon her knowledge of her nephew's threatened purpose combined.

'In telling you most of this, I have simply repeated Pierre's account, which I wrote down at the time. But here what he had to say came to a sudden break; for, the next morning, when Madame Babette rose, Virginie was missing, and it was some time before either she, or Pierre, or Morin, could get the slightest clue to the missing girl.

'And now I must take up the story as it was told to the Intendant Fléchier by the old gardener Jacques, with whom Clément had been lodging on his first arrival in Paris. The old man could not, I dare say, remember half as much of what had happened as Pierre did; the former had the dulled memory of age, while Pierre had evidently thought over the whole series of events as a story—as a play, if one may call it so— during the solitary hours in his after-life, wherever they were passed, whether in lonely camp watches, or in the foreign prison where he had to drag out many years. Clément had, as I said, returned to the gardener's garret after he had been dismissed from the Hôtel Duguesclin. There were several reasons for his thus doubling back. One was, that he put nearly the whole breadth of Paris between him and an enemy; though why Morin was an enemy, and to what extent he carried his dislike or hatred, Clément could not tell, of course. The next reason for returning to Jacques was, no doubt, the conviction that, in multiplying his residences, he multiplied the chances against his being suspected and recognized. And then, again, the old man was in his secret, and his ally, although perhaps but a feeble kind of one. It was through Jacques that the plan of communication, by means of a nosegay of pinks, had been devised; and it was Jacques who procured him the last disguise that Clément was to use in Paris—as he hoped and trusted. It was that

of a respectable shopkeeper of no particular class ;
a dress that would have seemed perfectly suitable to
the young man who would naturally have worn it ;
and yet, as Clément put it on, and adjusted it—giving
it a sort of finish and elegance which I always noticed
about his appearance, and which I believed was innate
in the wearer—I have no doubt it seemed like the
usual apparel of a gentleman. No coarseness of texture,
nor clumsiness of cut, could disguise the nobleman of
thirty descents, it appeared ; for, immediately on
arriving at the place of rendezvous, he was recognized
by the men placed there on Morin's information to
seize him. Jacques, following at a little distance, with
a bundle under his arm containing articles of feminine
disguise for Virginie, saw four men attempt Clément's
arrest—saw him, quick as lightning, draw a sword
hitherto concealed in a clumsy stick—saw his agile
figure spring to his guard,—and saw him defend himself with the rapidity and art of a man skilled in arms.
But what good did it do ? as Jacques piteously used
to ask, Monsieur Fléchier told me. A great blow from
a heavy club on the sword-arm of Monsieur de Créquy
laid it helpless and immovable by his side. Jacques
always thought that that blow came from one of the
spectators, who by this time had collected round the
scene of the affray. The next instant, his master—
his little marquis—was down among the feet of the
crowd, and though he was up again before he had
received much damage—so active and light was my
poor Clément—it was not before the old gardener had
hobbled forwards, and, with many an old-fashioned
oath and curse, proclaimed himself a partisan of the
losing side—a follower of a çi-devant aristocrat. It
was quite enough. He received one or two good blows,
which were, in fact, aimed at his master ; and then,
almost before he was aware, he found his arms pinioned
behind him with a woman's garter, which one of the
viragos in the crowd had made no scruple of pulling off
in public, as soon as she heard for what purpose it was
wanted. Poor Jacques was stunned and unhappy,—

his master was out of sight, on before; and the old
gardener scarce knew whither they were taking him.
His head ached from the blows which had fallen upon
it; it was growing dark,—June day though it was,
—and when first he seems to have become exactly
aware of what had happened to him, it was when he
was turned into one of the larger rooms of the Abbaye,
in which all were put who had no other allotted place
wherein to sleep. One or two iron lamps hung from
the ceiling by chains, giving a dim light for a little
circle. Jacques stumbled forwards over a sleeping
body lying on the ground. The sleeper wakened up
enough to complain; and the apology of the old man
in reply caught the ear of his master, who, until this
time, could hardly have been aware of the straits and
difficulties of his faithful Jacques. And there they
sat,—against a pillar, the live-long night, holding one
another's hands, and each restraining expressions of
pain, for fear of adding to the other's distress. That
night made them intimate friends, in spite of the
difference of age and rank. The disappointed hopes,
the acute suffering of the present, the apprehensions
of the future, made them seek solace in talking of the
past. Monsieur de Créquy and the gardener found
themselves disputing with interest in which chimney
of the stack the starling used to build,—the starling
whose nest Clément sent to Urian, you remember,—
and discussing the merits of different espalier-pears
which grew, and may grow still, in the old garden of
the Hôtel de Créquy. Towards morning both fell
asleep. The old man wakened first. His frame was
deadened to suffering, I suppose, for he felt relieved of
his pain; but Clément moaned and cried in feverish
slumber. His broken arm was beginning to inflame
his blood. He was, besides, much injured by some
kicks from the crowd as he fell. As the old man looked
sadly on the white, baked lips, and the flushed cheeks,
contorted with suffering even in his sleep, Clément
gave a sharp cry, which disturbed his miserable neighbours, all slumbering around in uneasy attitudes. They

bade him with curses be silent; and then turning round, tried again to forget their own misery in sleep. For you see, the bloodthirsty canaille* had not been sated with guillotining and hanging all the nobility they could find, but were now informing, right and left, even against each other; and when Clément and Jacques were in the prison, there were few of gentle blood in the place, and fewer still of gentle manners. At the sound of the angry words and threats, Jacques thought it best to awaken his master from his feverish uncomfortable sleep, lest he should provoke more enmity; and, tenderly lifting him up, he tried to adjust his own body, so that it should serve as a rest and a pillow for the younger man. The motion aroused Clément, and he began to talk in a strange, feverish way, of Virginie, too,—whose name he would not have breathed in such a place had he been quite himself. But Jacques had as much delicacy of feeling as any lady in the land, although, mind you, he knew neither how to read nor write,—and bent his head low down, so that his master might tell him in a whisper what messages he was to take to Mademoiselle de Créquy, in case——Poor Clément, he knew it must come to that! No escape for him now, in Norman disguise or otherwise! Either by gathering fever or guillotine, death was sure of his prey. Well! when that happened, Jacques was to go and find Mademoiselle de Créquy, and tell her that her cousin loved her at the last as he had loved her at the first; but that she should never have heard another word of his attachment from his living lips; that he knew he was not good enough for her, his queen; and that no thought of earning her love by his devotion had prompted his return to France, only that, if possible, he might have the great privilege of serving her whom he loved. And then he went off into rambling talk about petit-maîtres, and such kind of expressions, said Jacques to Fléchier, the Intendant, little knowing what a clue that one word gave to much of the poor lad's suffering.

'The summer morning came slowly on in that dark

prison, and when Jacques could look round—his master
was now sleeping on his shoulder, still the uneasy
starting sleep of fever,—he saw that there were many
women among the prisoners. (I have heard some of
those who have escaped from the prisons say, that the
look of despair and agony that came into the faces of
the prisoners on first wakening, as the sense of their
situation grew upon them, was what lasted the longest
in the memory of the survivors. This look, they said,
passed away from the women's faces sooner than it did
from those of the men.)

'Poor old Jacques kept falling asleep, and plucking
himself up again for fear lest, if he did not attend to
his master, some harm might come to the swollen
helpless arm. Yet his weariness grew upon him in
spite of all his efforts, and at last he felt as if he must
give way to the irresistible desire, if only for five
minutes. But just then there was a bustle at the door.
Jacques opened his eyes wide to look.

' " The gaoler is early with breakfast," said some
one, lazily.

' " It is the darkness of this accursed place that
makes us think it early," said another.

' All this time a parley was going on at the door.
Some one came in ; not the gaoler—a woman. The
door was shut to and locked behind her. She only
advanced a step or two ; for it was too sudden a change,
out of the light into that dark shadow, for any one to
see clearly for the first few minutes. Jacques had his
eyes fairly open now ; and was wide awake. It was
Mademoiselle de Créquy, looking bright, clear, and
resolute. The faithful heart of the old man read that
look like an open page. Her cousin should not die
there on her behalf, without at least the comfort of
her sweet presence.

' " Here he is," he whispered, as her gown would
have touched him in passing, without her perceiving
him, in the heavy obscurity of the place.

' " The good God bless you, my friend ! " she murmured, as she saw the attitude of the old man, propped

against a pillar, and holding Clément in his arms, as
if the young man had been a helpless baby, while one
of the poor gardener's hands supported the broken
limb in the easiest position. Virginie sat down by the
old man, and held out her arms. Softly she moved
Clément's head to her own shoulder ; softly she trans-
ferred the task of holding the arm to herself. Clément
lay on the floor, but she supported him, and Jacques
was at liberty to arise and stretch and shake his stiff
weary old body. He then sat down at a little distance,
and watched the pair until he fell asleep. Clément
had muttered " Virginie," as they half roused him by
their movements out of his stupor ; but Jacques
thought he was only dreaming ; nor did he seem fully
awake when once his eyes opened, and he looked full at
Virginie's face bending over him, and growing crimson
under his gaze, though she never stirred, for fear of
hurting him if she moved. Clément looked in silence,
until his heavy eyelids came slowly down, and he fell
into his oppressive slumber again. Either he did not
recognize her, or she came in too completely as a part
of his sleeping visions for him to be disturbed by her
appearance there.

' When Jacques awoke it was full daylight—at least
as full as it would ever be in that place. His breakfast—the gaol-allowance of bread and vin ordinaire—
was by his side. He must have slept soundly. He
looked for his master. He and Virginie had recognized
each other now,—hearts, as well as appearance. They
were smiling into each other's faces, as if that dull
vaulted room in the grim Abbaye were the sunny
gardens of Versailles, with music and festivity all
abroad. Apparently they had much to say to each
other ; for whispered questions and answers never
ceased.

' Virginie had made a sling for the poor broken
arm ; nay, she had obtained two splinters of wood in
some way, and one of their fellow-prisoners—having,
it appeared, some knowledge of surgery—had set it.
Jacques felt more desponding by far than they did, for

he was suffering from the night he had passed, which told upon his aged frame ; while they must have heard some good news, as it seemed to him, so bright and happy did they look. Yet Clément was still in bodily pain and suffering, and Virginie, by her own act and deed, was a prisoner in that dreadful Abbaye, whence the only issue was the guillotine. But they were together : they loved : they understood each other at length.

'When Virginie saw that Jacques was awake, and languidly munching his breakfast, she rose from the wooden stool on which she was sitting, and went to him, holding out both hands, and refusing to allow him to rise, while she thanked him with pretty eagerness for all his kindness to Monsieur. Monsieur himself came towards him,—following Virginie,—but with tottering steps, as if his head was weak and dizzy, to thank the poor old man, who, now on his feet, stood between them, ready to cry while they gave him credit for faithful actions which he felt to have been almost involuntary on his part,—for loyalty was like an instinct in the good old days, before your educational cant had come up. And so two days went on. The only event was the morning call for the victims, a certain number of whom were summoned to trial every day. And to be tried was to be condemned. Every one of the prisoners became grave, as the hour for their summons approached. Most of the victims went to their doom with uncomplaining resignation, and for awhile after their departure there was comparative silence in the prison. But, by and by,—so said Jacques,—the conversation or amusements began again. Human nature cannot stand the perpetual pressure of such keen anxiety, without an effort to relieve itself by thinking of something else. Jacques said that Monsieur and Mademoiselle were for ever talking together of the past days,—it was " Do you remember this ? " or, " Do you remember that ? " perpetually. He sometimes thought they forgot where they were, and what was before them. But Jacques did not, and every day he trembled more and more as the list was called over.

'The third morning of their incarceration, the gaoler brought in a man whom Jacques did not recognize, and therefore did not at once observe ; for he was waiting, as in duty bound, upon his master and his sweet young lady (as he always called her in repeating the story). He thought that the new introduction was some friend of the gaoler, as the two seemed well acquainted, and the latter stayed a few minutes talking with his visitor before leaving him in the prison. So Jacques was surprised when, after a short time had elapsed, he looked round, and saw the fierce stare with which the stranger was regarding Monsieur and Mademoiselle de Créquy, as the pair sat at breakfast,—the said breakfast being laid as well as Jacques knew how, on a bench fastened into the prison wall,—Virginie sitting on her low stool, and Clément half lying on the ground by her side, and submitting gladly to be fed by her pretty white fingers ; for it was one of her fancies, Jacques said, to do all she could for him, in consideration of his broken arm. And, indeed, Clément was wasting away daily ; for he had received other injuries, internal and more serious than that to his arm, during the mêlée which had ended in his capture. The stranger made Jacques conscious of his presence by a sigh, which was almost a groan. All three prisoners looked round at the sound. Clément's face expressed little but scornful indifference ; but Virginie's face froze into stony hate. Jacques said he never saw such a look, and hoped that he never should again. Yet after that first revelation of feeling, her look was steady and fixed in another direction to that in which the stranger stood,—still motionless—still watching. He came a step nearer at last.

' "Mademoiselle," he said. Not the quivering of an eyelash showed that she heard him. "Mademoiselle ! " he said again, with an intensity of beseeching that made Jacques—not knowing who he was—almost pity him, when he saw his young lady's obdurate face.

' There was perfect silence for a space of time which Jacques could not measure. Then again the voice, hesitatingly, saying, "Monsieur!" Clément could not hold the same icy countenance as Virginie; he turned his head with an impatient gesture of disgust; but even that emboldened the man.

' "Monsieur, do ask Mademoiselle to listen to me,—just two words!"

' "Mademoiselle de Créquy only listens to whom she chooses." Very haughtily my Clément would say that, I am sure.

' "But, Mademoiselle,"—lowering his voice, and coming a step or two nearer. Virginie must have felt his approach, though she did not see it; for she drew herself a little on one side, so as to put as much space as possible between him and her. "Mademoiselle, it is not too late. I can save you; but to-morrow your name is down on the list. I can save you, if you will listen."

' Still no word or sign. Jacques did not understand the affair. Why was she so obdurate to one who might be ready to include Clément in the proposal, as far as Jacques knew?

' The man withdrew a little, but did not offer to leave the prison. He never took his eyes off Virginie; he seemed to be suffering from some acute and terrible pain as he watched her.

' Jacques cleared away the breakfast-things as well as he could. Purposely, as I suspect, he passed near the man.

' "Hist!" said the stranger. "You are Jacques, the gardener, arrested for assisting an aristocrat. I know the gaoler. You shall escape, if you will. Only take this message from me to Mademoiselle. You heard. She will not listen to me: I did not want her to come here. I never knew she was here, and she will die to-morrow. They will put her beautiful round throat under the guillotine. Tell her, good old man, tell her how sweet life is; and how I can save her; and how I will not ask for more than just to see her from time to time. She is so young; and death is annihilation, you know. Why does she hate me so?

I want to save her ; I have done her no harm.  Good
old man, tell her how terrible death is ; and that she
will die to-morrow, unless she listens to me."

  ' Jacques saw no harm in repeating this message.
Clément listened in silence, watching Virginie with an
air of infinite tenderness.

  ' " Will you not try him, my cherished one ? " he
said.  " Towards you he may mean well " (which
makes me think that Virginie had never repeated to
Clément the conversation which she had overheard
that last night at Madame Babette's) ; " you would
be in no worse a situation than you were before ! "

  ' " No worse, Clément ! and I should have known
what you were, and have lost you.  My Clément ! "
said she, reproachfully.

  ' " Ask him," said she, turning to Jacques, suddenly,
" if he can save Monsieur de Créquy as well,—if he
can ?—O Clément, we might escape to England ;  we
are but young."  And she hid her face on his shoulder.

  ' Jacques returned to the stranger, and asked him
Virginie's question.  His eyes were fixed on the cousins ;
he was very pale, and the twitchings or contortions,
which must have been involuntary whenever he was
agitated, convulsed his whole body.

  ' He made a long pause.  " I will save mademoiselle
and monsieur, if she will go straight from prison to the
mairie, and be my wife."

  ' " Your wife ! "  Jacques could not help exclaiming.
" That she will never be—never ! "

  ' " Ask her ! " said Morin, hoarsely.

  ' But almost before Jacques thought he could have
fairly uttered the words, Clément caught their meaning.

  ' " Begone ! " said he ;  " not one word more."  Virginie touched the old man as he was moving away.
" Tell him he does not know how he makes me welcome
Death."  And smiling, as if triumphant, she turned
again to Clément.

  ' The stranger did not speak as Jacques gave him
the meaning, not the words, of their replies.  He was
going away, but stopped.  A minute or two afterwards,

he beckoned to Jacques. The old gardener seems to have thought it undesirable to throw away even the chance of assistance from such a man as this, for he went forwards to speak to him.

' " Listen ! I have influence with the gaoler. He shall let thee pass out with the victims to-morrow. No one will notice it, or miss thee——. They will be led to trial,—even at the last moment, I will save her, if she sends me word she relents. Speak to her, as the time draws on. Life is very sweet,—tell her how sweet. Speak to him ; he will do more with her than thou canst. Let him urge her to live. Even at the last, I will be at the Palais de Justice,—at the Grève. I have followers,—I have interest. Come among the crowd that follow the victims,—I shall see thee. It will be no worse for him, if she escapes "——

' " Save my master, and I will do all," said Jacques.

' " Only on my one condition," said Morin, doggedly ; and Jacques was hopeless of that condition ever being fulfilled. But he did not see why his own life might not be saved. By remaining in prison until the next day, he should have rendered every service in his power to his master and the young lady. He, poor fellow, shrank from death ; and he agreed with Morin to escape, if he could, by the means Morin suggested, and to bring him word if Mademoiselle de Créquy relented. (Jacques had no expectation that she would ; but I fancy he did not think it necessary to tell Morin of this conviction of his.) This bargaining with so base a man for so slight a thing as life, was the only flaw that I heard of in the old gardener's behaviour. Of course, the mere reopening of the subject was enough to stir Virginie to displeasure. Clément urged her, it is true ; but the light he had gained upon Morin's motions, made him rather try to set the case before her in as fair a manner as possible than use any persuasive arguments. And, even as it was, what he said on the subject made Virginie shed tears—the first that had fallen from her since she entered the prison. So, they were summoned and went together, at the fatal call of the muster-roll of victims the next morning. He, feeble from his wounds and his injured health; she, calm and serene, only petitioning to be allowed to walk next to him, in order that she might hold him up when he turned faint and giddy from his extreme suffering.

'Together they stood at the bar; together they were condemned. As the words of judgement were pronounced, Virginie turned to Clément, and embraced him with passionate fondness. Then, making him lean on her, they marched out towards the Place de la Grève.

'Jacques was free now. He had told Morin how fruitless his efforts at persuasion had been; and, scarcely caring to note the effect of his information upon the man, he had devoted himself to watching Monsieur and Mademoiselle de Créquy. And now he followed them to the Place de la Grève. He saw them mount the platform; saw them kneel down together till plucked up by the impatient officials; could see that she was urging some request to the executioner; the end of which seemed to be, that Clément advanced first to the guillotine, was executed (and just at this moment there was a stir among the crowd, as of a man pressing forward towards the scaffold). Then she, standing with her face to the guillotine, slowly made the sign of the cross, and knelt down.

'Jacques covered his eyes, blinded with tears. The report of a pistol made him look up. She was gone— another victim in her place—and where there had been the little stir in the crowd not five minutes before, some men were carrying off a dead body. A man had shot himself, they said. Pierre told me who that man was.'

## CHAPTER IX

AFTER a pause, I ventured to ask what became of
Madame de Créquy, Clément's mother.

'She never made any inquiry about him again,'
said my lady. 'She must have known that he was
dead; though how, we never could tell. Medlicott
remembered afterwards that it was about, if not on—
Medlicott to this day declares that it was on the very
Monday, June the nineteenth, when her son was executed, that Madame de Créquy left off her rouge, and
took to her bed, as one bereaved and hopeless. It
certainly was about that time; and Medlicott—who
was deeply impressed by that dream of Madame de
Créquy's (the relation of which I told you had had
such an effect on my lord), in which she had seen
the figure of Virginie—as the only light object amid
much surrounding darkness as of night, smiling and
beckoning Clément on—on—till at length the bright
phantom stopped, motionless, and Madame de Créquy's
eyes began to penetrate the murky darkness, and to
see closing around her the gloomy dripping walls which
she had once seen and never forgotten—the walls of
the vault of the chapel of the De Créquys in Saint
Germain l'Auxerrois; and there the two last of the
Créquys laid them down among their forefathers, and
Madame de Créquy had wakened to the sound of the
great door, which led to the open air, being locked
upon her—I say Medlicott, who was predisposed by
this dream to look out for the supernatural, always
declared that Madame de Créquy was made conscious,
in some mysterious way, of her son's death, on the
very day and hour when it occurred, and that after
that she had no more anxiety, but was only conscious
of a kind of stupefying despair.'

'And what became of her, my lady?' asked I,
repeating my question.

'What could become of her?' replied Lady Ludlow.
'She never could be induced to rise again, though she

lived more than a year after her son's departure. She
kept her bed; her room darkened, her face turned
towards the wall, whenever any one besides Medlicott
was in the room. She hardly ever spoke, and would
have died of starvation but for Medlicott's tender care,
in putting a morsel to her lips every now and then,
feeding her, in fact, just as an old bird feeds her young
ones. In the height of summer my lord and I left
London. We would fain have taken her with us into
Scotland, but the doctor (we had the old doctor from
Leicester Square) forbade her removal; and this time
he gave such good reasons against it that I acquiesced.
Medlicott and a maid were left with her. Every care
was taken of her. She survived till our return. Indeed,
I thought she was in much the same state as I had
left her in, when I came back to London. But Medlicott spoke of her as much weaker; and one morning,
on awakening, they told me she was dead. I sent for
Medlicott, who was in sad distress, she had become so
fond of her charge. She said that, about two o'clock,
she had been awakened by unusual restlessness on
Madame de Créquy's part; that she had gone to her
bedside, and found the poor lady feebly but perpetually
moving her wasted arm up and down—and saying to
herself in a wailing voice: "I did not bless him when
he left me—I did not bless him when he left me!"
Medlicott gave her a spoonful or two of jelly, and sat
by her, stroking her hand, and soothing her till she
seemed to fall asleep. But in the morning she was
dead.'

'It is a sad story, your ladyship,' said I, after a while.

'Yes, it is. People seldom arrive at my age without
having watched the beginning, middle, and end of
many lives and many fortunes. We do not talk about
them, perhaps; for they are often so sacred to us,
from having touched into the very quick of our own
hearts, as it were, or into those of others who are dead
and gone, and veiled over from human sight, that we
cannot tell the tale as if it was a mere story. But
young people should remember that we have had this

solemn experience of life, on which to base our opinions
and form our judgements, so that they are not mere
untried theories. I am not alluding to Mr. Horner
just now, for he is nearly as old as I am—within ten
years, I daresay—but I am thinking of Mr. Gray, with
his endless plans for some new thing—schools, education, Sabbaths, and what not. Now he has not seen
what all this leads to.'

' It is a pity he has not heard your ladyship tell the
story of poor Monsieur de Créquy.'

' Not at all a pity, my dear. A young man like
him, who, both by position and age, must have had
his experience confined to a very narrow circle, ought
not to set up his opinion against mine ; he ought not
to require reasons from me, nor to need such explanation of my arguments (if I condescend to argue), as
going into relation of the circumstances on which my
arguments are based in my own mind, would be.'

' But, my lady, it might convince him,' I said, with
perhaps injudicious perseverance.

' And why should he be convinced ? ' she asked, with
gentle inquiry in her tone. ' He has only to acquiesce.
Though he is appointed by Mr. Croxton, I am the
lady of the manor, as he must know. But it is with
Mr. Horner that I must have to do about this unfortunate lad Gregson. I am afraid there will be no
method of making him forget his unlucky knowledge.
His poor brains will be intoxicated with the sense of
his powers, without any counterbalancing principles to
guide him. Poor fellow ! I am quite afraid it will end
in his being hanged ! '

The next day Mr. Horner came to apologize and
explain. He was evidently—as I could tell from his
voice, as he spoke to my lady in the next room—
extremely annoyed at her ladyship's discovery of the
education he had been giving to this boy. My lady
spoke with great authority, and with reasonable grounds
of complaint. Mr. Horner was well acquainted with
her thoughts on the subject, and had acted in defiance
of her wishes. He acknowledged as much, and should

on no account have done it, in any other instance, without her leave.

'Which I could never have granted you,' said my lady.

But this boy had extraordinary capabilities; would, in fact, have taught himself much that was bad, if he had not been rescued, and another direction given to his powers. And in all Mr. Horner had done, he had had her ladyship's service in view. The business was getting almost beyond his power, so many letters and so much account-keeping was required by the complicated state in which things were.

Lady Ludlow felt what was coming—a reference to the mortgage for the benefit of my lord's Scottish estates, which, she was perfectly aware, Mr. Horner considered as having been a most unwise proceeding—and she hastened to observe :

'All this may be very true, Mr. Horner, and I am sure I should be the last person to wish you to over-work or distress yourself ; but of that we will talk another time. What I am now anxious to remedy is, if possible, the state of this poor little Gregson's mind. Would not hard work in the fields be a wholesome and excellent way of enabling him to forget ? '

'I was in hopes, my lady, that you would have permitted me to bring him up to act as a kind of clerk,' said Mr. Horner, jerking out his project abruptly.

'A what ? ' asked my lady, in infinite surprise.

'A kind of—of assistant, in the way of copying letters and doing up accounts. He is already an excellent penman and very quick at figures.'

'Mr. Horner,' said my lady, with dignity, 'the son of a poacher and vagabond ought never to have been able to copy letters relating to the Hanbury estates ; and, at any rate, he shall not. I wonder how it is that, knowing the use he has made of his power of reading a letter, you should venture to propose such an employment for him as would require his being in your confidence, and you the trusted agent of this family. Why, every secret (and every ancient and honourable family has its secrets, as you know, Mr. Horner!) would be learnt off by heart, and repeated to the first comer!'

'I should have hoped to have trained him, my lady, to understand the rules of discretion.'

'Trained! Train a barn-door fowl to be a pheasant, Mr. Horner! That would be the easier task. But you did right to speak of discretion rather than honour. Discretion looks to the consequences of actions—honour looks to the action itself, and is an instinct rather than a virtue. After all, it is possible, you might have trained him to be discreet.'

Mr. Horner was silent. My lady was softened by his not replying, and began, as she always did in such cases, to fear lest she had been too harsh. I could tell that by her voice and by her next speech, as well as if I had seen her face.

'But I am sorry you are feeling the pressure of the affairs; I am quite aware that I have entailed much additional trouble upon you by some of my measures; I must try and provide you with some suitable assistance. Copying letters and doing up accounts, I think you said?'

Mr. Horner had certainly had a distant idea of turning the little boy, in process of time, into a clerk; but he had rather urged this possibility of future usefulness beyond what he had at first intended, in speaking of it to my lady as a palliation of his offence, and he certainly was very much inclined to retract his statement that the letter-writing, or any other business, had increased, or that he was in the slightest want of help of any kind, when my lady, after a pause of consideration, suddenly said:

'I have it. Miss Galindo will, I am sure, be glad to assist you. I will speak to her myself. The payment we should make to a clerk would be of real service to her!'

I could hardly help echoing Mr. Horner's tone of surprise as he said—

'Miss Galindo!

For, you must be told who Miss Galindo was; at least, told as much as I know. Miss Galindo had lived in the village for many years, keeping house on the smallest possible means, yet always managing to maintain a servant. And this servant was invariably chosen because she had some infirmity that made her undesirable to every one else. I believe Miss Galindo had had lame and blind and hump-backed maids. She had even at one time taken in a girl hopelessly gone in consumption, because if not she would have had to go to the workhouse, and not have had enough to eat. Of course the poor creature could not perform a single duty usually required of a servant, and Miss Galindo herself was both servant and nurse.

Her present maid was scarcely four feet high, and bore a terrible character for ill-temper. Nobody but Miss Galindo would have kept her; but, as it was, mistress and servant squabbled perpetually, and were, at heart, the best of friends. For it was one of Miss Galindo's peculiarities to do all manner of kind and self-denying actions, and to say all manner of pro-voking things. Lame, blind, deformed, and dwarf, all came in for scoldings without number: it was only the consumptive girl that never had heard a sharp word. I don't think any of her servants liked her the worse for her peppery temper, and passionate odd ways, for they knew her real and beautiful kindness of heart; and, besides, she had so great a turn for humour, that very often her speeches amused as much or more than they irritated; and, on the other side, a piece of witty impudence from her servant would occasionally tickle her so much and so suddenly, that she would burst out laughing in the middle of her passion.

But the talk about Miss Galindo's choice and manage-ment of her servants was confined to village gossip, and had never reached my Lady Ludlow's ears, though doubtless Mr. Horner was well acquainted with it. What my lady knew of her amounted to this. It was the custom in those days for the wealthy ladies of the county to set on foot a repository, as it was called, in the assize-town. The ostensible manager of this repository was generally a decayed gentlewoman, a clergyman's widow, or so forth. She was, however, controlled by a committee of ladies; and paid by them in proportion to the amount of goods she sold; and these goods were the small manufactures of ladies of little or no fortune, whose names, if they chose it, were only signified by initials.

Poor water-colour drawings, in indigo and Indian ink; screens, ornamented with moss and dried leaves; paintings on velvet, and such faintly ornamental works were displayed on one side of the shop. It was always reckoned a mark of characteristic gentility in the repository, to have only common heavy-framed sash-windows, which admitted very little light, so I never was quite certain of the merit of these Works of Art, as they were entitled. But, on the other side, where the Useful Work placard was put up, there was a great variety of articles, of whose unusual excellence every one might judge. Such fine sewing, and stitching, and button-holing! Such bundles of soft delicate knitted stockings and socks; and, above all, in Lady Ludlow's eyes, such hanks of the finest spun flaxen thread!

And the most delicate dainty work of all was done by Miss Galindo, as Lady Ludlow very well knew. Yet, for all their fine sewing, it sometimes happened that Miss Galindo's patterns were of an old-fashioned kind; and the dozen night-caps, may-be, on the materials for which she had expended bonâ-fide money, and on the making-up, no little time and eyesight, would lie for months in a yellow neglected heap; and at such times, it was said, Miss Galindo was more amusing than usual, more full of dry drollery and humour; just as at the times when an order came in to X. (the initial she had chosen) for a stock of well-paying things, she sat and stormed at her servant as she stitched away. She herself explained her practice in this way:—

'When everything goes wrong, one would give up breathing if one could not lighten one's heart by a joke.

But when I've to sit still from morning till night, I must have something to stir my blood, or I should go off into an apoplexy, so I set to, and quarrel with Sally.'

Such were Miss Galindo's means and manner of living in her own house. Out of doors, and in the village, she was not popular, although she would have been sorely missed had she left the place. But she asked too many home questions (not to say impertinent) respecting the domestic economies (for even the very poor like to spend their bit of money their own way), and would open cupboards to find out hidden extravagances, and question closely respecting the weekly amount of butter, till one day she met with what would have been a rebuff to any other person, but which she rather enjoyed than otherwise.

She was going into a cottage, and in the doorway met the good woman chasing out a duck, and apparently unconscious of her visitor.

'Get out, Miss Galindo!' she cried, addressing the duck. 'Get out! O, I ask your pardon,' she continued, as if seeing the lady for the first time. 'It's only that weary duck that will come in. Get out, Miss Gal——' (to the duck).

'And so you call it after me, do you?' inquired her visitor.

'O, yes, ma'am, my master would have it so, for he said, sure enough the unlucky bird was always poking herself where she was not wanted.'

'Ha, ha! very good! And so your master is a wit, is he? Well! tell him to come up and speak to me to-night about my parlour chimney, for there is no one like him for chimney doctoring.'

And the master went up, and was so won over by Miss Galindo's merry ways, and sharp insight into the mysteries of his various kinds of business (he was a mason, chimney-sweeper, and ratcatcher), that he came home and abused his wife the next time she called the duck the name by which he himself had christened her.

But odd as Miss Galindo was in general, she could

be as well-bred a lady as any one when she chose.
And choose she always did when my Lady Ludlow
was by. Indeed, I don't know the man, woman, or
child, that did not instinctively turn out its best side
to her ladyship. So she had no notion of the qualities
which, I am sure, made Mr. Horner think that Miss
Galindo would be most unmanageable as a clerk, and
heartily wish that the idea had never come into my
lady's head. But there it was; and he had annoyed
her ladyship already more than he liked to-day, so
he could not directly contradict her, but only urge
difficulties which he hoped might prove insuperable.
But every one of them Lady Ludlow knocked down.
Letters to copy? Doubtless. Miss Galindo could come
up to the Hall; she should have a room to herself;
she wrote a beautiful hand; and writing would save
her eyesight. 'Capability with regard to accounts?'
My lady would answer for that too; and for more
than Mr. Horner seemed to think it necessary to inquire
about. Miss Galindo was by birth and breeding a lady
of the strictest honour, and would, if possible, forget
the substance of any letters that passed through her
hands; at any rate, no one would ever hear of them
again from her. 'Remuneration?' Oh! as for that,
Lady Ludlow would herself take care that it was
managed in the most delicate manner possible. She
would send to invite Miss Galindo to tea at the Hall
that very afternoon, if Mr. Horner would only give
her ladyship the slightest idea of the average length
of time that my lady was to request Miss Galindo to
sacrifice to her daily. 'Three hours! Very well.'
Mr. Horner looked very grave as he passed the windows
of the room where I lay. I don't think he liked the
idea of Miss Galindo as a clerk.

Lady Ludlow's invitations were like royal commands.
Indeed, the village was too quiet to allow the inhabitants to have many evening engagements of any kind.
Now and then, Mr. and Mrs. Horner gave a tea and
supper to the principal tenants and their wives, to
which the clergyman was invited, and Miss Galindo,

Mrs. Medlicott, and one or two other spinsters and widows. The glory of the supper-table on these occasions was invariably furnished by her ladyship : it was a cold roasted peacock, with his tail stuck out as if in life. Mrs. Medlicott would take up the whole morning arranging the feathers in the proper semicircle, and was always pleased with the wonder and admiration it excited. It was considered a due reward and fitting compliment to her exertions that Mr. Horner always took her in to supper, and placed her opposite to the magnificent dish, at which she sweetly smiled all the time they were at table. But since Mrs. Horner had had the paralytic stroke these parties had been given up ; and Miss Galindo wrote a note to Lady Ludlow in reply to her invitation, saying that she was entirely disengaged, and would have great pleasure in doing herself the honour of waiting upon her ladyship.

Whoever visited my lady took their meals with her, sitting on the dais, in the presence of all my former companions. So I did not see Miss Galindo until some time after tea ; as the young gentlewomen had had to bring her their sewing and spinning, to hear the remarks of so competent a judge. At length her ladyship brought her visitor into the room where I lay,—it was one of my bad days, I remember,—in order to have her little bit of private conversation. Miss Galindo was dressed in her best gown, I am sure, but I had never seen anything like it except in a picture, it was so old-fashioned. She wore a white muslin apron, delicately embroidered, and put on a little crookedly, in order, as she told us, even Lady Ludlow, before the evening was over, to conceal a spot whence the colour had been discharged by a lemon-stain. This crookedness had an odd effect, especially when I saw that it was intentional ; indeed, she was so anxious about her apron's right adjustment in the wrong place, that she told us straight out why she wore it so, and asked her ladyship if the spot was properly hidden, at the same time lifting up her apron and showing her how large it was.

'When my father was alive, I always took his right arm, so, and used to remove any spotted or discoloured breadths to the left side, if it was a walking-dress. That's the convenience of a gentleman. But widows and spinsters must do what they can. Ah, my dear (to me)! when you are reckoning up the blessings in your lot,—though you may think it a hard one in some respects,—don't forget how little your stockings want darning, as you are obliged to lie down so much! I would rather knit two pairs of stockings than darn one, any day.'

'Have you been doing any of your beautiful knitting lately?' asked my lady, who had now arranged Miss Galindo in the pleasantest chair, and taken her own little wicker-work one, and, having her work in her hands, was ready to try and open the subject.

'No, and alas! your ladyship. It is partly the hot weather's fault, for people seem to forget that winter must come; and partly, I suppose, that every one is stocked who has the money to pay four-and-sixpence a pair for stockings.'

'Then may I ask if you have any time in your active days at liberty?' said my lady, drawing a little nearer to her proposal, which I fancy she found it a little awkward to make.

'Why, the village keeps me busy, your ladyship, when I have neither knitting or sewing to do. You know I took X. for my letter at the repository, because it stands for Xantippe,* who was a great scold in old times, as I have learnt. But I'm sure I don't know how the world would get on without scolding, your ladyship. It would go to sleep, and the sun would stand still.'

'I don't think I could bear to scold, Miss Galindo,' said her ladyship, smiling.

'No! because your ladyship has people to do it for you. Begging your pardon, my lady, it seems to me the generality of people may be divided into saints, scolds, and sinners. Now, your ladyship is a saint, because you have a sweet and holy nature, in the first place ; and have people to do your anger and vexation for you, in the second place. And Jonathan Walker is a sinner, because he is sent to prison. But here am I, half way, having but a poor kind of disposition at best, and yet hating sin, and all that leads to it, such as wasting and extravagance, and gossiping,—and yet all this lies right under my nose in the village, and I am not saint enough to be vexed at it ; and so I scold. And though I had rather be a saint, yet I think I do good in my way.'

' No doubt you do, dear Miss Galindo,' said Lady Ludlow. ' But I am sorry to hear that there is so much that is bad going on in the village,—very sorry.'

' O, your ladyship ! then I am sorry I brought it out. It was only by way of saying, that when I have no particular work to do at home, I take a turn abroad, and set my neighbours to rights, just by way of steering clear of Satan.

> For Satan finds some mischief still
> For idle hands to do,*

you know, my lady.'

There was no leading into the subject by delicate degrees, for Miss Galindo was evidently so fond of talking, that, if asked a question, she made her answer so long, that before she came to an end of it, she had wandered far away from the original starting-point. So Lady Ludlow plunged at once into what she had to say.

' Miss Galindo, I have a great favour to ask of you.'

' My lady, I wish I could tell you what a pleasure it is to hear you say so,' replied Miss Galindo, almost with tears in her eyes ; so glad were we all to do anything for her ladyship,. which could be called a free service and not merely a duty.

' It is this. Mr. Horner tells me that the business-letters, relating to the estate, are multiplying so much that he finds it impossible to copy them all himself, and I therefore require the services of some confidential and discreet person to copy these letters, and occasionally to go through certain accounts. Now, there is a very pleasant little sitting-room very near to Mr. Horner's office (you know Mr. Horner's office ? on the other side of the stone hall ?), and if I could prevail upon you to come here to breakfast and afterwards sit there for three hours every morning, Mr. Horner should bring or send you the papers——'

Lady Ludlow stopped. Miss Galindo's countenance had fallen. There was some great obstacle in her mind to her wish for obliging Lady Ludlow.

' What would Sally do ? ' she asked at length. Lady Ludlow had not a notion who Sally was. Nor if she had had a notion, would she have had a conception of the perplexities that poured into Miss Galindo's mind, at the idea of leaving her rough forgetful dwarf without the perpetual monitorship of her mistress. Lady Ludlow, accustomed to a household where everything went on noiselessly, perfectly, and by clock-work, conducted by a number of highly-paid, well-chosen, and accomplished servants, had not a conception of the nature of the rough material from which her servants came. Besides, in her establishment, so that the result was good, no one inquired if the small economies had been observed in the production. Whereas every penny—every halfpenny, was of consequence to Miss Galindo ; and visions of squandered drops of milk and wasted crusts of bread filled her mind with dismay. But she swallowed all her apprehensions down, out of her regard for Lady Ludlow, and desire to be of service to her. No one knows how great a trial it was to her when she thought of Sally, unchecked and unscolded for three hours every morning. But all she said was :

' " Sally, go to the Deuce." I beg your pardon, my lady, if I was talking to myself ; it 's a habit I have got into of keeping my tongue in practice, and I am not quite aware when I do it. Three hours every morning ! I shall be only too proud to do what I can for your ladyship ; and I hope Mr. Horner will not be too impatient with me at first. You know, perhaps,

that I was nearly being an authoress once, and that
seems as if I was destined to "employ my time in
writing." '

' No, indeed ; we must return to the subject of the
clerkship afterwards, if you please. An authoress,
Miss Galindo ! You surprise me ! '

' But, indeed, I was.· All was quite ready. Doctor
Burney*used to teach me music : not that I ever could
learn, but it was a fancy of my poor father's. And
his daughter wrote a book, and they said she was but
a very young lady, and nothing but a music-master's
daughter ; so why should not I try ? '

' Well ? '

' Well ! I got paper and half-a-hundred good pens,
a bottle of ink, all ready——'

' And then——'

' O, it ended in my having nothing to say, when
I sat down to write. But sometimes, when I get hold
of a book, I wonder why I let such a poor reason stop
me. It does not others.'

' But I think it was very well it did, Miss Galindo,'
said her ladyship. ' I am extremely against women
usurping men's employments, as they are very apt to
do. But perhaps, after all, the notion of writing a book
improved your hand. It is one of the most legible
I ever saw.'

' I despise z's without tails,' said Miss Galindo, with
a good deal of gratified pride at my lady's praise.
Presently, my lady took her to look at a curious old
cabinet, which Lord Ludlow had picked up at the
Hague ; and while they were out of the room on this
errand, I suppose the question of remuneration was
settled, for I heard no more of it.

When they came back, they were talking of Mr. Gray.
Miss Galindo was unsparing in her expressions of
opinion about him : going much farther than my lady
—in her language, at least.

' A little blushing man like him, who can't say bo
to a goose without hesitating and colouring, to come to
this village—which is as good a village as ever lived—

and cry us down for a set of sinners, as if we had all
committed murder and that other thing!—I have no
patience with him, my lady. And then, how is he to
help us to heaven, by teaching us our a b, ab—b a, ba?
And yet, by all accounts, that's to save poor children's
souls. O, I knew your ladyship would agree with me.
I am sure my mother was as good a creature as ever
breathed the blessed air; and if she's not gone to
heaven, I don't want to go there; and she could not
spell a letter decently. And does Mr. Gray think God
took note of that?'

'I was sure you would agree with me, Miss Galindo,'
said my lady. 'You and I can remember how this
talk about education—Rousseau, and his writings—
stirred up the French people to their Reign of Terror,
and all those bloody scenes.'

'I'm afraid that Rousseau and Mr. Gray are birds
of a feather,' replied Miss Galindo, shaking her head.
'And yet there is some good in the young man, too.
He sat up all night with Billy Davis, when his wife
was fairly worn out with nursing him.'

'Did he, indeed!' said my lady, her face lighting
up, as it always did when she heard of any kind or
generous action, no matter who performed it. 'What
a pity he is bitten with these new revolutionary ideas,
and is so much for disturbing the established order of
society!'

When Miss Galindo went, she left so favourable an
impression of her visit on my lady, that she said to
me with a pleased smile:

'I think I have provided Mr. Horner with a far
better clerk than he would have made of that lad
Gregson in twenty years. And I will send the lad to
my lord's grieve, in Scotland, that he may be kept out
of harm's way.'

But something happened to the lad before this purpose could be accomplished.

## CHAPTER X

THE next morning, Miss Galindo made her appearance, and, by some mistake, unusual in my lady's well-trained servants, was shown into the room where I was trying to walk; for a certain amount of exercise was prescribed for me, painful although the exertion had become.

She brought a little basket along with her; and while the footman was gone to inquire my lady's wishes (for I don't think that Lady Ludlow expected Miss Galindo so soon to assume her clerkship; nor, indeed, had Mr. Horner any work of any kind ready for his new assistant to do), she launched out into conversation with me.

' It was a sudden summons, my dear! However, as I have often said to myself, ever since an occasion long ago, if Lady Ludlow ever honours me by asking for my right hand, I'll cut it off, and wrap the stump up so tidily she shall never find out it bleeds. But, if I had had a little more time, I could have mended my pens*better. You see, I have had to sit up pretty late to get these sleeves made '—and she took out of her basket a pair of brown-holland over-sleeves, very much such as a grocer's apprentice wears—' and I had only time to make seven or eight pens, out of some quills Farmer Thomson gave me last autumn. As for ink, I'm thankful to say, that's always ready; an ounce of steel filings, an ounce of nut-gall, and a pint of water (tea, if you're extravagant, which, thank Heaven! I'm not), put all in a bottle, and hang it up behind the house door, so that the whole gets a good shaking every time you slam it to—and even if you are in a passion and bang it, as Sally and I often do, it is all the better for it—and there's my ink ready for use; ready to write my lady's will with, if need be.'

' O, Miss Galindo!' said I, ' don't talk so; my lady's will! and she not dead yet.'

' And if she were, what would be the use of talking

of making her will! Now, if you were Sally, I should
say, "Answer me that, you goose!" But, as you're
a relation of my lady's, I must be civil, and only say,
"I can't think how you can talk so like a fool!" To
be sure, poor thing, you're lame!'

I do not know how long she would have gone on;
but my lady came in, and I, released from my duty
of entertaining Miss Galindo, made my limping way
into the next room. To tell the truth, I was rather
afraid of Miss Galindo's tongue, for I never knew what
she would say next.

After a while my lady came, and began to look in
the bureau for something; and as she looked she said:

'I think Mr. Horner must have made some mistake,
when he said he had so much work that he almost
required a clerk, for this morning he cannot find anything for Miss Galindo to do; and there she is, sitting
with her pen behind her ear, waiting for something to
write. I am come to find her my mother's letters, for
I should like to have a fair copy made of them. O,
here they are! don't trouble yourself, my dear child.'

When my lady returned again, she sat down and
began to talk of Mr. Gray.

'Miss Galindo says she saw him going to hold a
prayer-meeting in a cottage. Now, that really makes
me unhappy, it is so like what Mr. Wesley used to
do in my younger days; and since then we have had
rebellion in the American colonies and the French
Revolution. You may depend upon it, my dear, making
religion and education common—vulgarizing them, as
it were—is a bad thing for a nation. A man who
hears prayers read in the cottage where he has just
supped on bread and bacon, forgets the respect due
to a church: he begins to think that one place is as
good as another, and, by and by, that one person is
as good as another; and after that, I always find that
people begin to talk of their rights, instead of thinking
of their duties. I wish Mr. Gray had been more tract-
able, and had left well alone. What do you think
I heard this morning? Why, that the Home Hill

estate, which niches into the Hanbury property, was bought by a Baptist baker from Birmingham!'

'A Baptist baker!' I exclaimed. I had never seen a Dissenter, to my knowledge; but, having always heard them spoken of with horror, I looked upon them almost as if they were rhinoceroses. I wanted to see a live Dissenter, I believe, and yet I wished it were over. I was almost surprised when I heard that any of them were engaged in such peaceful occupations as baking.

'Yes! so Mr. Horner tells me. A Mr. Lambe, I believe. But, at any rate, he is a Baptist, and has been in trade. What with his schismatism and Mr. Gray's methodism, I am afraid all the primitive character of this place will vanish.'

From what I could hear, Mr. Gray seemed to be taking his own way; at any rate, more than he had done when he first came to the village, when his natural timidity had made him defer to my lady, and seek her consent and sanction before embarking in any new plan. But newness was a quality Lady Ludlow especially disliked. Even in the fashions of dress and furniture, she clung to the old, to the modes which had prevailed when she was young; and, though she had a deep personal regard for Queen Charlotte (to whom, as I have already said, she had been maid-of-honour), yet there was a tinge of Jacobitism about her, such as made her extremely dislike to hear Prince Charles Edward called the Young Pretender, as many loyal people did in those days, and made her fond of telling of the thorn-tree in my lord's park in Scotland, which had been planted by bonny Queen Mary herself, and before which every guest in the Castle of Monkshaven was expected to stand bare-headed, out of respect to the memory and misfortunes of the royal planter.

We might play at cards, if we so chose, on a Sunday; at least, I suppose we might, for my lady and Mr. Mountford used to do so often when I first went. But we must neither play cards, nor read, nor sew, on the fifth of November and on the thirtieth of January,* but must go to church, and meditate all the rest of the day—and very hard work meditating was. I would far rather have scoured a room. That was the reason, I suppose, why a passive life was seen to be better discipline for me than an active one.

But I am wandering away from my lady, and her dislike to all innovation. Now, it seemed to me, as far as I heard, that Mr. Gray was full of nothing but new things, and that what he first did was to attack all our established institutions, both in the village and the parish, and also in the nation. To be sure, I heard of his ways of going on principally from Miss Galindo, who was apt to speak more strongly than accurately.

'There he goes,' she said, 'clucking up the children just like an old hen, and trying to teach them about their salvation and their souls, and I don't know what—things that it is just blasphemy to speak about out of church. And he potters old people about reading their Bibles. I am sure I don't want to speak disrespectfully about the Holy Scriptures, but I found old Job Horton busy reading his Bible yesterday. Says I, "What are you reading, and where did you get it, and who gave it you?" So he made answer, "That he was reading Susannah and the Elders, for that he had read Bel and the Dragon till he could pretty near say it off by heart, and they were two as pretty stories as ever he had read, and that it was a caution to him what bad old chaps there were in the world." Now, as Job is bed-ridden, I don't think he is likely to meet with the Elders, and I say that I think repeating his Creed, the Commandments, and the Lord's Prayer, and, maybe, throwing in a verse of the Psalms, if he wanted a bit of a change, would have done him far more good than his pretty stories, as he called them. And what's the next thing our young parson does? Why, he tries to make us all feel pitiful for the black slaves, and leaves little pictures of negroes about, with the question printed below, "Am I not a man and a brother?" just as if I was to be hail-fellow-well-met with every negro footman. They do say he takes no sugar in his tea, because he thinks he sees spots of blood in it. Now I call that superstition.'

The next day it was a still worse story.

'Well, my dear! and how are you? My lady sent me in to sit a bit with you, while Mr. Horner looks out some papers for me to copy. Between ourselves, Mr. Steward Horner does not like having me for a clerk. It is all very well he does not; for, if he were decently civil to me, I might want a chaperone, you know, now poor Mrs. Horner is dead.' This was one of Miss Galindo's grim jokes. 'As it is, I try to make him forget I'm a woman. I do everything as ship-shape as a masculine man-clerk. I see he can't find a fault—writing good, spelling correct, sums all right. And then he squints up at me with the tail of his eye, and looks glummer than ever, just because I'm a woman—as if I could help that. I have gone good lengths to set his mind at ease. I have stuck my pen behind my ear, I have made him a bow instead of a curtsy, I have whistled—not a tune, I can't pipe up that—nay, if you won't tell my lady, I don't mind telling you that I have said "Confound it!" and "Zounds!" I can't get any farther. For all that, Mr. Horner won't forget I am a lady, and so I am not half the use I might be, and if it were not to please my Lady Ludlow, Mr. Horner and his books might go hang (see how natural that came out!). And there is an order for a dozen nightcaps for a bride, and I am so afraid I shan't have time to do them. Worst of all, there's Mr. Gray taking advantage of my absence to seduce Sally!'

'To seduce Sally! Mr. Gray!'

'Pooh, pooh, child! There's many a kind of seduction. Mr. Gray is seducing Sally to want to go to church. There has he been twice at my house, while I have been away in the mornings, talking to Sally about the state of her soul and that sort of thing. But when I found the meat all roasted to a cinder, I said, "Come, Sally, let's have no more praying when beef is down at the fire. Pray at six o'clock in the morning

and nine at night, and I won't hinder you." So she
sauced me, and said something about Martha and
Mary,* implying that, because she had let the beef get
so overdone that I declare I could hardly find a bit
fit for Nancy Pole's sick grandchild, she had chosen
the better part. I was very much put about, I own,
and perhaps you'll be shocked at what I said—indeed,
I don't know if it was right myself—but I told her
I had a soul as well as she, and if it was to be saved
by my sitting still and thinking about salvation and
never doing my duty, I thought I had as good a right
as she had to be Mary, and save my soul. So, that
afternoon, I sat quite still, and it was really a comfort,
for I am often too busy, I know, to pray as I ought.
There is first one person wanting me, and then another,
and the house and the food and the neighbours to
see after. So, when tea-time comes, there enters my
maid with her hump on her back, and her soul to be
saved. "Please, ma'am, did you order the pound of
butter ?"—"No, Sally," I said, shaking my head,
"this morning I did not go round by Hale's farm,
and this afternoon I have been employed in spiritual
things."

'Now, our Sally likes tea and bread-and-butter
above everything, and dry bread was not to her taste.

'"I'm thankful," said the impudent hussy, "that
you have taken a turn towards godliness. It will be
my prayers, I trust, that's given it you."

'I was determined not to give her an opening
towards the carnal subject of butter, so she lingered
still, longing to ask leave to run for it. But I gave
her none, and munched my dry bread myself, thinking
what a famous cake I could make for little Ben Pole
with the bit of butter we were saving ; and when Sally
had had her butterless tea, and was in none of the best
of tempers because Martha had not bethought herself
of the butter, I just quietly said :

'"Now, Sally, to-morrow we'll try to hash that beef
well, and to remember the butter, and to work out our
salvation all at the same time, for I don't see why it

can't all be done, as God has set us to do it all." But I heard her at it again about Mary and Martha, and I have no doubt that Mr. Gray will teach her to consider me a lost sheep.'

I had heard so many little speeches about Mr. Gray from one person or another, all speaking against him, as a mischief-maker, a setter-up of new doctrines, and of a fanciful standard of life (and you may be sure that, where Lady Ludlow led, Mrs. Medlicott and Adams were certain to follow, each in their different ways showing the influence my lady had over them), that I believe I had grown to consider him as a very instrument of evil, and to expect to perceive in his face marks of his presumption, and arrogance, and impertinent interference. It was now many weeks since I had seen him, and when he was one morning shown into the blue drawing-room (into which I had been removed for a change), I was quite surprised to see how innocent and awkward a young man he appeared, confused even more than I was at our unexpected tête-à-tête. He looked thinner, his eyes more eager, his expression more anxious, and his colour came and went more than it had done when I had seen him last. I tried to make a little conversation, as I was, to my own surprise, more at my ease than he was; but his thoughts were evidently too much preoccupied for him to do more than answer me with monosyllables.

Presently my lady came in. Mr. Gray twitched and coloured more than ever; but plunged into the middle of his subject at once.

'My lady, I cannot answer it to my conscience, if I allow the children of this village to go on any longer the little heathens that they are. I must do something to alter their condition. I am quite aware that your ladyship disapproves of many of the plans which have suggested themselves to me; but nevertheless I must do something, and I am come now to your ladyship to ask respectfully, but firmly, what you would advise me to do.'

His eyes were dilated, and I could almost have said

they were full of tears with his eagerness. But I am sure it is a bad plan to remind people of decided opinions which they have once expressed, if you wish them to modify those opinions. Now, Mr. Gray had done this with my lady; and though I do not mean to say she was obstinate, yet she was not one to retract.

She was silent for a moment or two before she replied.

'You ask me to suggest a remedy for an evil of the existence of which I am not conscious,' was her answer —very coldly, very gently given. 'In Mr. Mountford's time I heard no such complaints: whenever I see the village children (and they are not unfrequent visitors at this house, on one pretext or another), they are well and decently behaved.'

'Oh, madam, you cannot judge,' he broke in. 'They are trained to respect you in word and deed; you are the highest they ever look up to; they have no notion of a higher.'

'Nay, Mr. Gray,' said my lady, smiling, 'they are as loyally disposed as any children can be. They come up here every fourth of June, and drink his Majesty's health, and have buns, and (as Margaret Dawson can testify) they take a great and respectful interest in all the pictures I can show them of the Royal family.'

'But, madam, I think of something higher than any earthly dignities.'

My lady coloured at the mistake she had made; for she herself was truly pious. Yet when she resumed the subject, it seemed to me as if her tone was a little sharper than before.

'Such want of reverence is, I should say, the clergyman's fault. You must excuse me, Mr. Gray, if I speak plainly.'

'My lady, I want plain-speaking. I myself am not accustomed to those ceremonies and forms which are, I suppose, the etiquette in your ladyship's rank of life, and which seem to hedge you in from any power of mine to touch you. Among those with whom I have passed my life hitherto, it has been the custom to speak plainly out what we have felt earnestly. So, instead of needing any apology from your ladyship for straightforward speaking, I will meet what you say at once, and admit that it is the clergyman's fault, in a great measure, when the children of his parish swear, and curse, and are brutal, and ignorant of all saving grace; nay, some of them of the very name of God. And because this guilt of mine, as the clergyman of this parish, lies heavy on my soul, and every day leads but from bad to worse, till I am utterly bewildered how to do good to children who escape from me as if I were a monster, and who are growing up to be men fit for and capable of any crime, but those requiring wit or sense, I come to you, who seem to me all-powerful, as far as material power goes—for your ladyship only knows the surface of things, and barely that, that pass in your village—to help me with advice, and such outward help as you can give.'

Mr. Gray had stood up and sat down once or twice while he had been speaking, in an agitated, nervous kind of way, and now he was interrupted by a violent fit of coughing, after which he trembled all over.

My lady rang for a glass of water, and looked much distressed.

'Mr. Gray,' said she, 'I am sure you are not well; and that makes you exaggerate childish faults into positive evils. It is always the case with us when we are not strong in health. I hear of you exerting yourself in every direction: you over-work yourself, and the consequence is, that you imagine us all worse people than we are.'

And my lady smiled very kindly and pleasantly at him, as he sat, a little panting, a little flushed, trying to recover his breath. I am sure that now they were brought face to face, she had quite forgotten all the offence she had taken at his doings when she heard of them from others; and, indeed, it was enough to soften any one's heart to see that young, almost boyish face, looking in such anxiety and distress.

'O, my lady, what shall I do?' he asked, as soon as he could recover breath, and with such an air of humility that I am sure no one who had seen it could have ever thought him conceited again. 'The evil of this world is too strong for me. I can do so little. It is all in vain. It was only to-day——' And again the cough and agitation returned.

'My dear Mr. Gray,' said my lady (the day before, I could never have believed she could have called him My dear), 'you must take the advice of an old woman about yourself. You are not fit to do anything just now but attend to your own health: rest, and see a doctor (but, indeed, I will take care of that), and when you are pretty strong again, you will find that you have been magnifying evils to yourself.'

'But, my lady, I cannot rest. The evils do exist, and the burden of their continuance lies on my shoulders. I have no place to gather the children together in, that I may teach them the things necessary to salvation. The rooms in my own house are too small; but I have tried them. I have money of my own; and, as your ladyship knows, I tried to get a piece of leasehold property on which to build a school-house at my own expense. Your ladyship's lawyer comes forward, at your instructions, to enforce some old feudal right, by which no building is allowed on leasehold property without the sanction of the lady of the manor. It may be all very true; but it was a cruel thing to do,—that is, if your ladyship had known (which I am sure you do not) the real moral and spiritual state of my poor parishioners. And now I come to you to know what I am to do. Rest! I cannot rest, while children whom I could possibly save are being left in their ignorance, their blasphemy, their uncleanness, their cruelty. It is known through the village that your ladyship disapproves of my efforts, and opposes all my plans. If you think them wrong, foolish, ill-digested (I have been a student, living in a college, and eschewing all society but that of pious men, until now: I may not judge for the best, in my ignorance of this sinful human nature), tell me of better plans and wiser projects for accomplishing my end; but do not bid me rest, with Satan compassing me round, and stealing souls away.'

'Mr. Gray,' said my lady, 'there may be some truth in what you have said. I do not deny it, though I think, in your present state of indisposition and excitement, you exaggerate it much. I believe—nay, the experience of a pretty long life has convinced me—that education is a bad thing, if given indiscriminately. It unfits the lower orders for their duties, the duties to which they are called by God, of submission to those placed in authority over them, of contentment with that state of life to which it has pleased God to call them, and of ordering themselves lowly and reverently to all their betters. I have made this conviction of mine tolerably evident to you; and have expressed distinctly my disapprobation of some of your ideas. You may imagine, then, that I was not well pleased when I found that you had taken a rood or more of Farmer Hale's land, and were laying the foundations of a school-house. You had done this without asking for my permission, which, as Farmer Hale's liege lady, ought to have been obtained legally, as well as asked for out of courtesy. I put a stop to what I believed to be calculated to do harm to a village, to a population in which, to say the least of it, I may be supposed to take as much interest as you can do. How can reading and writing, and the multiplication-table (if you choose to go so far), prevent blasphemy, and uncleanness and cruelty? Really, Mr. Gray, I hardly like to express myself so strongly on the subject in your present state of health, as I should do at any other time. It seems to me that books do little; character much; and character is not formed from books.'

'I do not think of character: I think of souls. I must get some hold upon these children, or what will become of them in the next world? I must be found to have some power beyond what they have, and which they are rendered capable of appreciating, before they will listen to me. At present, physical force is all they look up to ; and I have none.'

' Nay, Mr. Gray, by your own admission, they look up to me.'

' They would not do anything your ladyship disliked if it was likely to come to your knowledge ; but if they could conceal it from you, the knowledge of your dislike to a particular line of conduct would never make them cease from pursuing it.'

' Mr. Gray '—surprise in her air, and some little indignation—' they and their fathers have lived on the Hanbury lands for generations ! '

' I cannot help it, madam. I am telling you the truth, whether you believe me or not.' There was a pause ; my lady looking perplexed, and somewhat ruffled ; Mr. Gray as though hopeless and wearied out. ' Then, my lady,' said he, at last, rising as he spoke, ' you can suggest nothing to ameliorate the state of things which, I do assure you, does exist on your lands, and among your tenants. Surely, you will not object to my using Farmer Hale's great barn every Sabbath ? He will allow me the use of it, if your ladyship will grant your permission.'

' You are not fit for any extra work at present ' (and indeed he had been coughing very much all through the conversation). ' Give me time to consider of it. Tell me what you wish to teach. You will be able to take care of your health and grow stronger while I consider. It shall not be the worse for you, if you leave it in my hands for a time.'

My lady spoke very kindly ; but he was in too excited a state to recognize the kindness, while the idea of delay was evidently a sore irritation. I heard him say : ' And I have so little time in which to do my work. Lord ! lay not this sin to my charge.'

But my lady was speaking to the old butler, for whom, at her sign, I had rung the bell some little time before. Now she turned round.

' Mr. Gray, I find I have some bottles of Malmsey, of the vintage of seventeen hundred and seventy-eight, yet left. Malmsey, as perhaps you know, used to be considered a specific for coughs arising from weakness. You must permit me to send you half-a-dozen bottles, and, depend upon it, you will take a more cheerful view of life and its duties before you have finished them, especially if you will be so kind as to see Doctor Trevor, who is coming to see me in the course of the week. By the time you are strong enough to work, I will try and find some means of preventing the children from using such bad language, and otherwise annoying you.'

'My lady, it is the sin, and not the annoyance. I wish I could make you understand.' He spoke with some impatience; poor fellow, he was too weak, exhausted, and nervous. 'I am perfectly well; I can set to work to-morrow; I will do anything not to be oppressed with the thought of how little I am doing. I do not want your wine. Liberty to act in the manner I think right, will do me far more good. But it is of no use. It is pre-ordained that I am to be nothing but a cumberer of the ground. I beg your ladyship's pardon for this call.'

He stood up, and then turned dizzy. My lady looked on, deeply hurt, and not a little offended. He held out his hand to her, and I could see that she had a little hesitation before she took it. He then saw me, I almost think, for the first time; and put out his hand once more, drew it back, as if undecided, put it out again, and finally took hold of mine for an instant in his damp, listless hand, and was gone.

Lady Ludlow was dissatisfied with both him and herself, I was sure. Indeed, I was dissatisfied with the result of the interview myself. But my lady was not one to speak out her feelings on the subject; nor was I one to forget myself, and begin on a topic which she did not begin. She came to me, and was very tender with me; so tender, that that, and the thoughts of Mr. Gray's sick, hopeless, disappointed look, nearly made me cry.

'You are tired, little one,' said my lady. 'Go and

lie down in my room, and hear what Medlicott and
I can decide upon in the way of strengthening dainties
for that poor young man, who is killing himself with
his over-sensitive conscientiousness.'

' O, my lady ! ' said I, and then I stopped.

' Well.   What ? ' asked she.

' If you would but let him have Farmer Hale's barn
at once, it would do him more good than all.'

' Pooh, pooh, child ! ' though I don't think she was
displeased, ' he is not fit for more work just now.
I shall go and write for Doctor Trevor.'

And, for the next half-hour, we did nothing but
arrange physical comforts and cures for poor Mr. Gray.
At the end of the time, Mrs. Medlicott said :

' Has your ladyship heard that Harry Gregson has
fallen from a tree, and broken his thigh-bone, and is
like to be a cripple for life ? '

' Harry Gregson !   That black-eyed lad who read
my letter ?   It all comes from over-education ! '


## CHAPTER XI

BUT I don't see how my lady could think it was
over-education that made Harry Gregson break his
thigh, for the manner in which he met with the accident
was this :—

Mr. Horner, who had fallen sadly out of health since
his wife's death, had attached himself greatly to Harry
Gregson.   Now, Mr. Horner had a cold manner to
every one, and never spoke more than was necessary,
at the best of times.   And, latterly, it had not been
the best of times with him.   I dare say, he had had
some causes for anxiety (of which I knew nothing)
about my lady's affairs ; and he was evidently annoyed
by my lady's whim (as he once inadvertently called it)
of placing Miss Galindo under him in the position of
a clerk.   Yet he had always been friends, in his quiet
way, with Miss Galindo, and she devoted herself to
her new occupation with diligence and punctuality,

although more than once she had moaned to me over the orders for needlework which had been sent to her, and which, owing to her occupation in the service of Lady Ludlow, she had been unable to fulfil.

The only living creature to whom the staid Mr. Horner could be said to be attached, was Harry Gregson. To my lady he was a faithful and devoted servant, looking keenly after her interests, and anxious to forward them at any cost of trouble to himself. But the more shrewd Mr. Horner was, the more probability was there of his being annoyed at certain peculiarities of opinion which my lady held with a quiet, gentle pertinacity ; against which no arguments, based on mere worldly and business calculations, made any way. This frequent opposition to views which Mr. Horner entertained, although it did not interfere with the sincere respect which the lady and the steward felt for each other, yet prevented any warmer feeling of affection from coming in. It seems strange to say it, but I must repeat it—the only person for whom, since his wife's death, Mr. Horner seemed to feel any love, was the little imp Harry Gregson, with his bright, watchful eyes, his tangled hair hanging right down to his eyebrows, for all the world like a Skye terrier. This lad, half gipsy and whole poacher, as many people esteemed him, hung about the silent, respectable, staid Mr. Horner, and followed his steps with something of the affectionate fidelity of the dog which he resembled. I suspect, this demonstration of attachment to his person on Harry Gregson's part was what won Mr. Horner's regard. In the first instance, the steward had only chosen the lad out as the cleverest instrument he could find for his purpose ; and I don't mean to say that, if Harry had not been almost as shrewd as Mr. Horner himself was, both by original disposition and subsequent experience, the steward would have taken to him as he did, let the lad have shown ever so much affection for him.

But even to Harry Mr. Horner was silent. Still, it was pleasant to find himself in many ways so readily

understood ; to perceive that the crumbs of knowledge
he let fall were picked up by his little follower, and
hoarded like gold ; that here was one to hate the
persons and things whom Mr. Horner coldly disliked,
and to reverence and admire all those for whom he
had any regard. Mr. Horner had never had a child,
and unconsciously, I suppose, something of the paternal
feeling had begun to develop itself in him towards
Harry Gregson. I heard one or two things from different people, which have always made me fancy that
Mr. Horner secretly and almost unconsciously hoped
that Harry Gregson might be trained so as to be first
his clerk, and next his assistant, and finally his successor in his stewardship to the Hanbury estates.

Harry's disgrace with my lady, in consequence of his
reading the letter, was a deeper blow to Mr. Horner
than his quiet manner would ever have led any one
to suppose, or than Lady Ludlow ever dreamed of
inflicting, I am sure.

Probably Harry had a short, stern rebuke from
Mr. Horner at the time, for his manner was always
hard even to those he cared for the most. But Harry's
love was not to be daunted or quelled by a few sharp
words. I dare say, from what I heard of them afterwards, that Harry accompanied Mr. Horner in his
walk over the farm the very day of the rebuke ; his
presence apparently unnoticed by the agent, by whom
his absence would have been painfully felt nevertheless. That was the way of it, as I have been told.
Mr. Horner never bade Harry go with him ; never
thanked him for going, or being at his heels ready to
run on any errands, straight as the crow flies to his
point, and back to heel in as short a time as possible.
Yet, if Harry were away, Mr. Horner never inquired
the reason from any of the men who might be supposed
to know whether he was detained by his father, or
otherwise engaged ; he never asked Harry himself
where he had been. But Miss Galindo said that those
labourers who knew Mr. Horner well, told her that he
was always more quick-eyed to shortcomings, more

savage-like in fault-finding, on those days when the
lad was absent.

Miss Galindo, indeed, was my great authority for
most of the village news which I heard. She it was
who gave me the particulars of poor Harry's accident.

'You see, my dear,' she said, 'the little poacher has
taken some unaccountable fancy to my master.' (This
was the name by which Miss Galindo always spoke of
Mr. Horner to me, ever since she had been, as she
called it, appointed his clerk.)

'Now, if I had twenty hearts to lose, I never could
spare a bit of one of them for that good, grey, square,
severe man. But different people have different tastes,
and here is that little imp of a gipsy-tinker ready to
turn slave for my master; and, odd enough, my
master,—who, I should have said beforehand, would
have made short work of imp, and imp's family, and
have sent Hall, the Bang-beggar,* after them in no
time—my master, as they tell me, is in his way quite
fond of the lad, and if he could, without vexing my
lady too much, he would have made him what the
folks here call a Latiner. However, last night, it seems
that there was a letter of some importance forgotten
(I can't tell you what it was about, my dear, though
I know perfectly well, but "*service oblige*," as well as
"noblesse," and you must take my word for it that it
was important, and one that I am surprised my master
could forget), till too late for the post. (The poor,
good, orderly man is not what he was before his wife's
death.) Well, it seems that he was sore annoyed by
his forgetfulness, and well he might be. And it was
all the more vexatious, as he had no one to blame but
himself. As for that matter, I always scold somebody
else when I'm in fault; but I suppose my master
would never think of doing that, else it's a mighty
relief. However, he could eat no tea, and was altogether put out and gloomy. And the little faithful
imp-lad, perceiving all this, I suppose, got up like a
page in an old ballad, and said he would run for his
life across country to Comberford, and see if he could

not get there before the bags were made up. So my
master gave him the letter, and nothing more was
heard of the poor fellow till this morning, for the father
thought his son was sleeping in Mr. Horner's barn, as
he does occasionally, it seems, and my master, as was
very natural, that he had gone to his father's.'

'And he had fallen down the old stone quarry, had
he not?'

'Yes, sure enough. Mr. Gray had been up here
fretting my lady with some of his new-fangled schemes,
and because the young man could not have it all his
own way, from what I understand, he was put out,
and thought he would go home by the back lane,
instead of through the village, where the folks would
notice if the parson looked glum. But, however, it
was a mercy, and I don't mind saying so, aye, and
meaning it too, though it may be like Methodism, for,
as Mr. Gray walked by the quarry, he heard a groan,
and at first he thought it was a lamb fallen down;
and he stood still, and then he heard it again; and
then, I suppose, he looked down and saw Harry. So
he let himself down by the boughs of the trees to the
ledge where Harry lay half-dead, and with his poor
thigh broken. There he had lain ever since the night
before: he had been returning to tell the master that
he had safely posted the letter, and the first words he
said, when they recovered him from the exhausted
state he was in, were' (Miss Galindo tried hard not
to whimper, as she said it), '"It was in time, sir.
I see'd it put in the bag with my own eyes."'

'But where is he?' asked I. 'How did Mr. Gray
get him out?'

'Aye! there it is, you see. Why, the old gentleman
(I daren't say Devil in Lady Ludlow's house) is not
so black as he is painted; and Mr. Gray must have
a deal of good in him, as I say at times; and then
at others, when he has gone against me, I can't bear
him, and think hanging too good for him. But he
lifted the poor lad, as if he had been a baby, I suppose,
and carried him up the great ledges that were formerly

used for steps; and laid him soft and easy on the
wayside grass, and ran home and got help and a door,
and had him carried to his house, and laid on his bed ;
and then somehow, for the first time either he or any
one else perceived it, he himself was all over blood—
his own blood—he had broken a blood-vessel ; and
there he lies in the little dressing-room, as white and as
still as if he were dead ; and the little imp in Mr. Gray's
own bed, sound asleep, now his leg is set, just as if linen
sheets and a feather bed were his native element,
as one may say. Really, now he is doing so well, I've
no patience with him, lying there where Mr. Gray ought
to be. It is just what my lady always prophesied would
come to pass, if there was any confusion of ranks.'

'Poor Mr. Gray !' said I, thinking of his flushed
face, and his feverish, restless ways, when he had been
calling on my lady not an hour before his exertions
on Harry's behalf. And I told Miss Galindo how ill
I had thought him.

'Yes,' said she. 'And that was the reason my lady
had sent for Doctor Trevor. Well, it has fallen out
admirably, for he looked well after that old donkey of
a Prince, and saw that he made no blunders.'

Now 'that old donkey of a Prince' meant the village
surgeon, Mr. Prince, between whom and Miss Galindo
there was war to the knife, as they often met in the
cottages, when there was illness, and she had her queer,
odd recipes, which he, with his grand pharmacopoeia,
held in infinite contempt, and the consequence of their
squabbling had been, not long before this very time,
that he had established a kind of rule, that into whatever sick-room Miss Galindo was admitted, there he
refused to visit. But Miss Galindo's prescriptions and
visits cost nothing, and were often backed by kitchen-
physic ; so, though it was true that she never came
but she scolded about something or other, she was
generally preferred as medical attendant to Mr. Prince.

'Yes, the old donkey is obliged to tolerate me, and
be civil to me ; for, you see, I got there first, and had
possession, as it were, and yet my lord the donkey

likes the credit of attending the parson, and being in
consultation with so grand a county-town doctor as
Doctor Trevor.  And Doctor Trevor is an old friend of
mine' (she sighed a little, some time I may tell you
why), 'and treats me with infinite bowing and respect;
so the donkey, not to be out of medical fashion, bows
too, though it is sadly against the grain: and he pulled
a face as if he had heard a slate-pencil gritting against
a slate, when I told Doctor Trevor I meant to sit up
with the two lads, for I call Mr. Gray little more than
a lad, and a pretty conceited one, too, at times.'

'But why should you sit up, Miss Galindo?  It will
tire you sadly.'

'Not it.  You see, there is Gregson's mother to keep
quiet; for she sits by her lad, fretting and sobbing,
so that I'm afraid of her disturbing Mr. Gray; and
there's Mr. Gray to keep quiet, for Doctor Trevor says
his life depends on it; and there is medicine to be
given to the one, and bandages to be attended to for
the other; and the wild horde of gipsy brothers and
sisters to be turned out, and the father to be held in
from showing too much gratitude to Mr. Gray, who
can't bear it,—and who is to do it all but me?  The
only servant is old lame Betty, who once lived with
me, and *would* leave me because she said I was always
bothering—(there was a good deal of truth in what she
said, I grant, but she need not have said it; a good
deal of truth is best let alone at the bottom of the well),
and what can she do,—deaf as ever she can be, too?'

So Miss Galindo went her ways; but not the less
was she at her post in the morning; a little crosser
and more silent than usual; but the first was not to
be wondered at, and the last was rather a blessing.

Lady Ludlow had been extremely anxious both about
Mr. Gray and Harry Gregson.  Kind and thoughtful in
any case of illness and accident, she always was; but
somehow, in this, the feeling that she was not quite—
what shall I call it?—'friends' seems hardly the right
word to use, as to the possible feeling between the
Countess Ludlow and the little vagabond messenger,

who had only once been in her presence,—that she had hardly parted from either as she could have wished to do, had death been near, made her more than usually anxious.  Doctor Trevor was not to spare obtaining the best medical advice the county could afford; whatever he ordered in the way of diet, was to be prepared under Mrs. Medlicott's own eye, and sent down from the Hall to the Parsonage.  As Mr. Horner had given somewhat similar directions, in the case of Harry Gregson at least, there was rather a multiplicity of counsellors and dainties, than any lack of them.  And, the second night, Mr. Horner insisted on taking the superintendence of the nursing himself, and sat and snored by Harry's bedside, while the poor, exhausted mother lay by her child,—thinking that she watched him, but in reality fast asleep, as Miss Galindo told us; for, distrusting any one's powers of watching and nursing but her own, she had stolen across the quiet village street in cloak and dressing-gown, and found Mr. Gray in vain trying to reach the cup of barley-water which Mr. Horner had placed just beyond his reach.

In consequence of Mr. Gray's illness, we had to have a strange curate to do duty; a man who dropped his h's, and hurried through the service, and yet had time enough to stand in my lady's way, bowing to her as she came out of church, and so subservient in manner, that I believe that sooner than remain unnoticed by a countess, he would have preferred being scolded, or even cuffed.  Now I found out, that great as was my lady's liking and approval of respect, nay, even reverence, being paid to her as a person of quality,—a sort of tribute to her Order, which she had no individual right to remit, or, indeed, not to exact,—yet she, being personally simple, sincere, and holding herself in low esteem, could not endure anything like the servility of Mr. Crosse, the temporary curate.  She grew absolutely to loathe his perpetual smiling and bowing; his instant agreement with the slightest opinion she uttered; his veering round as she blew the wind.  I have often said that my lady did not talk much, as she might have

done had she lived among her equals.  But we all
loved her so much, that we had learnt to interpret
all her little ways pretty truly ; and I knew what
particular turns of her head, and contractions of her
delicate fingers meant, as well as if she had expressed
herself in words.  I began to suspect that my lady
would be very thankful to have Mr. Gray about again,
and doing his duty even with a conscientiousness that
might amount to worrying himself, and fidgeting others ;
and although Mr. Gray might hold her opinions in as
little esteem as those of any simple gentlewoman, she
was too sensible not to feel how much flavour there
was in his conversation, compared to that of Mr. Crosse,
who was only her tasteless echo.

As for Miss Galindo, she was utterly and entirely
a partisan of Mr. Gray's, almost ever since she had
begun to nurse him during his illness.

'You know, I never set up for reasonableness, my
lady.  So I don't pretend to say, as I might do if
I were a sensible woman and all that,—that I am
convinced by Mr. Gray's arguments of this thing or
t'other.  For one thing, you see, poor fellow ! he has
never been able to argue, or hardly indeed to speak,
for Doctor Trevor has been very peremptory.  So
there's been no scope for arguing !  But what I mean
is this :—When I see a sick man thinking always of
others, and never of himself ; patient, humble—a trifle
too much at times, for I've caught him praying to be
forgiven for having neglected his work as a parish
priest' (Miss Galindo was making horrible faces, to
keep back tears, squeezing up her eyes in a way which
would have amused me at any other time, but when
she was speaking of Mr. Gray) ; 'when I see a downright good, religious man, I'm apt to think he's got
hold of the right clue, and that I can do no better
than hold on by the tails of his coat and shut my eyes,
if we've got to go over doubtful places on our road to
Heaven.  So, my lady, you must excuse me, if, when
he gets about again, he is all agog about a Sunday-
school, for if he is, I shall be agog too, and perhaps

twice as bad as him, for, you see, I've a strong constitution compared to his, and strong ways of speaking and acting. And I tell your ladyship this now, because I think from your rank—and still more, if I may say so, for all your kindness to me long ago, down to this very day—you've a right to be first told of anything about me. Change of opinion I can't exactly call it, for I don't see the good of schools and teaching A B C, any more than I did before, only Mr. Gray does, so I'm to shut my eyes, and leap over the ditch to the side of education. I've told Sally already, that if she does not mind her work, but stands gossiping with Nelly Mather, I'll teach her her lessons; and I've never caught her with old Nelly since.'

I think Miss Galindo's desertion to Mr. Gray's opinions in this matter hurt my lady just a little bit; but she only said:

' Of course, if the parishioners wish for it, Mr. Gray must have his Sunday-school. I shall, in that case, withdraw my opposition. I am sorry I cannot change my opinions as easily as you.'

My lady made herself smile as she said this. Miss Galindo saw it was an effort to do so. She thought a minute before she spoke again.

' Your ladyship has not seen Mr. Gray as intimately as I have done. That's one thing. But, as for the parishioners, they will follow your ladyship's lead in everything; so there is no chance of their wishing for a Sunday-school.'

' I have never done anything to make them follow my lead, as you call it, Miss Galindo,' said my lady, gravely.

' Yes, you have,' replied Miss Galindo, bluntly. And then, correcting herself, she said, ' Begging your ladyship's pardon, you have. Your ancestors have lived here time out of mind, and have owned the land on which their forefathers have lived ever since there were forefathers. You yourself were born amongst them, and have been like a little queen to them ever since, I might say, and they've never known your ladyship

do anything but what was kind and gentle; but I'll
leave fine speeches about your ladyship to Mr. Crosse.
Only you, my lady, lead the thoughts of the parish;
and save some of them a world of trouble, for they
could never tell what was right if they had to think
for themselves. It's all quite right that they should
be guided by you, my lady,—if only you would agree
with Mr. Gray.'

'Well,' said my lady, 'I told him only the last day
that he was here, that I would think about it. I do
believe I could make up my mind on certain subjects
better if I were left alone, than while being constantly
talked to about them.'

My lady said this in her usual soft tones; but the
words had a tinge of impatience about them; indeed,
she was more ruffled than I had often seen her; but,
checking herself in an instant, she said:

'You don't know how Mr. Horner drags in this
subject of education apropos of everything. Not that
he says much about it at any time: it is not his way.
But he cannot let the thing alone.'

'I know why, my lady,' said Miss Galindo. 'That
poor lad, Harry Gregson, will never be able to earn
his livelihood in any active way, but will be lame for
life. Now, Mr. Horner thinks more of Harry than of
any one else in the world,—except, perhaps, your ladyship.' Was it not a pretty companionship for my lady?
'And he has schemes of his own for teaching Harry;
and if Mr. Gray could but have his school, Mr. Horner
and he think Harry might be schoolmaster, as your
ladyship would not like to have him coming to you
as steward's clerk. I wish your ladyship would fall
into this plan; Mr. Gray has it so at heart.'

Miss Galindo looked wistfully at my lady, as she
said this. But my lady only said, drily, and rising at
the same time, as if to end the conversation:

'So! Mr. Horner and Mr. Gray seem to have gone
a long way in advance of my consent to their plans.'

'There!' exclaimed Miss Galindo, as my lady left
the room, with an apology for going away; 'I have

gone and done mischief with my long, stupid tongue. To be sure, people plan a long way ahead of to-day ; more especially when one is a sick man, lying all through the weary day on a sofa.'

'My lady will soon get over her annoyance,' said I, as it were apologetically. I only stopped Miss Galindo's self-reproaches to draw down her wrath upon myself.

'And has not she a right to be annoyed with me, if she likes, and to keep annoyed as long as she likes ? Am I complaining of her, that you need tell me that ? Let me tell you, I have known my lady these thirty years ; and if she were to take me by the shoulders, and turn me out of the house, I should only love her the more. So don't you think to come between us with any little mincing, peace-making speeches. I have been a mischief-making parrot, and I like her the better for being vexed with me. So good-bye to you, Miss ; and wait till you know Lady Ludlow as well as I do, before you next think of telling me she will soon get over her annoyance ! ' And off Miss Galindo went.

I could not exactly tell what I had done wrong ; but I took care never again to come in between my lady and her by any remark about the one to the other ; for I saw that some most powerful bond of grateful affection made Miss Galindo almost worship my lady.

Meanwhile, Harry Gregson was limping a little about in the village, still finding his home in Mr. Gray's house ; for there he could most conveniently be kept under the doctor's eye, and receive the requisite care, and enjoy the requisite nourishment. As soon as he was a little better, he was to go to Mr. Horner's house ; but, as the steward lived some distance out of the way, and was much from home, he had agreed to leave Harry at the house to which he had first been taken, until he was quite strong again ; and the more willingly, I suspect, from what I heard afterwards, because Mr. Gray gave up all the little strength of speaking which he had, to teaching Harry in the very manner which Mr. Horner most desired.

As for Gregson the father—he—wild man of the
woods, poacher, tinker, jack-of-all-trades—was getting
tamed by this kindness to his child.  Hitherto his hand
had been against every man, as every man's had been
against him.  That affair before the justice, which I
told you about, when Mr. Gray and even my lady had
interested themselves to get him released from unjust
imprisonment, was the first bit of justice he had ever
met with ; it attracted him to the people, and attached
him to the spot on which he had but squatted for
a time.  I am not sure if any of the villagers were
grateful to him for remaining in their neighbourhood,
instead of decamping as he had often done before, for
good reasons, doubtless, of personal safety.  Harry was
only one out of a brood of ten or twelve children, some
of whom had earned for themselves no good character
in service :  one, indeed, had been actually transported,
for a robbery committed in a distant part of the
county ;  and the tale was yet told in the village of
how Gregson the father came back from the trial in
a state of wild rage, striding through the place, and
uttering oaths of vengeance to himself, his great black
eyes gleaming out of his matted hair, and his arms
working by his side, and now and then tossed up in
his impotent despair.  As I heard the account, his
wife followed him, child-laden and weeping.  After
this, they had vanished from the country for a time,
leaving their mud hovel locked up, and the door-key,
as the neighbours said, buried in a hedge-bank.  The
Gregsons had reappeared much about the same time
that Mr. Gray came to Hanbury.  He had either never
heard of their evil character, or considered that it gave
them all the more claims upon his Christian care ; and
the end of it was, that this rough, untamed, strong
giant of a heathen was loyal slave to the weak, hectic,
nervous, self-distrustful parson.  Gregson had also a
kind of grumbling respect for Mr. Horner : he did not
quite like the steward's monopoly of his Harry : the
mother submitted to that with a better grace, swallow-
ing down her maternal jealousy in the prospect of her

child's advancement to a better and more respectable
position than that in which his parents had struggled
through life. But Mr. Horner, the steward, and Gregson, the poacher and squatter, had come into disagreeable contact too often in former days for them to be
perfectly cordial at any future time. Even now, when
there was no immediate cause for anything but gratitude for his child's sake on Gregson's part, he would
skulk out of Mr. Horner's way, if he saw him coming ;
and it took all Mr. Horner's natural reserve and
acquired self-restraint to keep him from occasionally
holding up his father's life as a warning to Harry.
Now Gregson had nothing of this desire for avoidance
with regard to Mr. Gray. The poacher had a feeling
of physical protection towards the parson ; while the
latter had shown the moral courage, without which
Gregson would never have respected him, in coming
right down upon him more than once in the exercise
of unlawful pursuits, and simply and boldly telling
him he was doing wrong, with such a quiet reliance
upon Gregson's better feeling, at the same time, that
the strong poacher could not have lifted a finger against
Mr. Gray, though it had been to save himself from
being apprehended and taken to the lock-ups the very
next hour. He had rather listened to the parson's bold
words with an approving smile, much as Mr. Gulliver*
might have hearkened to a lecture from a Lilliputian.
But when brave words passed into kind deeds, Gregson's heart mutely acknowledged its master and keeper.
And the beauty of it all was, that Mr. Gray knew
nothing of the good work he had done, or recognised
himself as the instrument which God had employed.
He thanked God, it is true, fervently and often, that
the work was done ; and loved the wild man for his
rough gratitude ; but it never occurred to the poor
young clergyman, lying on his sick-bed, and praying,
as Miss Galindo had told us he did, to be forgiven for
his unprofitable life, to think of Gregson's reclaimed
soul as anything with which he had had to do. It
was now more than three months since Mr. Gray had

been at Hanbury Court. During all that time, he
had been confined to his house, if not to his sick-
bed, and he and my lady had never met since their
last discussion and difference about Farmer Hale's
barn.

This was not my dear lady's fault; no one could
have been more attentive in every way to the slightest
possible want of either of the invalids, especially of
Mr. Gray. And she would have gone to see him at
his own house, as she sent him word, but that her foot
had slipped upon the polished oak staircase, and her
ancle had been sprained.

So we had never seen Mr. Gray since his illness,
when one November day he was announced as wishing
to speak to my lady. She was sitting in her room—
the room in which I lay now pretty constantly—and I
remember she looked startled, when word was brought
to her of Mr. Gray's being at the Hall.

She could not go to him, she was too lame for that,
so she bade him be shown into where she sat.

'Such a day for him to go out!' she exclaimed,
looking at the fog which had crept up to the windows,
and was sapping the little remaining life in the brilliant
Virginian creeper leaves that draperied the house on
the terrace side.

He came in white, trembling, his large eyes wild and
dilated. He hastened up to Lady Ludlow's chair, and,
to my surprise, took one of her hands and kissed it,
without speaking, yet shaking all over.

'Mr. Gray!' said she, quickly, with sharp, tremulous
apprehension of some unknown evil. 'What is it?
There is something unusual about you.'

'Something unusual has occurred,' replied he,
forcing his words to be calm, as with a great effort.
'A gentleman came to my house, not half-an-hour ago
—a Mr. Howard. He came straight from Vienna.'

'My son!' said my dear lady, stretching out her
arms in dumb questioning attitude.

'The Lord gave and the Lord taketh away. Blessed
be the name of the Lord.'

But my poor lady could not echo the words. He was the last remaining child. And once she had been the joyful mother of nine.

## CHAPTER XII

I AM ashamed to say what feeling became strongest in my mind about this time. Next to the sympathy we all of us felt for my dear lady in her deep sorrow, I mean. For that was greater and stronger than anything else, however contradictory you may think it, when you hear all.

It might arise from my being so far from well at the time, which produced a diseased mind in a diseased body; but I was absolutely jealous for my father's memory, when I saw how many signs of grief there were for my lord's death, he having done next to nothing for the village and parish, which now changed, as it were, its daily course of life, because his lordship died in a far-off city. My father had spent the best years of his manhood in labouring hard, body and soul, for the people amongst whom he lived. His family, of course, claimed the first place in his heart; he would have been good for little, even in the way of benevolence, if they had not. But close after them he cared for his parishioners and neighbours. And yet, when he died, though the church-bells tolled, and smote upon our hearts with hard, fresh pain at every beat, the sounds of every-day life still went on, close pressing around us,—carts and carriages, street-cries, distant barrel-organs (the kindly neighbours kept them out of our street): life, active, noisy life, pressed on our acute consciousness of Death, and jarred upon it as on a quick nerve.

And when we went to church,—my father's own church,—though the pulpit-cushions were black, and many of the congregation had put on some humble sign of mourning, yet it did not alter the whole material aspect of the place. And yet what was Lord Ludlow's relation to Hanbury, compared to my father's work and place in——?

O ! it was very wicked in me ! I think if I had seen my lady,—if I had dared to ask to go to her, I should not have felt so miserable, so discontented. But she sat in her own room, hung with black, all, even over the shutters. She saw no light but that which was artificial—candles, lamps, and the like—for more than a month. Only Adams went near her. Mr. Gray was not admitted, though he called daily. Even Mrs. Medlicott did not see her for near a fortnight. The sight of my lady's griefs, or rather the recollection of it, made Mrs. Medlicott talk far more than was her wont. She told us, with many tears, and much gesticulation, even speaking German at times, when her English would not flow, that my lady sat there, a white figure in the middle of the darkened room ; a shaded lamp near her, the light of which fell on an open Bible,—the great family Bible. It was not opened at any chapter, or consoling verse ; but at the page whereon were registered the births of her nine children. Five had died in infancy,—sacrificed to the cruel system which forbade the mother to suckle her babies. Four had lived longer ; Urian had been the first to die, Ughtred-Mortimar, Earl Ludlow, the last.

My lady did not cry, Mrs. Medlicott said. She was quite composed ; very still, very silent. She put aside everything that savoured of mere business ; sent people to Mr. Horner for that. But she was proudly alive to every possible form which might do honour to the last of her race.

In those days, expresses were slow things, and forms still slower. Before my lady's directions could reach Vienna, my lord was buried. There was some talk (so Mrs. Medlicott said) about taking the body up, and bringing him to Hanbury. But his executors,—connexions on the Ludlow side,—demurred to this. If he were removed to England, he must be carried on to Scotland, and interred with his Monkshaven forefathers. My lady, deeply hurt, withdrew from the discussion before it degenerated to an unseemly contest. But all the more, for this understood mortification of my lady's, did the whole village and estate of Hanbury assume every outward sign of mourning. The church-bells tolled morning and evening. The church itself was draped in black inside. Hatchments* were placed everywhere, where hatchments could be put. All the tenantry spoke in hushed voices for more than a week, scarcely daring to observe that all flesh, even that of an Earl Ludlow, and the last of the Hanburys, was but grass after all. The very Fighting Lion closed its front door, front shutters it had none, and those who needed drink stole in at the back, and were silent and maudlin over their cups, instead of riotous and noisy. Miss Galindo's eyes were swollen up with crying, and she told me, with a fresh burst of tears, that even hump-backed Sally had been found sobbing over her Bible, and using a pocket-handkerchief for the first time in her life; her aprons having hitherto stood her in the necessary stead, but not being sufficiently in accordance with etiquette to be used when mourning over an earl's premature decease.

If it was in this way out of the Hall, ' you might work it by the rule of three,' as Miss Galindo used to say, and judge what it was in the Hall. We none of us spoke but in a whisper: we tried not to eat; and indeed the shock had been so really great, and we did really care so much for my lady, that for some days we had but little appetite. But after that, I fear our sympathy grew weaker, while our flesh grew stronger. But we still spoke low, and our hearts ached whenever we thought of my lady sitting there alone in the darkened room, with the light ever falling on that one solemn page.

We wished, O how I wished that she would see Mr. Gray! But Adams said, she thought my lady ought to have a bishop come to see her. Still no one had authority enough to send for one.

Mr. Horner all this time was suffering as much as any one. He was too faithful a servant of the great

Hanbury family, though now the family had dwindled
down to a fragile old lady, not to mourn acutely over
its probable extinction. He had, besides, a deeper
sympathy and reverence with, and for, my lady in all
things, than probably he ever cared to show, for his
manners were always measured and cold. He suffered
from sorrow. He also suffered from wrong. My lord's
executors kept writing to him continually. My lady
refused to listen to mere business, saying she intrusted
all to him. But the ' all ' was more complicated than I
ever thoroughly understood. As far as I comprehended
the case, it was something of this kind :—There had
been a mortgage raised on my lady's property of Hanbury, to enable my lord, her husband, to spend money
in cultivating his Scotch estates, after some new fashion
that required capital. As long as my lord, her son,
lived, who was to succeed to both the estates after her
death, this did not signify ; so she had said and felt ;
and she had refused to take any steps to secure the
repayment of capital, or even the payment of the
interest of the mortgage from the possible representa-
tives and possessors of the Scotch estates, to the possible owner of the Hanbury property ; saying it ill
became her to calculate on the contingency of her son's
death.

But he had died, childless, unmarried. The heir of
the Monkshaven property was an Edinburgh advocate,
a far-away kinsman of my lord's : the Hanbury property, at my lady's death, would go to the descendants
of a third son of the Squire Hanbury in the days of
Queen Anne.

This complication of affairs was most grievous to
Mr. Horner. He had always been 'opposed to the
mortgage ; had hated the payment of the interest, as
obliging my lady to practise certain economies which,
though she took care to make them as personal as
possible, he disliked as derogatory to the family. Poor
Mr. Horner ! He was so cold and hard in his manner, so
curt and decisive in his speech, that I don't think we
any of us did him justice. Miss Galindo was almost the

first, at this time, to speak a kind word of him, or to
take thought of him at all, any farther than to get out
of his way when we saw him approaching.

'I don't think Mr. Horner is well,' she said one day,
about three weeks after we had heard of my lord's
death. 'He sits resting his head on his hand, and
hardly hears me when I speak to him.'

But I thought no more of it, as Miss Galindo did not
name it again. My lady came amongst us once more.
From elderly she had become old; a little, frail, old
lady, in heavy black drapery, never speaking about nor
alluding to her great sorrow; quieter, gentler, paler
than ever before; and her eyes dim with much weeping, never witnessed by mortal.

She had seen Mr. Gray at the expiration of the month
of deep retirement. But I do not think that even to
him she had said one word of her own particular individual sorrow. All mention of it seemed buried deep
for evermore. One day, Mr. Horner sent word that he
was too much indisposed to attend to his usual business
at the Hall; but he wrote down some directions and
requests to Miss Galindo, saying that he would be at his
office early the next morning. The next morning he
was dead!

Miss Galindo told my lady. Miss Galindo herself
cried plentifully, but my lady, although very much
distressed, could not cry. It seemed a physical impos-
sibility, as if she had shed all the tears in her power.
Moreover, I almost think her wonder was far greater
that she herself lived than that Mr. Horner died. It
was almost natural that so faithful a servant should
break his heart, when the family he belonged to lost
their stay, their heir and their last hope.

Yes! Mr. Horner was a faithful servant. I do not
think there are many so faithful now; but, perhaps,
that is an old woman's fancy of mine. When his will
came to be examined, it was discovered that, soon after
Harry Gregson's accident, Mr. Horner had left the few
thousands (three, I think,) of which he was possessed,
in trust for Harry's benefit, desiring his executors to

see that the lad was well educated in certain things, for which Mr. Horner had thought that he had shown especial aptitude; and there was a kind of implied apology to my lady in one sentence, where he stated that Harry's lameness would prevent his being ever able to gain his living by the exercise of any mere bodily faculties, ' as had been wished by a lady whose wishes' he, the testator, ' was bound to regard.'

But there was a codicil to the will, dated since Lord Ludlow's death—feebly written by Mr. Horner himself, as if in preparation only for some more formal manner of bequest; or, perhaps, only as a mere temporary arrangement till he could see a lawyer, and have a fresh will made. In this he revoked his previous bequest to Harry Gregson. He only left two hundred pounds to Mr. Gray to be used, as that gentleman thought best, for Harry Gregson's benefit. With this one exception, he bequeathed all the rest of his savings to my lady, with a hope that they might form a nest-egg, as it were, towards the paying off of the mortgage which had been such a grief to him during his life. I may not repeat all this in lawyer's phrase; I heard it through Miss Galindo, and she might make mistakes. Though, indeed, she was very clear-headed, and soon earned the respect of Mr. Smithson, my lady's lawyer from Warwick. Mr. Smithson knew Miss Galindo a little before, both personally and by reputation; but I don't think he was prepared to find her installed as steward's clerk, and, at first, he was inclined to treat her, in this capacity, with polite contempt. But Miss Galindo was both a lady and a spirited, sensible woman, and she could put aside her self-indulgence in eccentricity of speech and manner whenever she chose. Nay more; she was usually so talkative, that if she had not been amusing and warm-hearted, one might have thought her wearisome occasionally. But, to meet Mr. Smithson, she came out daily in her Sunday gown; she said no more than was required in answer to his questions; her books and papers were in thorough order, and methodically kept; her statements of matters-of-fact

accurate, and to be relied on. She was amusingly
conscious of her victory over his contempt of a woman-
clerk and his preconceived opinion of her unpractical
eccentricity.

'Let me alone, said she, one day when she came in
to sit awhile with me. 'That man is a good man—
a sensible man—and, I have no doubt, he is a good
lawyer; but he can't fathom women yet. I make no
doubt he'll go back to Warwick, and never give credit
again to those people who made him think me half-
cracked to begin with. O, my dear, he did! He
showed it twenty times worse than my poor dear
master ever did. It was a form to be gone through to
please my lady, and, for her sake, he would hear my
statements and see my books. It was keeping a woman
out of harm's way, at any rate, to let her fancy herself
useful. I read the man. And, I am thankful to say,
he cannot read me. At least, only one side of me.
When I see an end to be gained, I can behave myself
accordingly. Here was a man who thought that a
woman in a black silk gown was a respectable, orderly
kind of person; and I was a woman in a black silk
gown. He believed that a woman could not write
straight lines, and required a man to tell her that two
and two made four. I was not above ruling my books,
and had Cocker a little more at my fingers' ends than
he had. But my greatest triumph has been holding my
tongue. He would have thought nothing of my books,
or my sums, or my black silk gown, if I had spoken
unasked. So I have buried more sense in my bosom
these ten days than ever I have uttered in the whole
course of my life before. I have been so curt, so abrupt,
so abominably dull, that I'll answer for it he thinks me
worthy to be a man. But I must go back to him, my
dear, so good-bye to conversation and you.'

But though Mr. Smithson might be satisfied with
Miss Galindo, I am afraid she was the only part of the
affair with which he was content. Everything else
went wrong. I could not say who told me so—but
the conviction of this seemed to pervade the house. I

never knew how much we had all looked up to the silent,
gruff Mr. Horner for decisions, until he was gone.   My
lady herself was a pretty good woman of business, as
women of business go.   Her father, seeing that she
would be the heiress of the Hanbury property, had
given her a training which was thought unusual in
those days, and she liked to feel herself queen regnant,
and to have to decide in all cases between herself and
her tenantry.   But, perhaps, Mr. Horner would have
done it more wisely ; not but what she always attended
to him at last.   She would begin by saying, pretty
clearly and promptly, what she would have done, and
what she would not have done.   If Mr. Horner approved
of it, he bowed, and set about obeying her directly ;
if he disapproved of it, he bowed, and lingered so long
before he obeyed her, that she forced his opinion out of
him with her ' Well, Mr. Horner ! and what have you
to say against it ? '   For she always understood his
silence as well as if he had spoken.   But the estate was
pressed for ready money, and Mr. Horner had grown
gloomy and languid since the death of his wife, and
even his own personal affairs were not in the order in
which they had been a year or two before, for his old
clerk had gradually become superannuated, or, at any
rate, unable by the superfluity of his own energy and
wit to supply the spirit that was wanting in Mr. Horner.

Day after day Mr. Smithson seemed to grow more
fidgety, more annoyed at the state of affairs.   Like
every one else employed by Lady Ludlow, as far as I
could learn, he had an hereditary tie to the Hanbury
family.   As long as the Smithsons had been lawyers,
they had been lawyers to the Hanburys ; always coming in on all great family occasions, and better able to
understand the characters, and connect the links of
what had once been a large and scattered family, than
any individual thereof had ever been.

As long as a man was at the head of the Hanburys,
the lawyers had simply acted as servants, and had only
given their advice when it was required.   But they had
assumed a different position on the memorable occasion

of the mortgage : they had remonstrated against it. My lady had resented this remonstrance, and a slight unspoken coolness had existed between her and the father of this Mr. Smithson ever since.

I was very sorry for my lady. Mr. Smithson was inclined to blame Mr. Horner for the disorderly state in which he found some of the outlying farms, and for the deficiencies in the annual payment of rents. Mr. Smithson had too much good feeling to put this blame into words ; but my lady's quick instinct led her to reply to a thought, the existence of which she perceived ; and she quietly told the truth, and explained how she had interfered repeatedly to prevent Mr. Horner from taking certain desirable steps, which were discordant to her hereditary sense of right and wrong between landlord and tenant. She also spoke of the want of ready money as a misfortune that could be remedied, by more economical personal expenditure on her own part ; by which individual saving, it was possible that a reduction of fifty pounds a year might have been accomplished. But as soon as Mr. Smithson touched on larger economies, such as either affected the welfare of others, or the honour and standing of the great House of Hanbury, she was inflexible. Her establishment consisted of somewhere about forty servants, of whom nearly as many as twenty were unable to perform their work properly, and yet would have been hurt if they had been dismissed ; so they had the credit of fulfilling duties, while my lady paid and kept their substitutes. Mr. Smithson made a calculation, and would have saved some hundreds a year by pensioning off these old servants. But my lady would not hear of it. Then, again, I know privately that he urged her to allow some of us to return to our homes. Bitterly we should have regretted the separation from Lady Ludlow ; but we would have gone back gladly, had we known at the time that her circumstances required it : but she would not listen to the proposal for a moment.

' If I cannot act justly towards every one, I will give up a plan which has been a source of much satisfaction ;

at least, I will not carry it out to such an extent in future. But to these young ladies, who do me the favour to live with me at present, I stand pledged. I cannot go back from my word, Mr. Smithson. We had better talk no more of this.'

As she spoke, she entered the room where I lay. She and Mr. Smithson were coming for some papers contained in the bureau. They did not know I was there, and Mr. Smithson started a little when he saw me, as he must have been aware that I had overheard something. But my lady did not change a muscle of her face. All the world might overhear her kind, just, pure sayings, and she had no fear of their misconstruction. She came up to me, and kissed me on the forehead, and then went to search for the required papers.

' I rode over the Conington farms yesterday, my lady. I must say I was quite grieved to see the condition they are in ; all the land that is not waste is utterly exhausted with working successive white crops. Not a pinch of manure laid on the ground for years. I must say that a greater contrast could never have been presented than that between Harding's farm and the next fields—fences in perfect order, rotation crops, sheep eating down the turnips on the waste lands—everything that could be desired.'

' Whose farm is that ? ' asked my lady.

' Why, I am sorry to say, it was on none of your ladyship's that I saw such good methods adopted. I hoped it was, I stopped my horse to inquire. A queer-looking man, sitting on his horse like a tailor, watching his men with a couple of the sharpest eyes I ever saw, and dropping his h's at every word, answered my question, and told me it was his. I could not go on asking him who he was ; but I fell into conversation with him, and I gathered that he had earned some money in trade in Birmingham, and had bought the estate (five hundred acres, I think he said), on which he was born, and now was setting himself to cultivate it in downright earnest, going to Holkham and Woburn, and half the country over, to get himself up on the subject.'

'It would be Brooke, that dissenting baker from Birmingham,' said my lady in her most icy tone. 'Mr. Smithson, I am sorry I have been detaining you so long, but I think these are the letters you wished to see.'

If her ladyship thought by this speech to quench Mr. Smithson she was mistaken. Mr. Smithson just looked at the letters, and went on with the old subject.

'Now, my lady, it struck me that if you had such a man to take poor Horner's place, he would work the rents and the land round most satisfactorily. I should not despair of inducing this very man to undertake the work. I should not mind speaking to him myself on the subject, for we got capital friends over a snack of luncheon that he asked me to share with him.'

Lady Ludlow fixed her eyes on Mr. Smithson as he spoke, and never took them off his face until he had ended. She was silent a minute before she answered.

'You are very good, Mr. Smithson, but I need not trouble you with any such arrangements. I am going to write this afternoon to Captain James, a friend of one of my sons, who has, I hear, been severely wounded at Trafalgar,* to request him to honour me by accepting Mr. Horner's situation.'

'A Captain James! A captain in the navy! going to manage your ladyship's estate!'

'If he will be so kind. I shall esteem it a condescension on his part; but I hear that he will have to resign his profession, his state of health is so bad, and a country life is especially prescribed for him. I am in some hopes of tempting him here, as I learn he has but little to depend on if he gives up his profession.'

'A Captain James! an invalid captain!'

'You think I am asking too great a favour,' continued my lady. (I never could tell how far it was simplicity, or how far a kind of innocent malice, that made her misinterpret Mr. Smithson's words and looks as she did.) 'But he is not a post-captain, only a commander, and his pension will be but small. I may be able, by offering him country air and a healthy occupation, to restore him to health.'

'Occupation! My lady, may I ask how a sailor is to manage land? Why, your tenants will laugh him to scorn.'

'My tenants, I trust, will not behave so ill as to laugh at any one I choose to set over them. Captain James has had experience in managing men. He has remarkable practical talents, and great common sense, as I hear from every one. But, whatever he may be, the affair rests between him and myself. I can only say I shall esteem myself fortunate if he comes.'

There was no more to be said, after my lady spoke in this manner. I had heard her mention Captain James before, as a middy who had been very kind to her son Urian. I thought I remembered then, that she had mentioned that his family circumstances were not very prosperous. But, I confess, that little as I knew of the management of land, I quite sided with Mr. Smithson. He, silently prohibited from again speaking to my lady on the subject, opened his mind to Miss Galindo, from whom I was pretty sure to hear all the opinions and news of the household and village. She had taken a great fancy to me, because she said I talked so agreeably. I believe it was because I listened so well.

'Well, have you heard the news,' she began, 'about this Captain James? A sailor,—with a wooden leg, I have no doubt. What would the poor, dear, deceased master have said to it, if he had known who was to be his successor? My dear, I have often thought of the postman's bringing me a letter as one of the pleasures I shall miss in heaven. But, really, I think Mr. Horner may be thankful he has got out of the reach of news; or else he would hear of Mr. Smithson's having made up to the Birmingham baker, and of this one-legged Captain, coming to dot-and-go-one over the estate. I suppose he will look after the labourers through a spy-glass. I only hope he won't stick in the mud with his wooden leg; for I, for one, won't help him out. Yes, I would,' said she, correcting herself; 'I would, for my lady's sake.'

'But are you sure he has a wooden leg ? ' asked
I. 'I heard Lady Ludlow tell Mr. Smithson about
him, and she only spoke of him as wounded.'

'Well, sailors are almost always wounded in the leg.
Look at Greenwich Hospital !* I should say there were
twenty one-legged pensioners to one without an arm
there. But say he has got half-a-dozen legs, what is
he to do with managing land ? I shall think him very
impudent if he comes, taking advantage of my lady's
kind heart.'

However, come he did. In a month from that time,
the carriage was sent to meet Captain James ; just as
three years before it had been sent to meet me. His
coming had been so much talked about that we were
all as curious as possible to see him, and to know how
so unusual an experiment, as it seemed to us, would
answer. But, before I tell you anything about our new
agent, I must speak of something quite as interesting,
and I really think quite as important. And this was
my lady's making friends with Harry Gregson. I do
believe she did it for Mr. Horner's sake ; but, of course,
I can only conjecture why my lady did anything. But
I heard one day, from Mary Legard, that my lady
had sent for Harry to come and see her, if he was well
enough to walk so far ; and the next day he was shown
into the room he had been in once before under such
unlucky circumstances.

The lad looked pale enough, as he stood propping
himself up on his crutch, and the instant my lady saw
him, she bade John Footman place a stool for him to
sit down upon while she spoke to him. It might be
his paleness that gave his whole face a more refined
and gentle look ; but I suspect it was that the boy
was apt to take impressions, and that Mr. Horner's
grave, dignified ways, and Mr. Gray's tender and quiet
manners, had altered him ; and then the thoughts of
illness and death seem to turn many of us into gentlemen, and gentlewomen, as long as such thoughts are
in our minds. We cannot speak loudly or angrily at
such times ; we are not apt to be eager about mere

worldly things, for our very awe at our quickened sense
of the nearness of the invisible world, makes us calm
and serene about the petty trifles of to-day.  At least,
I know that was the explanation Mr. Gray once gave
me of what we all thought the great improvement in
Harry Gregson's way of behaving.

My lady hesitated so long about what she had best
say, that Harry grew a little frightened at her silence.
A few months ago it would have surprised me more
than it did now; but since my lord her son's death,
she had seemed altered in many ways,—more uncertain
and distrustful of herself, as it were.

At last she said, and I think the tears were in her
eyes: ' My poor little fellow, you have had a narrow
escape with your life since I saw you last.'

To this there was nothing to be said but ' Yes; '
and again there was silence.

' And you have lost a good, kind friend, in Mr.
Horner.'

The boy's lips worked, and I think he said, ' Please,
don't.'  But I can't be sure; at any rate, my lady
went on:

' And so have I,—a good, kind friend, he was to
both of us; and to you he wished to show his kindness in even a more generous way than he has done.
Mr. Gray has told you about his legacy to you, has
he not ? '

There was no sign of eager joy on the lad's face, as
if he realised the power and pleasure of having what
to him must have seemed like a fortune.

' Mr. Gray said as how he had left me a matter of
money.'

' Yes, he has left you two hundred pounds.'

' But I would rather have had him alive, my lady,'
he burst out, sobbing as if his heart would break.

' My lad, I believe you.  We would rather have had
our dead alive, would we not ?  and there is nothing
in money that can comfort us for their loss.  But you
know—Mr. Gray has told you—who has appointed us
all our times to die.  Mr. Horner was a good, just

man ; and has done well and kindly, both by me and
you. You perhaps do not know ' (and now I understood what my lady had been making up her mind to
say to Harry, all the time she was hesitating how to
begin) ' that Mr. Horner, at one time, meant to leave
you a great deal more ; probably all he had, with the
exception of a legacy to his old clerk, Morrison. But
he knew that this estate—on which my forefathers had
lived for six hundred years—was in debt, and that
I had no immediate chance of paying off this debt ;
and yet he felt that it was a very sad thing for an old
property like this to belong in part to those other men,
who had lent the money. You understand me, I think,
my little man ? ' said she, questioning Harry's face.

He had left off crying, and was trying to understand,
with all his might and main ; and I think he had got
a pretty good general idea of the state of affairs ;
though probably he was puzzled by the term ' the
estate being in debt.' But he was sufficiently interested to want my lady to go on ; and he nodded
his head at her, to signify this to her.

'So Mr. Horner took the money which he once
meant to be yours, and has left the greater part of it
to me, with the intention of helping me to pay off this
debt I have told you about. It will go a long way,
and I shall try hard to save the rest, and then I shall
die happy in leaving the land free from debt.' She
paused. 'But I shall not die happy in thinking of
you. I do not know if having money, or even having
a great estate and much honour, is a good thing for
any of us. But God sees fit that some of us should
be called to this condition, and it is our duty then
to stand by our posts, like brave soldiers. Now,
Mr. Horner intended you to have this money first.
I shall only call it borrowing it from you, Harry
Gregson, if I take it and use it to pay off the debt.
I shall pay Mr. Gray interest on this money, because
he is to stand as your guardian, as it were, till you
come of age ; and he must fix what ought to be done
with it, so as to fit you for spending the principal

rightly when the estate can repay it you. I suppose,
now, it will be right for you to be educated. That
will be another snare that will come with your money.
But have courage, Harry. Both education and money
may be used rightly, if we only pray against the
temptations they bring with them.'

Harry could make no answer, though I am sure he
understood it all. My lady wanted to get him to talk
to her a little, by way of becoming acquainted with
what was passing in his mind; and she asked him
what he would like to have done with his money, if he
could have part of it now? To such a simple question,
involving no talk about feelings, his answer came
readily enough.

'Build a cottage for father, with stairs in it, and
give Mr. Gray a school-house. O, father does so want
Mr. Gray for to have his wish! Father saw all the
stones lying quarried and hewn on Farmer Hale's land;
Mr. Gray had paid for them all himself. And father
said he would work night and day, and little Tommy
should carry mortar, if the parson would let him,
sooner than that he should be fretted and frabbed
as he was, with no one giving him a helping hand or
a kind word.'

Harry knew nothing of my lady's part in the affair;
that was very clear. My lady kept silence.

'If I might have a piece of my money, I would buy
land from Mr. Brooke: he has got a bit to sell just
at the corner of Hendon Lane, and I would give it
to Mr. Gray; and, perhaps, if your ladyship thinks
I may be learned again, I might grow up into the
schoolmaster.'

'You are a good boy,' said my lady. 'But there
are more things to be thought of, in carrying out such
a plan, than you are aware of. However, it shall be
tried.'

'The school, my lady?' I exclaimed, almost thinking
she did not know what she was saying.

'Yes, the school. For Mr. Horner's sake, for Mr.
Gray's sake, and last, not least, for this lad's sake,

I will give the new plan a trial. Ask Mr. Gray to come up to me this afternoon about the land he wants. He need not go to a Dissenter for it. And tell your father he shall have a good share in the building of it, and Tommy shall carry the mortar.'

' And I may be schoolmaster ? ' asked Harry, eagerly.

' We'll see about that,' said my lady, amused. ' It will be some time before that plan comes to pass, my little fellow.'

And now to return to Captain James. My first account of him was from Miss Galindo.

' He 's not above thirty ; and I must just pack up my pens and my paper, and be off ; for it would be the height of impropriety for me to be staying here as his clerk. It was all very well in the old master's days. But here am I, not fifty till next May, and this young, unmarried man, who is not even a widower ! O, there would be no end of gossip. Besides, he looks as askance at me as I do at him. My black silk gown had no effect. He 's afraid I shall marry him. But I won't ; he may feel himself quite safe from that. And Mr. Smithson has been recommending a clerk to my lady. She would far rather keep me on ; but I can't stop. I really could not think it proper.'

'What sort of a looking man is he ? '

' O, nothing particular. Short, and brown, and sun-burnt. I did not think it became me to look at him. Well, now for the nightcaps. I should have grudged any one else doing them, for I have got such a pretty pattern ! '

But, when it came to Miss Galindo's leaving, there was a great misunderstanding between her and my lady. Miss Galindo had imagined that my lady had asked her as a favour to copy the letters, and enter the accounts, and had agreed to do the work without a notion of being paid for so doing. She had, now and then, grieved over a very profitable order for needle-work passing out of her hands on account of her not having time to do it, because of her occupation at the Hall ; but she had never hinted this to my lady, but

gone on cheerfully at her writing as long as her clerkship was required.  My lady was annoyed that she
had not made her intention of paying Miss Galindo
more clear, in the first conversation she had had with
her; but I suppose that she had been too delicate to
be very explicit with regard to money matters; and
now Miss Galindo was quite hurt at my lady's wanting
to pay her for what she had done in such right-down
good-will.

'No,' Miss Galindo said; '"my own dear lady, you
may be as angry with me as you like, but don't offer
me money.  Think of six-and-twenty years ago, and
poor Arthur, and as you were to me then!  Besides,
I wanted money—I don't disguise it—for a particular
purpose; and when I found that (God bless you for
asking me!) I could do you a service, I turned it over
in my mind, and I gave up one plan and took up
another, and it's all settled now.  Bessy is to leave
school and come and live with me.  Don't, please, offer
me money again.  You don't know how glad I have
been to do anything for you.  Have not I, Margaret
Dawson?  Did you not hear me say, one day, I would
cut off my hand for my lady; for am I a stock or
a stone, that I should forget kindness?  O, I have
been so glad to work for you.  And now Bessy is
coming here; and no one knows anything about her—
as if she had done anything wrong, poor child!'

'Dear Miss Galindo,' replied my lady, 'I will never
ask you to take money again.  Only I thought it was
quite understood between us.  And, you know, you
have taken money for a set of morning wrappers,
before now.'

'Yes, my lady; but that was not confidential.
Now I was so proud to have something to do for you
confidentially.'

'But who is Bessy?' asked my lady.  'I do not
understand who she is, or why she is to come and live
with you.  Dear Miss Galindo, you must honour me
by being confidential with me in your turn!'

## CHAPTER XIII

I HAD always understood that Miss Galindo had once been in much better circumstances, but I had never liked to ask any questions respecting her. But about this time many things came out respecting her former life, which I will try and arrange; not, however, in the order in which I heard them, but rather as they occurred.

Miss Galindo was the daughter of a clergyman in Westmoreland. Her father was the younger brother of a baronet, his ancestor having been one of those of James the First's creation. This baronet-uncle of Miss Galindo was one of the queer, out-of-the-way people who were bred at that time, and in that northern district of England. I never heard much of him from any one, besides this one great fact: that he had early disappeared from his family, which indeed only consisted of a brother and sister who died unmarried, and lived no one knew where,—somewhere on the Continent, it was supposed, for he had never returned from the grand tour which he had been sent to make, according to the general fashion of the day, as soon as he left Oxford. He corresponded occasionally with his brother the clergyman; but the letters passed through a banker's hands; the banker being pledged to secrecy, and, as he told Mr. Galindo, having the penalty, if he broke his pledge, of losing the whole profitable business, and of having the management of the baronet's affairs taken out of his hands, without any advantage accruing to the inquirer, for Sir Lawrence had told Messrs. Graham that, in case his place of residence was revealed by them, not only would he cease to bank with them, but instantly take measures to baffle any future inquiries as to his whereabouts, by removing to some distant country.

Sir Lawrence paid a certain sum of money to his brother's account every year; but the time of this payment varied, and it was sometimes eighteen or nineteen months between the deposits; then, again, it would not be above a quarter of the time, showing that he intended it to be annual, but, as this intention was never expressed in words, it was impossible to rely upon it, and a great deal of this money was swallowed up by the necessity Mr. Galindo felt himself under of living in the large, old, rambling family mansion, which had been one of Sir Lawrence's rarely expressed desires. Mr. and Mrs. Galindo often planned to live upon their own small fortune and the income derived from the living (a vicarage, of which the great tithes went to Sir Lawrence as lay impropriator), so as to put by the payments made by the baronet, for the benefit of Laurentia—our Miss Galindo. But I suppose they found it difficult to live economically in a large house, even though they had it rent free. They had to keep up with hereditary neighbours and friends, and could hardly help doing it in the hereditary manner.

One of these neighbours, a Mr. Gibson, had a son a few years older than Laurentia. The families were sufficiently intimate for the young people to see a good deal of each other: and I was told that this young Mr. Mark Gibson was an unusually prepossessing man (he seemed to have impressed every one who spoke of him to me as being a handsome, manly, kind-hearted fellow), just what a girl would be sure to find most agreeable. The parents either forgot that their children were growing up to man's and woman's estate, or thought that the intimacy and probable attachment would be no bad thing, even if it did lead to a marriage. Still, nothing was ever said by young Gibson till later on, when it was too late, as it turned out. He went to and from Oxford; he shot and fished with Mr. Galindo, or came to the Mere to skate in winter-time; was asked to accompany Mr. Galindo to the Hall, as the latter returned to the quiet dinner with his wife and daughter; and so, and so, it went on, nobody much knew how, until one day, when Mr. Galindo received a formal letter from his brother's bankers, announcing Sir Lawrence's death, of malaria fever, at Albano, and

congratulating Sir Hubert on his accession to the
estates and the baronetcy. 'The king is dead—Long
live the king!' as I have since heard that the French
express it.

Sir Hubert and his wife were greatly surprised. Sir
Lawrence was but two years older than his brother;
and they had never heard of any illness till they heard
of his death. They were sorry; very much shocked;
but still a little elated at the succession to the baronetcy
and estates. The London bankers had managed everything well. There was a large sum of ready money in
their hands, at Sir Hubert's service, until he should
touch his rents, the rent-roll being eight thousand
a-year. And only Laurentia to inherit it all! Her
mother, a poor clergyman's daughter, began to plan
all sorts of fine marriages for her; nor was her father
much behind his wife in his ambition. They took her
up to London, when they went to buy new carriages,
and dresses, and furniture. And it was then and there
she made my lady's acquaintance. How it was that
they came to take a fancy to each other, I cannot say.
My lady was of the old nobility,—grand, composed,
gentle, and stately in her ways. Miss Galindo must
always have been hurried in her manner, and her
energy must have shown itself in inquisitiveness and
oddness even in her youth. But I don't pretend to
account for things: I only narrate them. And the
fact was this:—that the elegant, fastidious Countess
was attracted to the country girl, who on her part
almost worshipped my lady. My lady's notice of their
daughter made her parents think, I suppose, that there
was no match that she might not command; she, the
heiress of eight thousand a-year, and visiting about
among earls and dukes. So when they came back to
their old Westmoreland Hall, and Mark Gibson rode
over to offer his hand and his heart, and prospective
estate of nine hundred a-year to his old companion
and playfellow, Laurentia, Sir Hubert and Lady
Galindo made very short work of it. They refused
him plumply themselves; and when he begged to be

allowed to speak to Laurentia, they found some excuse
for refusing him the opportunity of so doing, until they
had talked to her themselves, and brought up every
argument and fact in their power to convince her—
a plain girl, and conscious of her plainness—that
Mr. Mark Gibson had never thought of her in the
way of marriage till after her father's accession to his
fortune; and that it was the estate—not the young
lady—that he was in love with. I suppose it will
never be known in this world how far this supposition
of theirs was true. My Lady Ludlow had always
spoken as if it was; but perhaps events, which came
to her knowledge about this time, altered her opinion.
At any rate, the end of it was, Laurentia refused Mark,
and almost broke her heart in doing so. He discovered
the suspicions of Sir Hubert and Lady Galindo, and
that they had persuaded their daughter to share in
them. So he flung off with high words, saying that
they did not know a true heart when they met with
one; and that, although he had never offered till after
Sir Lawrence's death, yet that his father knew all
along that he had been attached to Laurentia, only
that he, being the eldest of five children, and having
as yet no profession, had had to conceal, rather than
to express, an attachment, which, in those days, he
had believed was reciprocated. He had always meant
to study for the bar, and the end of all he had hoped
for had been to earn a moderate income, which he
might ask Laurentia to share. This, or something like
it, was what he said. But his reference to his father
cut two ways. Old Mr. Gibson was known to be very
keen about money. It was just as likely that he
would urge Mark to make love to the heiress, now she
was an heiress, as that he would have restrained him
previously, as Mark said he had done. When this
was repeated to Mark, he became proudly reserved, or
sullen, and said that Laurentia, at any rate, might
have known him better. He left the country, and
went up to London to study law soon afterwards; and
Sir Hubert and Lady Galindo thought they were well

rid of him. But Laurentia never ceased reproaching herself, and never did to her dying day, as I believe. The words, 'She might have known me better,' told to her by some kind friend or other, rankled in her mind, and were never forgotten. Her father and mother took her up to London the next year; but she did not care to visit—dreaded going out even for a drive, lest she should see Mark Gibson's reproachful eyes—pined and lost her health. Lady Ludlow saw this change with regret, and was told the cause by Lady Galindo, who, of course, gave her own version of Mark's conduct and motives. My lady never spoke to Miss Galindo about it, but tried constantly to interest and please her. It was at this time that my lady told Miss Galindo so much about her own early life, and about Hanbury, that Miss Galindo resolved, if ever she could, she would go and see the old place which her friend loved so well. The end of it all was, that she came to live there, as we know.

But a great change was to come first. Before Sir Hubert and Lady Galindo had left London on this, their second visit, they had a letter from the lawyer, whom they employed, saying that Sir Lawrence had left an heir, his legitimate child by an Italian woman of low rank; at least, legal claims to the title and property had been sent into him on the boy's behalf. Sir Lawrence had always been a man of adventurous and artistic, rather than of luxurious tastes; and it was supposed, when all came to be proved at the trial, that he was captivated by the free, beautiful life they lead in Italy, and had married this Neapolitan fisherman's daughter, who had people about her shrewd enough to see that the ceremony was legally performed. She and her husband had wandered about the shores of the Mediterranean for years, leading a happy, careless, irresponsible life, unencumbered by any duties except those connected with a rather numerous family. It was enough for her that they never wanted money, and that her husband's love was always continued to her. She hated the name of England—wicked, cold,

heretic England—and avoided the mention of any
subjects connected with her husband's early life. So
that, when he died at Albano, she was almost roused
out of her vehement grief to anger with the Italian
doctor, who declared that he must write to a certain
address to announce the death of Lawrence Galindo.
For some time, she feared lest English barbarians
might come down upon her, making a claim to the
children. She hid herself and them in the Abruzzi,
living upon the sale of what furniture and jewels Sir
Lawrence had died possessed of. When these failed,
she returned to Naples, which she had not visited since
her marriage. Her father was dead ; but her brother
inherited some of his keenness. He interested the
priests, who made inquiries and found that the Galindo
succession was worth securing to an heir of the true
faith. They stirred about it, obtained advice at the
English Embassy ; and hence that letter to the lawyers,
calling upon Sir Hubert to relinquish title and property,
and to refund what money he had expended. He was
vehement in his opposition to this claim. He could not
bear to think of his brother having married a foreigner
—a papist, a fisherman's daughter ; nay, of his having
become a papist himself. He was in despair at the
thought of his ancestral property going to the issue of
such a marriage. He fought tooth and nail, making
enemies of his relations, and losing almost all his own
private property ; for he would go on against the
lawyer's advice, long after every one was convinced
except himself and his wife. At last he was conquered.
He gave up his living in gloomy despair. He would
have changed his name if he could, so desirous was he
to obliterate all tie between himself and the mongrel
papist baronet and his Italian mother, and all the
succession of children and nurses who came to take
possession of the Hall soon after Mr. Hubert Galindo's
departure, stayed there one winter, and then flitted
back to Naples with gladness and delight. Mr. and
Mrs. Hubert Galindo lived in London. He had obtained a curacy somewhere in the city. They would

have been thankful now if Mr. Mark Gibson had
renewed his offer. No one could accuse him of mer-
cenary motives if he had done so. Because he did
not come forward, as they wished, they brought his
silence up as a justification of what they had previously
attributed to him. I don't know what Miss Galindo
thought herself; but Lady Ludlow has told me how
she shrank from hearing her parents abuse him. Lady
Ludlow supposed that he was aware that they were
living in London. His father must have known the
fact, and it was curious if he had never named it to
his son. Besides, the name was very uncommon; and
it was unlikely that it should never come across him,
in the advertisements of charity sermons which the
new and rather eloquent curate of Saint Mark's East
was asked to preach. All this time Lady Ludlow never
lost sight of them, for Miss Galindo's sake. And when
the father and mother died, it was my lady who
upheld Miss Galindo in her determination not to apply
for any provision to her cousin, the Italian baronet,
but rather to live upon the hundred a-year which had
been settled on her mother and the children of his
son Hubert's marriage by the old grandfather, Sir
Lawrence.

Mr. Mark Gibson had risen to some eminence as
a barrister on the Northern Circuit; but had died
unmarried in the lifetime of his father, a victim (so
people said) to intemperance. Doctor Trevor, the
physician who had been called in to Mr. Gray and
Harry Gregson, had married a sister of his. And that
was all my lady knew about the Gibson family. But
who was Bessy?

That mystery and secret came out, too, in process
of time. Miss Galindo had been to Warwick, some
years before I arrived at Hanbury, on some kind of
business or shopping, which can only be transacted in
a county town. There was an old Westmoreland connexion between her and Mrs. Trevor, though I believe
the latter was too young to have been made aware of
her brother's offer to Miss Galindo at the time when it

took place ; and such affairs, if they are unsuccessful,
are seldom spoken about in the gentleman's family
afterwards. But the Gibsons and Galindos had been
county neighbours too long for the connexion not to
be kept up between two members settled far away
from their early homes. Miss Galindo always desired
her parcels to be sent to Doctor Trevor's, when she
went to Warwick for shopping purposes. If she were
going any journey, and the coach did not come through
Warwick as soon as she arrived (in my lady's coach or
otherwise) from Hanbury, she went to Doctor Trevor's
to wait. She was as much expected to sit down to the
household meals as if she had been one of the family ;
and in after years it was Mrs. Trevor who managed
her repository business for her.

So, on the day I spoke of, she had gone to Doctor
Trevor's to rest, and possibly to dine. The post, in
those times, came in at all hours of the morning ; and
Doctor Trevor's letters had not arrived until after his
departure on his morning round. Miss Galindo was
sitting down to dinner with Mrs. Trevor and her seven
children, when the Doctor came in. He was flurried
and uncomfortable, and hurried the children away as
soon as he decently could. Then (rather feeling Miss
Galindo's presence an advantage, both as a present
restraint on the violence of his wife's grief, and as a
consoler when he was absent on his afternoon round),
he told Mrs. Trevor of her brother's death. He had
been taken ill on circuit, and had hurried back to his
chambers in London, only to die. She cried terribly ;
but Doctor Trevor said afterwards, he never noticed
that Miss Galindo cared much about it one way or
another. She helped him to soothe his wife, promised
to stay with her all the afternoon instead of returning
to Hanbury, and afterwards offered to remain with her
while the Doctor went to attend the funeral. When
they heard of the old love-story between the dead man
and Miss Galindo,—brought up by mutual friends in
Westmoreland, in the review which we are all inclined
to take of the events of a man's life when he comes to

die,—they tried to remember Miss Galindo's speeches and ways of going on during this visit. She was a little pale, a little silent; her eyes were sometimes swollen, and her nose red; but she was at an age when such appearances are generally attributed to a bad cold in the head, rather than to any more sentimental reason. They felt towards her as towards an old friend, a kindly, useful, eccentric old maid. She did not expect more, or wish them to remember that she might once have had other hopes, and more youthful feelings. Doctor Trevor thanked her very warmly for staying with his wife, when he returned home from London (where the funeral had taken place). He begged Miss Galindo to stay with them, when the children were gone to bed, and she was preparing to leave the husband and wife by themselves. He told her and his wife many particulars—then paused—then went on—

'And Mark has left a child—a little girl——'

'But he never was married,' exclaimed Mrs. Trevor.

'A little girl,' continued her husband, 'whose mother, I conclude, is dead. At any rate, the child was in possession of his chambers; she and an old nurse, who seemed to have the charge of everything, and has cheated poor Mark, I should fancy, not a little.'

'But the child!' asked Mrs. Trevor, still almost breathless with astonishment. 'How do you know it is his?'

'The nurse told me it was, with great appearance of indignation at my doubting it. I asked the little thing her name, and all I could get was "Bessy!" and a cry of "Me wants papa!" The nurse said the mother was dead, and she knew no more about it than that Mr. Gibson had engaged her to take care of the little girl, calling it his child. One or two of his lawyer friends, whom I met with at the funeral, told me they were aware of the existence of the child.'

'What is to be done with her?' asked Mrs. Trevor.

'Nay, I don't know,' replied he. 'Mark has hardly left assets enough to pay his debts, and your father is not inclined to come forward.'

That night, as Doctor Trevor sat in his study, after his wife had gone to bed, Miss Galindo knocked at his door. She and he had a long conversation. The result was that he accompanied Miss Galindo up to town the next day ; that they took possession of the little Bessy, and she was brought down, and placed at nurse at a farm in the country near Warwick, Miss Galindo undertaking to pay one-half the expense, and to furnish her with clothes, and Dr. Trevor undertaking that the remaining half should be furnished by the Gibson family, or by himself in their default.

Miss Galindo was not fond of children, and I daresay she dreaded taking this child to live with her for more reasons than one. My Lady Ludlow could not endure any mention of illegitimate children. It was a principle of hers that society ought to ignore them. And I believe Miss Galindo had always agreed with her until now, when the thing came home to her womanly heart. Still she shrank from having this child of some strange woman under her roof. She went over to see it from time to time ; she worked at its clothes long after every one thought she was in bed ; and, when the time came for Bessy to be sent to school, Miss Galindo laboured away more diligently than ever, in order to pay the increased expense. For the Gibson family had, at first, paid their part of the compact, but with unwillingness and grudging hearts ; then they had left it off altogether, and it fell hard on Doctor Trevor with his twelve children ; and, latterly, Miss Galindo had taken upon herself almost all the burden. One can hardly live and labour, and plan and make sacrifices, for any human creature, without learning to love it. And Bessy loved Miss Galindo, too, for all the poor girl's scanty pleasures came from her, and Miss Galindo had always a kind word, and, latterly, many a kind caress, for Mark Gibson's child ; whereas, if she went to Doctor Trevor's for her holiday, she was overlooked and neglected in that bustling family, who seemed to think that if she had comfortable board and lodging under their roof, it was enough.

I am sure, now, that Miss Galindo had often longed to have Bessy to live with her; but, as long as she could pay for her being at school, she did not like to take so bold a step as bringing her home, knowing what the effect of the consequent explanation would be on my lady. And as the girl was now more than seventeen, and past the age when young ladies are usually kept at school, and as there was no great demand for governesses in those days, and as Bessy had never been taught any trade by which to earn her own living, why, I don't exactly see what could have been done but for Miss Galindo to bring her to her own home in Hanbury. For, although the child had grown up lately, in a kind of unexpected manner, into a young woman, Miss Galindo might have kept her at school for a year longer, if she could have afforded it; but this was impossible when she became Mr. Horner's clerk, and relinquished all the payment of her repository work; and perhaps, after all, she was not sorry to be compelled to take the step she was longing for. At any rate, Bessy came to live with Miss Galindo in a very few weeks from the time when Captain James set Miss Galindo free to superintend her own domestic economy again.

For a long time, I knew nothing about this new inhabitant of Hanbury. My lady never mentioned her in any way. This was in accordance with Lady Ludlow's well-known principles. She neither saw nor heard, nor was in any way cognisant of the existence of those who had no legal right to exist at all. If Miss Galindo had hoped to have an exception made in Bessy's favour, she was mistaken. My lady sent a note inviting Miss Galindo herself to tea one evening, about a month after Bessy came; but Miss Galindo 'had a cold and could not come.' The next time she was invited, she 'had an engagement at home'— a step nearer to the absolute truth. And the third time, she 'had a young friend staying with her whom she was unable to leave.' My lady accepted every excuse as bonâ fide, and took no further notice. I

missed Miss Galindo very much ; we all did ; for, in
the days when she was clerk, she was sure to come in
and find the opportunity of saying something amusing
to some of us before she went away.  And I, as an
invalid, or perhaps from natural tendency, was particularly fond of little bits of village gossip.  There
was no Mr. Horner—he even had come in, now and
then, with formal, stately pieces of intelligence—and
there was no Miss Galindo, in these days.  I missed
her much.  And so did my lady, I am sure.  Behind
all her quiet, sedate manner, I am certain her heart
ached sometimes for a few words from Miss Galindo,
who seemed to have absented herself altogether from
the Hall now Bessy was come.

Captain James might be very sensible, and all that ;
but not even my lady could call him a substitute for
the old familiar friends.  He was a thorough sailor, as
sailors were in those days—swore a good deal, drank
a good deal (without its ever affecting him in the
least), and was very prompt and kind-hearted in all
his actions ; but he was not accustomed to women, as
my lady once said, and would judge in all things for
himself.  My lady had expected, I think, to find some
one who would take his notions on the management of
her estate from her ladyship's own self ; but he spoke
as if he were responsible for the good management of
the whole, and must, consequently, be allowed full
liberty of action.  He had been too long in command
over men at sea to like to be directed by a woman in
anything he undertook, even though that woman was
my lady.  I suppose this was the common-sense my
lady spoke of ; but when common-sense goes against
us, I don't think we value it quite so much as we
ought to do.

Lady Ludlow was proud of her personal superintendence of her own estate.  She liked to tell us how
her father used to take her with him in his rides, and
bid her observe this and that, and on no account to
allow such and such things to be done.  But I have
heard that the first time she told all this to Captain

James, he told her point-blank that he had heard from
Mr. Smithson that the farms were much neglected and
the rents sadly behind-hand, and that he meant to set
to in good earnest and study agriculture, and see how
he could remedy the state of things. My lady would,
I am sure, be greatly surprised, but what could she
do ? Here was the very man she had chosen herself,
setting to with all his energy to conquer the defect of
ignorance, which was all that those who had presumed
to offer her ladyship advice had ever had to say against
him. Captain James read Arthur Young's ' Tours '*in
all his spare time, as long as he was an invalid ; and
shook his head at my lady's accounts as to how the
land had been cropped or left fallow from time immemorial. Then he set to, and tried too many new
experiments at once. My lady looked on in dignified
silence ; but all the farmers and tenants were in an
uproar, and prophesied a hundred failures. Perhaps
fifty did occur ; they were only half as many as Lady
Ludlow had feared ; but they were twice as many,
four, eight times as many as the captain had anticipated. His openly-expressed disappointment made
him popular again. The rough country people could
not have understood silent and dignified regret at the
failure of his plans ; but they sympathised with a man
who swore at his ill success—sympathised, even while
they chuckled over his discomfiture. Mr. Brooke, the
retired tradesman, did not cease blaming him for not
succeeding, and for swearing. ' But what could you
expect from a sailor ? ' Mr. Brooke asked, even in my
lady's hearing ; though he might have known Captain
James was my lady's own personal choice, from the
old friendship Mr. Urian had always shown for him.
I think it was this speech of the Birmingham baker's
that made my lady determine to stand by Captain
James, and encourage him to try again. For she
would not allow that her choice had been an unwise
one, at the bidding (as it were) of a Dissenting
tradesman ; the only person in the neighbourhood,
too, who had flaunted about in coloured clothes,

when all the world was in mourning for my lady's only son.

Captain James would have thrown the agency up at once, if my lady had not felt herself bound to justify the wisdom of her choice, by urging him to stay. He was much touched by her confidence in him, and swore a great oath, that the next year he would make the land such as it had never been before for produce. It was not my lady's way to repeat anything she had heard, especially to another person's disadvantage. So I don't think she ever told Captain James of Mr. Brooke's speech about a sailor's being likely to mismanage the property; and the captain was too anxious to succeed in this, the second year of his trial, to be above going to the flourishing, shrewd Mr. Brooke, and asking for his advice as to the best method of working the estate. I dare say, if Miss Galindo had been as intimate as formerly at the Hall, we should all of us have heard of this new acquaintance of the agent's long before we did. As it was, I am sure my lady never dreamed that the captain, who held opinions that were even more Church and King than her own, could ever have made friends with a Baptist baker from Birmingham, even to serve her ladyship's own interests in the most loyal manner.

We heard of it first from Mr. Gray, who came now often to see my lady, for neither he nor she could forget the solemn tie which the fact of his being the person to acquaint her with my lord's death had created between them. For true and holy words spoken at that time, though having no reference to aught below the solemn subjects of life and death, had made her withdraw her opposition to Mr. Gray's wish about establishing a village school. She had sighed a little, it is true, and was even yet more apprehensive than hopeful as to the result; but, almost as if as a memorial to my lord, she had allowed a kind of rough schoolhouse to be built on the green, just by the church; and had gently used the power she undoubtedly had, in expressing her strong wish that the boys might only be taught to read and write, and the first four rules of arithmetic; while the girls were only to learn to read, and to add up in their heads, and the rest of the time to work at mending their own clothes, knitting stockings, and spinning. My lady presented the school with more spinning-wheels than there were girls, and requested that there might be a rule that they should have spun so many hanks of flax, and knitted so many pairs of stockings, before they ever were taught to read at all. After all, it was but making the best of a bad job with my poor lady—but life was not what it had been to her. I remember well the day that Mr. Gray pulled some delicately fine yarn (and I was a good judge of those things) out of his pocket, and laid it and a capital pair of knitted stockings before my lady, as the first-fruits, so to say, of his school. I recollect seeing her put on her spectacles, and carefully examine both productions. Then she passed them to me.

'This is well, Mr. Gray. I am much pleased. You are fortunate in your schoolmistress. She has had both proper knowledge of womanly things and much patience. Who is she? One out of our village?'

'My lady,' said Mr. Gray, stammering and colouring in his old fashion, 'Miss Bessy is so very kind as to teach all those sorts of things—Miss Bessy, and Miss Galindo, sometimes.'

My lady looked at him over her spectacles: but she only repeated the words 'Miss Bessy,' and paused, as if trying to remember who such a person could be; and he, if he had then intended to say more, was quelled by her manner, and dropped the subject. He went on to say that he had thought it his duty to decline the subscription to his school offered by Mr. Brooke, because he was a Dissenter; that he (Mr. Gray) feared that Captain James, through whom Mr. Brooke's offer of money had been made, was offended at his refusing to accept it from a man who held heterodox opinions; nay, whom Mr. Gray suspected of being infected by Dodwell's heresy.[*]

'I think there must be some mistake,' said my lady, 'or I have misunderstood you. Captain James would never be sufficiently with a schismatic to be employed by that man Brooke in distributing his charities. I should have doubted, until now, if Captain James knew him.'

'Indeed, my lady, he not only knows him, but is intimate with him, I regret to say. I have repeatedly seen the captain and Mr. Brooke walking together; going through the fields together; and people do say——'

My lady looked up in interrogation at Mr. Gray's pause.

'I disapprove of gossip, and it may be untrue; but people do say that Captain James is very attentive to Miss Brooke.'

'Impossible!' said my lady, indignantly. 'Captain James is a loyal and religious man. I beg your pardon, Mr. Gray, but it is impossible.'


CHAPTER XIV

LIKE many other things which have been declared to be impossible, this report of Captain James being attentive to Miss Brooke turned out to be very true.

The mere idea of her agent being on the slightest possible terms of acquaintance with the Dissenter, the tradesman, the Birmingham democrat, who had come to settle in our good, orthodox, aristocratic, and agricultural Hanbury, made my lady very uneasy. Miss Galindo's misdemeanour in having taken Miss Bessy to live with her, faded into a mistake, a mere error of judgement, in comparison with Captain James's intimacy at Yeast House, as the Brookes called their ugly square-built farm. My lady talked herself quite into complacency with Miss Galindo, and even Miss Bessy was named by her, the first time I had ever been aware that my lady recognised her existence; but—I recollect it was a long rainy afternoon, and I sat with her ladyship, and we had time and opportunity for a long uninterrupted talk—whenever we had been silent for a little while she began again, with something like a wonder how it was that Captain James could ever have commenced an acquaintance with ' that man Brooke.' My lady recapitulated all the times she could remember, that anything had occurred, or been said by Captain James which she could now understand as throwing light upon the subject.

' He said once that he was anxious to bring in the Norfolk system of cropping, and spoke a good deal about Mr. Coke*of Holkham (who, by the way, was no more a Coke than I am—collateral in the female line— which counts for little or nothing among the great old commoners' families of pure blood), and his new ways of cultivation ; of course new men bring in new ways, but it does not follow that either are better than the old ways. However, Captain James has been very anxious to try turnips and bone manure, and he really is a man of such good sense and energy, and was so sorry last year about the failure, that I consented ; and now I begin to see my error. I have always heard that town bakers adulterate their flour with bone-dust ; and, of course, Captain James would be aware of this, and go to Brooke to inquire where the article was to be purchased.'

My lady always ignored the fact which had some-times, I suspect, been brought under her very eyes during her drives, that Mr. Brooke's few fields were in a state of far higher cultivation than her own ; so she could not, of course, perceive that there was any wisdom to be gained from asking the advice of the tradesman turned farmer.

But by-and-by this fact of her agent's intimacy with the person whom in the whole world she most disliked (with that sort of dislike in which a large amount of uncomfortableness is combined—the dislike which con-scientious people sometimes feel to another without knowing why, and yet which they cannot indulge in with comfort to themselves without having a moral reason why), came before my lady in many shapes.

For, indeed, I am sure that Captain James was not
a man to conceal or be ashamed of one of his actions.
I cannot fancy his ever lowering his strong loud clear
voice, or having a confidential conversation with any
one. When his crops had failed, all the village had
known it. He complained, he regretted, he was angry,
or owned himself a ――― fool, all down the village
street; and the consequence was that, although he
was a far more passionate man than Mr. Horner, all
the tenants liked him far better. People, in general,
take a kindlier interest in any one, the workings of
whose mind and heart they can watch and understand,
than in a man who only lets you know what he has
been thinking about and feeling, by what he does.
But Harry Gregson was faithful to the memory of
Mr. Horner. Miss Galindo has told me that she used
to watch him hobble out of the way of Captain James,
as if to accept his notice, however good-naturedly
given, would have been a kind of treachery to his
former benefactor. But Gregson (the father) and the
new agent rather took to each other; and one day,
much to my surprise, I heard that the 'poaching,
tinkering vagabond,' as people used to call Gregson
when I first had come to live at Hanbury, had been
appointed gamekeeper; Mr. Gray standing godfather,
as it were, to his trustworthiness, if he were trusted
with anything; which I thought at the time was
rather an experiment, only it answered, as many of
Mr. Gray's deeds of daring did. It was curious how
he was growing to be a kind of autocrat in the village;
and how unconscious he was of it. He was as shy
and awkward and nervous as ever in any affair that
was not of some moral consequence to him. But as
soon as he was convinced that a thing was right, he
'shut his eyes and ran and butted at it like a ram,'
as Captain James once expressed it, in talking over
something Mr. Gray had done. People in the village
said, 'they never knew what the parson would be at
next;' or they might have said, 'where his reverence
would next turn up.' For I have heard of his marching

right into the middle of a set of poachers, gathered together for some desperate midnight enterprise, or walking into a public-house that lay just beyond the bounds of my lady's estate, and in that extra-parochial piece of ground I named long ago, and which was considered the rendezvous of all the ne'er-do-weel characters for miles round, and where a parson and a constable were held in much the same kind of esteem as unwelcome visitors. And yet Mr. Gray had his long fits of depression, in which he felt as if he were doing nothing, making no way in his work, useless and unprofitable, and better out of the world than in it. In comparison with the work he had set himself to do, what he did seemed to be nothing. I suppose it was constitutional, those attacks of lowness of spirits which he had about this time ; perhaps a part of the nervousness which made him always so awkward when he came to the Hall. Even Mrs. Medlicott, who almost worshipped the ground he trod on, as the saying is, owned that Mr. Gray never entered one of my lady's rooms without knocking down something, and too often breaking it. He would much sooner have faced a desperate poacher than a young lady any day. At least so we thought.

I do not know how it was that it came to pass that my lady became reconciled to Miss Galindo about this time. Whether it was that her ladyship was weary of the unspoken coolness with her old friend ; or that the specimens of delicate sewing and fine spinning at the school had mollified her towards Miss Bessy ; but I was surprised to learn one day that Miss Galindo and her young friend were coming that very evening to tea at the Hall. This information was given me by Mrs. Medlicott, as a message from my lady, who further went on to desire that certain little preparations should be made in her own private sitting-room, in which the greater part of my days were spent. From the nature of these preparations, I became quite aware that my lady intended to do honour to her expected visitors. Indeed, Lady Ludlow never forgave by halves, as I

have known some people do. Whoever was coming
as a visitor to my lady, peeress, or poor nameless girl,
there was a certain amount of preparation required,
in order to do them fitting honour. I do not mean
to say that the preparation was of the same degree
of importance in each case. I dare say, if a peeress
had come to visit us at the Hall, the covers would
have been taken off the furniture in the white drawing-
room (they never were uncovered all the time I stayed
at the Hall), because my lady would wish to offer her
the ornaments and luxuries which this grand visitor
(who never came—I wish she had! I did so want to
see that furniture uncovered!) was accustomed to at
home, and to present them to her in the best order
in which my lady could. The same rule, modified,
held good with Miss Galindo. Certain things, in which
my lady knew she took an interest, were laid out
ready for her to examine on this very day; and, what
was more, great books of prints were laid out, such
as I remembered my lady had had brought forth to
beguile my own early days of illness,—Mr. Hogarth's
works, and the like,—which I was sure were put out
for Miss Bessy.

No one knows how curious I was to see this mysterious Miss Bessy—twenty times more mysterious, of
course, for want of her surname. And then again (to
try and account for my great curiosity, of which in
recollection I am more than half ashamed), I had been
leading the quiet monotonous life of a crippled invalid
for many years,—shut up from any sight of new faces;
and this was to be the face of one whom I had thought
about so much and so long,—Oh! I think I might be
excused.

Of course, they drank tea in the great hall, with the
four young gentlewomen, who, with myself, formed
the small bevy now under her ladyship's charge. Of
those who were at Hanbury when first I came, none
remained; all were married, or gone once more to live
at some home which could be called their own, whether
the ostensible head were father or brother. I myself

was not without some hopes of a similar kind. My
brother Harry was now a curate in Westmoreland,
and wanted me to go and live with him, as eventually
I did for a time. But that is neither here nor there
at present. What I am talking about is Miss Bessy.

After a reasonable time had elapsed, occupied as I
well knew by the meal in the great hall,—the measured,
yet agreeable conversation afterwards,—and a certain
promenade around the hall, and through the drawing-
rooms, with pauses before different pictures, the history
or subject of each of which was invariably told by my
lady to every new visitor,—a sort of giving them the
freedom of the old family-seat, by describing the kind
and nature of the great progenitors who had lived there
before the narrator,—I heard the steps approaching
my lady's room where I lay. I think I was in such
a state of nervous expectation, that if I could have
moved easily, I should have got up and run away.
And yet I need not have been, for Miss Galindo was
not in the least altered (her nose a little redder, to be
sure, but then that might only have had a temporary
cause in the private crying I know she would have had
before coming to see her dear Lady Ludlow once again).
But I could almost have pushed Miss Galindo away,
as she intercepted me in my view of the mysterious
Miss Bessy.

Miss Bessy was, as I knew, only about eighteen, but
she looked older. Dark hair, dark eyes, a tall, firm
figure, a good, sensible face, with a serene expression,
not in the least disturbed by what I had been thinking
must be such awful circumstances as a first introduction to my lady, who had so disapproved of her very
existence : those are the clearest impressions I remember of my first interview with Miss Bessy. She seemed
to observe us all, in her quiet manner, quite as much as
I did her ; but she spoke very little ; occupied herself,
indeed, as my lady had planned, with looking over
the great books of engravings. I think I must have
(foolishly) intended to make her feel at her ease, by
my patronage ; but she was seated far away from my

sofa, in order to command the light, and really seemed
so unconcerned at her unwonted circumstances, that
she did not need my countenance or kindness. One
thing I did like—her watchful look at Miss Galindo
from time to time: it showed that her thoughts and
sympathy were ever at Miss Galindo's service, as indeed
they well might be. When Miss Bessy spoke, her voice
was full and clear, and what she said, to the purpose,
though there was a slight provincial accent in her way
of speaking. After a while, my lady set us two to
play at chess, a game which I had lately learnt at
Mr. Gray's suggestion. Still we did not talk much
together, though we were becoming attracted towards
each other, I fancy.

'You will play well,' said she. 'You have only
learnt about six months, have you? And yet you can
nearly beat me, who have been at it as many years.'

'I began to learn last November. I remember
Mr. Gray's bringing me "Philidor on Chess," one very
foggy, dismal day.'

What made her look up so suddenly, with bright
inquiry in her eyes? What made her silent for a
moment, as if in thought, and then go on with something, I know not what, in quite an altered tone?

My lady and Miss Galindo went on talking, while
I sat thinking. I heard Captain James's name mentioned pretty frequently; and at last my lady put
down her work, and said, almost with tears in her eyes:

'I could not—I cannot believe it. He must be aware
she is a schismatic; a baker's daughter; and he is
a gentleman by virtue and feeling, as well as by his
profession, though his manners may be at times a little
rough. My dear Miss Galindo, what will this world
come to?'

Miss Galindo might possibly be aware of her own
share in bringing the world to the pass which now
dismayed my lady,—for, of course, though all was now
over and forgiven, yet Miss Bessy's being received into
a respectable maiden lady's house, was one of the
portents as to the world's future which alarmed her

ladyship; and Miss Galindo knew this,—but, at any rate, she had too lately been forgiven herself not to plead for mercy for the next offender against my lady's delicate sense of fitness and propriety,—so she replied:

'Indeed, my lady, I have long left off trying to conjecture what makes Jack fancy Gill, or Gill Jack. It's best to sit down quiet under the belief that marriages are made for us, somewhere out of this world, and out of the range of this world's reasons and laws. I'm not so sure that I should settle it down that they were made in Heaven; t'other place seems to me as likely a workshop; but, at any rate, I've given up troubling my head as to why they take place. Captain James is a gentleman; I make no doubt of that ever since I saw him stop to pick up old Goody Blake (when she tumbled down on the slide last winter) and then swear at a little lad who was laughing at her, and cuff him till he tumbled down crying; but we must have bread somehow, and though I like it better baked at home in a good sweet brick oven, yet, as some folks never can get it to rise, I don't see why a man may not be a baker. You see, my lady, I look upon baking as a simple trade, and as such lawful. There is no machine comes in to take away a man's or woman's power of earning their living, like the spinning-jenny (the old busybody that she is), to knock up all our good old women's livelihood, and send them to their graves before their time. There's an invention of the enemy, if you will!'

'That's very true!' said my lady, shaking her head.

'But baking bread is wholesome, straightforward elbow-work. They have not got to inventing any contrivance for that yet, thank Heaven! It does not seem to me natural, nor according to Scripture, that iron and steel (whose brows can't sweat) should be made to do man's work. And so I say, all those trades where iron and steel do the work ordained to man at the Fall, are unlawful, and I never stand up for them. But say this baker Brooke did knead his bread, and make it rise, and then that people, who had, perhaps, no good ovens, came to him, and bought his good light bread, and in this manner he turned an honest penny, and got rich ; why, all I say, my lady, is this,—I dare say he would have been born a Hanbury, or a lord, if he could ; and if he was not, it is no fault of his, that I can see, that he made good bread (being a baker by trade), and got money, and bought his land. It was his misfortune, not his fault, that he was not a person of quality by birth.'

'That's very true,' said my lady, after a moment's pause for consideration. 'But, although he was a baker, he might have been a Churchman. Even your eloquence, Miss Galindo, shan't convince me that that is not his own fault.'

'I don't see even that, begging your pardon, my lady,' said Miss Galindo, emboldened by the first success of her eloquence. 'When a Baptist is a baby, if I understand their creed aright, he is not baptized ; and, consequently, he can have no godfathers and godmothers to do anything for him in his baptism ; you agree to that, my lady ? '

My lady would rather have known what her acquiescence would lead to, before acknowledging that she could not dissent from this first proposition ; still she gave her tacit agreement by bowing her head.

'And, you know, our godfathers and godmothers are expected to promise and vow three things in our name, when we are little babies, and can do nothing but squall for ourselves. It is a great privilege, but don't let us be hard upon those who have not had the chance of godfathers and godmothers. Some people, we know, are born with silver spoons,—that's to say, a godfather to give one things, and teach one one's catechism, and see that we're confirmed into good church-going Christians,—and others with wooden ladles in their mouths. These poor last folks must just be content to be godfatherless orphans, and Dissenters, all their lives ; and if they are tradespeople into the bargain, so much the worse for them ; but let us be humble Christians, my dear lady, and not hold our heads too high because we were born orthodox quality.'

'You go on too fast, Miss Galindo! I can't follow you. Besides, I do believe dissent to be an invention of the Devil's. Why can't they believe as we do? It's very wrong. Besides, it's schism and heresy, and, you know, the Bible says that's as bad as witchcraft.'

My lady was not convinced, as I could see. After Miss Galindo had gone, she sent Mrs. Medlicott for certain books out of the great old library upstairs, and had them made up into a parcel under her own eye.

'If Captain James comes to-morrow, I will speak to him about these Brookes. I have not hitherto liked to speak to him, because I did not wish to hurt him, by supposing there could be any truth in the reports about his intimacy with them. But now I will try and do my duty by him and them. Surely, this great body of divinity will bring them back to the true church.'

I could not tell, for though my lady read me over the titles, I was not any the wiser as to their contents. Besides, I was much more anxious to consult my lady as to my own change of place. I showed her the letter I had that day received from Harry; and we once more talked over the expediency of my going to live with him, and trying what entire change of air would do to re-establish my failing health. I could say anything to my lady, she was so sure to understand me rightly. For one thing, she never thought of herself, so I had no fear of hurting her by stating the truth. I told her how happy my years had been while passed under her roof; but that now I had begun to wonder whether I had not duties elsewhere, in making a home for Harry,—and whether the fulfilment of these duties, quiet ones they must needs be in the case of such a cripple as myself, would not prevent my sinking into the querulous habit of thinking and talking into which I found myself occasionally falling. Add to which, there was the prospect of benefit from the more bracing air of the north.

It was then settled that my departure from Hanbury,

my happy home for so long, was to take place before many weeks had passed. And as, when one period of life is about to be shut up for ever, we are sure to look back upon it with fond regret, so I, happy enough in my future prospects, could not avoid recurring to all the days of my life in the Hall, from the time when I came to it, a shy, awkward girl, scarcely past childhood, to now, when a grown woman,—past childhood—almost, from the very character of my illness, past youth,—I was looking forward to leaving my lady's house (as a residence) for ever. As it has turned out, I never saw either her or it again. Like a piece of seawreck, I have drifted away from those days: quiet, happy, eventless days, very happy to remember!

I thought of good, jovial Mr. Mountford,—and his regrets that he might not keep a pack, ' a very small pack,' of harriers, and his merry ways, and his love of good eating; of the first coming of Mr. Gray, and my lady's attempt to quench his sermons, when they tended to enforce any duty connected with education. And now we had an absolute school-house in the village; and since Miss Bessy's drinking tea at the Hall, my lady had been twice inside it, to give directions about some fine yarn she was having spun for table-napery. And her ladyship had so outgrown her old custom of dispensing with sermon or discourse, that even during the temporary preaching of Mr. Crosse, she had never had recourse to it, though I believe she would have had all the congregation on her side if she had.

And Mr. Horner was dead, and Captain James reigned in his stead. Good, steady, severe, silent Mr. Horner! with his clock-like regularity, and his snuff-coloured clothes, and silver buckles! I have often wondered which one misses most when they are dead and gone,—the bright creatures full of life, who are hither and thither and everywhere, so that no one can reckon upon their coming and going, with whom stillness and the long quiet of the grave seems utterly irreconcilable, so full are they of vivid motion and passion,—or the slow, serious people, whose movements —nay, whose very words, seem to go by clock-work; who never appear much to affect the course of our life while they are with us, but whose methodical ways show themselves, when they are gone, to have been intertwined with our very roots of daily existence. I think I miss these last the most, although I may have loved the former best. Captain James never was to me what Mr. Horner was, though the latter had hardly changed a dozen words with me at the day of his death. Then Miss Galindo! I remembered the time, as if it had been only yesterday, when she was but a name—and a very odd one—to me; then she was a queer, abrupt, disagreeable, busy old maid. Now I loved her dearly, and I found out that I was almost jealous of Miss Bessy.

Mr. Gray I never thought of with love; the feeling was almost reverence with which I looked upon him. I have not wished to speak much of myself, or else I could have told you how much he had been to me during these long, weary years of illness. But he was almost as much to every one, rich and poor, from my lady down to Miss Galindo's Sally.

The village, too, had a different look about it. I am sure I could not tell you what caused the change; but there were no more lounging young men to form a group at the cross-road, at a time of day when young men ought to be at work. I don't say this was all Mr. Gray's doing, for there really was so much to do in the fields that there was but little time for lounging now-a-days. And the children were hushed up in school, and better behaved out of it, too, than in the days when I used to be able to go my lady's errands in the village. I went so little about now, that I am sure I can't tell who Miss Galindo found to scold; and yet she looked so well and so happy that I think she must have had her accustomed portion of that wholesome exercise.

Before I left Hanbury, the rumour that Captain James was going to marry Miss Brooke, Baker Brooke's eldest daughter, who had only a sister to share his property with her, was confirmed. He himself announced it to my lady; nay, more, with a courage, gained, I suppose, in his former profession, where, as I have heard, he had led his ship into many a post of danger, he asked her ladyship, the Countess Ludlow, if he might bring his bride-elect (the Baptist baker's daughter!) and present her to my lady!

I am glad I was not present when he made this request; I should have felt so much ashamed for him, and I could not have helped being anxious till I heard my lady's answer, if I had been there. Of course she acceded; but I can fancy the grave surprise of her look. I wonder if Captain James noticed it.

I hardly dared ask my lady, after the interview had taken place, what she thought of the bride-elect; but I hinted my curiosity, and she told me, that if the young person had applied to Mrs. Medlicott for the situation of cook, and Mrs. Medlicott had engaged her, she thought that it would have been a very suitable arrangement. I understood from this how little she thought a marriage with Captain James, R.N., suitable.

About a year after I left Hanbury, I received a letter from Miss Galindo; I think I can find it.—Yes, this is it.

'Hanbury, May 4, 1811.

' DEAR MARGARET,

' You ask for news of us all. Don't you know there is no news in Hanbury? Did you ever hear of an event here? Now, if you have answered "Yes" in your own mind to these questions, you have fallen into my trap, and never were more mistaken in your life. Hanbury is full of news; and we have more events on our hands than we know what to do with. I will take them in the order of the newspapers—births, deaths, and marriages. In the matter of births, Jenny Lucas has had twins not a week ago. Sadly too much of a good thing, you'll say. Very true: but then they died; so their birth did not much signify. My cat has kittened, too; she has had three kittens, which again you may observe is too much of a good thing;

and so it would be, if it were not for the next item of intelligence I shall lay before you. Captain and Mrs. James have taken the old house next Pearson's; and the house is overrun with mice, which is just as fortunate for me as the King of Egypt's rat-ridden kingdom was to Dick Whittington. For my cat's kittening decided me to go and call on the bride, in hopes she wanted a cat; which she did, like a sensible woman, as I do believe she is, in spite of Baptism, Bakers, Bread, and Birmingham, and something worse than all, which you shall hear about, if you'll only be patient. As I had got my best bonnet on—the one I bought when poor Lord Ludlow was last at Hanbury in '99—I thought it a great condescension in myself (always remembering the date of the Galindo Baronetcy) to go and call on the bride; though I don't think so much of myself in my every-day clothes, as you know. But who should I find there but my Lady Ludlow! She looks as frail and delicate as ever, but is, I think, in better heart ever since that old city merchant of a Hanbury took it into his head that he was a cadet of the Hanburys of Hanbury, and left her that handsome legacy. I'll warrant you the mortgage was paid off pretty fast; and Mr. Horner's money— or my lady's money, or Harry Gregson's money, call it which you will,—is invested in his name, all right and tight, and they do talk of his being captain of his school, or Grecian,* or something, and going to college, after all! Harry Gregson the poacher's son! Well! to be sure, we are living in strange times!

'But I have not done with the marriages yet. Captain James's is all very well, but no one cares for it now, we are all so full of Mr. Gray's. Yes, indeed, Mr. Gray is going to be married, and to nobody else but my little Bessy! I tell her she will have to nurse him half the days of her life, he is such a frail little body. But she says she does not care for that; so that his body holds his soul, it is enough for her. She has a good spirit, and a brave heart, has my Bessy! It is a great advantage that she won't have to mark her clothes over again; for when she had knitted herself her last set of stockings, I told her to put G for Galindo, if she did not choose to put it for Gibson, for she should be my child if she was no one else's. And now, you see, it stands for Gray. So there are two marriages, and what more would you have? And she promises to take another of my kittens.

'Now, as to deaths, old Farmer Hale is dead—poor old man, I should think his wife thought it a good riddance, for he beat her every day that he was drunk, and he never was sober, in spite of Mr. Gray. I don't think (as I tell him) that Mr. Gray would ever have found courage to speak to Bessy as long as Farmer Hale lived, he took the old gentleman's sins so much to heart, and seemed to think it was all his fault for not being able to make a sinner into a saint. The parish bull is dead too. I never was so glad in my life. But they say we are to have a new one in his place. In the meantime I cross the common in peace, which is convenient just now, when I have so often to go to Mr. Gray's to see about furnishing.

'Now you think I have told you all the Hanbury news, don't you? Not so. The very greatest thing of all is to come. I won't tantalize you, but just out with it, for you would never guess it. My Lady Ludlow has given a party, just like any plebeian amongst us. We had tea and toast in the blue drawing-room, old John Footman waiting, with Tom Diggles, the lad that used to frighten away crows in Farmer Hale's fields, following in my lady's livery, hair powdered and everything. Mrs. Medlicott made tea in my lady's own room. My lady looked like a splendid fairy queen of mature age, in black velvet, and the old lace, which I have never seen her wear before since my lord's death. But the company? you'll say. Why we had the parson of Clover, and the parson of Headleigh, and the parson of Merribank, and the three parsonesses; and Farmer Donkin and two Miss Donkins; and Mr. Gray (of course), and myself and Bessy; and Captain and Mrs. James; yes, and Mr. and Mrs.

Brooke: think of that! I am not so sure the parsons liked it; but he was there. For he has been helping Captain James to get my lady's land into order; and then his daughter married the agent; and Mr. Gray (who ought to know) says, after all, Baptists are not such bad people; and he was right against them at one time, as you may remember. Mrs. Brooke is a rough diamond, to be sure. People have said that of me, I know. But, being a Galindo, I learnt manners in my youth, and can take them up when I choose. But Mrs. Brooke never learnt manners, I'll be bound. When John Footman handed her the tray with the tea-cups, she looked up at him as if she were sorely puzzled by that way of going on. I was sitting next to her, so I pretended not to see her perplexity, and put her cream and sugar in for her, and was all ready to pop it into her hands,—when who should come up, but that impudent lad Tom Diggles (I call him lad, for all his hair is powdered, for you know that it is not natural grey hair), with his tray full of cakes and what not, all as good as Mrs. Medlicott could make them. By this time, I should tell you, all the parsonesses were looking at Mrs. Brooke, for she had shown her want of breeding before; and the parsonesses, who were just a step above her in manners, were very much inclined to smile at her doings and sayings. Well! what does she do but pull out a clean Bandanna pocket-handkerchief, all red and yellow silk, spread it over her best silk gown; it was, like enough, a new one, for I had it from Sally, who had it from her cousin Molly, who is dairy-woman at the Brookes', that the Brookes were mighty set-up with an invitation to drink tea at the Hall. There we were, Tom Diggles even on the grin (I wonder how long it is since he was own brother to a scarecrow, only not so decently dressed) and Mrs. Parsoness of Headleigh,— I forget her name, and it's no matter, for she's an ill-bred creature, I hope Bessy will behave herself better,—was right-down bursting with laughter, and as near a hee-haw as ever a donkey was, when what

does my lady do ? Ay ! there 's my own dear Lady
Ludlow, God bless her ! She takes out her own pocket-
handkerchief, all snowy cambric, and lays it softly
down on her velvet lap, for all the world as if she did
it every day of her life, just like Mrs. Brooke, the
baker's wife ; and when the one got up to shake the
crumbs into the fireplace, the other did just the same.
But with such a grace ! and such a look at us all !
Tom Diggles went red all over ; and Mrs. Parsoness
of Headleigh scarce spoke for the rest of the evening ;
and the tears came into my old silly eyes ; and Mr.
Gray, who was before silent and awkward, in a way
which I tell Bessy she must cure him of, was made so
happy by this pretty action of my lady's, that he
talked away all the rest of the evening, and was the
life of the company.

'Oh! Margaret Dawson, I sometimes wonder if
you're the better off for leaving us. To be sure, you're
with your brother, and blood is blood. But when I
look at my lady and Mr. Gray, for all they're so
different, I would not change places with any in
England.'

Alas ! alas ! I never saw my dear lady again. She
died in eighteen hundred and fourteen, and Mr. Gray
did not long survive her. As I dare say you know,
the Reverend Henry Gregson is now vicar of Hanbury,
and his wife is the daughter of Mr. Gray and Miss
Bessy.

# AN ACCURSED RACE

WE have our prejudices in England. Or, if that assertion offends any of my readers, I will modify it: we have had our prejudices in England. We have tortured Jews; we have burnt Catholics and Protestants, to say nothing of a few witches and wizards. We have satirised Puritans, and we have dressed-up Guys. But, after all, I do not think we have been so bad as our Continental friends. To be sure, our insular position has kept us free, to a certain degree, from the inroads of alien races; who, driven from one land of refuge, steal into another equally unwilling to receive them; and where, for long centuries, their presence is barely endured, and no pains is taken to conceal the repugnance which the natives of 'pure blood' experience towards them.

There yet remains a remnant of the miserable people called Cagots in the valleys of the Pyrenees; in the Landes near Bourdeaux; and, stretching up on the west side of France, their numbers become larger in Lower Brittany. Even now, the origin of these families is a word of shame to them among their neighbours; although they are protected by the law, which confirmed them in the equal rights of citizens about the end of the last century. Before then they had lived, for hundreds of years, isolated from all those who boasted of pure blood, and they had been, all this time, oppressed by cruel local edicts. They were truly what they were popularly called, The Accursed Race.

All distinct traces of their origin are lost. Even at the close of that period which we call the Middle Ages, this was a problem which no one could solve; and as the traces, which even then were faint and uncertain, have vanished away one by one, it is a complete mystery at the present day. Why they were accursed in the first instance, why isolated from their kind, no one knows. From the earliest accounts of their state that are yet remaining to us, it seems that the names which they gave each other were ignored by the population they lived amongst, who spoke of them as Crestiaa,* or Cagots, just as we speak of animals by their generic names. Their houses or huts were always placed at some distance out of the villages of the country-folk, who unwillingly called in the services of the Cagots as carpenters, or tilers, or slaters—trades which seemed appropriated by this unfortunate race— who were forbidden to occupy land, or to bear arms, the usual occupations of those times. .They had some small right of pasturage on the common lands, and in the forests: but the number of their cattle and live- stock was strictly limited by the earliest laws relating to the Cagots. They were forbidden by one act to have more than twenty sheep, a pig, a ram, and six geese. The pig was to be fattened and killed for winter food; the fleece of the sheep was to clothe them; but, if the said sheep had lambs, they were forbidden to eat them. Their only privilege arising from this increase was, that they might choose out the strongest and finest in preference to keeping the old sheep. At Martinmas*the authorities of the commune came round, and counted over the stock of each Cagot. If he had more than his appointed number, they were forfeited; half went to the commune, and half to the baillie, or chief magistrate of the commune. The poor beasts were limited as to the amount of common land which they might stray over in search of grass. While the cattle of the inhabitants of the commune might wander hither and thither in search of the sweetest herbage, the deepest shade, or the coolest pool in which to stand on the hot days, and lazily switch their dappled sides, the Cagot sheep and pig had to learn imaginary bounds, beyond which if they strayed, any one might snap them up, and kill them, reserving a part of the flesh for his own use, but graciously restoring the inferior parts to their original owner. Any damage done by the sheep was, however, fairly appraised, and the Cagot paid no more for it than any other man would have done.

Did a Cagot leave his poor cabin, and venture into the towns, even to render services required of him in the way of his trade, he was bidden, by all the municipal laws, to stand by and remember his rude old state. In all the towns and villages in the large districts extending on both sides of the Pyrenees—in all that part of Spain—they were forbidden to buy or sell anything eatable, to walk in the middle (esteemed the better) part of the streets, to come within the gates before sunrise, or to be found after sunset within the walls of the town. But still, as the Cagots were good-looking men, and (although they bore certain natural marks of their caste, of which I shall speak by-and-by) were not easily distinguished by casual passers-by from other men, they were compelled to wear some distinctive peculiarity which should arrest the eye; and, in the greater number of towns, it was decreed that the outward sign of a Cagot should be a piece of red cloth sewed conspicuously on the front of his dress. In other towns, the mark of Cagoterie was the foot of a duck or a goose hung over their left shoulder, so as to be seen by any one meeting them. After a time, the more convenient badge of a piece of yellow cloth cut out in the shape of a duck's foot, was adopted. If any Cagot was found in any town or village without his badge, he had to pay a fine of five sous, and to lose his dress. He was expected to shrink away from any passer-by, for fear that their clothes should touch each other; or else to stand still in some corner or by-place. If the Cagots were thirsty during the days which they passed in those towns where their presence was barely suffered, they had no means of quenching their thirst, for they were forbidden to enter into the little cabarets or taverns. Even the water gushing out of the common fountain was prohibited to them. Far away, in their own squalid village, there was the Cagot fountain, and they were not allowed to drink of any other water. A Cagot woman having to make purchases in the town, was liable to be flogged out of it if she went to buy anything except on a Monday—a day on which all other people who could, kept their houses for fear of coming in contact with the accursed race.

In the Pays Basque, the prejudices—and for some time the laws—ran stronger against them than any which I have hitherto mentioned. The Basque Cagot was not allowed to possess sheep. He might keep a pig for provision, but his pig had no right of pasturage. He might cut and carry grass for the ass, which was the only other animal he was permitted to own; and this ass was permitted, because its existence was rather an advantage to the oppressor, who constantly availed himself of the Cagot's mechanical skill, and was glad to have him and his tools easily conveyed from one place to another.

The race was repulsed by the State. Under the small local governments they could hold no post whatsoever. And they were barely tolerated by the Church, although they were good Catholics, and zealous frequenters of the mass. They might only enter the churches by a small door set apart for them, through which no one of the pure race ever passed. This door was low, so as to compel them to make an obeisance. It was occasionally surrounded by sculpture, which invariably represented an oak-branch with a dove above it. When they were once in, they might not go to the holy water used by others. They had a bénitier* of their own; nor were they allowed to share in the consecrated bread when that was handed round to the believers of the pure race. The Cagots stood afar off, near the door. There were certain boundaries —imaginary lines—in the nave and in the aisles which they might not pass. In one or two of the more tolerant of the Pyrenean villages, the blessed bread was offered to the Cagots, the priest standing on one side of the boundary, and giving the pieces of bread on a long wooden fork to each person successively

When the Cagot died, he was interred apart, in a plot of burying-ground on the north side of the cemetery.

Under such laws and prescriptions as I have described, it is no wonder that he was generally too poor to have much property for his children to inherit; but certain descriptions of it were forfeited to the commune. The only possession which all who were not of his own race refused to touch, was his furniture. That was tainted, infectious, unclean—fit for none but Cagots.

When such were, for at least three centuries, the prevalent usages and opinions with regard to this oppressed race, it is not surprising that we read of occasional outbursts of ferocious violence on their part. In the Basses-Pyrenées, for instance, it is only about a hundred years since, that the Cagots of Rehouilhes rose up against the inhabitants of the neighbouring town of Lourdes, and got the better of them, by their magical powers, as it is said. The people of Lourdes were conquered and slain, and their ghastly, bloody heads served the triumphant Cagots for balls to play at ninepins with! The local parliaments had begun, by this time, to perceive how oppressive was the ban of public opinion under which the Cagots lay, and were not inclined to enforce too severe a punishment. Accordingly, the decree of the parliament of Toulouse condemned only the leading Cagots concerned in this affray to be put to death, and that henceforward and for ever no Cagot was to be permitted to enter the town of Lourdes by any gate but that called Capdet-pourtet: they were only to be allowed to walk under the rain-gutters, and neither to sit, eat, nor drink in the town. If they failed in observing any of these rules, the parliament decreed, in the spirit of Shylock, that the disobedient Cagots should have two strips of flesh, weighing never more than two ounces a-piece, cut out from each side of their spines.

In the fourteenth, fifteenth, and sixteenth centuries, it was considered no more a crime to kill a Cagot than to destroy obnoxious vermin. A 'nest of Cagots,' as the old accounts phrase it, had assembled in a deserted castle of Mauvezin, about the year sixteen hundred; and, certainly, they made themselves not very agreeable neighbours, as they seemed to enjoy their reputation of magicians; and, by some acoustic secrets which were known to them, all sorts of moanings and groanings were heard in the neighbouring forests, very much to the alarm of the good people of the pure race; who could not cut off a withered branch for firewood, but some unearthly sound seemed to fill the air, nor drink water which was not poisoned, because the Cagots would persist in filling their pitchers at the same running stream. Added to these grievances, the various pilferings perpetually going on in the neighbourhood made the inhabitants of the adjacent towns and hamlets believe that they had a very sufficient cause for wishing to murder all the Cagots in the Château de Mauvezin. But it was surrounded by a moat, and only accessible by a drawbridge; besides which, the Cagots were fierce and vigilant. Some one, however, proposed to get into their confidence; and for this purpose he pretended to fall ill close to their path, so that on returning to their stronghold they perceived him, and took him in, restored him to health, and made a friend of him. One day, when they were all playing at ninepins in the woods, their treacherous friend left the party on pretence of being thirsty, and went back into the castle, drawing up the bridge after he had passed over it, and so cutting off their means of escape into safety. Then, going up to the highest part of the castle, he blew a horn, and the pure race, who were lying in wait on the watch for some such signal, fell upon the Cagots at their games, and slew them all. For this murder I find no punishment decreed in the parliament of Toulouse, or elsewhere.

As any intermarriage with the pure race was strictly forbidden, and as there were books kept in every commune in which the names and habitations of the reputed Cagots were written, these unfortunate people had no hope of ever becoming blended with the rest of the population. Did a Cagot marriage take place, the couple were serenaded with satirical songs. They also had minstrels, and many of their romances are still current in Brittany; but they did not attempt to make any reprisals of satire or abuse. Their disposition was amiable, and their intelligence great. Indeed, it required both these qualities, and their great love of mechanical labour, to make their lives tolerable.

At last, they began to petition that they might receive some protection from the laws; and, towards the end of the seventeenth century, the judicial power took their side. But they gained little by this. Law could not prevail against custom: and, in the ten or twenty years just preceding the first French revolution, the prejudice in France against the Cagots amounted to fierce and positive abhorrence.

At the beginning of the sixteenth century, the Cagots of Navarre complained to the Pope that they were excluded from the fellowship of men, and accursed by the Church, because their ancestors had given help to a certain Count Raymond of Toulouse in his revolt against the Holy See. They entreated his holiness not to visit upon them the sins of their fathers. The Pope issued a bull—on the thirteenth of May, fifteen hundred and fifteen—ordering them to be well-treated and to be admitted to the same privileges as other men. He charged Don Juan de Santa Maria of Pampeluna to see to the execution of this bull. But Don Juan was slow to help, and the poor Spanish Cagots grew impatient, and resolved to try the secular power. They accordingly applied to the Cortes of Navarre, and were opposed on a variety of grounds. First, it was stated that their ancestors had had 'nothing to do with Raymond Count of Toulouse, or with any such knightly personage; that they were in fact descendants of Gehazi, servant of Elisha (second book of Kings, fifth chapter, twenty-seventh verse), who had been accursed by his master for his fraud upon Naaman, and doomed, he and his descendants, to be lepers for evermore. Name, Cagots or Gahets; Gahets, Gehazites. What can be more clear? And if that is not enough, and you tell us that the Cagots are not lepers now; we reply that there are two kinds of leprosy, one perceptible and the other imperceptible, even to the person suffering from it. Besides, it is the country talk, that where the Cagot treads, the grass withers, proving the unnatural heat of his body. Many credible and trustworthy witnesses will also tell you that, if a Cagot holds a freshly-gathered apple in his hand, it will shrivel and wither up in an hour's time as much as if it had been kept for a whole winter in a dry room. They are born with tails; although the parents are cunning enough to pinch them off immediately. Do you doubt this? If it is not true, why do the children of the pure race delight in sewing on sheep's tails to the dress of any Cagot who is so absorbed in his work as not to perceive them? And their bodily smell is so horrible and detestable that it shows that they must be heretics of some vile and pernicious description, for do we not read of the incense of good workers, and the fragrance of holiness?'

Such were literally the arguments by which the Cagots were thrown back into a worse position than ever, as far as regarded their rights as citizens. The Pope insisted that they should receive all their ecclesiastical privileges. The Spanish priests said nothing; but tacitly refused to allow the Cagots to mingle with the rest of the faithful, either dead or alive. The accursed race obtained laws in their favour from the Emperor Charles the Fifth; which, however, there was no one to carry into effect. As a sort of revenge for their want of submission, and for their impertinence in daring to complain, their tools were all taken away from them by the local authorities: an old man and all his family died of starvation, being no longer allowed to fish.

They could not emigrate. Even to remove their poor mud habitations, from one spot to another, excited anger and suspicion. To be sure, in sixteen hundred and ninety-five, the Spanish government ordered the alcaldes* to search out all the Cagots, and to expel them before two months had expired, under pain of having fifty ducats to pay for every Cagot remaining in

Spain at the expiration of that time. The inhabitants of the villages rose up and flogged out any of the miserable race who might be in their neighbourhood ; but the French were on their guard against this enforced irruption, and refused to permit them to enter France. Numbers were hunted up into the inhospitable Pyrenees, and there died of starvation, or became a prey to wild beasts. They were obliged to wear both gloves and shoes when they were thus put to flight, otherwise the stones and herbage they trod upon, and the balustrades of the bridges that they handled in crossing, would, according to popular belief, have become poisonous.

And all this time, there was nothing remarkable or disgusting in the outward appearance of this unfortunate people. There was nothing about them to countenance the idea of their being lepers—the most natural mode of accounting for the abhorrence in which they were held. They were repeatedly examined by learned doctors, whose experiments, although singular and rude, appear to have been made in a spirit of humanity. For instance, the surgeons of the king of Navarre, in sixteen hundred, bled twenty-two Cagots, in order to examine and analyse their blood. They were young and healthy people of both sexes ; and the doctors seem to have expected that they should have been able to extract some new kind of salt from their blood which might account for the wonderful heat of their bodies. But their blood was just like that of other people. Some of these medical men have left us a description of the general appearance of this unfortunate race, at a time when they were more numerous and less intermixed than they are now. The families existing in the south and west of France, who are reputed to be of Cagot descent at this day, are, like their ancestors, tall, largely made, and powerful in frame ; fair and ruddy in complexion, with gray-blue eyes, in which some observers see a pensive heaviness of look. Their lips are thick, but well-formed. Some of the reports name their sad expression of countenance with surprise and suspicion—'They are not gay, like other folk.' The wonder would be if they were. Dr. Guyon, the medical man of the last century who has left the clearest report on the health of the Cagots, speaks of the vigorous old age they attain to. In one family alone, he found a man of seventy-four years of age; a woman as old, gathering cherries; and another woman, aged eighty-three, was lying on the grass, having her hair combed by her great-grandchildren. Dr. Guyon and other surgeons examined into the subject of the horribly infectious smell which the Cagots were said to leave behind them, and upon everything they touched; but they could perceive nothing unusual on this head. They also examined their ears, which, according to common belief (a belief existing to this day), were differently shaped from those of other people; being round and gristly, without the lobe of flesh into which the ear-ring is inserted. They decided that most of the Cagots whom they examined had the ears of this round shape; but they gravely added, that they saw no reason why this should exclude them from the good-will of men, and from the power of holding office in Church and State. They recorded the fact, that the children of the towns ran baaing after any Cagot who had been compelled to come into the streets to make purchases, in allusion to this peculiarity of the shape of the ear, which bore some resemblance to the ears of the sheep as they are cut by the shepherds in this district. Dr. Guyon names the case of a beautiful Cagot girl, who sang most sweetly, and prayed to be allowed to sing canticles in the organ-loft. The organist, more musician than bigot, allowed her to come; but the indignant congregation, finding out whence proceeded that clear fresh voice, rushed up to the organ-loft, and chased the girl out, bidding her 'remember her ears,' and not commit the sacrilege of singing praises to God along with the pure race.

But this medical report of Dr. Guyon's—bringing facts and arguments to confirm his opinion, that there

was no physical reason why the Cagots should not
be received on terms of social equality by the rest of
the world—did no more for his clients than the legal
decrees promulgated two centuries before had done.
The French proved the truth of the saying in Hudibras,

> He that's convinced against his will
> Is of the same opinion still.*

And, indeed, the being convinced by Dr. Guyon that
they ought to receive Cagots as fellow-creatures, only
made them more rabid in declaring that they would not.
One or two little occurrences which are recorded, show
that the bitterness of the repugnance to the Cagots
was in full force at the time just preceding the first
French revolution.  There was a M. d'Abedos, the
curate of Lourbes, and brother to the seigneur of the
neighbouring castle, who was living in seventeen
hundred and eighty ; he was well-educated for the
time, a travelled man, and sensible and moderate in
all respects but that of his abhorrence of the Cagots :
he would insult them from the very altar, calling out
to them, as they stood afar off, ' Oh !  ye Cagots,
damned for evermore ! '  One day, a half-blind Cagot
stumbled and touched the censer borne before this
Abbé de Lourbes.  He was immediately turned out of
the church, and forbidden ever to re-enter it.  One
does not know how to account for the fact, that the
very brother of this bigoted abbé, the seigneur of the
village, went and married a Cagot girl ; but so it was,
and the abbé brought a legal process against him, and
had his estates taken from him, solely on account of
his marriage, which reduced him to the condition of
a Cagot, against whom the old law was still in force.
The descendants of this Seigneur de Lourbes are simple
peasants at this very day, working on the lands which
belonged to their grandfather.

This prejudice against mixed marriages remained
prevalent until very lately.  The tradition of the Cagot
descent lingered among the people, long after the laws
against the accursed race were abolished.  A Breton
girl, within the last few years, having two lovers each

of reputed Cagot descent, employed a notary to examine their pedigrees, and see which of the two had least Cagot in him; and to that one she gave her hand. In Brittany the prejudice seems to have been more virulent than anywhere else. M. Emile Souvestre records proofs of the hatred borne to them in Brittany so recently as in eighteen hundred and thirty-five. Just lately a baker at Hennebon, having married a girl of Cagot descent, lost all his custom. The godfather and godmother of a Cagot child became Cagots themselves by the Breton laws, unless, indeed, the poor little baby died before attaining a certain number of days. They had to eat the butchers' meat condemned as unhealthy; but, for some unknown reason, they were considered to have a right to every cut loaf turned upside down, with its cut side towards the door, and might enter any house in which they saw a loaf in this position, and carry it away with them. About thirty years ago, there was the skeleton of a hand hanging up as an offering in a Breton Church near Quimperle, and the tradition was, that it was the hand of a rich Cagot who had dared to take holy water out of the usual bénitier, some time at the beginning of the reign of Louis the Sixteenth; which an old soldier witnessing, he lay in wait, and the next time the offender approached the bénitier he cut off his hand, and hung it up, dripping with blood, as an offering to the patron saint of the church. The poor Cagots in Brittany petitioned against their opprobrious name, and begged to be distinguished by the appellation of Malandrins. To English ears one is much the same as the other, as neither conveys any meaning; but, to this day, the descendants of the Cagots do not like to have this name applied to them, preferring that of Malandrin.

The French Cagots tried to destroy all the records of their pariah descent, in the commotions of seventeen hundred and eighty-nine; but if writings have disappeared, the tradition yet remains, and points out such and such a family as Cagot, or Malandrin, or Oiselier, according to the old terms of abhorrence.

There are various ways in which learned men have attempted to account for the universal repugnance in which this well-made, powerful race are held. Some say that the antipathy to them took its rise in the days when leprosy was a dreadfully prevalent disease; and that the Cagots are more liable than any other men to a kind of skin disease, not precisely leprosy, but resembling it in some of its symptoms; such as dead whiteness of complexion, and swellings of the face and extremities. There was also some resemblance to the ancient Jewish custom in respect to lepers, in the habit of the people; who, on meeting a Cagot, called out, 'Cagote? Cagote?' to which they were bound to reply, 'Perlute! perlute!'* Leprosy is not properly an infectious complaint, in spite of the horror in which the Cagot furniture, and the cloth woven by them, are held in some places; the disorder is hereditary, and hence (say this body of wise men, who have troubled themselves to account for the origin of Cagoterie) the reasonableness and the justice of preventing any mixed marriages, by which this terrible tendency to leprous complaints might be spread far and wide. Another authority says, that though the Cagots are fine-looking men, hard-working, and good mechanics, yet they bear in their faces, and show in their actions, reasons for the detestation in which they are held: their glance, if you meet it, is the jettatura, or evil-eye, and they are spiteful, and cruel, and deceitful above all other men. All these qualities they derive from their ancestor Gehazi, the servant of Elisha, together with their tendency to leprosy.

Again, it is said that they are descended from the Arian Goths, who were permitted to live in certain places in Guienne and Languedoc, after their defeat by King Clovis,* on condition that they abjured their heresy, and kept themselves separate from all other men for ever. The principal reason alleged in support of this supposition of their Gothic descent, is the specious one of derivation,—Chiens Gots, Cans Gots, Cagots, equivalent to Dogs of Goths.

Again, they were thought to be Saracens, coming from Syria. In confirmation of this idea, was the belief that all Cagots were possessed by a horrible smell. The Lombards, also, were an unfragrant race, or so reputed among the Italians: witness Pope Stephen's letter to Charlemagne,* dissuading him from marrying Bertha, daughter of Didier, King of Lombardy. The Lombards boasted of Eastern descent, and were noisome. The Cagots were noisome, and therefore must be of Eastern descent. What could be clearer? In addition, there was the proof to be derived from the name Cagot, which those maintaining the opinion of their Saracen descent held to be Chiens, or Chasseurs des Gots, because the Saracens chased the Goths out of Spain. Moreover, the Saracens were originally Mahometans, and as such obliged to bathe seven times a-day: whence the badge of the duck's foot. A duck was a water-bird: Mahometans bathed in the water. Proof upon proof!

In Brittany the common idea was, they were of Jewish descent. Their unpleasant smell was again pressed into service. The Jews, it was well known, had this physical infirmity, which might be cured either by bathing in a certain fountain in Egypt—which was a long way from Brittany—or by anointing themselves with the blood of a Christian child. Blood gushed out of the body of every Cagot on Good Friday. No wonder, if they were of Jewish descent. It was the only way of accounting for so portentous a fact. Again, the Cagots were capital carpenters, which gave the Bretons every reason to believe that their ancestors were the very Jews who made the cross. When first the tide of emigration set from Brittany to America, the oppressed Cagots crowded to the ports, seeking to go to some new country, where their race might be unknown. Here was another proof of their descent from Abraham and his nomadic people; and, the forty years' wandering in the wilderness and the Wandering Jew himself, were pressed into the service to prove that the Cagots derived their restlessness and love of change from their ancestors, the Jews. The Jews, also, practised arts-magic, and the Cagots sold bags of wind to the Breton sailors, enchanted maidens to love them— maidens who never would have cared for them, unless they had been previously enchanted—made hollow rocks and trees give out strange and unearthly noises, and sòld the magical herb called bon-succès. It is true enough that, in all the early acts of the fourteenth century, the same laws apply to Jews as to Cagots, and the appellations seem used indiscriminately; but their fair complexions, their remarkable devotion to all the ceremonies of the Catholic Church, and many other circumstances, conspire to forbid our believing them to be of Hebrew descent.

Another very plausible idea is, that they are the descendants of unfortunate individuals afflicted with goîtres, which is, even to this day, not an uncommon disorder in the gorges and valleys of the Pyrenees. Some have even derived the word goître from Got, or Goth; but their name, Crestiaa, is not unlike Cretin, and the same symptoms of idiotism were not unusual among the Cagots; although sometimes, if old tradi- tion is to be credited, their malady of the brain took rather the form of violent delirium, which attacked them at new and full moons. Then the workmen laid down their tools, and rushed off from their labour to play mad pranks up and down the country. Perpetual motion was required to alleviate the agony of fury that seized upon the Cagots at such times. In this desire for rapid movement, the attack resembled the Nea- politan tarantella;[*] while in the mad deeds they per- formed during such attacks, they were not unlike the northern Berserker.[*] In Béarn especially, those suffer- ing from this madness were dreaded by the pure race; the Béarnais, going to cut their wooden clogs in the great forests that lay around the base of the Pyrenées, feared above all things to go too near the periods when the Cagoutelle seized on the oppressed and accursed people; from whom it was then the oppressors' turn to fly. A man was living within the memory of some, who had married a Cagot wife; he used to beat her right soundly when he saw the first symptoms of the Cagoutelle, and, having reduced her to a wholesome state of exhaustion and insensibility, he locked her up until the moon had altered her shape in the heavens. If he had not taken such decided steps, say the oldest inhabitants, there is no knowing what might have happened.

From the thirteenth to the end of the eighteenth century, there are facts enough to prove the universal abhorrence in which this unfortunate race was held; whether called Cagots, or Gahets in Pyrenean districts, Caqueaux in Brittany, or Vaqueros in Asturias. The great French revolution brought some good out of its fermentation of the people: the more intelligent among them tried to overcome the prejudice against the Cagots.

In seventeen hundred and eighteen, there was a famous cause tried at Biarritz relating to Cagot rights and privileges. There was a wealthy miller, Etienne Arnauld by name, of the race of Gotz, Quagotz, Bisigotz, Astragotz, or Gahetz, as his people are described in the legal document. He married an heiress, a Gotte (or Cagot) of Biarritz; and the newly-married, well-to-do couple saw no reason why they should stand near the door in the church, nor why he should not hold some civil office in the commune, of which he was the principal inhabitant. Accordingly, he petitioned the law that he and his wife might be allowed to sit in the gallery of the church, and that he might be relieved from his civil disabilities. This wealthy white miller, Etienne Arnauld, pursued his rights with some vigour against the Baillie of Labourd, the dignitary of the neighbourhood. Whereupon the inhabitants of Biarritz met in the open air, on the eighth of May, to the number of one hundred and fifty; approved of the conduct of the Baillie in rejecting Arnauld, made a subscription, and gave all power to their lawyers to defend the cause of the pure race against Etienne Arnauld—'that stranger,' who, having married a girl of Cagot blood, ought also to be expelled from the holy places. This lawsuit was carried through all the local courts, and ended by an appeal to the highest court in Paris; where a decision was given against Basque superstitions; and Etienne Arnauld was thenceforward entitled to enter the gallery of the church.

Of course, the inhabitants of Biarritz were all the more ferocious for having been conquered; and, four years later, a carpenter, Miguel Legaret, suspected of Cagot descent, having placed himself in the church among other people, was dragged out by the abbé and two of the jurats of the parish. Legaret defended himself with a sharp knife at the time, and went to law afterwards; the end of which was, that the abbé and his two accomplices were condemned to a public confession of penitence, to be uttered while on their knees at the church door, just after high mass. They appealed to the parliament of Bourdeaux against this decision, but met with no better success than the opponents of the miller Arnauld. Legaret was confirmed in his right of standing where he would in the parish church. That a living Cagot had equal rights with other men in the town of Biarritz seemed now ceded to them; but a dead Cagot was a different thing. The inhabitants of pure blood struggled long and hard to be interred apart from the abhorred race. The Cagots were equally persistent in claiming to have a common buryingground. Again the texts of the Old Testament were referred to, and the pure blood quoted triumphantly the precedent of Uzziah the leper (twenty-sixth chapter of the second book of Chronicles), who was buried in the field of the Sepulchres of the Kings, not in the sepulchres themselves. The Cagots pleaded that they were healthy and able-bodied; with no taint of leprosy near them. They were met by the strong argument so difficult to be refuted, which I quoted before. Leprosy was of two kinds, perceptible and imperceptible. If the Cagots were suffering from the latter kind, who could tell whether they were free from it or not? That decision must be left to the judgement of others.

One sturdy Cagot family alone, Belone by name,

kept up a lawsuit, claiming the privilege of common sepulture, for forty-two years; although the curé of Biarritz had to pay one hundred livres for every Cagot not interred in the right place. The inhabitants indemnified the curate for all these fines.

M. de Romagne, Bishop of Tarbes, who died in seventeen hundred and sixty-eight, was the first to allow a Cagot to fill any office in the Church. To be sure, some were so spiritless as to reject office when it was offered to them, because, by so claiming their equality, they had to pay the same taxes as other men, instead of the Rancale or poll-tax levied on the Cagots; the collector of which had also a right to claim a piece of bread of a certain size for his dog at every Cagot dwelling.

Even in the present century, it has been necessary in some churches for the archdeacon of the district, followed by all his clergy, to pass out of the small door previously appropriated to the Cagots, in order to mitigate the superstition which, even so lately, made the people refuse to mingle with them in the house of God. A Cagot once played the congregation at Larroque a trick suggested by what I have just named. He slily locked the great parish-door of the church, while the greater part of the inhabitants were assisting at mass inside; put gravel into the lock itself, so as to prevent the use of any duplicate key,—and had the pleasure of seeing the proud pure-blooded people file out with bended head, through the small low door used by the abhorred Cagots.

We are naturally shocked at discovering, from facts such as these, the causeless rancour with which innocent and industrious people were so recently persecuted. The moral of the history of the accursed race may, perhaps, be best conveyed in the words of an epitaph on Mrs. Mary Hand, who lies buried in the churchyard of Stratford-on-Avon

> 'What faults you saw in me,
>   Pray strive to shun;
> And look at home; there's
>   Something to be done.'

# THE
# DOOM OF THE GRIFFITHS

## CHAPTER I

I HAVE always been much interested by the traditions
which are scattered up and down North Wales relating
to Owen Glendower*(Owain Glendwr is the national
spelling of the name), and I fully enter into the feeling
which makes the Welsh peasant still look upon him as
the hero of his country. There was great joy among
many of the inhabitants of the principality, when the
subject of the Welsh prize poem at Oxford, some fifteen
or sixteen years ago, was announced to be 'Owain
Glendwr.' It was the most proudly national subject
that had been given for years.

Perhaps, some may not be aware that this redoubted
chieftain is, even in the present days of enlightenment,
as famous among his illiterate countrymen for his
magical powers as for his patriotism. He says himself—or Shakespeare says it for him, which is much the
same thing—

> 'At my nativity
> The front of heaven was full of fiery shapes
> Of burning cressets  . . . .
> . . . . I can call spirits from the vasty deep.'

And few among the lower orders in the principality would
think of asking Hotspur's irreverent question in reply.

Among other traditions preserved relative to this
part of the Welsh hero's character, is the old family
prophecy which gives title to this tale. When Sir
David Gam,*' as black a traitor as if he had been born
in Builth,' sought to murder Owen at Machynlleth,
there was one with him whose name Glendwr little
dreamed of having associated with his enemies. Rhys

ap Gryfydd, his 'old familiar friend,' his relation, his more than brother, had consented unto his blood. Sir David Gam might be forgiven, but one whom he had loved, and who had betrayed him, could never be forgiven. Glendwr was too deeply read in the human heart to kill him. No, he let him live on, the loathing and scorn of his compatriots, and the victim of bitter remorse. The mark of Cain was upon him.

But before he went forth—while yet he stood a prisoner, cowering beneath his conscience before Owain Glendwr—that chieftain passed a doom upon him and his race :

'I doom thee to live, because I know thou wilt pray for death. Thou shalt live on beyond the natural term of the life of man, the scorn of all good men. The very children shall point to thee with hissing tongue, and say, "There goes one who would have shed a brother's blood !" For I loved thee more than a brother, oh Rhys ap Gryfydd ! Thou shalt live on to see all of thy house, except the weakling in arms, perish by the sword. Thy race shall be accursed. Each generation shall see their lands melt away like snow ; yea, their wealth shall vanish, though they may labour night and day to heap up gold. And when nine generations have passed from the face of the earth, thy blood shall no longer flow in the veins of any human being. In those days the last male of thy race shall avenge me. The son shall slay the father.'

Such was the traditionary account of Owain Glendwr's speech to his once-trusted friend. And it was declared that the doom had been fulfilled in all things ; that, live in as miserly a manner as they would, the Griffiths never were wealthy and prosperous—indeed, that their worldly stock diminished without any visible cause.

But the lapse of many years had almost deadened the wonder-inspiring power of the whole curse. It was only brought forth from the hoards of Memory when some untoward event happened to the Griffiths family ; and in the eighth generation the faith in the prophecy

was nearly destroyed, by the marriage of the Griffiths
of that day, to a Miss Owen, who, unexpectedly, by
the death of a brother, became an heiress—to no considerable amount, to be sure, but enough to make
the prophecy appear reversed.  The heiress and her
husband removed from his small patrimonial estate in
Merionethshire, to her heritage in Caenarvonshire, and
for a time the prophecy lay dormant.

If you go from Tremadoc to Criccaeth you pass by
the parochial church of Ynysynhanarn, situated in
a boggy valley running from the mountains, which
shoulder up to the Rivals, down to Cardigan Bay.
This tract of land has every appearance of having been
redeemed at no distant period of time from the sea,
and has all the desolate rankness often attendant upon
such marshes.  But the valley beyond, similar in
character, had yet more of gloom at the time of which
I write.  In the higher part there were large plantations of firs, set too closely to attain any size, and
remaining stunted in height and scrubby in appearance.
Indeed, many of the smaller and more weakly had
died, and the bark had fallen down on the brown soil
neglected and unnoticed.  These trees had a ghastly
appearance, with their white trunks, seen by the dim
light which struggled through the thick boughs above.
Nearer to the sea, the valley assumed a more open,
though hardly a more cheerful character ; it looked
dark and overhung by sea-fog through the greater
part of the year, and even a farm-house, which usually
imparts something of cheerfulness to a landscape, failed
to do so here.  This valley formed the greater part of
the estate to which Owen Griffiths became entitled by
right of his wife.  In the higher part of the valley was
situated the family mansion, or rather dwelling-house,
for ' mansion,' is too grand a word to apply to the
clumsy, but substantially-built Bodowen.  It was
square and heavy-looking, with just that much pretension to ornament necessary to distinguish it from
the mere farm-house.

In this dwelling Mrs. Owen Griffiths bore her husband

two sons—Llewellyn, the future Squire, and Robert, who was early destined for the Church. The only difference in their situation, up to the time when Robert was entered at Jesus College, was that the elder was invariably indulged by all around him, while Robert was thwarted and indulged by turns; that Llewellyn never learned anything from the poor Welsh parson who was nominally his private tutor; while occasionally Squire Griffiths made a great point of enforcing Robert's diligence, telling him that, as he had his bread to earn, he must pay attention to his learning. There is no knowing how far the very irregular education he had received would have carried Robert through his college examinations; but, luckily for him in this respect, before such a trial of his learning came round, he heard of the death of his elder brother, after a short illness, brought on by a hard drinking-bout. Of course, Robert was summoned home, and it seemed quite as much of course, now that there was no necessity for him to ' earn his bread by his learning,' that he should not return to Oxford. So the half-educated, but not unintelligent, young man continued at home, during the short remainder of his parent's lifetime.

His was not an uncommon character. In general he was mild, indolent, and easily managed; but once thoroughly roused, his passions were vehement and fearful. He seemed, indeed, almost afraid of himself, and in common hardly dared to give way to justifiable anger—so much did he dread losing his self-control. Had he been judiciously educated, he would, probably, have distinguished himself in those branches of litera-ture which call for taste and imagination, rather than any exertion of reflection or judgement. As it was, his literary taste showed itself in making collections of Cambrian antiquities of every description, till his stock of Welsh MSS. would have excited the envy of Dr. Pugh* himself, had he been alive at the time of which I write.

There is one characteristic of Robert Griffiths which

I have omitted to note, and which was peculiar among
his class. He was no hard drinker; whether it was
that his head was very easily affected, or that his
partially-refined taste led him to dislike intoxication
and its attendant circumstances, I cannot say; but
at five-and-twenty Robert Griffiths was habitually
sober—a thing so rare in Llyn, that he was almost
shunned as a churlish, unsociable being, and passed much
of his time in solitude.

About this time, he had to appear in some case that
was tried at the Caernarvon assizes; and while there,
was a guest at the house of his agent, a shrewd, sensible
Welsh attorney, with one daughter, who had charms
enough to captivate Robert Griffiths. Though he
remained only a few days at her father's house, they
were sufficient to decide his affections, and short was
the period allowed to elapse before he brought home
a mistress to Bodowen. The new Mrs. Griffiths was
a gentle, yielding person, full of love toward her
husband, of whom, nevertheless, she stood something
in awe, partly arising from the difference in their ages,
partly from his devoting much time to studies of which
she could understand nothing.

She soon made him the father of a blooming little
daughter, called Augharad after her mother. Then
there came several uneventful years in the household
of Bodowen; and when the old women had one and
all declared that the cradle would not rock again,
Mrs. Griffiths bore the son and heir. His birth was
soon followed by his mother's death: she had been
ailing and low-spirited during her pregnancy, and she
seemed to lack the buoyancy of body and mind
requisite to bring her round after her time of trial.
Her husband, who loved her all the more from having
few other claims on his affections, was deeply grieved
by her early death, and his only comforter was the
sweet little boy whom she had left behind. That part
of the Squire's character, which was so tender, and
almost feminine, seemed called forth by the helpless
situation of the little infant, who stretched out his

arms to his father with the same earnest cooing that happier children make use of to their mother alone. Augharad was almost neglected, while the little Owen was king of the house; still, next to his father, none tended him so lovingly as his sister. She was so accustomed to give way to him that it was no longer a hardship. By night and by day Owen was the constant companion of his father, and increasing years seemed only to confirm the custom. It was an un-natural life for the child, seeing no bright little faces peering into his own (for Augharad was, as I said before, five or six years older, and her face, poor motherless girl, was often anything but bright), hearing no din of clear ringing voices, but day after day sharing the otherwise solitary hours of his father, whether in the dim room, surrounded by wizard-like antiquities, or pattering his little feet to keep up with his ' tada ' in his mountain rambles or shooting excursions. When the pair came to some little foaming brook, where the stepping-stones were far and wide, the father carried his little boy across with the tenderest care; when the lad was weary, they rested, he cradled in his father's arms, or the Squire would lift him up and carry him to his home again. The boy was indulged (for his father felt flattered by the desire) in his wish of sharing his meals and keeping the same hours. All this indulgence did not render Owen unamiable, but it made him wilful, and not a happy child. He had a thoughtful look, not common to the face of a young boy. He knew no games, no merry sports; his information was of an imaginative and speculative character. His father delighted to interest him in his own studies, without considering how far they were healthy for so young a mind.

Of course Squire Griffiths was not unaware of the prophecy which was to be fulfilled in his generation. He would occasionally refer to it when among his friends, with sceptical levity; but in truth it lay nearer to his heart than he chose to acknowledge. His strong imagination rendered him peculiarly impressible

on such subjects; while his judgement, seldom exercised
or fortified by severe thought, could not prevent his
continually recurring to it. He used to gaze on the
half-sad countenance of the child, who sat looking up
into his face with his large dark eyes, so fondly yet
so inquiringly, till the old legend swelled around his
heart, and became too painful for him not to require
sympathy. Besides, the overpowering love he bore to
the child seemed to demand fuller vent than tender
words; it made him like, yet dread, to upbraid its
object for the fearful contrast foretold. Still Squire
Griffiths told the legend, in a half-jesting manner, to
his little son, when they were roaming over the wild
heaths in the autumn days, 'the saddest of the year,'
or while they sat in the oak-wainscoted room, surrounded by mysterious relics that gleamed strangely
forth by the flickering fire-light. The legend was
wrought into the boy's mind, and he would crave, yet
tremble, to hear it told over and over again, while the
words were intermingled with caresses and questions as
to his love. Occasionally his loving words and actions
were cut short by his father's light yet bitter speech—
'Get thee away, my lad; thou knowest not what is
to come of all this love.'

When Augharad was seventeen, and Owen eleven or
twelve, the rector of the parish in which Bodowen was
situated, endeavoured to prevail on Squire Griffiths to
send the boy to school. Now, this rector had many
congenial tastes with his parishioner, and was his only
intimate; and, by repeated arguments, he succeeded
in convincing the Squire that the unnatural life Owen
was leading was in every way injurious. Unwillingly
was the father wrought to part from his son; but he
did at length send him to the Grammar School at
Bangor, then under the management of an excellent
classic. Here Owen showed that he had more talents
than the rector had given him credit for, when he
affirmed that the lad had been completely stupefied
by the life he led at Bodowen. He bade fair to do
credit to the school in the peculiar branch of learning

for which it was famous.  But he was not popular
among his schoolfellows.  He was wayward, though,
to a certain degree, generous and unselfish ;  he was
reserved but gentle, except when the tremendous bursts
of passion (similar in character to those of his father)
forced their way.

On his return from school one Christmas-time, when
he had been a year or so at Bangor, he was stunned
by hearing that the undervalued Augharad was about
to be married to a gentleman of South Wales, residing
near Aberystwith.   Boys seldom appreciate their
sisters ;  but Owen thought of the many slights with
which he had requited the patient Augharad, and he
gave way to bitter regrets, which, with a selfish want
of control over his words, he kept expressing to his
father, until the Squire was thoroughly hurt and
chagrined at the repeated exclamations of ' What shall
we do when Augharad is gone ? '  ' How dull we shall
be when Augharad is married ! '  Owen's holidays were
prolonged a few weeks, in order that he might be
present at the wedding ;  and when all the festivities
were over, and the bride and bridegroom had left
Bodowen, the boy and his father really felt how much
they missed the quiet, loving Augharad.  She had
performed so many thoughtful, noiseless little offices,
on which their daily comfort depended ;  and now she
was gone, the household seemed to miss the spirit that
peacefully kept it in order ;  the servants roamed about
in search of commands and directions, the rooms had
no longer the unobtrusive ordering of taste to make
them cheerful, the very fires burned dim, and were
always sinking down into dull heaps of grey ashes.
Altogether Owen did not regret his return to Bangor,
and this also the mortified parent perceived.  Squire
Griffiths was a selfish parent.

Letters in those days were a rare occurrence.  Owen
usually received one during his half-yearly absences
from home, and occasionally his father paid him a visit.
This half-year the boy had no visit, nor even a letter,
till very near the time of his leaving school, and then

he was astounded by the intelligence that his father
was married again.

Then came one of his paroxysms of rage; the more
disastrous in its effects upon his character because it
could find no vent in action. Independently of
slight to the memory of the first wife, which children
are so apt to fancy such an action implies, Owen had
hitherto considered himself (and with justice) the first
object of his father's life. They had been so much to
each other; and now a shapeless, but too real something had come between him and his father there for
ever. He felt as if his permission should have been
asked, as if he should have been consulted. Certainly
he ought to have been told of the intended event.
So the Squire felt, and hence his constrained letter,
which had so much increased the bitterness of Owen's
feelings.

With all this anger, when Owen saw his stepmother,
he thought he had never seen so beautiful a woman
for her age; for she was no longer in the bloom of
youth, being a widow when his father married her.
Her manners, to the Welsh lad, who had seen little of
female grace among the families of the few antiquarians
with whom his father visited, were so fascinating that
he watched her with a sort of breathless admiration.
Her measured grace, her faultless movements, her tones
of voice, sweet, till the ear was sated with their sweet-
ness, made Owen less angry at his father's marriage.
Yet he felt, more than ever, that the cloud was between
him and his father; that the hasty letter he had sent
in answer to the announcement of his wedding was
not forgotten, although no allusion was ever made to
it. He was no longer his father's confidant—hardly
ever his father's companion, for the newly-married wife
was all in all to the Squire, and his son felt himself
almost a cipher, where he had so long been everything.
The lady herself had ever the softest consideration for
her stepson; almost too obtrusive was the attention
paid to his wishes, but still he fancied that the heart
had no part in the winning advances. There was

a watchful glance of the eye that Owen once or twice caught when she had imagined herself unobserved, and many other nameless little circumstances, that gave him a strong feeling of want of sincerity in his stepmother. Mrs. Owen brought with her into the family her little child by her first husband, a boy nearly three years old. He was one of those elfish, observant, mocking children, over whose feelings you seem to have no control: agile and mischievous, his little practical jokes, at first performed in ignorance of the pain he gave, but afterward proceeding to a malicious pleasure in suffering, really seemed to afford some ground to the superstitious notion of some of the common people that he was a fairy changeling.

Years passed on ; and as Owen grew older he became more observant. He saw, even in his occasional visits at home (for from school he had passed on to college), that a great change had taken place in the outward manifestations of his father's character ; and, by degrees, Owen traced this change to the influence of his stepmother ; so slight, so imperceptible to the common observer, yet so resistless in its effects. Squire Griffiths caught up his wife's humbly advanced opinions, and, unawares to himself, adopted them as his own, defying all argument and opposition. It was the same with her wishes ; they met with their fulfilment, from the extreme and delicate art with which she insinuated them into her husband's mind, as his own. She sacrificed the show of authority for the power. At last, when Owen perceived some oppressive act in his father's conduct toward his dependants, or some unaccountable thwarting of his own wishes, he fancied he saw his stepmother's secret influence thus displayed, however much she might regret the injustice of his father's actions in her conversations with him when they were alone. His father was fast losing his temperate habits, and frequent intoxication soon took its usual effect upon the temper. Yet even here was the spell of his wife upon him. Before her he placed a restraint upon his passion, yet she was perfectly aware of his irritable disposition, and directed it hither and thither with the same apparent ignorance of the tendency of her words.

Meanwhile Owen's situation became peculiarly mortifying to a youth whose early remembrances afforded such a contrast to his present state. As a child, he had been elevated to the consequence of a man before his years gave any mental check to the selfishness which such conduct was likely to engender; he could remember when his will was law to the servants and dependants, and his sympathy necessary to his father: now he was as a cipher in his father's house; and the Squire, estranged in the first instance by a feeling of the injury he had done his son in not sooner acquainting him with his purposed marriage, seemed rather to avoid than to seek him as a companion, and too frequently showed the most utter indifference to the feelings and wishes which a young man of a high and independent spirit might be supposed to indulge.

Perhaps Owen was not fully aware of the force of all these circumstances; for an actor in a family drama is seldom unimpassioned enough to be perfectly observant. But he became moody and soured; brooding over his unloved existence, and craving with a human heart after sympathy.

This feeling took more full possession of his mind when he had left college, and returned home to lead an idle and purposeless life. As the heir, there was no worldly necessity for exertion: his father was too much of a Welsh squire to dream of the moral necessity, and he himself had not sufficient strength of mind to decide at once upon abandoning a place and mode of life which abounded in daily mortifications; yet to this course his judgement was slowly tending, when some circumstances occurred to detain him at Bodowen.

It was not to be expected that harmony would long be preserved, even in appearance, between an unguarded and soured young man, such as Owen, and his wary stepmother, when he had once left college, and come, not as a visitor, but as the heir to his father's

house. Some cause of difference occurred, where the
woman subdued her hidden anger sufficiently to become
convinced that Owen was not entirely the dupe she
had believed him to be. Henceforward there was no
peace between them. Not in vulgar altercations did
this show itself ; but in moody reserve on Owen's part,
and in undisguised and contemptuous pursuance of her
own plans by his stepmother. Bodowen was no longer
a place where, if Owen was not loved or attended to,
he could at least find peace, and care for himself : he
was thwarted at every step, and in every wish, by his
father's desire apparently, while the wife sat by with
a smile of triumph on her beautiful lips.

So Owen went forth at the early day dawn, sometimes roaming about on the shore or the upland,
shooting or fishing, as the season might be, but oftener
' stretched in indolent repose '*on the short, sweet grass,
indulging in gloomy and morbid reveries. He would
fancy that this mortified state of existence was a dream,
a horrible dream, from which he should awake and find
himself again the sole object and darling of his father.
And then he would start up and strive to shake off the
incubus. There was the molten sunset of his childish
memory ; the gorgeous crimson piles of glory in the
west, fading away into the cold, calm light of the rising
moon, while here and there a cloud floated across the
western heaven, like a seraph's wing, in its flaming
beauty ; the earth was the same as in his childhood's
days, full of gentle evening sounds, and the harmonies
of twilight—the breeze came sweeping low over the
heather and blue-bells by his side, and the turf was
sending up its evening incense of perfume. But life,
and heart, and hope were changed for ever since those
bygone days !

Or he would seat himself in a favourite niche of the
rocks on Moel Gêst, hidden by a stunted growth of
the whitty, or mountain-ash, from general observation
with a rich-tinted cushion of stone-crop for his feet, and
a straight precipice of rock rising just above. Here
would he sit for hours, gazing idly at the bay below

with its background of purple hills, and the little fishing-sail on its bosom, showing white in the sunbeam, and gliding on in such harmony with the quiet beauty of the glassy sea ; or he would pull out an old school-volume, his companion for years, and in morbid accordance with the dark legend that still lurked in the recesses of his mind—a shape of gloom in those innermost haunts awaiting its time to come forth in distinct outline—would he turn to the old Greek dramas which treat of a family foredoomed by an avenging Fate. The worn page opened of itself at the play of the Œdipus Tyrannus,* and Owen dwelt with the craving of disease upon the prophecy so nearly resembling that which concerned himself. With his consciousness of neglect, there was a sort of self-flattery in the consequence which the legend gave him. He almost wondered how they durst, with slights and insults, thus provoke the Avenger.

The days drifted onward. Often he would vehemently pursue some sylvan sport, till thought and feeling were lost in the violence of bodily exertion. Occasionally his evenings were spent at a small public-house, such as stood by the unfrequented wayside, where the welcome, hearty though bought, seemed so strongly to contrast with the gloomy negligence of home—unsympathizing home.

One evening (Owen might be four or five-and-twenty), wearied with a day's shooting on the Clenneny Moors, he passed by the open door of ' The Goat ' at Penmorfa. The light and the cheeriness within tempted him, poor self-exhausted man ! as it has done many a one more wretched in worldly circumstances, to step in, and take his evening meal where at least his presence was of some consequence. It was a busy day in that little hostel. A flock of sheep, amounting to some hundreds, had arrived at Penmorfa, on their road to England, and thronged the space before the house. Inside was the shrewd, kind-hearted hostess, bustling to and fro, with merry greetings for every tired drover who was to pass the night in her house, while the sheep were penned in

a field close by. Ever and anon, she kept attending
to the second crowd of guests, who were celebrating
a rural wedding in her house. It was busy work to
Martha Thomas, yet her smile never flagged ; and when
Owen Griffiths had finished his evening meal she was
there, ready with a hope that it had done him good,
and was to his mind, and a word of intelligence that
the wedding-folk were about to dance in the kitchen,
and the harper was the famous Edward of Corwen.

Owen, partly from good-natured compliance with
his hostess's implied wish, and partly from curiosity,
lounged to the passage which led to the kitchen—not
the every-day, working, cooking kitchen which was
beyond, but a good-sized room where the mistress sat
when her work was done, and where the country people
were commonly entertained at such merry-makings as
the present. The lintels of the door formed a frame
for the animated picture which Owen saw within, as
he leaned against the wall in the dark passage. The
red light of the fire, with every now and then a falling
piece of turf sending forth a fresh blaze, shone full
upon four young men who were dancing a measure
something like a Scotch reel, keeping admirable time
in their rapid movements to the capital tune the harper
was playing. They had their hats on when Owen first
took his stand, but as they grew more and more
animated they flung them away, and presently their
shoes were kicked off with like disregard to the spot
where they might happen to alight. Shouts of applause
followed any remarkable exertion of agility, in which
each seemed to try to excel his companions. At length,
wearied and exhausted, they sat down, and the harper
gradually changed to one of those wild, inspiring
national airs for which he was so famous. The thronged
audience sat earnest and breathless, and you might
have heard a pin drop, except when some maiden
passed hurriedly, with flaring candle and busy look,
through to the real kitchen beyond. When he had
finished playing his beautiful theme on ' The march of
the men of Harlech,' he changed the measure again to

'Tri chant o' bunnan' (Three hundred pounds), and immediately a most unmusical-looking man began chanting 'Pennillion,' or a sort of recitative stanzas, which were soon taken up by another, and this amusement lasted so long that Owen grew weary, and was thinking of retreating from his post by the door, when some little bustle was occasioned, on the opposite side of the room, by the entrance of a middle-aged man, and a young girl, apparently his daughter. The man advanced to the bench occupied by the seniors of the party, who welcomed him with the usual pretty Welsh greeting, 'Pa sut mae dy galon?' ('How is thy heart?') and drinking his health, passed on to him the cup of excellent *cwrw*.* The girl, evidently a village belle, was as warmly greeted by the young men, while the girls eyed her rather askance with a half-jealous look, which Owen set down to the score of her extreme prettiness. Like most Welsh women, she was of middle size as to height, but beautifully made, with the most perfect yet delicate roundness in every limb. Her little mob-cap was carefully adjusted to a face which was excessively pretty, though it never could be called handsome. It also was round, with the slightest tendency to the oval shape, richly coloured, though somewhat olive in complexion, with dimples in cheek and chin, and the most scarlet lips Owen had ever seen, that were too short to meet over the small pearly teeth. The nose was the most defective feature ; but the eyes were splendid. They were so long, so lustrous, yet at times so very soft under their thick fringe of eyelash ! The nut-brown hair was carefully braided beneath the border of delicate lace : it was evident the little village beauty knew how to make the most of all her attractions, for the gay colours which were displayed in her neckerchief were in complete harmony with the complexion.

Owen was much attracted, while yet he was amused, by the evident coquetry the girl displayed, collecting around her a whole bevy of young fellows, for each of whom she seemed to have some gay speech, some

attractive look or action. In a few minutes, young
Griffiths of Bodowen was at her side, brought thither
by a variety of idle motives, and as her undivided
attention was given to the Welsh heir, her admirers,
one by one, dropped off, to seat themselves by some
less fascinating but more attentive fair one. The more
Owen conversed with the girl, the more he was taken ;
she had more wit and talent than he had fancied
possible ; a self-abandon and thoughtfulness, to boot,
that seemed full of charms ; and then her voice was
so clear and sweet, and her actions so full of grace,
that Owen was fascinated before he was well aware,
and kept looking into her bright, blushing face, till her
uplifted flashing eye fell beneath his earnest gaze.

While it thus happened that they were silent—she
from confusion at the unexpected warmth of his admiration, he from an unconsciousness of anything but the
beautiful changes in her flexile countenance—the man
whom Owen took for her father came up and addressed
some observation to his daughter, from whence he
glided into some commonplace though respectful remark
to Owen, and at length engaging him in some slight
local conversation, he led the way to the account
of a spot on the peninsula of Penthryn, where teal
abounded, and concluded with begging Owen to allow
him to show him the exact place, saying that whenever the young Squire felt so inclined, if he would
honour him by a call at his house, he would take him
across in his boat. While Owen listened, his attention
was not so much absorbed as to be unaware that the
little beauty at his side was refusing one or two who
endeavoured to draw her from her place by invitations
to dance. Flattered by his own construction of her
refusals, he again directed all his attention to her, till
she was called away by her father, who was leaving
the scene of festivity. Before he left he reminded
Owen of his promise, and added,

'Perhaps, Sir, you do not know me. My name is
Ellis Pritchard, and I live at Ty Glas, on this side of
Moel Gêst ; any one can point it out to you.'

When the father and daughter had left, Owen slowly prepared for his ride home ; but, encountering the hostess, he could not resist asking a few questions relative to Ellis Pritchard and his pretty daughter. She answered shortly but respectfully, and then said rather hesitatingly—

'Master Griffiths, you know the triad, "Tri pheth tebyg y naill i'r llall, ysgnbwr heb yd, mail deg heb ddiawd, a merch deg heb ei geirda" (Three things are alike : a fine barn without corn, a fine cup without drink, a fine woman without her reputation).' She hastily quitted him, and Owen rode slowly to his unhappy home.

Ellis Pritchard, half farmer and half fisherman, was shrewd, and keen, and worldly ; yet he was good-natured, and sufficiently generous to have become rather a popular man among his equals. He had been struck with the young Squire's attention to his pretty daughter, and was not insensible to the advantages to be derived from it. Nest would not be the first peasant girl, by any means, who had been transplanted to a Welsh manor-house as its mistress ; and, accordingly, her father had shrewdly given the admiring young man some pretext for further opportunities of seeing her.

As for Nest herself, she had somewhat of her father's worldliness, and was fully alive to the superior station of her new admirer, and quite prepared to slight all her old sweethearts on his account. But then she had something more of feeling in her reckoning ; she had not been insensible to the earnest yet comparatively refined homage which Owen paid her ; she had noticed his expressive and occasionally handsome countenance with admiration, and was flattered by his so imme-diately singling her out from her companions. As to the hint which Martha Thomas had thrown out, it is enough to say that Nest was very giddy, and that she was motherless. She had high spirits and a great love of admiration, or, to use a softer term, she loved to please ; men, women, and children, all, she delighted to gladden with her smile and voice. She coquetted,

and flirted, and went to the extreme lengths of Welsh
courtship, till the seniors of the village shook their
heads, and cautioned their daughters against her
acquaintance. If not absolutely guilty, she had too
frequently been on the verge of guilt.

Even at the time, Martha Thomas's hint made but
little impression on Owen, for his senses were otherwise
occupied ; but in a few days the recollection thereof
had wholly died away, and one warm glorious summer's
day, he bent his steps toward Ellis Pritchard's with
a beating heart ; for, except some very slight flirta-
tions at Oxford, Owen had never been touched ; his
thoughts, his fancy, had been otherwise engaged.

Ty Glas was built against one of the lower rocks of
Moel Gêst, which, indeed, formed a side to the low
lengthy house. The materials of the cottage were the
shingly stones which had fallen from above, plastered
rudely together, with deep recesses for the small oblong
windows. Altogether, the exterior was much ruder
than Owen had expected ; but inside there seemed no
lack of comforts. The house was divided into two
apartments, one large, roomy, and dark, into which
Owen entered immediately ; and before the blushing
Nest came from the inner chamber (for she had seen
the young Squire coming, and hastily gone to make
some alteration in her dress), he had had time to look
around him, and note the various little particulars of
the room. Beneath the window (which commanded
a magnificent view) was an oaken dresser, replete with
drawers and cupboards, and brightly polished to a rich
dark colour. In the farther part of the room, Owen
could at first distinguish little, entering as he did from
the glaring sunlight, but he soon saw that there were
two oaken beds, closed up after the manner of the
Welsh : in fact, the dormitories of Ellis Pritchard and
the man who served under him, both on sea and on
land. There was the large wheel used for spinning
wool, left standing on the middle of the floor, as if
in use only a few minutes before ; and around the
ample chimney hung flitches of bacon, dried kids'-flesh,

and fish, that was in process of smoking for winter's store.

Before Nest had shyly dared to enter, her father, who had been mending his nets down below, and seen Owen winding up to the house, came in and gave him a hearty yet respectful welcome ; and then Nest, downcast and blushing, full of the consciousness which her father's advice and conversation had not failed to inspire, ventured to join them. To Owen's mind this reserve and shyness gave her new charms.

It was too bright, too hot, too anything, to think of going to shoot teal till later in the day, and Owen was delighted to accept a hesitating invitation to share the noonday meal. Some ewe-milk cheese, very hard and dry, oat-cake, slips of the dried kids'-flesh broiled, after having been previously soaked in water for a few minutes, delicious butter and fresh buttermilk, with a liquor called ' diod griafol ' (made from the berries of the *Sorbus aucuparia*,* infused in water and then fermented), composed the frugal repast; but there was something so clean and neat, and withal such a true welcome, that Owen had seldom enjoyed a meal so much. Indeed, at that time of day the Welsh squires differed from the farmers more in the plenty and rough abundance of their manner of living than in the refinement of style of their table.

At the present day, down in Llyn, the Welsh gentry are not a whit behind their Saxon equals in the expensive elegances of life ; but then (when there was but one pewter-service in all Northumberland) there was nothing in Ellis Pritchard's mode of living that grated on the young Squire's sense of refinement.

Little was said by that young pair of wooers during the meal : the father had all the conversation to himself, apparently heedless of the ardent looks and inattentive mien of his guest. As Owen became more serious in his feelings, he grew more timid in their expression, and at night, when they returned from their shooting-excursion, the caress he gave Nest was almost as bashfully offered as received.

This was but the first of a series of days devoted to Nest in reality, though at first he thought some little disguise of his object was necessary. The past, the future, was all forgotten in those happy days of love.

And every worldly plan, every womanly wile was put in practice by Ellis Pritchard and his daughter, to render his visits agreeable and alluring. Indeed, the very circumstance of his being welcome was enough to attract the poor young man, to whom the feeling so produced was new and full of charms. He left a home where the certainty of being thwarted made him chary in expressing his wishes; where no tones of love ever fell on his ear, save those addressed to others; where his presence or absence was a matter of utter indifference; and when he entered Ty Glas, all, down to the little cur which, with clamorous barkings, claimed a part of his attention, seemed to rejoice. His account of his day's employment found a willing listener in Ellis; and when he passed on to Nest, busy at her wheel or at her churn, the deepened colour, the conscious eye, and the gradual yielding of herself up to his lover-like caress, had worlds of charms. Ellis Pritchard was a tenant on the Bodowen estate, and therefore had reasons in plenty for wishing to keep the young Squire's visits secret; and Owen, unwilling to disturb the sunny calm of these halcyon days by any storm at home, was ready to use all the artifice which Ellis suggested as to the mode of his calls at Ty Glas. Nor was he unaware of the probable, nay, the hoped-for termination of these repeated days of happiness. He was quite conscious that the father wished for nothing better than the marriage of his daughter to the heir of Bodowen; and when Nest had hidden her face in his neck, which was encircled by her clasping arms, and murmured into his ear her acknowledgement of love, he felt only too desirous of finding some one to love him for ever. Though not highly principled, he would not have tried to obtain Nest on other terms save those of marriage: he did so pine after enduring love, and fancied he should have bound her heart for evermore to his, when they had taken the solemn oaths of matrimony.

There was no great difficulty attending a secret marriage at such a place and at such a time. One gusty autumn day, Ellis ferried them round Penthryn to Llandutrwyn, and there saw his little Nest become future Lady of Bodowen.

How often do we see giddy, coquetting, restless girls become sobered by marriage ? A great object in life is decided ; one on which their thoughts have been running in all their vagaries, and they seem to verify the beautiful fable of Undine.* A new soul beams out in the gentleness and repose of their future lives. An indescribable softness and tenderness takes place of the wearying vanity of their former endeavours to attract admiration. Something of this sort took place in Nest Pritchard. If at first she had been anxious to attract the young Squire of Bodowen, long before her marriage this feeling had merged into a truer love than she had ever felt before ; and now that he was her own, her husband, her whole soul was bent toward making him amends, as far as in her lay, for the misery which, with a woman's tact, she saw that he had to endure at his home. Her greetings were abounding in delicately-expressed love ; her study of his tastes unwearying, in the arrangement of her dress, her time, her very thoughts.

No wonder that he looked back on his wedding-day with a thankfulness which is seldom the result of unequal marriages. No wonder that his heart beat aloud as formerly when he wound up the little path to Ty Glas, and saw—keen though the winter's wind might be—that Nest was standing out at the door to watch for his dimly-seen approach, while the candle flared in the little window as a beacon to guide him aright.

The angry words and unkind actions of home fell deadened on his heart ; he thought of the love that was surely his, and of the new promise of love that a short time would bring forth, and he could almost have smiled at the impotent efforts to disturb his peace.

A few more months, and the young father was greeted by a feeble little cry, when he hastily entered Ty Glas, one morning early, in consequence of a summons conveyed mysteriously to Bodowen; and the pale mother, smiling, and feebly holding up her babe to its father's kiss, seemed to him even more lovely than the bright gay Nest who had won his heart at the little inn of Penmorfa.

But the curse was at work! The fulfilment of the prophecy was nigh at hand!

## CHAPTER II

IT was the autumn after the birth of their boy: it had been a glorious summer, with bright, hot, sunny weather; and now the year was fading away as seasonably into mellow days, with mornings of silver mists and clear frosty nights. The blooming look of the time of flowers was past and gone; but instead there were even richer tints abroad in the sun-coloured leaves, the lichens, the golden-blossomed furze: if it was the time of fading, there was a glory in the decay.

Nest, in her loving anxiety to surround her dwelling with every charm for her husband's sake, had turned gardener, and the little corners of the rude court before the house were filled with many a delicate mountain-flower, transplanted more for its beauty than its rarity. The sweetbrier bush may even yet be seen, old and grey, which she and Owen planted a green slipling beneath the window of her little chamber. In those moments Owen forgot all besides the present; all the cares and griefs he had known in the past, and all that might await him of woe and death in the future. The boy, too, was as lovely a child as the fondest parent was ever blessed with; and crowed with delight, and clapped his little hands, as his mother held him in her

arms at the cottage-door to watch his father's ascent
up the rough path that led to Ty Glas, one bright
autumnal morning; and when the three entered the
house together, it was difficult to say which was the
happiest. Owen carried his boy, and tossed and played
with him, while Nest sought out some little article of
work, and seated herself on the dresser beneath the
window, where, now busily plying the needle, and then
again looking at her husband, she eagerly told him the
little pieces of domestic intelligence, the winning ways
of the child, the result of yesterday's fishing, and such
of the gossip of Penmorfa as came to the ears of the
now retired Nest. She noticed that, when she mentioned any little circumstance which bore the slightest
reference to Bodowen, her husband appeared chafed
and uneasy, and at last avoided anything that might
in the least remind him of home. In truth, he had
been suffering much of late from the irritability of his
father, shown in trifles to be sure, but not the less
galling on that account.

While they were thus talking, and caressing each
other and the child, a shadow darkened the room, and
before they could catch a glimpse of the object that
had occasioned it, it vanished, and Squire Griffiths
lifted the door-latch and stood before them. He stood
and looked—first on his son, so different (in his buoyant
expression of content and enjoyment, with his noble
child in his arms, like a proud and happy father, as
he was) from the depressed, moody young man he
too often appeared at Bodowen; then on Nest—poor,
trembling, sickened Nest!—who dropped her work,
but yet durst not stir from her seat on the dresser,
while she looked to her husband as if for protection
from his father.

The Squire was silent, as he glared from one to
the other, his features white with restrained passion.
When he spoke, his words came most distinct in their
forced composure. It was to his son he addressed
himself:

'That woman! who is she?'

Owen hesitated one moment, and then replied, in a steady, yet quiet voice :

'Father, that woman is my wife.'

He would have added some apology for the long concealment of his marriage ; have appealed to his father's forgiveness ; but the foam flew from Squire Owen's lips as he burst forth with invective against Nest :—

'You have married her ! It is as they told me ! Married Nest Pritchard yr buten !* And you stand there as if you had not disgraced yourself for ever and ever with your accursed wiving ! And the fair harlot sits there, in her mocking modesty, practising the mimming airs that will become her state as future Lady of Bodowen. But I will move heaven and earth before that false woman darken the doors of my father's house as mistress ! '

All this was said with such rapidity that Owen had no time for the words that thronged to his lips. 'Father ! ' (he burst forth at length) 'Father, who-soever told you that Nest Pritchard was a harlot told you a lie as false as hell ! Ay ! a lie as false as hell ! ' he added, in a voice of thunder, while he advanced a step or two nearer to the Squire. And then, in a lower tone, he said :

'She is as pure as your own wife ; nay, God help me ! as the dear, precious mother who brought me forth, and then left me—with no refuge in a mother's heart—to struggle on through life alone. I tell you Nest is as pure as that dear, dead mother ! '

'Fool—poor fool ! '*

At this moment the child—the little Owen—who had kept gazing from one angry countenance to the other, and with earnest look, trying to understand what had brought the fierce glare into the face where till now he had read nothing but love, in some way attracted the Squire's attention, and increased his wrath.

'Yes ! ' he continued, 'poor, weak fool that you are, hugging the child of another as if it were your own offspring ! ' Owen involuntarily caressed the affrighted child, and half smiled at the implication of his father's words. This the Squire perceived, and raising his voice to a scream of rage, he went on :

' I bid you, if you call yourself my son, to cast away that miserable, shameless woman's offspring ; cast it away this instant—this instant ! '

In his ungovernable rage, seeing that Owen was far from complying with his command, he snatched the poor infant from the loving arms that held it, and throwing it to its mother, left the house inarticulate with fury.

Nest—who had been pale and still as marble during this terrible dialogue, looking on and listening as if fascinated by the words that smote her heart—opened her arms to receive and cherish her precious babe ; but the boy was not destined to reach the white refuge of her breast. The furious action of the Squire had been almost without aim, and the infant fell against the sharp edge of the dresser down on to the stone floor.

Owen sprang up to take the child, but he lay so still, so motionless, that the awe of death came over the father, and he stooped down to gaze more closely. At that moment, the upturned, filmy eyes rolled convulsively—a spasm passed along the body—and the lips, yet warm with kissing, quivered into everlasting rest.

A word from her husband told Nest all. She slid down from her seat, and lay by her little son as corpse-like as he, unheeding all the agonizing endearments and passionate adjurations of her husband. And that poor, desolate husband and father ! Scarce one little quarter of an hour, and he had been so blessed in his consciousness of love ! the bright promise of many years on his infant's face, and the new, fresh soul beaming forth in its awakened intelligence. And there it was ; the little clay image, that would never more gladden up at the sight of him, nor stretch forth to meet his embrace ; whose inarticulate, yet most eloquent cooings might haunt him in his dreams, but

would never more be heard in waking life again ! And
by the dead babe, almost as utterly insensate, the poor
mother had fallen in a merciful faint—the slandered,
heart-pierced Nest ! Owen struggled against the sick-
ness that came over him, and busied himself in vain
attempts at her restoration.

It was now near noon-day, and Ellis Pritchard came
home, little dreaming of the sight that awaited him ;
but, though stunned, he was able to take more effectual
measures for his poor daughter's recovery than Owen
had done.

By-and-by she showed symptoms of returning sense,
and was placed in her own little bed in a darkened
room, where, without ever waking to complete consciousness, she fell asleep. Then it was that her
husband, suffocated by pressure of miserable thought,
gently drew his hand from her tightened clasp, and
printing one long soft kiss on her white waxen forehead, hastily stole out of the room, and out of the
house.

Near the base of Moel Gêst—it might be a quarter
of a mile from Ty Glas—was a little neglected solitary
copse, wild and tangled with the trailing branches of
the dog-rose and the tendrils of the white bryony.
Toward the middle of this thicket lay a deep crystal
pool—a clear mirror for the blue heavens above—and
round the margin floated the broad green leaves of the
water-lily, and when the regal sun shone down in his
noonday glory the flowers arose from their cool depths
to welcome and greet him. The copse was musical
with many sounds ; the warbling of birds rejoicing in
its shades, the ceaseless hum of the insects that hovered
over the pool, the chime of the distant waterfall, the
occasional bleating of the sheep from the mountain-
top, were all blended into the delicious harmony of
nature.

It had been one of Owen's favourite resorts when
he had been a lonely wanderer—a pilgrim in search of
love in the years gone by. And thither he went, as
if by instinct, when he left Ty Glas ; quelling the

uprising agony till he should reach that little solitary
spot.

It was the time of day when a change in the aspect
of the weather so frequently takes place ; and the little
pool was no longer the reflection of a blue and sunny
sky : it sent back the dark and slaty clouds above,
and, every now and then, a rough gust shook the
painted autumn leaves from their branches, and all
other music was lost in the sound of the wild winds
piping down from the moorlands, which lay up and
beyond the clefts in the mountain-side.  Presently the
rain came on and beat down in torrents.

But Owen heeded it not.  He sat on the dank ground,
his face buried in his hands, and his whole strength,
physical and mental, employed in quelling the rush of
blood, which rose and boiled and gurgled in his brain
as if it would madden him.

The phantom of his dead child rose ever before him,
and seemed to cry aloud for vengeance.  And when
the poor young man thought upon the victim whom he
required in his wild longing for revenge, he shuddered,
for it was his father !

Again and again he tried not to think ; but still
the circle of thought came round, eddying through his
brain.  At length he mastered his passions, and they
were calm ; then he forced himself to arrange some
plan for the future.

He had not, in the passionate hurry of the moment,
seen that his father had left the cottage before he was
aware of the fatal accident that befell the child.  Owen
thought he had seen all ; and once he planned to go to
the Squire and tell him of the anguish of heart he had
wrought, and awe him, as it were, by the dignity of
grief.  But then again he durst not—he distrusted his
self-control—the old prophecy rose up in its horror—
he dreaded his doom.

At last he determined to leave his father for ever ;
to take Nest to some distant country where she might
forget her first-born, and where he himself might gain
a livelihood by his own exertions.

But when he tried to descend to the various little
arrangements which were involved in the execution of
this plan, he remembered that all his money (and in
this respect Squire Griffiths was no niggard) was locked
up in his escritoire at Bodowen. In vain he tried to
do away with this matter-of-fact difficulty; go to
Bodowen he must: and his only hope—nay his determination—was to avoid his father.

He rose and took a by-path to Bodowen. The house
looked even more gloomy and desolate than usual in
the heavy down-pouring rain, yet Owen gazed on it
with something of regret—for sorrowful as his days in
it had been, he was about to leave it for many, many
years, if not for ever. He entered by a side-door,
opening into a passage that led to his own room, where
he kept his books, his guns, his fishing-tackle, his
writing-materials, et cetera.

Here he hurriedly began to select the few articles
he intended to take; for, besides the dread of inter-
ruption, he was feverishly anxious to travel far that
very night, if only Nest was capable of performing the
journey. As he was thus employed, he tried to conjecture what his father's feelings would be on finding
that his once-loved son was gone away for ever. Would
he then awaken to regret for the conduct which had
driven him from home, and bitterly think on the loving
and caressing boy who haunted his footsteps in former
days? Or, alas! would he only feel that an obstacle
to his daily happiness—to his contentment with his
wife, and his strange, doting affection for the child—
was taken away? Would they make merry over the
heir's departure? Then he thought of Nest—the young
childless mother, whose heart had not yet realized her
fullness of desolation. Poor Nest! so loving as she
was, so devoted to her child—how should he console
her? He pictured her away in a strange land, pining
for her native mountains, and refusing to be comforted
because her child was not.

Even this thought of the home-sickness that might
possibly beset Nest hardly made him hesitate in his

determination ; so strongly had the idea taken possession of him that only by putting miles and leagues
between him and his father could he avert the doom
which seemed blending itself with the very purposes
of his life as long as he stayed in proximity with the
slayer of his child.

He had now nearly completed his hasty work of
preparation, and was full of tender thoughts of his
wife, when the door opened, and the elfish Robert
peered in, in search of some of his brother's possessions.
On seeing Owen he hesitated, but then came boldly
forward, and laid his hand on Owen's arm, saying,
' Nesta yr buten !  How is Nest yr buten ? '
He looked maliciously into Owen's face to mark the
effect of his words, but was terrified at the expression
he read there.  He started off and ran to the door,
while Owen tried to check himself, saying continually,
' He is but a child.  He does not understand the
meaning of what he says.  He is but a child ! '  Still
Robert, now in fancied security, kept calling out his
insulting words, and Owen's hand was on his gun,
grasping it as if to restrain his rising fury.

But when Robert passed on daringly to mocking
words relating to the poor dead child, Owen could bear
it no longer ;  and before the boy was well aware, Owen
was fiercely holding him in an iron clasp with one hand,
while he struck him hard with the other.

In a minute he checked himself.  He paused, relaxed
his grasp, and, to his horror, he saw Robert sink to
the ground ;  in fact, the lad was half-stunned, half-
frightened, and thought it best to assume insensibility.

Owen—miserable Owen—seeing him lie there prostrate, was bitterly repentant, and would have dragged
him to the carved settle, and done all he could to
restore him to his senses, but at this instant the Squire
came in.

Probably, when the household at Bodowen rose that
morning, there was but one among them ignorant of
the heir's relation to Nest Pritchard and her child ;
for secret as he had tried to make his visits to Ty Glas,

they had been too frequent not to be noticed, and
Nest's altered conduct—no longer frequenting dances
and merry-makings—was a strongly corroborative circumstance. But Mrs. Griffiths' influence reigned para-
mount, if unacknowledged, at Bodowen, and till she
sanctioned the disclosure, none would dare to tell the
Squire.

Now, however, the time drew near when it suited
her to make her husband aware of the connexion his
son had formed; so, with many tears, and much
seeming reluctance, she broke the intelligence to him—
taking good care, at the same time, to inform him
of the light character Nest had borne. Nor did she
confine this evil reputation to her conduct before her
marriage, but insinuated that even to this day she was
a 'woman of the grove and brake'—for centuries
the Welsh term of opprobrium for the loosest female
characters.

Squire Griffiths easily tracked Owen to Ty Glas;
and without any aim but the gratification of his furious
anger, followed him to upbraid as we have seen. But
he left the cottage even more enraged against his son
than he had entered it, and returned home to hear the
evil suggestions of the stepmother. He had heard a
slight scuffle in which he caught the tones of Robert's
voice, as he passed along the hall, and an instant afterwards he saw the apparently lifeless body of his little
favourite dragged along by the culprit Owen—the
marks of strong passion yet visible on his face. Not
loud, but bitter and deep were the evil words which
the father bestowed on the son; and as Owen stood
proudly and sullenly silent, disdaining all exculpation
of himself in the presence of one who had wrought him
so much graver—so fatal an injury—Robert's mother
entered the room. At sight of her natural emotion
the wrath of the Squire was redoubled, and his wild
suspicions that this violence of Owen's to Robert was
a premeditated act appeared like the proven truth
through the mists of rage. He summoned domestics
as if to guard his own and his wife's life from the

attempts of his son; and the servants stood wondering around—now gazing at Mrs. Griffiths, alternately scolding and sobbing, while she tried to restore the lad from his really bruised and half-unconscious state; now at the fierce and angry Squire; and now at the sad and silent Owen. And he—he was hardly aware of their looks of wonder and terror; his father's words fell on a deadened ear; for before his eyes there rose a pale dead babe, and in that lady's violent sounds of grief he heard the wailing of a more sad, more hopeless mother. For by this time the lad Robert had opened his eyes, and though evidently suffering a good deal from the effects of Owen's blows, was fully conscious of all that was passing around him.

Had Owen been left to his own nature, his heart would have worked itself to doubly love the boy whom he had injured; but he was stubborn from injustice, and hardened by suffering. He refused to vindicate himself; he made no effort to resist the imprisonment the Squire had decreed, until a surgeon's opinion of the real extent of Robert's injuries was made known. It was not until the door was locked and barred, as if upon some wild and furious beast, that the recollection of poor Nest, without his comforting presence, came into his mind. Oh! thought he, how she would be wearying, pining for his tender sympathy; if, indeed, she had recovered the shock of mind sufficiently to be sensible of consolation! What would she think of his absence? Could she imagine he believed his father's words, and had left her, in this her sore trouble and bereavement? The thought maddened him, and he looked around for some mode of escape.

He had been confined in a small unfurnished room on the first floor, wainscoted, and carved all round, with a massy door, calculated to resist the attempts of a dozen strong men, even had he afterward been able to escape from the house unseen, unheard. The window was placed (as is common in old Welsh houses) over the fireplace; with branching chimneys on either hand, forming a sort of projection on the outside. By

this outlet his escape was easy, even had he been less
determined and desperate than he was. And when he
had descended, with a little care, a little winding, he
might elude all observation and pursue his original
intention of going to Ty Glas.

The storm had abated, and watery sunbeams were
gilding the bay, as Owen descended from the window,
and, stealing along in the broad afternoon shadows,
made his way to the little plateau of green turf in the
garden at the top of a steep precipitous rock, down the
abrupt face of which he had often dropped, by means
of a well-secured rope, into the small sailing-boat (his
father's present, alas! in days gone by) which lay
moored in the deep sea-water below. He had always
kept his boat there, because it was the nearest available spot to the house; but before he could reach the
place—unless, indeed, he crossed a broad sun-lighted
piece of ground in full view of the windows on that
side of the house, and without the shadow of a single
sheltering tree or shrub—he had to skirt round a rude
semicircle of underwood, which would have been considered as a shrubbery had any one taken pains with
it. Step by step he stealthily moved along—hearing
voices now, again seeing his father and stepmother in
no distant walk, the Squire evidently caressing and
consoling his wife, who seemed to be urging some point
with great vehemence, again forced to crouch down to
avoid being seen by the cook, returning from the rude
kitchen-garden with a handful of herbs. This was the
way the doomed heir of Bodowen left his ancestral
house for ever, and hoped to leave behind him his
doom. At length he reached the plateau—he breathed
more freely. He stooped to discover the hidden coil
of rope, kept safe and dry in a hole under a great
round flat piece of rock: his head was bent down;
he did not see his father approach, nor did he hear
his footstep for the rush of blood to his head in the
stooping effort of lifting the stone; the Squire had
grappled with him before he rose up again, before he
fully knew whose hands detained him, now, when his

liberty of person and action seemed secure.  He made
a vigorous struggle to free himself ; he wrestled with
his father for a moment—he pushed him hard, and
drove him on to the great displaced stone, all unsteady
in its balance.

Down went the Squire, down into the deep waters
below—down after him went Owen, half consciously,
half unconsciously, partly compelled by the sudden
cessation of any opposing body, partly from a vehement
irrepressible impulse to rescue his father.  But he had
instinctively chosen a safer place in the deep sea-water
pool than that into which his push had sent his father.
The Squire had hit his head with much violence against
the side of the boat, in his fall ; it is, indeed, doubtful
whether he was not killed before ever he sank into the
sea.  But Owen knew nothing save that the awful
doom seemed even now present.  He plunged down,
he dived below the water in search of the body, which
had none of the elasticity of life to buoy it up ; he
saw his father in those depths, he clutched at him,
he brought him up and cast him, a dead weight, into
the boat, and, exhausted by the effort, he had begun
himself to sink again before he instinctively strove to
rise and climb into the rocking boat.  There lay his
father, with a deep dent in the side of his head where
the skull had been fractured by his fall ; his face
blackened by the arrested course of the blood.  Owen
felt his pulse, his heart—all was still.  He called him
by his name.

'Father, father ! ' he cried, ' come back ! come back !
You never knew how I loved you ! how I could love
you still—if—Oh God ! '

And the thought of his little child rose before him.
' Yes, father,' he cried afresh, ' you never knew how
he fell—how he died !  Oh, if I had but had patience
to tell you !  If you would but have borne with me
and listened !  And now it is over !  Oh father !
father ! '

Whether she had heard this wild wailing voice, or
whether it was only that she missed her husband and

wanted him for some little every-day question, or, as was perhaps more likely, she had discovered Owen's escape, and come to inform her husband of it, I do not know, but on the rock, right above his head, as it seemed, Owen heard his stepmother calling her husband.

He was silent, and softly pushed the boat right under the rock till the sides grated against the stones, and the overhanging branches concealed him and it from all not on a level with the water. Wet as he was, he lay down by his dead father the better to conceal himself ; and, somehow, the action recalled those early days of childhood—the first in the Squire's widowhood —when Owen had shared his father's bed, and used to waken him in the morning to hear one of the old Welsh legends. How long he lay thus—body chilled, and brain hard-working through the heavy pressure of a reality as terrible as a nightmare—he never knew ; but at length he roused himself up to think of Nest.

Drawing out a great sail, he covered up the body of his father with it where he lay in the bottom of the boat. Then with his numbed hands he took the oars, and pulled out into the more open sea toward Criccaeth. He skirted along the coast till he found a shadowed cleft in the dark rocks ; to that point he rowed, and anchored his boat close in land. Then he mounted, staggering, half longing to fall into the dark waters and be at rest—half instinctively finding out the surest foot-rests on that precipitous face of rock, till he was high up, safe landed on the turfy summit. He ran off, as if pursued, toward Penmorfa ; he ran with maddened energy. Suddenly he paused, turned, ran again with the same speed, and threw himself prone on the summit, looking down into his boat with straining eyes to see if there had been any movement of life—any displacement of a fold of sail-cloth. It was all quiet deep down below, but as he gazed the shifting light gave the appearance of a slight movement. Owen ran to a lower part of the rock, stripped, plunged into the water, and swam to the boat. When there, all was still—awfully still! For a minute or two, he dared not lift up the cloth. Then reflecting that the same terror might beset him again—of leaving his father unaided while yet a spark of life lingered— he removed the shrouding cover. The eyes looked into his with a dead stare! He closed the lids and bound up the jaw. Again he looked. This time he raised himself out of the water and kissed the brow.

'It was my doom, father! It would have been better if I had died at my birth!'

Daylight was fading away. Precious daylight! He swam back, dressed, and set off afresh for Penmorfa. When he opened the door of Ty Glas, Ellis Pritchard looked at him reproachfully, from his seat in the darkly-shadowed chimney corner.

'You're come at last,' said he. 'One of our kind (*i.e.*, station) would not have left his wife to mourn by herself over her dead child; nor would one of our kind have let his father kill his own true son. I've a good mind to take her from you for ever.'

'I did not tell him,' cried Nest, looking piteously at her husband; 'he made me tell him part, and guessed the rest.'

She was nursing her babe on her knee as if it was alive. Owen stood before Ellis Pritchard.

'Be silent,' said he, quietly. 'Neither words nor deeds but what are decreed can come to pass. I was set to do my work, this hundred years and more. The time waited for me, and the man waited for me. I have done what was foretold of me for generations!'

Ellis Pritchard knew the old tale of the prophecy, and believed in it in a dull, dead kind of way, but somehow never thought it would come to pass in his time. Now, however, he understood it all in a moment, though he mistook Owen's nature so much as to believe that the deed was intentionally done, out of revenge for the death of his boy; and viewing it in this light, Ellis thought it little more than a just punishment for the cause of all the wild despairing sorrow he had seen his only child suffer during the hours of this long

afternoon.  But he knew the law would not so regard
it.  Even the lax Welsh law of those days could not
fail to examine into the death of a man of Squire
Griffiths' standing.  So the acute Ellis thought how
he could conceal the culprit for a time.

'Come,' said he;  'don't look so scared!  It was
your doom, not your fault;' and he laid a hand on
Owen's shoulder.

'You're wet,' said he, suddenly.  'Where have you
been?  Nest, your husband is dripping, drookit*wet.
That's what makes him look so blue and wan.'

Nest softly laid her baby in its cradle;  she was
half stupefied with crying, and had not understood to
what Owen alluded, when he spoke of his doom being
fulfilled, if indeed she had heard the words.

Her touch thawed Owen's miserable heart.

'Oh, Nest!' said he, clasping her in his arms;  'do
you love me still—can you love me, my own darling?'

'Why not?' asked she, her eyes filling with tears.
'I only love you more than ever, for you were my
poor baby's father!'

'But, Nest—  Oh, tell her, Ellis!  *you* know.'

'No need, no need!' said Ellis.  'She's had enough
to think on.  Bustle, my girl, and get out my Sunday
clothes.'

'I don't understand,' said Nest, putting her hand
up to her head.  'What is to tell?  and why are you
so wet?  God help me for a poor crazed thing, for
I cannot guess at the meaning of your words and your
strange looks!  I only know my baby is dead!' and
she burst into tears.

'Come, Nest!  go and fetch him a change, quick!'
and as she meekly obeyed, too languid to strive further
to understand, Ellis said rapidly to Owen, in a low
hurried voice,

'Are you meaning that the Squire is dead?  Speak
low, lest she hear!  Well, well, no need to talk about
how he died.  It was sudden, I see;  and we must all
of us die;  and he'll have to be buried.  It's well the
night is near.  And I should not wonder now if you'd

like to travel for a bit; it would do Nest a power of good; and then—there's many a one goes out of his own house and never comes back again; and—I trust he's not lying in his own house—and there's a stir for a bit, and a search, and a wonder—and, by-and-by, the heir just steps in, as quiet as can be. And that's what you'll do, and bring Nest to Bodowen after all. Nay, child, better stockings nor those; find the blue woollens I bought at Llanrwst fair. Only don't lose heart. It's done now and can't be helped. It was the piece of work set you to do from the days of the Tudors, they say. And he deserved it. Look in yon cradle. So tell us where he is, and I'll take heart of grace and see what can be done for him.'

But Owen sat wet and haggard, looking into the peat fire as if for visions of the past, and never heeding a word Ellis said. Nor did he move when Nest brought the armful of dry clothes.

'Come, rouse up, man!' said Ellis, growing impatient.

But he neither spoke nor moved.

'What is the matter, father?' asked Nest, bewildered.

Ellis kept on watching Owen for a minute or two, till, on his daughter's repetition of the question, he said, 'Ask him yourself, Nest.'

'Oh, husband, what is it?' said she, kneeling down and bringing her face to a level with his.

'Don't you know?' said he, heavily. 'You won't love me when you do know. And yet it was not my doing. It was my doom.'

'What does he mean, father?' asked Nest, looking up; but she caught a gesture from Ellis urging her to go on questioning her husband.

'I will love you, husband, whatever has happened. Only let me know the worst.'

A pause, during which Nest and Ellis hung breathless.

'My father is dead, Nest.'

Nest caught her breath with a sharp gasp.

'God forgive him!' said she, thinking on her babe.

'God forgive *me!*' said Owen.

'You did not—' Nest stopped.

'Yes, I did. Now you know it. It was my doom.
How could I help it? The devil helped me—he placed
the stone so that my father fell. I jumped into the
water to save him. I did, indeed, Nest. I was nearly
drowned myself.' But he was dead—dead—killed by
the fall!'

'Then he is safe at the bottom of the sea?' said
Ellis, with hungry eagerness.

'No, he is not; he lies in my boat,' said Owen,
shivering a little, more at the thought of his last
glimpse at his father's face than from cold.

'Oh, husband, change your wet clothes!' pleaded
Nest, to whom the death of the old man was simply
a horror with which she had nothing to do, while her
husband's discomfort was a present trouble.

While she helped him to take off the wet garments
which he would never have had energy enough to
remove of himself, Ellis was busy preparing food, and
mixing a great tumbler of spirits and hot water. He
stood over the unfortunate young man and compelled
him to eat and drink, and made Nest, too, taste some
mouthfuls—all the while planning in his own mind
how best to conceal what had been done, and who
had done it; not altogether without a certain feeling
of vulgar triumph in the reflection that Nest, as she
stood there, carelessly dressed, dishevelled in her grief,
was in reality the mistress of Bodowen, than which
Ellis Pritchard had never seen a grander house, though
he believed such might exist.

By dint of a few dexterous questions he found out all
he wanted to know from Owen, as he ate and drank.
In fact, it was almost a relief to Owen to dilute the
horror by talking about it. Before the meal was done,
if meal it could be called, Ellis knew all he cared to know.

'Now, Nest, on with your cloak and haps. Pack up
what needs to go with you, for both you and your husband must be half way to Liverpool by to-morrow's

morn. I'll take you past Rhyl Sands in my fishing-boat, with yours in tow; and, once over the dangerous part, I'll return with my cargo of fish, and learn how much stir there is at Bodowen. Once safe hidden in Liverpool, no one will know where you are, and you may stay quiet till your time comes for returning.'

'I will never come home again,' said Owen, doggedly. 'The place is accursed!'

'Hoot! be guided by me, man. Why, it was but an accident, after all! And we'll land at the Holy Island, at the Point of Llyn; there is an old cousin of mine, the parson, there—for the Pritchards have known better days, Squire—and we'll bury him there. It was but an accident, man. Hold up your head! You and Nest will come home yet and fill Bodowen with children, and I'll live to see it.'

'Never!' said Owen. 'I am the last male of my race, and the son has murdered his father!'

Nest came in laden and cloaked. Ellis was for hurrying them off. The fire was extinguished, the door was locked.

'Here, Nest, my darling, let me take your bundle while I guide you down the steps.' But her husband bent his head, and spoke never a word. Nest gave her father the bundle (already loaded with such things as he himself had seen fit to take), but clasped another softly and tightly.

'No one shall help me with this,' said she, in a low voice.

Her father did not understand her; her husband did, and placed his strong helping arm round her waist, and blessed her.

'We will all go together, Nest,' said he. 'But where?' and he looked up at the storm-tossed clouds coming up from windward.

'It is a dirty night,' said Ellis, turning his head round to speak to his companions at last. 'But never fear, we'll weather it!' And he made for the place where his vessel was moored. Then he stopped and thought a moment.

'Stay here!' said he, addressing his companions.
'I may meet folk, and I shall, maybe, have to hear
and to speak. You wait here till I come back for
you.' So they sat down close together in a corner of
the path.

'Let me look at him, Nest!' said Owen.

She took her little dead son out from under her
shawl; they looked at his waxen face long and tenderly;
kissed it, and covered it up reverently and softly.

'Nest,' said Owen, at last, 'I feel as though my
father's spirit had been near us, and as if it had bent
over our poor little one. A strange chilly air met me
as I stooped over him. I could fancy the spirit of our
pure, blameless child guiding my father's safe over the
paths of the sky to the gates of heaven, and escaping
those accursed dogs of hell that were darting up from
the north in pursuit of souls not five minutes since.'

'Don't talk so, Owen,' said Nest, curling up to him
in the darkness of the copse. 'Who knows what may
be listening?'

The pair were silent, in a kind of nameless terror,
till they heard Ellis Pritchard's loud whisper. 'Where
are ye? Come along, soft and steady. There were
folk about even now, and the Squire is missed, and
madam in a fright.'

They went swiftly down to the little harbour, and
embarked on board Ellis's boat. The sea heaved and
rocked even there; the torn clouds went hurrying
overhead in a wild tumultuous manner.

They put out into the bay; still in silence, except
when some word of command was spoken by Ellis, who
took the management of the vessel. They made for
the rocky shore, where Owen's boat had been moored.
It was not there. It had broken loose and disappeared.

Owen sat down and covered his face. This last
event, so simple and natural in itself, struck on his
excited and superstitious mind in an extraordinary
manner. He had hoped for a certain reconciliation, so
to say, by laying his father and his child both in one
grave. But now it appeared to him as if there was

to be no forgiveness; as if his father revolted even
in death against any such peaceful union. Ellis took
a practical view of the case. If the Squire's body was
found drifting about in a boat known to belong to his
son, it would create terrible suspicion as to the manner
of his death. At one time in the evening, Ellis had
thought of persuading Owen to let him bury the Squire
in a sailor's grave; or, in other words, to sew him up
in a spare sail, and, weighting it well, sink it for ever.
He had not broached the subject, from a certain fear
of Owen's passionate repugnance to the plan; otherwise, if he had consented, they might have returned to
Penmorfa, and passively awaited the course of events,
secure of Owen's succession to Bodowen, sooner or
later; or if Owen was too much overwhelmed by what
had happened, Ellis would have advised him to go
away for a short time, and return when the buzz and
the talk was over.

Now it was different. It was absolutely necessary
that they should leave the country for a time. Through
those stormy waters they must plough their way that
very night. Ellis had no fear—would have had no
fear, at any rate, with Owen as he had been a week,
a day ago; but with Owen wild, despairing, helpless,
fate-pursued, what could he do?

They sailed into the tossing darkness, and were never
more seen of men.

The house of Bodowen has sunk into damp, dark
ruins; and a Saxon stranger holds the lands of the
Griffiths.

# THE POOR CLARE

## CHAPTER I

DECEMBER 12th, 1747.—My life has been strangely bound up with extraordinary incidents, some of which occurred before I had any connexion with the principal actors in them, or, indeed, before I even knew of their existence. I suppose most old men are, like me, more given to looking back upon their own career with a kind of fond interest and affectionate remembrance, than to watching the events—though these may have far more interest for the multitude—immediately passing before their eyes. If this should be the case with the generality of old people, how much more so with me ! . . . . If I am to enter upon that strange story connected with poor Lucy, I must begin a long way back. I myself only came to the knowledge of her family history after I knew her ; but, to make the tale clear to any one else, I must arrange events in the order in which they occurred—not that in which I became acquainted with them.

There is a great old hall in the north-east of Lancashire, in a part they call the Trough of Bolland, adjoining that other district named Craven. Starkey Manor-House is rather like a number of rooms clustered round a grey, massive old keep than a regularly-built hall. Indeed, I suppose that the house only consisted of the great tower in the centre, in the days when the Scots made their raids terrible as far south as this ; and that after the Stuarts came in, and there was a little more security of property in those parts, the Starkeys of that time added the lower building, which runs, two stories high, all round the base of the keep.

There has been a grand garden laid out in my days, on the southern slope near the house; but when I first knew the place, the kitchen-garden at the farm was the only piece of cultivated ground belonging to it. The deer used to come within sight of the drawing-room windows, and might have browsed quite close up to the house if they had not been too wild and shy. Starkey Manor-House itself stood on a projection or peninsula of high land, jutting out from the abrupt hills that form the sides of the Trough of Bolland. These hills were rocky and bleak enough towards their summit; lower down they were clothed with tangled copsewood and green depths of fern, out of which a grey giant of an ancient forest-tree would tower here and there, throwing up its ghastly white branches, as if in imprecation, to the sky. These trees, they told me, were the remnants of that forest which existed in the days of the Heptarchy,* and were even then noted as landmarks. No wonder that their upper and more exposed branches were leafless, and that the dead bark had peeled away, from sapless old age.

Not far from the house there were a few cottages, apparently of the same date as the keep, probably built for some retainers of the family, who sought shelter—they and their families and their small flocks and herds—at the hands of their feudal lord. Some of them had pretty much fallen to decay. They were built in a strange fashion. Strong beams had been sunk firm in the ground at the requisite distance, and their other ends had been fastened together, two and two, so as to form the shape of one of those rounded waggon-headed gipsy-tents, only very much larger. The spaces between were filled with mud, stones, osiers, rubbish, mortar—anything to keep out the weather. The fires were made in the centre of these rude dwellings, a hole in the roof forming the only chimney. No Highland hut or Irish cabin could be of rougher construction.

The owner of this property, at the beginning of the present century, was a Mr. Patrick Byrne Starkey.

His family had kept to the old faith,[*] and were staunch
Roman Catholics, esteeming it even a sin to marry
any one of Protestant descent, however willing he or
she might have been to embrace the Romish religion.
Mr. Patrick Starkey's father had been a follower of
James the Second; and, during the disastrous Irish
campaign of that monarch, he had fallen in love with
an Irish beauty, a Miss Byrne, as zealous for her religion
and for the Stuarts as himself. He had returned to
Ireland after his escape to France, and married her,
bearing her back to the court of St. Germains. But
some licence on the part of the disorderly gentlemen
who surrounded King James in his exile, had insulted
his beautiful wife, and disgusted him; so he removed
from St. Germains to Antwerp, whence, in a few years'
time, he quietly returned to Starkey Manor-House—
some of his Lancashire neighbours having lent their
good offices to reconcile him to the powers that
were. He was as firm a Catholic as ever, and as
staunch an advocate for the Stuarts and the divine
right of kings; but his religion almost amounted to
asceticism, and the conduct of those with whom he
had been brought in such close contact at St. Germains
would little bear the inspection of a stern moralist.
So he gave his allegiance where he could not give his
esteem, and learned to respect sincerely the upright
and moral character of one whom he yet regarded as
an usurper. King William's government had little
need to fear such a one. So he returned, as I have
said, with a sobered heart and impoverished fortunes,
to his ancestral house, which had fallen sadly to ruin
while the owner had been a courtier, a soldier, and an
exile. The roads into the Trough of Bolland were
little more than cart-ruts; indeed, the way up to the
house lay along a ploughed field before you came to
the deer-park. Madam, as the country-folk used to
call Mrs. Starkey, rode on a pillion behind her husband,
holding on to him with a light hand by his leather
riding-belt. Little master (he that was afterwards
Squire Patrick Byrne Starkey) was held on to his pony

by a serving-man. A woman past middle age walked, with a firm and strong step, by the cart that held much of the baggage ; and, high up on the mails and boxes, sat a girl of dazzling beauty, perched lightly on the topmost trunk, and swaying herself fearlessly to and fro, as the cart rocked and shook in the heavy roads of late autumn. The girl wore the Antwerp faille, or black Spanish mantle over her head, and altogether her appearance was such that the old cottager, who described the procession to me many years after, said that all the country-folk took her for a foreigner. Some dogs, and the boy who held them in charge, made up the company. They rode silently along, looking with grave, serious eyes at the people, who came out of the scattered cottages to bow or curtsy to the real Squire, 'come back at last,' and gazed after the little procession with gaping wonder, not deadened by the sound of the foreign language in which the few necessary words that passed among them were spoken. One lad, called from his staring by the Squire to come and help about the cart, accompanied them to the Manor-House. He said that when the lady had descended from her pillion, the middle-aged woman whom I have described as walking while the others rode, stepped quickly forward, and taking Madame Starkey (who was of a slight and delicate figure) in her arms, she lifted her over the threshold, and set her down in her husband's house, at the same time uttering a passionate and outlandish blessing. The Squire stood by, smiling gravely at first ; but when the words of blessing were pronounced, he took off his fine feathered hat, and bent his head. The girl with the black mantle stepped onward into the shadow of the dark hall, and kissed the lady's hand ; and that was all the lad could tell to the group that gathered round him on his return, eager to hear everything, and to know how much the Squire had given him for his services.

From all I could gather, the Manor-House, at the time of the Squire's return, was in the most dilapidated

state. The stout grey walls remained firm and entire ;
but the inner chambers had been used for all kinds
of purposes. The great withdrawing-room had been
a barn ; the state tapestry-chamber had held wool,
and so on. But, by-and-by, they were cleared out ;
and if the Squire had no money to spend on new
furniture, he and his wife had the knack of making
the best of the old. He was no despicable joiner ; she
had a kind of grace in whatever she did, and imparted
an air of elegant picturesqueness to whatever she
touched. Besides, they had brought many rare things
from the Continent ; perhaps I should rather say,
things that were rare in that part of England—
carvings, and crosses, and beautiful pictures. And
then, again, wood was plentiful in the Trough of
Bolland, and great log-fires danced and glittered in all
the dark, old rooms, and gave a look of home and
comfort to everything.

Why do I tell you all this ? I have little to do
with the Squire and Madame Starkey ; and yet I dwell
upon them, as if I were unwilling to come to the real
people with whom my life was so strangely mixed up.
Madam had been nursed in Ireland by the very woman
who lifted her in her arms, and welcomed her to her
husband's home in Lancashire. Excepting for the
short period of her own married life, Bridget Fitzgerald
had never left her nursling. Her marriage—to one
above her in rank—had been unhappy. Her husband
had died, and left her in even greater poverty than that
in which she was when he had first met with her. She
had one child, the beautiful daughter who came riding
on the waggon-load of furniture that was brought to
the Manor-House. Madame Starkey had taken her
again into her service when she became a widow. She
and her daughter had followed ' the mistress ' in all
her fortunes ; they had lived at St. Germains and at
Antwerp, and were now come to her home in Lancashire. As soon as Bridget had arrived there, the Squire
gave her a cottage of her own, and took more pains
in furnishing it for her than he did in anything else

out of his own house. It was only nominally her
residence. She was constantly up at the great house;
indeed, it was but a short cut across the woods from
her own home to the home of her nursling. Her
daughter Mary, in like manner, moved from one house
to the other at her own will. Madam loved both
mother and child dearly. They had great influence
over her, and, through her, over her husband. Whatever Bridget or Mary willed was sure to come to pass.
They were not disliked; for, though wild and passionate, they were also generous by nature. But the
other servants were afraid of them, as being in secret
the ruling spirits of the household. The Squire had
lost his interest in all secular things; Madam was
gentle, affectionate, and yielding. Both husband and
wife were tenderly attached to each other and to their
boy; but they grew more and more to shun the
trouble of decision on any point; and hence it was
that Bridget could exert such despotic power. But if
every one else yielded to her 'magic of a superior
mind,' her daughter not unfrequently rebelled. She
and her mother were too much alike to agree. There
were wild quarrels between them, and wilder recon-
ciliations. There were times when, in the heat of
passion, they could have stabbed each other. At all
other times they both—Bridget especially—would
have willingly laid down their lives for one another.
Bridget's love for her child lay very deep—deeper than
that daughter ever knew; or I should think she would
never have wearied of home as she did, and prayed
her mistress to obtain for her some situation—as
waiting-maid—beyond the seas, in that more cheerful
continental life, among the scenes of which so many
of her happiest years had been spent. She thought,
as youth thinks, that life would last for ever, and that
two or three years were but a small portion of it to
pass away from her mother, whose only child she was.
Bridget thought differently, but was too proud ever
to show what she felt. If her child wished to leave
her, why—she should go. But people said Bridget

became ten years older in the course of two months at this time. She took it that Mary wanted to leave her. The truth was, that Mary wanted for a time to leave the place, and to seek some change, and would thankfully have taken her mother with her. Indeed, when Madame Starkey had gotten her a situation with some grand lady abroad, and the time drew near for her to go, it was Mary who clung to her mother with passionate embrace, and, with floods of tears, declared that she would never leave her; and it was Bridget who at last loosened her arms, and, grave and tearless herself, bade her keep her word, and go forth into the wide world. Sobbing aloud, and looking back continually, Mary went away. Bridget was still as death, scarcely drawing her breath, or closing her stony eyes; till at last she turned back into her cottage, and heaved a ponderous old settle against the door. There she sat, motionless, over the grey ashes of her extinguished fire, deaf to Madam's sweet voice, as she begged leave to enter and comfort her nurse. Deaf, stony, and motionless, she sat for more than twenty hours; till, for the third time, Madam came across the snowy path from the great house, carrying with her a young spaniel, which had been Mary's pet up at the hall, and which had not ceased all night long to seek for its absent mistress, and to whine and moan after her. With tears Madam told this story, through the closed door— tears excited by the terrible look of anguish, so steady, so immovable—so the same to-day as it was yesterday—on her nurse's face. The little creature in her arms began to utter its piteous cry, as it shivered with the cold. Bridget stirred; she moved—she listened. Again that long whine; she thought it was for her daughter; and what she had denied to her nursling and mistress she granted to the dumb creature that Mary had cherished. She opened the door, and took the dog from Madam's arms. Then Madam came in, and kissed and comforted the old woman, who took but little notice of her or anything. And sending up Master Patrick to the hall for fire and food, the sweet young lady never left her nurse all that night. Next day, the Squire himself came down, carrying a beautiful foreign picture: Our Lady of the Holy Heart, the Papists call it. It is a picture of the Virgin, her heart pierced with arrows, each arrow representing one of her great woes. That picture hung in Bridget's cottage when I first saw her; I have that picture now.

Years went on. Mary was still abroad. Bridget was still and stern, instead of active and passionate. The little dog, Mignon, was indeed her darling. I have heard that she talked to it continually; although, to most people, she was so silent. The Squire and Madam treated her with the greatest consideration, and well they might; for to them she was as devoted and faithful as ever. Mary wrote pretty often, and seemed satisfied with her life. But at length the letters ceased —I hardly know whether before or after a great and terrible sorrow came upon the house of the Starkeys. The Squire sickened of a putrid fever; and Madam caught it in nursing him, and died. You may be sure, Bridget let no other woman tend her but herself; and in the very arms that had received her at her birth, that sweet young woman laid her head down, and gave up her breath. The Squire recovered, in a fashion. He was never strong—he had never the heart to smile again. He fasted and prayed more than ever; and people did say that he tried to cut off the entail, and leave all the property away to found a monastery abroad, of which he prayed that some day little Squire Patrick might be the reverend father. But he could not do this, for the strictness of the entail and the laws against the Papists. So he could only appoint gentlemen of his own faith as guardians to his son, with many charges about the lad's soul, and a few about the land, and the way it was to be held while he was a minor. Of course, Bridget was not forgotten. He sent for her as he lay on his death-bed, and asked her if she would rather have a sum down, or have a small annuity settled upon her. She said at once she would have a sum down; for she thought of her daughter, and how she could bequeath the money to her, whereas an annuity would have died with her. So the Squire left her her cottage for life, and a fair sum of money. And then he died, with as ready and willing a heart as, I suppose, ever any gentleman took out of this world with him. The young Squire was carried off by his guardians, and Bridget was left alone.

I have said that she had not heard from Mary for some time. In her last letter, she had told of travelling about with her mistress, who was the English wife of some great foreign officer, and had spoken of her chances of making a good marriage, without naming the gentleman's name, keeping it rather back as a pleasant surprise to her mother; his station and fortune being, as I had afterwards reason to know, far superior to anything she had a right to expect. Then came a long silence; and Madam was dead, and the Squire was dead; and Bridget's heart was gnawed by anxiety, and she knew not whom to ask for news of her child. She could not write, and the Squire had managed her communication with her daughter. She walked off to Hurst; and got a good priest there— one whom she had known at Antwerp—to write for her. But no answer came. It was like crying into the awful stillness of night.

One day, Bridget was missed by those neighbours who had been accustomed to mark her goings-out and comings-in. She had never been sociable with any of them; but the sight of her had become a part of their daily lives, and slow wonder arose in their minds, as morning after morning came, and her house-door remained closed, her window dead from any glitter, or light of fire within. At length, some one tried the door; it was locked. Two or three laid their heads together, before daring to look in through the blank, unshuttered window. But, at last, they summoned up courage; and then saw that Bridget's absence from their little world was not the result of accident or death, but of premeditation. Such small articles of furniture as could be secured from the effects of time and damp by being packed up, were stowed away in boxes. The picture of the Madonna was taken down, and gone. In a word, Bridget had stolen away from her home, and left no trace whither she was departed. I knew afterwards that she and her little dog had wandered off on the long search for her lost daughter. She was too illiterate to have faith in letters, even had she had the means of writing and sending many. But she had faith in her own strong love, and believed that her passionate instinct would guide her to her child. Besides, foreign travel was no new thing to her, and she could speak enough of French to explain the object of her journey, and had, moreover, the advantage of being, from her faith, a welcome object of charitable hospitality at many a distant convent. But the country people round Starkey Manor-House knew nothing of all this. They wondered what had become of her, in a torpid, lazy fashion, and then left off thinking of her altogether. Several years passed. Both Manor-House and cottage were deserted. The young Squire lived far away under the direction of his guardians. There were inroads of wool and corn into the sitting-rooms of the Hall ; and there was some low talk, from time to time, among the hinds and country people, whether it would not be as well to break into old Bridget's cottage, and save such of her goods as were left from the moth and rust which must be making sad havoc. But this idea was always quenched by the recollection of her strong character and passionate anger ; and tales of her masterful spirit, and vehement force of will, were whispered about, till the very thought of offending her, by touching any article of hers, became invested with a kind of horror : it was believed that, dead or alive, she would not fail to avenge it.

Suddenly she came home ; with as little noise or note of preparation as she had departed. One day, some one noticed a thin, blue curl of smoke ascending from her chimney. Her door stood open to the noon-day sun ; and, ere many hours had elapsed, some one had seen an old travel-and-sorrow-stained woman

dipping her pitcher in the well; and said, that the
dark, solemn eyes that looked up at him were more
like Bridget Fitzgerald's than any one else's in this
world; and yet, if it were she, she looked as if she
had been scorched in the flames of hell, so brown, and
scared, and fierce a creature did she seem.  By-and-by
many saw her; and those who met her eye once cared
not to be caught looking at her again.  She had got
into the habit of perpetually talking to herself; nay,
more, answering herself, and varying her tones according to the side she took at the moment.  It was no
wonder that those who dared to listen outside her door
at night believed that she held converse with some
spirit; in short, she was unconsciously earning for
herself the dreadful reputation of a witch.

Her little dog, which had wandered half over the
Continent with her, was her only companion; a dumb
remembrancer of happier days.  Once he was ill; and
she carried him more than three miles, to ask about
his management from one who had been groom to the
last Squire, and had then been noted for his skill in
all diseases of animals.  Whatever this man did, the
dog recovered; and they who heard her thanks, intermingled with blessings (that were rather promises of
good fortune than prayers), looked grave at his good
luck when, next year, his ewes twinned, and his
meadow-grass was heavy and thick.

Now it so happened that, about the year seventeen
hundred and eleven, one of the guardians of the young
Squire, a certain Sir Philip Tempest, bethought him
of the good shooting there must be on his ward's
property; and, in consequence, he brought down four
or five gentlemen, of his friends, to stay for a week or
two at the Hall.  From all accounts, they roystered
and spent pretty freely.  I never heard any of their
names but one, and that was Squire Gisborne's.  He
was hardly a middle-aged man then; he had been
much abroad, and there, I believe, he had known Sir
Philip Tempest, and done him some service.  He was
a daring and dissolute fellow in those days: careless

and fearless, and one who would rather be in a quarrel than out of it. He had his fits of ill-temper beside, when he would spare neither man nor beast. Otherwise, those who knew him well used to say he had a good heart, when he was neither drunk, nor angry, nor in any way vexed. He had altered much when I came to know him.

One day, the gentlemen had all been out shooting, and with but little success, I believe; anyhow, Mr. Gisborne had none, and was in a black humour accordingly. He was coming home, having his gun loaded, sportsman-like, when little Mignon crossed his path, just as he turned out of the wood by Bridget's cottage. Partly for wantonness, partly to vent his spleen upon some living creature, Mr. Gisborne took his gun, and fired—he had better have never fired gun again than aimed that unlucky shot: he hit Mignon, and at the creature's sudden cry, Bridget came out, and saw at a glance what had been done. She took Mignon up in her arms, and looked hard at the wound; the poor dog looked at her with his glazing eyes, and tried to wag his tail and lick her hand, all covered with blood. Mr. Gisborne spoke in a kind of sullen penitence:

'You should have kept the dog out of my way— a little poaching varmint.'

At this very moment, Mignon stretched out his legs and stiffened in her arms—her lost Mary's dog, who had wandered and sorrowed with her for years. She walked right into Mr. Gisborne's path, and fixed his unwilling, sullen look with her dark and terrible eye.

'Those never throve that did me harm,' said she. 'I'm alone in the world, and helpless; the more do the Saints in Heaven hear my prayers. Hear me, ye blessed ones! hear me while I ask for sorrow on this bad, cruel man. He has killed the only creature that loved me—the dumb beast that I loved. Bring down heavy sorrow on his head for it, O ye Saints! He thought that I was helpless, because he saw me lonely and poor ; but are not the armies of Heaven for the like of me ? '

' Come, come,' said he, half-remorseful, but not one whit afraid. ' Here 's a crown to buy thee another dog. Take it, and leave off cursing ! I care none for thy threats.'

' Don't you ? ' said she, coming a step closer, and changing her imprecatory cry for a whisper which made the gamekeeper's lad, following Mr. Gisborne, creep all over. ' You shall live to see the creature you love best, and who alone loves you—aye, a human creature, but as innocent and fond as my poor, dead darling—you shall see this creature, for whom death would be too happy, become a terror and a loathing to all, for this blood's sake. Hear me, O holy Saints, who never fail them that have no other help ! '

She threw up her right hand, filled with poor Mignon's life-drops ; they spirted, one or two of them, on his shooting-dress,—an ominous sight to the follower. But the master only laughed a little, forced, scornful laugh, and went on to the Hall. Before he got there, however, he took out a gold piece, and bade the boy carry it to the old woman on his return to the village. The lad was ' afeared,' as he told me in after years ; he came to the cottage, and hovered about, not daring to enter. He peeped through the window at last ; and by the flickering wood-flame he saw Bridget kneeling before the picture of Our Lady of the Holy Heart, with dead Mignon lying between her and the Madonna. She was praying wildly, as her outstretched arms betokened. The lad shrank away in redoubled terror ; and contented himself with slipping the gold-piece under the ill-fitting door. The next day it was thrown out upon the midden ; and there it lay, no one daring to touch it.

Meanwhile Mr. Gisborne, half curious, half uneasy, thought to lessen his uncomfortable feelings by asking Sir Philip who Bridget was ? He could only describe her—he did not know her name. Sir Philip was equally at a loss. But an old servant of the Starkeys, who had resumed his livery at the Hall on this occasion—

a scoundrel whom Bridget had saved from dismissal
more than once during her palmy days—said :—

'It will be the old witch, that his worship means.
She needs a ducking, if ever woman did, does that
Bridget Fitzgerald.'

'Fitzgerald!' said both the gentlemen at once. But
Sir Philip was the first to continue :—

'I must have no talk of ducking her, Dickon. Why,
she must be the very woman poor Starkey bade me
have a care of; but when I came here last she was
gone, no one knew where. I'll go and see her to-
morrow. But mind you, sirrah, if any harm comes
to her, or any more talk of her being a witch—I've
a pack of hounds at home, who can follow the scent of
a lying knave as well as ever they followed a dog-fox;
so take care how you talk about ducking a faithful old
servant of your dead master's.'

'Had she ever a daughter?' asked Mr. Gisborne,
after a while.

'I don't know—yes! I've a notion she had; a kind
of waiting-woman to Madame Starkey.'

'Please your worship,' said humbled Dickon,
'Mistress Bridget had a daughter—one Mistress
Mary—who went abroad, and has never been heard on
since; and folk do say that has crazed her mother.'

Mr. Gisborne shaded his eyes with his hand.

'I could wish she had not cursed me,' he muttered.
'She may have power—no one else could.' After
a while, he said aloud, no one understanding rightly
what he meant, 'Tush! it is impossible!'—and called
for claret; and he and the other gentlemen set-to to
a drinking-bout.

# CHAPTER II

I NOW come to the time in which I myself was mixed up with the people that I have been writing about. And to make you understand how I became connected with them, I must give you some little account of myself. My father was the younger son of a Devonshire gentleman of moderate property; my eldest uncle succeeded to the estate of his forefathers, my second became an eminent attorney in London, and my father took orders. Like most poor clergymen, he had a large family; and I have no doubt was glad enough when my London uncle, who was a bachelor, offered to take charge of me, and bring me up to be his successor in business.

In this way I came to live in London, in my uncle's house, not far from Gray's Inn,* and to be treated and esteemed as his son, and to labour with him in his office. I was very fond of the old gentleman. He was the confidential agent of many country squires, and had attained to his present position as much by knowledge of human nature as by knowledge of law; though he was learned enough in the latter. He used to say his business was law, his pleasure heraldry. From his intimate acquaintance with family history, and all the tragic courses of life therein involved, to hear him talk, at leisure times, about any coat of arms that came across his path was as good as a play or a romance. Many cases of disputed property, dependent on a love of genealogy, were brought to him, as to a great authority on such points. If the lawyer who came to consult him was young, he would take no fee, only give him a long lecture on the importance of attending to heraldry; if the lawyer was of mature age and good standing, he would mulct him pretty well, and abuse him to me afterwards as negligent of one great branch of the profession. His house was in a stately new street called Ormond Street, and in it he had a handsome library; but all the books treated of things that were past; none of them planned or looked forward into the future. I worked away— partly for the sake of my family at home, partly because my uncle had really taught me to enjoy the kind of practice in which he himself took such delight. I suspect I worked too hard; at any rate, in seventeen hundred and eighteen I was far from well, and my good uncle was disturbed by my ill looks.

One day, he rang the bell twice into the clerk's room at the dingy office in Gray's Inn Lane. It was the summons for me, and I went into his private room just as a gentleman—whom I knew well enough by sight as an Irish lawyer of more reputation than he deserved—was leaving.

My uncle was slowly rubbing his hands together and considering. I was there two or three minutes before he spoke. Then he told me that I must pack up my portmanteau that very afternoon, and start that night by post-horse for West Chester. I should get there, if all went well, at the end of five days' time, and must then wait for a packet to cross over to Dublin; from thence I must proceed to a certain town named Kildoon, and in that neighbourhood I was to remain, making certain inquiries as to the existence of any descendants of the younger branch of a family to whom some valuable estates had descended in the female line. The Irish lawyer whom I had seen was weary of the case, and would willingly have given up the property, without further ado, to a man who appeared to claim them; but on laying his tables and trees before my uncle, the latter had foreseen so many possible prior claimants that the lawyer had begged him to undertake the management of the whole business. In his youth, my uncle would have liked nothing better than going over to Ireland himself, and ferreting out every scrap of paper or parchment, and every word of tradition respecting the family. As it was, old and gouty, he deputed me.

Accordingly, I went to Kildoon. I suspect I had something of my uncle's delight in following up a genealogical scent, for I very soon found out, when on the spot, that Mr. Rooney, the Irish lawyer, would have got both himself and the first claimant into a terrible scrape, if he had pronounced his opinion that the estates ought to be given up to him. There were three poor Irish fellows, each nearer of kin to the last possessor; but, a generation before, there was a still nearer relation, who had never been accounted for, nor his existence ever discovered by the lawyers, I venture to think, till I routed him out from the memory of some of the old dependants of the family. What had become of him? I travelled backwards and forwards; I crossed over to France, and came back again with a slight clue, which ended in my discovering that, wild and dissipated himself, he had left one child, a son, of yet worse character than his father; that this same Hugh Fitzgerald had married a very beautiful serving-woman of the Byrnes—a person below him in hereditary rank, but above him in character; that he had died soon after his marriage, leaving one child, whether a boy or a girl I could not learn, and that the mother had returned to live in the family of the Byrnes. Now, the chief of this latter family was serving in the Duke of Berwick's regiment, and it was long before I could hear from him; it was more than a year before I got a short, haughty letter—I fancy he had a soldier's contempt for a civilian, an Irishman's hatred for an Englishman, an exiled Jacobite's jealousy of one who prospered and lived tranquilly under the government he looked upon as an usurpation. 'Bridget Fitzgerald,' he said, ' had been faithful to the fortunes of his sister— had followed her abroad, and to England when Mrs. Starkey had thought fit to return. Both his sister and her husband were dead; he knew nothing of Bridget Fitzgerald at the present time: probably Sir Philip Tempest, his nephew's guardian, might be able to give me some information.' I have not given the little contemptuous terms; the way in which faithful

service was meant to imply more than it said—all that
has nothing to do with my story. Sir Philip, when
applied to, told me that he paid an annuity regularly
to an old woman named Fitzgerald, living at Coldholme
(the village near Starkey Manor-House). Whether she
had any descendants he could not say.

One bleak March evening, I came in sight of the
places described at the beginning of my story. I could
hardly understand the rude dialect in which the direction to old Bridget's house was given.

' Yo' see yon furleets,' all run together, gave me no
idea that I was to guide myself by the distant lights
that shone in the windows of the Hall, occupied for
the time by a farmer who held the post of steward,
while the Squire, now four or five and twenty, was
making the grand tour. However, at last, I reached
Bridget's cottage—a low, moss-grown place ; the
palings that had once surrounded it were broken and
gone ; and the underwood of the forest came up to
the walls, and must have darkened the windows. It
was about seven o'clock—not late to my London
notions—but, after knocking for some time at the
door and receiving no reply, I was driven to conjecture
that the occupant of the house was gone to bed. So
I betook myself to the nearest church I had seen, three
miles back on the road I had come, sure that close to
that I should find an inn of some kind ; and early the
next morning I set off back to Coldholme, by a field-
path which my host assured me I should find a shorter
cut than the road I had taken the night before. It
was a cold, sharp morning ; my feet left prints in the
sprinkling of hoar-frost that covered the ground ;
nevertheless, I saw an old woman, whom I instinctively
suspected to be the object of my search, in a sheltered
covert on one side of my path. I lingered and watched
her. She must have been considerably above the
middle size in her prime, for when she raised herself
from the stooping position in which I first saw her,
there was something fine and commanding in the
erectness of her figure. She drooped again in a minute

or two, and seemed looking for something on the ground, as, with bent head, she turned off from the spot where I gazed upon her, and was lost to my sight. I fancy I missed my way, and made a round in spite of the landlord's directions; for by the time I had reached Bridget's cottage she was there, with no semblance of hurried walk or discomposure of any kind. The door was slightly ajar. I knocked, and the majestic figure stood before me, silently awaiting the explanation of my errand. Her teeth were all gone, so the nose and chin were brought near together;* the gray eyebrows were straight, and almost hung over her deep, cavernous eyes, and the thick white hair lay in silvery masses over the low, wide, wrinkled forehead. For a moment, I stood uncertain how to shape my answer to the solemn questioning of her silence.

'Your name is Bridget Fitzgerald, I believe?'

She bowed her head in assent.

'I have something to say to you. May I come in? I am unwilling to keep you standing.'

'You cannot tire me,' she said, and at first she seemed inclined to deny me the shelter of her roof. But the next moment—she had searched the very soul in me with her eyes during that instant—she led me in, and dropped the shadowing hood of her grey, draping cloak, which had previously hid part of the character of her countenance. The cottage was rude and bare enough. But before the picture of the Virgin, of which I have made mention, there stood a little cup filled with fresh primroses. While she paid her reverence to the Madonna, I understood why she had been out seeking through the clumps of green in the sheltered copse. Then she turned round, and bade me be seated. The expression of her face, which all this time I was studying, was not bad, as the stories of my last night's landlord had led me to expect; it was a wild, stern, fierce, indomitable countenance, seamed and scarred by agonies of solitary weeping; but it was neither cunning nor malignant.

'My name is Bridget Fitzgerald,' said she, by way of opening our conversation.

'And your husband was Hugh Fitzgerald, of Knock-Mahon, near Kildoon, in Ireland?'

A faint light came into the dark gloom of her eyes.

'He was.'

'May I ask if you had any children by him?'

The light in her eyes grew quick and red. She tried to speak, I could see; but something rose in her throat and choked her, and until she could speak calmly, she would fain not speak at all before a stranger. In a minute or so she said:

'I had a daughter—one Mary Fitzgerald,'—then her strong nature mastered her strong will, and she cried out, with a trembling, wailing cry: 'Oh, man! what of her?—what of her?'

She rose from her seat, and came and clutched at my arm, and looked in my eyes. There she read, as I suppose, my utter ignorance of what had become of her child; for she went blindly back to her chair, and sat rocking herself and softly moaning, as if I were not there; I not daring to speak to the lone and awful woman. After a little pause, she knelt down before the picture of Our Lady of the Holy Heart, and spoke to her by all the fanciful and poetic names of the Litany.

'O Rose of Sharon! O Tower of David! O Star of the Sea! have ye no comfort for my sore heart? Am I for ever to hope? Grant me at least despair!' —and so on she went, heedless of my presence. Her prayers grew wilder and wilder, till they seemed to me to touch on the borders of madness and blasphemy. Almost involuntarily, I spoke as if to stop her.

'Have you any reason to think that your daughter is dead?'

She rose from her knees, and came and stood before me.

'Mary Fitzgerald is dead,' said she. 'I shall never see her again in the flesh. No tongue ever told me;

but I know she is dead. I have yearned so to see her, and my heart's will is fearful and strong: it would have drawn her to me before now, if she had been a wanderer on the other side of the world. I wonder often it has not drawn her out of the grave to come and stand before me, and hear me tell her how I loved her. For, sir, we parted unfriends.'

I knew nothing but the dry particulars needed for my lawyer's quest, but I could not help feeling for the desolate woman; and she must have read the unusual sympathy with her wistful eyes.

'Yes, sir, we did. She never knew how I loved her; and we parted unfriends; and I fear me that I wished her voyage might not turn out well, only meaning,—O blessed Virgin! you know I only meant that she should come home to her mother's arms as to the happiest place on earth; but my wishes are terrible—their power goes beyond my thought—and there is no hope for me, if my words brought Mary harm.'

'But,' I said, 'you do not know that she is dead. Even now, you hoped she might be alive. Listen to me,' and I told her the tale I have already told you, giving it all in the driest manner, for I wanted to recall the clear sense that I felt almost sure she had possessed in her younger days, and by keeping up her attention to details, restrain the vague wildness of her grief.

She listened with deep attention, putting from time to time such questions as convinced me I had to do with no common intelligence, however dimmed and shorn by solitude and mysterious sorrow. Then she took up her tale; and, in few brief words, told me of her wanderings abroad in vain search after her daughter; sometimes in the wake of armies, some-times in camp, sometimes in city. The lady, whose waiting-woman Mary had gone to be, had died soon after the date of her last letter home; her husband, the foreign officer, had been serving in Hungary, whither Bridget had followed him, but too late to find him. Vague rumours reached her that Mary had made a great marriage : and this sting of doubt was added,— whether the mother might not be close to her child under her new name, and even hearing of her every day, and yet never recognising the lost one under the appellation she then bore. At length the thought took possession of her, that it was possible that all this time Mary might be at home at Coldholme, in the Trough of Bolland, in Lancashire, in England ; and home came Bridget, in that vain hope, to her desolate hearth, and empty cottage. Here she had thought it safest to remain ; if Mary was in life, it was here she would seek for her mother.

I noted down one or two particulars out of Bridget's narrative that I thought might be of use to me : for I was stimulated to further search in a strange and extraordinary manner. It seemed as if it were impressed upon me, that I must take up the quest where Bridget had laid it down ; and this for no reason that had previously influenced me (such as my uncle's anxiety on the subject, my own reputation as a lawyer, and so on), but from some strange power which had taken possession of my will only that very morning, and which forced it in the direction it chose.

'I will go,' said I. 'I will spare nothing in the search. Trust to me. I will learn all that can be learnt. You shall know all that money, or pains, or wit can discover. It is true she may be long dead : but she may have left a child.'

'A child ! ' she cried, as if for the first time this idea had struck her mind. 'Hear him, Blessed Virgin ! he says she may have left a child. And you have never told me, though I have prayed so for a sign, waking or sleeping ! '

'Nay,' said I, 'I know nothing but what you tell me. You say you heard of her marriage.'

But she caught nothing of what I said. She was praying to the Virgin in a kind of ecstacy, which seemed to render her unconscious of my very presence.

From Coldholme I went to Sir Philip Tempest's. The wife of the foreign officer had been a cousin of his father's, and from him I thought I might gain some particulars as to the existence of the Count de la Tour d'Auvergne, and where I could find him; for I knew questions *de vive voix* aid the flagging recollection, and I was determined to lose no chance for want of trouble. But Sir Philip had gone abroad, and it would be some time before I could receive an answer. So I followed my uncle's advice, to whom I had mentioned how wearied I felt, both in body and mind, by my will-o'-the-wisp search. He immediately told me to go to Harrogate, there to await Sir Philip's reply. I should be near to one of the places connected with my search, Coldholme; not far from Sir Philip Tempest, in case he returned, and I wished to ask him any further questions; and, in conclusion, my uncle bade me try to forget all about my business for a time.

This was far easier said than done. I have seen a child on a common blown along by a high wind, without power of standing still and resisting the tempestuous force. I was somewhat in the same predicament as regarded my mental state. Something resistless seemed to urge my thoughts on, through every possible course by which there was a chance of attaining to my object. I did not see the sweeping moors when I walked out : when I held a book in my hand, and read the words, their sense did not penetrate to my brain. If I slept, I went on with the same ideas, always flowing in the same direction. This could not last long without having a bad effect on the body. I had an illness, which, although I was racked with pain, was a positive relief to me, as it compelled me to live in the present suffering, and not in the visionary researches I had been continually making before. My kind uncle came to nurse me ; and after the immediate danger was over, my life seemed to slip away in delicious languor for two or three months. I did not ask—so much did I dread falling into the

old channel of thought—whether any reply had been
received to my letter to Sir Philip. I turned my whole
imagination right away from all that subject. My
uncle remained with me until nigh midsummer, and
then returned to his business in London ; leaving me
perfectly well, although not completely strong. I was
to follow him in a fortnight ; when, as he said, ' we
would look over letters, and talk about several things.'
I knew what this little speech alluded to, and shrank
from the train of thought it suggested, which was so
intimately connected with my first feelings of illness.
However, I had a fortnight more to roam on those
invigorating Yorkshire moors.

In those days, there was one large, rambling inn at
Harrogate, close to the Medicinal Spring ; but it was
already becoming too small for the accommodation of
the influx of visitors, and many lodged round about,
in the farm-houses of the district. It was so early in
the season, that I had the inn pretty much to myself ;
and, indeed, felt rather like a visitor in a private house,
so intimate had the landlord and landlady become with
me during my long illness. She would chide me for
being out so late on the moors, or for having been too
long without food, quite in a motherly way ; while he
consulted me about vintages and wines, and taught me
many a Yorkshire wrinkle about horses. In my walks
I met other strangers from time to time. Even before
my uncle had left me, I had noticed, with half-torpid
curiosity, a young lady of very striking appearance,
who went about always accompanied by an elderly
companion,—hardly a gentlewoman, but with something in her look that prepossessed me in her favour.
The younger lady always put her veil down when any
one approached ; so it had been only once or twice,
when I had come upon her at a sudden turn in the
path, that I had even had a glimpse of her face. I am
not sure if it was beautiful, though in after-life I grew
to think it so. But it was at this time overshadowed
by a sadness that never varied : a pale, quiet, resigned
look of intense suffering, that irresistibly attracted

me,—not with love, but with a sense of infinite compassion for one so young yet so hopelessly unhappy.
The companion wore something of the same look:
quiet, melancholy, hopeless, yet resigned. I asked my
landlord who they were. He said they were called
Clarke, and wished to be considered as mother and
daughter; but that, for his part, he did not believe
that to be their right name, or that there was any such
relationship between them. They had been in the
neighbourhood of Harrogate for some time, lodging in a
remote farm-house. The people there would tell nothing
about them; saying that they paid handsomely, and
never did any harm; so why should they be speaking
of any strange things that might happen? That, as
the landlord shrewdly observed, showed there was
something out of the common way: he had heard
that the elderly woman was a cousin of the farmer's
where they lodged, and so the regard existing between
relations might help to keep them quiet.

'What did he think, then, was the reason for their
extreme seclusion?' asked I.

'Nay, he could not tell,—not he. He had heard that
the young lady, for all as quiet as she seemed, played
strange pranks at times.' He shook his head when
I asked him for more particulars, and refused to give
them, which made me doubt if he knew any, for he
was in general a talkative and communicative man.
In default of other interests, after my uncle left, I set
myself to watch these two people. I hovered about
their walks, drawn towards them with a strange fascination, which was not diminished by their evident
annoyance at so frequently meeting me. One day,
I had the sudden good fortune to be at hand when
they were alarmed by the attack of a bull, which, in
those unenclosed grazing districts, was a particularly
dangerous occurrence. I have other and more important things to relate, than to tell of the accident which
gave me an opportunity of rescuing them; it is enough
to say, that this event was the beginning of an acquaintance, reluctantly acquiesced in by them, but eagerly

prosecuted by me. I can hardly tell when intense curiosity became merged in love, but in less than ten days after my uncle's departure I was passionately enamoured of Mistress Lucy, as her attendant called her; carefully—for this I noted well—avoiding any address which appeared as if there was an equality of station between them. I noticed also that Mrs. Clarke, the elderly woman, after her first reluctance to allow me to pay them any attentions had been overcome, was cheered by my evident attachment to the young girl; it seemed to lighten her heavy burden of care, and she evidently favoured my visits to the farm-house where they lodged. It was not so with Lucy. A more attractive person I never saw, in spite of her depression of manner, and shrinking avoidance of me. I felt sure at once, that whatever was the source of her grief, it rose from no fault of her own. It was difficult to draw her into conversation; but when at times, for a moment or two, I beguiled her into talk, I could see a rare intelligence in her face, and a grave, trusting look in the soft, grey eyes that were raised for a minute to mine. I made every excuse I possibly could for going there. I sought wild flowers for Lucy's sake; I planned walks for Lucy's sake; I watched the heavens by night, in hopes that some unusual beauty of sky would justify me in tempting Mrs. Clarke and Lucy forth upon the moors, to gaze at the great purple dome above.

It seemed to me that Lucy was aware of my love; but that, for some motive which I could not guess, she would fain have repelled me; but then again I saw, or fancied I saw, that her heart spoke in my favour, and that there was a struggle going on in her mind, which at times (I loved so dearly) I could have begged her to spare herself, even though the happiness of my whole life should have been the sacrifice; for her complexion grew paler, her aspect of sorrow more hopeless, her delicate frame yet slighter. During this period I had written, I should say, to my uncle, to beg to be allowed to prolong my stay at Harrogate, not giving any reason;

but such was his tenderness towards me, that in a few days I heard from him, giving me a willing permission, and only charging me to take care of myself, and not use too much exertion during the hot weather.

One sultry evening I drew near the farm. The windows of their parlour were open, and I heard voices when I turned the corner of the house, as I passed the first window (there were two windows in their little ground-floor room). I saw Lucy distinctly ; but when I had knocked at their door—the house-door stood always ajar—she was gone, and I saw only Mrs. Clarke, turning over the work-things lying on the table, in a nervous and purposeless manner. I felt by instinct that a conversation of some importance was coming on, in which I should be expected to say what was my object in paying these frequent visits. I was glad of the opportunity. My uncle had several times alluded to the pleasant possibility of my bringing home a young wife, to cheer and adorn the old house in Ormond Street. He was rich, and I was to succeed him, and had, as I knew, a fair reputation for so young a lawyer. So on my side I saw no obstacle. It was true that Lucy was shrouded in mystery ; her name (I was convinced it was not Clarke), birth, parentage, and previous life were unknown to me. But I was sure of her goodness and sweet innocence, and although I knew that there must be something painful to be told, to account for her mournful sadness, yet I was willing to bear my share in her grief, whatever it might be.

Mrs. Clarke began, as if it was a relief to her to plunge into the subject.

'We have thought, sir—at least I have thought—that you knew very little of us, nor we of you, indeed ; not enough to warrant the intimate acquaintance we have fallen into. I beg your pardon, sir,' she went on, nervously ; 'I am but a plain kind of woman, and I mean to use no rudeness ; but I must say straight out that I—we—think it would be better for you not to come so often to see us. She is very unprotected, and '——

'Why should I not come to see you, dear madam?'
asked I, eagerly, glad of the opportunity of explaining
myself. 'I come, I own, because I have learnt to love
Mistress Lucy, and wish to teach her to love me.'

Mistress Clarke shook her head, and sighed.

'Don't, sir—neither love her, nor, for the sake of
all you hold sacred, teach her to love you! If I am
too late, and you love her already, forget her,—forget
these last few weeks. O! I should never have allowed
you to come!' she went on passionately; 'but what
am I to do? We are forsaken by all, except the great
God, and even He permits a strange and evil power
to afflict us,—what am I to do! Where is it to end?'
She wrung her hands in her distress; then she turned
to me: 'Go away, sir! go away, before you learn to
care any more for her. I ask it for your own sake—
I implore! You have been good and kind to us, and
we shall always recollect you with gratitude; but go
away now, and never come back to cross our fatal
path!'

'Indeed, madam,' said I, 'I shall do no such thing.
You urge it for my own sake. I have no fear, so urged—
nor wish, except to hear more—all. I cannot have
seen Mistress Lucy in all the intimacy of this last
fortnight, without acknowledging her goodness and
innocence; and without seeing—pardon me, madam—
that for some reason you are two very lonely women,
in some mysterious sorrow and distress. Now, though
I am not powerful myself, yet I have friends who are
so wise and kind that they may be said to possess
power. Tell me some particulars. Why are you in
grief—what is your secret—why are you here? I
declare solemnly that nothing you have said has
daunted me in my wish to become Lucy's husband;
nor will I shrink from any difficulty that, as such an
aspirant, I may have to encounter. You say you are
friendless—why cast away an honest friend? I will
tell you of people to whom you may write, and who
will answer any questions as to my character and
prospects. I do not shun inquiry.'

She shook her head again. 'You had better go away, sir. You know nothing about us.'

'I know your names,' said I, 'and I have heard you allude to the part of the country from which you came, which I happen to know as a wild and lonely place. There are so few people living in it that, if I chose to go there, I could easily ascertain all about you; but I would rather hear it from yourself.' You see I wanted to pique her into telling me something definite.

'You do not know our true names, sir,' said she, hastily.

'Well, I may have conjectured as much. But tell me, then, I conjure you. Give me your reasons for distrusting my willingness to stand by what I have said with regard to Mistress Lucy.'

'Oh, what can I do?' exclaimed she. 'If I am turning away a true friend, as he says?—Stay!' coming to a sudden decision—'I will tell you something—I cannot tell you all—you would not believe it. But, perhaps, I can tell you enough to prevent your going on in your hopeless attachment. I am not Lucy's mother.'

'So I conjectured,' I said. 'Go on.'

'I do not even know whether she is the legitimate or illegitimate child of her father. But he is cruelly turned against her; and her mother is long dead; and for a terrible reason, she has no other creature to keep constant to her but me. She—only two years ago—such a darling and such a pride in her father's house! Why, sir, there is a mystery that might happen in connection with her any moment; and then you would go away like all the rest; and, when you next heard her name, you would loathe her. Others, who have loved her longer, have done so before now. My poor child! whom neither God nor man has mercy upon—or, surely, she would die!'

The good woman was stopped by her crying. I confess, I was a little stunned by her last words; but only for a moment. At any rate, till I knew definitely what was this mysterious stain upon one so simple and pure as Lucy seemed, I would not desert her, and so I said; and she made me answer:—

'If you are daring in your heart to think harm of my child, sir, after knowing her as you have done, you are no good man yourself; but I am so foolish and helpless in my great sorrow, that I would fain hope to find a friend in you. I cannot help trusting that, although you may no longer feel toward her as a lover, you will have pity upon us; and perhaps by your learning you can tell us where to go for aid.'

'I implore you to tell me what this mystery is,' I cried, almost maddened by this suspense.

'I cannot,' said she, solemnly. 'I am under a deep vow of secrecy. If you are to be told, it must be by her.' She left the room, and I remained to ponder over this strange interview. I mechanically turned over the few books, and with eyes that saw nothing at the time, examined the tokens of Lucy's frequent presence in that room. When I got home at night, I remembered how all these trifles spoke of a pure and tender heart and innocent life.

Mistress Clarke returned; she had been crying sadly.

'Yes,' said she, 'it is as I feared: she loves you so much that she is willing to run the fearful risk of telling you all herself—she acknowledges it is but a poor chance; but your sympathy will be a balm, if you give it. To-morrow, come here at ten in the morning; and, as you hope for pity in your hour of agony, repress all show of fear or repugnance you may feel towards one so grievously afflicted.'

I half smiled. 'Have no fear,' I said. It seemed too absurd to imagine my feeling dislike to Lucy.

'Her father loved her well,' said she, gravely, 'yet he drove her out like some monstrous thing.'

Just at this moment came a peal of ringing laughter from the garden. It was Lucy's voice; it sounded as if she were standing just on one side of the open casement—and as though she were suddenly stirred to merriment—merriment verging on boisterousness, by the doings or sayings of some other person. I can scarcely say why, but the sound jarred on me inexpressibly. She knew the subject of our conversation, and must have been at least aware of the state of agitation her friend was in ; she herself usually so gentle and quiet. I half rose to go to the window, and satisfy my instinctive curiosity as to what had provoked this burst of ill-timed laughter ; but Mrs. Clarke threw her whole weight and power upon the hand with which she pressed and kept me down.

'For God's sake !' she said, white and trembling all over, 'sit still ; be quiet. Oh ! be patient. To-morrow you will know all. Leave us, for we are all sorely afflicted. Do not seek to know more about us.'

Again that laugh—so musical in sound, yet so discordant to my heart. She held me tight—tighter ; without positive violence I could not have risen. I was sitting with my back to the window, but I felt a shadow pass between the sun's warmth and me, and a strange shudder ran through my frame. In a minute or two she released me.

'Go,' repeated she. 'Be warned, I ask you once more. I do not think you can stand this knowledge that you seek. If I had had my own way, Lucy should never have yielded, and promised to tell you all. Who knows what may come of it ? '

'I am firm in my wish to know all. I return at ten to-morrow morning, and then expect to see Mistress Lucy herself.'

I turned away ; having my own suspicions, I confess, as to Mistress Clarke's sanity.

Conjectures as to the meaning of her hints, and uncomfortable thoughts connected with that strange laughter, filled my mind. I could hardly sleep. I rose early ; and long before the hour I had appointed, I was on the path over the common that led to the old farm-house where they lodged. I suppose that Lucy had passed no better a night than I ; for there she was also, slowly pacing with her even step, her eyes bent down, her whole look most saintly and pure. She started when I came close to her, and grew paler as I reminded her of my appointment, and spoke with something of the impatience of obstacles that, seeing her once more, had called up afresh in my mind. All strange and terrible hints, and giddy merriment were forgotten. My heart gave forth words of fire, and my tongue uttered them. Her colour went and came, as she listened; but, when I had ended my passionate speeches, she lifted her soft eyes to me, and said—

'But you know that you have something to learn about me yet. I only want to say this: I shall not think less of you—less well of you, I mean—if you, too, fall away from me when you know all. Stop!' said she, as if fearing another burst of mad words. 'Listen to me. My father is a man of great wealth. I never knew my mother; she must have died when I was very young. When first I remember anything, I was living in a great, lonely house, with my dear and faithful Mistress Clarke. My father, even, was not there; he was—he is—a soldier, and his duties lie abroad. But he came from time to time, and every time I think he loved me more and more. He brought me rarities from foreign lands, which prove to me now how much he must have thought of me during his absences. I can sit down and measure the depth of his lost love now, by such standards as these. I never thought whether he loved me or not, then; it was so natural, that it was like the air I breathed. Yet he was an angry man at times, even then; but never with me. He was very reckless, too; and, once or twice, I heard a whisper among the servants that a doom was over him, and that he knew it, and tried to drown his knowledge in wild activity, and even sometimes, sir, in wine. So I grew up in this grand mansion, in that lonely place. Everything around me seemed at my disposal, and I think every one loved me; I am sure I loved them. Till about two years ago—I remember it well—my father had come to England, to us; and he seemed so proud and so pleased with me and all I had done. And one day his tongue seemed loosened with wine, and he told me much that I had not known till then,—how dearly he had loved my mother, yet how his wilful usage had caused her death ; and then he went on to say how he loved me better than any creature on earth, and how, some day, he hoped to take me to foreign places, for that he could hardly bear these long absences from his only child. Then he seemed to change suddenly, and said, in a strange, wild way, that I was not to believe what he said ; that there was many a thing he loved better—his horse—his dog—I know not what.

' And 'twas only the next morning that, when I came into his room to ask his blessing as was my wont, he received me with fierce and angry words. " Why had I," so he asked, " been delighting myself in such wanton mischief—dancing over the tender plants in the flower-beds, all set with the famous Dutch bulbs he had brought from Holland ? " I had never been out of doors that morning, sir, and I could not conceive what he meant, and so I said ; and then he swore at me for a liar, and said I was of no true blood, for he had seen me doing all that mischief himself—with his own eyes. What could I say ? He would not listen to me, and even my tears seemed only to irritate him. That day was the beginning of my great sorrows. Not long after, he reproached me for my undue familiarity— all unbecoming a gentlewoman—with his grooms. I had been in the stable-yard, laughing and talking, he said. Now, sir, I am something of a coward by nature, and I had always dreaded horses ; besides that, my father's servants—those whom he brought with him from foreign parts—were wild fellows, whom I had always avoided, and to whom I had never spoken, except as a lady must needs from time to time speak to her father's people. Yet my father called me by names of which I hardly know the meaning, but my heart told me they were such as shame any modest woman ; and from that day he turned quite against me ;—nay, sir, not many weeks after that, he came in with a riding-whip in his hand ; and, accusing me harshly of

evil doings, of which I knew no more than you, sir,
he was about to strike me, and I, all in bewildering
tears, was ready to take his stripes as great kindness
compared to his harder words, when suddenly
he stopped his arm mid-way, gasped and staggered, crying
out, "The curse—the curse!" I looked up in terror.
In the great mirror opposite I saw myself, and right
behind, another wicked, fearful self, so like me that
my soul seemed to quiver within me, as though not
knowing to which similitude of body it belonged. My
father saw my double at the same moment, either in
its dreadful reality, whatever that might be, or in the
scarcely less terrible reflection in the mirror ; but what
came of it at that moment I cannot say, for I suddenly
swooned away ; and when I came to myself I was
lying in my bed, and my faithful Clarke sitting by me.
I was in my bed for days ; and even while I lay there my
double was seen by all, flitting about the house and
gardens, always about some mischievous or detestable
work. What wonder that every one shrank from me
in dread—that my father drove me forth at length,
when the disgrace of which I was the cause was past
his patience to bear. Mistress Clarke came with me ;
and here we try to live such a life of piety and prayer
as may in time set me free from the curse.'

All the time she had been speaking, I had been
weighing her story in my mind. I had hitherto put
cases of witchcraft on one side, as mere superstitions ;
and my uncle and I had had many an argument, he
supporting himself by the opinion of his good friend
Sir Matthew Hale.* Yet this sounded like the tale of
one bewitched ; or was it merely the effect of a life
of extreme seclusion telling on the nerves of a sensitive
girl ? My scepticism inclined me to the latter belief,
and when she paused I said :

'I fancy that some physician could have disabused
your father of his belief in visions '——

Just at that instant, standing as I was opposite to
her in the full and perfect morning light, I saw behind
her another figure,—a ghastly resemblance, complete

in likeness, so far as form and feature and minutest touch of dress could go, but with a loathsome demon soul looking out of the grey eyes, that were in turns mocking and voluptuous. My heart stood still within me ; every hair rose up erect ; my flesh crept with horror. I could not see the grave and tender Lucy— my eyes were fascinated by the creature beyond. I know not why, but I put out my hand to clutch it ; I grasped nothing but empty air, and my whole blood curdled to ice. For a moment I could not see ; then my sight came back, and I saw Lucy standing before me, alone, deathly pale, and, I could have fancied, almost, shrunk in size.

'IT has been near me ?' she said, as if asking a question.

The sound seemed taken out of her voice ; it was husky as the notes on an old harpsichord when the strings have ceased to vibrate. She read her answer in my face, I suppose, for I could not speak. Her look was one of intense fear, but that died away into an aspect of most humble patience. At length she seemed to force herself to face behind and around her : she saw the purple moors, the blue distant hills, quivering in the sunlight, but nothing else.

'Will you take me home ?' she said, meekly.

I took her by the hand, and led her silently through the budding heather—we dared not speak ; for we could not tell but that the dread creature was listening, although unseen,—but that IT might appear and push us asunder. I never loved her more fondly than now when—and that was the unspeakable misery—the idea of her was becoming so inextricably blended with the shuddering thought of IT. She seemed to understand what I must be feeling. She let go my hand, which she had kept clasped until then, when we reached the garden gate, and went forwards to meet her anxious friend, who was standing by the window looking for her. I could not enter the house : I needed silence, society, leisure, change—I knew not what—to shake off the sensation of that creature's presence. Yet

I lingered about the garden—I hardly know why; I partly suppose, because I feared to encounter the resemblance again on the solitary common, where it had vanished, and partly from a feeling of inexpressible compassion for Lucy. In a few minutes Mistress Clarke came forth and joined me. We walked some paces in silence.

'You know all now,' said she, solemnly.

'I saw IT,' said I, below my breath.

'And you shrink from us, now,' she said, with a hopelessness which stirred up all that was brave or good in me.

'Not a whit,' said I. 'Human flesh shrinks from encounter with the powers of darkness: and, for some reason unknown to me, the pure and holy Lucy is their victim.'

'The sins of the fathers shall be visited upon the children,' she said.

'Who is her father?' asked I. 'Knowing as much as I do, I may surely know more—know all. Tell me, I entreat you, madam, all that you can conjecture respecting this demoniac persecution of one so good.'

'I will; but not now. I must go to Lucy now. Come this afternoon, I will see you alone; and oh, sir! I will trust that you may yet find some way to help us in our sore trouble!'

I was miserably exhausted by the swooning affright which had taken possession of me. When I reached the inn, I staggered in like one overcome by wine. I went to my own private room. It was some time before I saw that the weekly post had come in, and brought me my letters. There was one from my uncle, one from my home in Devonshire, and one, re-directed over the first address, sealed with a great coat of arms. It was from Sir Philip Tempest: my letter of inquiry respecting Mary Fitzgerald had reached him at Liége, where it so happened that the Count de la Tour d'Auvergne was quartered at the very time. He remembered his wife's beautiful attendant; she had had high words with the deceased countess, respecting her intercourse with an English gentleman of good standing, who was also in the foreign service. The countess augured evil of his intentions; while Mary, proud and vehement, asserted that he would soon marry her, and resented her mistress's warnings as an insult. The consequence was, that she had left Madame de la Tour d'Auvergne's service, and, as the Count believed, had gone to live with the Englishman; whether he had married her, or not, he could not say. 'But,' added Sir Philip Tempest, 'you may easily hear what particulars you wish to know respecting Mary Fitzgerald from the Englishman himself, if, as I suspect, he is no other than my neighbour and former acquaintance, Mr. Gisborne, of Skipford Hall, in the West Riding. I am led to the belief that he is no other, by several small particulars, none of which are in themselves conclusive, but which, taken together, furnish a mass of presumptive evidence. As far as I could make out from the Count's foreign pronunciation, Gisborne was the name of the Englishman: I know that Gisborne of Skipford was abroad and in the foreign service at that time—he was a likely fellow enough for such an exploit, and, above all, certain expressions recur to my mind which he used in reference to old Bridget Fitzgerald, of Coldholme, whom he once encountered while staying with me at Starkey Manor-house. I remember that the meeting seemed to have produced some extraordinary effect upon his mind, as though he had suddenly discovered some connexion which she might have had with his previous life. I beg you to let me know if I can be of any further service to you. Your uncle once rendered me a good turn, and I will gladly repay it, so far as in me lies, to his nephew.'

I was now apparently close on the discovery which I had striven so many months to attain. But success had lost its zest. I put my letters down, and seemed to forget them all in thinking of the morning I had passed that very day. Nothing was real but the unreal presence, which had come like an evil blast across my

bodily eyes, and burnt itself down upon my brain.
Dinner came, and went away untouched. Early in
the afternoon I walked to the farm-house. I found
Mistress Clarke alone, and I was glad and relieved.
She was evidently prepared to tell me all I might wish
to hear.

'You asked me for Mistress Lucy's true name; it
is Gisborne,' she began.

'Not Gisborne of Skipford?' I exclaimed, breathless with anticipation.

'The same,' said she, quietly, not regarding my
manner. 'Her father is a man of note; although,
being a Roman Catholic, he cannot take that rank*in
this country to which his station entitles him. The
consequence is that he lives much abroad—has been
a soldier, I am told.'

'And Lucy's mother?' I asked.

She shook her head. 'I never knew her,' said she.
'Lucy was about three years old when I was engaged
to take charge of her. Her mother was dead.'

'But you know her name?—you can tell if it was
Mary Fitzgerald?'

She looked astonished. 'That was her name. But,
sir, how came you to be so well acquainted with it?
It was a mystery to the whole household at Skipford
Court. She was some beautiful young woman whom
he lured away from her protectors while he was abroad.
I have heard said he practised some terrible deceit upon
her, and when she came to know it, she was neither
to have nor to hold, but rushed off from his very arms,
and threw herself into a rapid stream and was drowned.
It stung him deep with remorse, but I used to think
the remembrance of the mother's cruel death made him
love the child yet dearer.'

I told her, as briefly as might be, of my researches
after the descendant and heir of the Fitzgeralds of
Kildoon, and added—something of my old lawyer
spirit returning into me for the moment—that I had
no doubt but that we should prove Lucy to be by right
possessed of large estates in Ireland.

No flush came over her grey face; no light into her eyes. 'And what is all the wealth in the whole world to that poor girl?' she said. 'It will not free her from the ghastly bewitchment which persecutes her. As for money, what a pitiful thing it is! it cannot touch her.'

'No more can the Evil Creature harm her,' I said. 'Her holy nature dwells apart, and cannot be defiled or stained by all the devilish arts in the whole world.'

'True! but it is a cruel fate to know that all shrink from her, sooner or later, as from one possessed—accursed.'

'How came it to pass?' I asked.

'Nay, I know not. Old rumours there are, that were bruited through the household at Skipford.'

'Tell me,' I demanded.

'They came from servants, who would fain account for everything. They say that, many years ago, Mr. Gisborne killed a dog belonging to an old witch at Coldholme; that she cursed, with a dreadful and mysterious curse, the creature, whatever it might be, that he should love best; and that it struck so deeply into his heart that for years he kept himself aloof from any temptation to love aught. But who could help loving Lucy?'

'You never heard the witch's name?' I gasped.

'Yes—they called her Bridget; they said he would never go near the spot again for terror of her. Yet he was a brave man!'

'Listen,' said I, taking hold of her arm, the better to arrest her full attention; 'if what I suspect holds true, that man stole Bridget's only child—the very Mary Fitzgerald who was Lucy's mother; if so, Bridget cursed him in ignorance of the deeper wrong he had done her. To this hour she yearns after her lost child, and questions the saints whether she be living or not. The roots of that curse lie deeper than she knows: she unwittingly banned him for a deeper guilt than that of killing a dumb beast. The sins of the fathers are indeed visited upon the children.'

'But,' said Mistress Clarke, eagerly, 'she would

never let evil rest on her own grandchild ? Surely, sir, if what you say be true, there are hopes for Lucy. Let us go—go at once, and tell this fearful woman all that you suspect, and beseech her to take off the spell she has put upon her innocent grandchild.'

It seemed to me, indeed, that something like this was the best course we could pursue. But first it was necessary to ascertain more than what mere rumour or careless hearsay could tell. My thoughts turned to my uncle—he could advise me wisely—he ought to know all. I resolved to go to him without delay ; but I did not choose to tell Mistress Clarke of all the visionary plans that flitted through my mind. I simply declared my intention of proceeding straight to London on Lucy's affairs. I bade her believe that my interest on the young lady's behalf was greater than ever, and that my whole time should be given up to her cause. I saw that Mistress Clarke distrusted me, because my mind was too full of thoughts for my words to flow freely. She sighed and shook her head, and said, ' Well, it is all right ! ' in such a tone that it was an implied reproach. But I was firm and constant in my heart, and I took confidence from that.

I rode to London. I rode long days drawn out into the lovely summer nights : I could not rest. I reached London. I told my uncle all, though in the stir of the great city the horror had faded away, and I could hardly imagine that he would believe the account I gave him of the fearful double of Lucy which I had seen on the lonely moor-side. But my uncle had lived many years, and learnt many things ; and, in the deep secrets of family history that had been confided to him, he had heard of cases of innocent people bewitched and taken possession of by evil spirits yet more fearful than Lucy's. For, as he said, to judge from all I told him, that resemblance had no power over her—she was too pure and good to be tainted by its evil, haunting presence. It had, in all probability, so my uncle conceived, tried to suggest wicked thoughts and to tempt to wicked actions ; but she, in her saintly maidenhood, had passed on undefiled by evil thought or deed. It could not touch her soul : but true, it set her apart from all sweet love or common human intercourse. My uncle threw himself with an energy more like six-and-twenty than sixty into the consideration of the whole case. He undertook the proving Lucy's descent, and volunteered to go and find out Mr. Gisborne, and obtain, firstly, the legal proofs of her descent from the Fitzgeralds of Kildoon, and, secondly, to try and hear all that he could respecting the working of the curse, and whether any and what means had been taken to exorcise that terrible appearance. For he told me of instances where, by prayers and long fasting, the evil possessor had been driven forth with howling and many cries from the body which it had come to inhabit ; he spoke of those strange New England cases*which had happened not so long before ; of Mr. Defoe,* who had written a book, wherein he had named many modes of subduing apparitions, and sending them back whence they came ; and, lastly, he spoke low of dreadful ways of compelling witches to undo their witchcraft. But I could not endure to hear of those tortures and burnings. I said that Bridget was rather a wild and savage woman than a malignant witch ; and, above all, that Lucy was of her kith and kin ; and that, in putting her to the trial, by water or by fire, we should be torturing—it might be to the death—the ancestress of her we sought to redeem.

My uncle thought awhile, and then said, that in this last matter I was right—at any rate, it should not be tried, with his consent, till all other modes of remedy had failed ; and he assented to my proposal that I should go myself and see Bridget, and tell her all.

In accordance with this, I went down once more to the wayside inn near Coldholme. It was late at night when I arrived there ; and, while I supped, I inquired of the landlord more particulars as to Bridget's ways. Solitary and savage had been her life for many years. Wild and despotic were her words and manner to those few people who came across her path. The country-folk did her imperious bidding, because they feared to disobey. If they pleased her, they prospered ; if, on the contrary, they neglected or traversed her behests, misfortune, small or great, fell on them and theirs. It was not detestation so much as an indefinable terror that she excited.

In the morning I went to see her. She was standing on the green outside her cottage, and received me with the sullen grandeur of a throneless queen. I read in her face that she recognized me, and that I was not unwelcome ; but she stood silent till I had opened my errand.

'I have news of your daughter,' said I, resolved to speak straight to all that I knew she felt of love, and not to spare her. 'She is dead !'

The stern figure scarcely trembled, but her hand sought the support of the door-post.

'I knew that she was dead,' said she, deep and low, and then was silent for an instant. 'My tears that should have flowed for her were burnt up long years ago. Young man, tell me about her.'

'Not yet,' said I, having a strange power given me of confronting one, whom, nevertheless, in my secret soul I dreaded.

'You had once a little dog,' I continued. The words called out in her more show of emotion than the intelligence of her daughter's death. She broke in upon my speech :—

'I had ! It was hers—the last thing I had of hers— and it was shot for wantonness ! It died in my arms. The man who killed that dog rues it to this day. For that dumb beast's blood, his best-beloved stands accursed.'

Her eyes distended, as if she were in a trance and saw the working of her curse. Again I spoke :—

'O woman !' I said, 'that best-beloved, standing accursed before men, is your dead daughter's child.'

The life, the energy, the passion came back to the eyes with which she pierced through me, to see if I spoke truth ; then, without another question or word, she threw herself on the ground with fearful vehemence, and clutched at the innocent daisies with convulsed hands.

'Bone of my bone ! flesh of my flesh ! have I cursed thee—and art thou accursed ? '

So she moaned, as she lay prostrate in her great agony. I stood aghast at my own work. She did not hear my broken sentences ; she asked no more, but the dumb confirmation which my sad looks had given that one fact, that her curse rested on her own daughter's child. The fear grew on me lest she should die in her strife of body and soul ; and then might not Lucy remain under the spell as long as she lived ?

Even at this moment, I saw Lucy coming through the woodland path that led to Bridget's cottage ; Mistress Clarke was with her : I felt at my heart that it was she, by the balmy peace which the look of her sent over me, as she slowly advanced, a glad surprise shining out of her soft quiet eyes. That was as her gaze met mine. As her looks fell on the woman lying stiff, convulsed on the earth, they became full of tender pity ; and she came forward to try and lift her up. Seating herself on the turf, she took Bridget's head into her lap ; and, with gentle touches, she arranged the dishevelled grey hair streaming thick and wild from beneath her mutch.

'God help her ! ' murmured Lucy. 'How she suffers ! '

At her desire we sought for water ; but when we returned, Bridget had recovered her wandering senses, and was kneeling with clasped hands before Lucy, gazing at that sweet sad face as though her troubled nature drank in health and peace from every moment's contemplation. A faint tinge on Lucy's pale cheeks showed me that she was aware of our return ; otherwise it appeared as if she was conscious of her influence for good over the passionate and troubled woman kneeling before her, and would not willingly avert her grave and loving eyes from that wrinkled and careworn countenance.

Suddenly—in the twinkling of an eye—the creature
appeared, there, behind Lucy; fearfully the same as to
outward semblance, but kneeling exactly as Bridget
knelt, and clasping her hands in jesting mimicry as
Bridget clasped hers in her ecstasy that was deepening
into a prayer. Mistress Clarke cried out—Bridget
arose slowly, her gaze fixed on the creature beyond:
drawing her breath with a hissing sound, never moving
her terrible eyes, that were steady as stone, she made a
dart at the phantom, and caught, as I had done, a
mere handful of empty air. We saw no more of the
creature—it vanished as suddenly as it came, but
Bridget looked slowly on, as if watching some receding
form. Lucy sat still, white, trembling, drooping—
I think she would have swooned if I had not been there
to uphold her. While I was attending to her, Bridget
passed us, without a word to any one, and, entering
her cottage, she barred herself in, and left us without.

All our endeavours were now directed to get Lucy
back to the house where she had tarried the night
before. Mistress Clarke told me that, not hearing from
me (some letter must have miscarried), she had grown
impatient and despairing, and had urged Lucy to the
enterprise of coming to seek her grandmother; not
telling her, indeed, of the dread reputation she possessed, or how we suspected her of having so fearfully
blighted that innocent girl; but, at the same time,
hoping much from the mysterious stirring of blood,
which Mistress Clarke trusted in for the removal of the
curse. They had come, by a different route from that
which I had taken, to a village inn not far from Coldholme, only the night before. This was the first interview between ancestress and descendant.

All through the sultry noon I wandered along the
tangled wood-paths of the old neglected forest, thinking
where to turn for remedy in a matter so complicated
and mysterious. Meeting a countryman, I asked my
way to the nearest clergyman, and went, hoping to
obtain some counsel from him. But he proved to be
a coarse and common-minded man, giving no time or

attention to the intricacies of a case, but dashing out a strong opinion involving immediate action. For instance, as soon as I named Bridget Fitzgerald, he exclaimed :—

' The Coldholme witch ! the Irish papist ! I'd have had her ducked long since but for that other papist, Sir Philip Tempest. He has had to threaten honest folk about here over and over again, or they'd have had her up before the justices for her black doings. And it's the law of the land that witches should be burnt !* Aye, and of Scripture, too, sir ! Yet you see a papist, if he's a rich squire, can overrule both law and Scripture. I'd carry a faggot myself to rid the country of her ! '

Such a one could give me no help. I rather drew back what I had already said ; and tried to make the parson forget it, by treating him to several pots of beer, in the village inn, to which we had adjourned for our conference at his suggestion. I left him as soon as I could, and returned to Coldholme, shaping my way past deserted Starkey Manor-House, and coming upon it by the back. At that side were the oblong remains of the old moat, the waters of which lay placid and motionless under the crimson rays of the setting sun ; with the forest-trees lying straight along each side, and their deep-green foliage mirrored to blackness in the burnished surface of the moat below—and the broken sun-dial at the end nearest the hall—and the heron, standing on one leg at the water's edge, lazily looking down for fish—the lonely and desolate house scarce needed the broken windows, the weeds on the door-sill, the broken shutter softly flapping to and fro in the twilight breeze, to fill up the picture of desertion and decay. I lingered about the place until the growing darkness warned me on. And then I passed along the path, cut by the orders of the last lady of Starkey Manor-House, that led me to Bridget's cottage. I resolved at once to see her ; and, in spite of closed doors —it might be of resolved will—she should see me. So I knocked at her door, gently, loudly, fiercely. I shook it so vehemently that at length the old hinges gave way, and with a crash it fell inwards, leaving me suddenly face to face with Bridget—I, red, heated, agitated with my so long-baffled efforts—she, stiff as any stone, standing right facing me, her eyes dilated with terror, her ashen lips trembling, but her body motionless. In her hands she held her crucifix, as if by that holy symbol she sought to oppose my entrance. At sight of me, her whole frame relaxed, and she sank back upon a chair. Some mighty tension had given way. Still her eyes looked fearfully into the gloom of the outer air, made more opaque by the glimmer of the lamp inside, which she had placed before the picture of the Virgin.

'Is she there?' asked Bridget, hoarsely.

'No! Who? I am alone. You remember me.'

'Yes,' replied she, still terror-stricken. 'But she —that creature—has been looking in upon me through that window all day long. I closed it up with my shawl; and then I saw her feet below the door, as long as it was light, and I knew she heard my very breathing —nay, worse, my very prayers; and I could not pray, for her listening choked the words ere they rose to my lips. Tell me, who is she?—what means that double girl I saw this morning? One had a look of my dead Mary; but the other curdled my blood, and yet it was the same!'

She had taken hold of my arm, as if to secure herself some human companionship. She shook all over with the slight, never-ceasing tremor of intense terror. I told her my tale, as I have told it you, sparing none of the details.

How Mistress Clarke had informed me that the resemblance had driven Lucy forth from her father's house—how I had disbelieved, until, with mine own eyes, I had seen another Lucy standing behind my Lucy, the same in form and feature, but with the demon-soul looking out of the eyes. I told her all, I say, believing that she—whose curse was working so upon the life of her innocent grandchild—was the only person who could find the remedy and the redemption. When I had done, she sat silent for many minutes.

" You love Mary's child ? ' she asked.

' I do, in spite of the fearful working of the curse—
I love her. Yet I shrink from her ever since that day
on the moor-side. And men must shrink from one so
accompanied ; friends and lovers must stand afar off.
Oh, Bridget Fitzgerald ! loosen the curse ! Set her
free ! '

' Where is she ? '

I eagerly caught at the idea that her presence was
needed, in order that, by some strange prayer or exorcism, the spell might be reversed.

' I will go and bring her to you,' I exclaimed. But
Bridget tightened her hold upon my arm.

' Not so,' said she, in a low, hoarse voice. ' It would
kill me to see her again as I saw her this morning. And
I must live till I have worked my work. Leave me ! '
said she, suddenly, and again taking up the cross. ' I
defy the demon I have called up. Leave me to wrestle
with it ! '

She stood up, as if in an ecstasy of inspiration, from
which all fear was banished. I lingered—why, I can
hardly tell—until once more she bade me begone. As
I went along the forest way, I looked back, and saw her
planting the cross in the empty threshold, where the
door had been.

The next morning Lucy and I went to seek her, to
bid her join her prayers with ours. The cottage stood
open and wide to our gaze. No human being was
there : the cross remained on the threshold, but Bridget
was gone.

## CHAPTER III.

WHAT was to be done next ? was the question that
I asked myself.  As for Lucy, she would fain have sub-
mitted to the doom that lay upon her.  Her gentleness
and piety, under the pressure of so horrible a life,
seemed over-passive to me.  She never complained.
Mrs. Clarke complained more than ever.  As for me,
I was more in love with the real Lucy than ever ; but
I shrunk from the false similitude with an intensity pro-
portioned to my love.  I found out by instinct that
Mrs. Clarke had occasional temptations to leave Lucy.
The good lady's nerves were shaken, and, from what
she said, I could almost have concluded that the object
of the Double was to drive away from Lucy this last
and almost earliest friend.  At times, I could scarcely
bear to own it, but I myself felt inclined to turn re-
creant ; and I would accuse Lucy of being too patient
—too resigned.  One after another, she won the little
children of Coldholme.  (Mrs. Clarke and she had
resolved to stay there, for was it not as good a place
as any other to such as they ?  and did not all our faint
hopes rest on Bridget ?—never seen or heard of now,
but still, we trusted, to come back, or give some token ?)
So, as I say, one after another, the little children came
about my Lucy, won by her soft tones, and her gentle
smiles, and kind actions.  Alas ! one after another they
fell away, and shrunk from her path with blanching
terror ;  and we too surely guessed the reason why.
It was the last drop.  I could bear it no longer.  I
resolved no more to linger around the spot, but to go
back to my uncle, and among the learned divines of the
city of London, seek for some power whereby to annul
the curse.

My uncle, meanwhile, had obtained all the requisite
testimonials relating to Lucy's descent and birth, from
the Irish lawyers, and from Mr. Gisborne.  The latter
gentleman had written from abroad (he was again serving in the Austrian army), a letter alternately passion

ately self-reproachful and stoically repellent. It was evident that when he thought of Mary—her short life— how he had wronged her, and of her violent death, he could hardly find words severe enough for his own conduct ; and from this point of view, the curse that Bridget had laid upon him and his was regarded by him as a prophetic doom, to the utterance of which she was moved by a Higher Power, working for the fulfilment of a deeper vengeance than for the death of the poor dog. But then, again, when he came to speak of his daughter, the repugnance which the conduct of the demoniac creature had produced in his mind, was but ill-disguised under a show of profound indifference as to Lucy's fate. One almost felt as if he would have been as content to put her out of existence, as he would have been to destroy some disgusting reptile that had invaded his chamber or his couch.

The great Fitzgerald property was Lucy's ; and that was all—was nothing.

My uncle and I sat in the gloom of a London November evening, in our house in Ormond Street. I was out of health, and felt as if I were in an inextricable coil of misery. Lucy and I wrote to each other, but that was little ; and we dared not see each other for dread of the fearful Third, who had more than once taken her place at our meetings. My uncle had, on the day I speak of, bidden prayers to be put up, on the ensuing Sabbath, in many a church and meeting-house in London, for one grievously tormented by an evil spirit. He had faith in prayers—I had none ; I was fast losing faith in all things. So we sat—he trying to interest me in the old talk of other days, I oppressed by one thought— when our old servant, Anthony, opened the door, and, without speaking, showed in a very gentlemanly and prepossessing man, who had something remarkable about his dress, betraying his profession to be that of the Roman Catholic priesthood. He glanced at my uncle first, then at me. It was to me he bowed.

'I did not give my name,' said he, 'because you would hardly have recognized it ; unless, sir, when in the north, you heard of Father Bernard, the chaplain at Stoney Hurst ? '*

I remembered afterwards that I had heard of him, but at the time I had utterly forgotten it ; so I professed myself a complete stranger to him ; while my ever-hospitable uncle, although hating a papist as much as it was in his nature to hate anything, placed a chair for the visitor, and bade Anthony bring glasses and a fresh jug of claret.

Father Bernard received this courtesy with the graceful ease and pleasant acknowledgment which belongs to the man of the world. Then he turned to scan me with his keen glance. After some slight conversation, entered into on his part, I am certain, with an intention of discovering on what terms of confidence I stood with my uncle, he paused, and said gravely—

'I am sent here with a message to you,' sir, from a woman to whom you have shown kindness, and who is one of my penitents, in Antwerp—one Bridget Fitzgerald.'

'Bridget Fitzgerald !' exclaimed I. 'In Antwerp ? Tell me, sir, all that you can about her.'

'There is much to be said,' he replied. 'But may I inquire if this gentleman—if your uncle is acquainted with the particulars of which you and I stand informed ? '

'All that I know, he knows,' said I, eagerly laying my hand on my uncle's arm, as he made a motion as if to quit the room.

'Then I have to speak before two gentlemen who, however they may differ from me in faith, are yet fully impressed with the fact, that there are evil powers going about continually to take cognizance of our evil thoughts ; and, if their Master gives them power, to bring them into overt action. Such is my theory of the nature of that sin, which I dare not disbelieve— as some sceptics would have us do—the sin of witchcraft. Of this deadly sin, you and I are aware, Bridget Fitzgerald has been guilty. Since you saw her last, many prayers have been offered in our churches, many

masses sung, many penances undergone, in order that,
if God and the Holy Saints so willed it, her sin might
be blotted out.    But it has not been so willed.'

'Explain to me,' said I, ' who you are, and how you
come connected with Bridget.   Why is she at Antwerp?
I pray you, sir, tell me more.   If I am impatient,
excuse me ;  I am ill and feverish, and in consequence
bewildered.'

There was something to me inexpressibly soothing
in the tone of voice with which he began to narrate, as
it were from the beginning, his acquaintance with
Bridget.

'I had known Mr. and Mrs. Starkey during their
residence abroad, and so it fell out naturally that, when
I came as chaplain to the Sherburnes at Stoney Hurst,
our acquaintance was renewed ; and thus I became the
confessor of the whole family, isolated as they were
from the offices of the Church, Sherburne being their
nearest neighbour who professed the true faith.    Of
course, you are aware that facts revealed in confession are sealed as in the grave ;  but I learnt enough of
Bridget's character to be convinced that I had to do
with no common woman ;  one powerful for good as for
evil.   I believe that I was able to give her spiritual
assistance from time to time, and that she looked upon
me as a servant of that Holy Church, which has such
wonderful power of moving men's hearts, and relieving
them of the burden of their sins.    I have known her
cross the moors on the wildest nights of storm, to confess and be absolved ;  and then she would return,
calmed and subdued, to her daily work about her mistress, no one witting where she had been during the
hours that most passed in sleep upon their beds.    After
her daughter's departure—after Mary's mysterious disappearance—I had to impose many a long penance, in
order to wash away the sin of impatient repining that
was fast leading her into the deeper guilt of blasphemy.
She set out on that long journey of which you have
possibly heard—that fruitless journey in search of Mary
—and during her absence, my superiors ordered my

return to my former duties at Antwerp, and for many years I heard no more of Bridget.

'Not many months ago, as I was passing homewards in the evening, along one of the streets near St. Jacques, leading into the Meer Straet, I saw a woman sitting crouched up under the shrine of the Holy Mother of Sorrows. Her hood was drawn over her head, so that the shadow caused by the light of the lamp above fell deep over her face; her hands were clasped round her knees. It was evident that she was some one in hopeless trouble, and as such it was my duty to stop and speak. I naturally addressed her first in Flemish, believing her to be one of the lower class of inhabitants. She shook her head, but did not look up. Then I tried French, and she replied in that language, but speaking it so indifferently, that I was sure she was either English or Irish, and consequently spoke to her in my own native tongue. She recognised my voice; and, starting up, caught at my robes, dragging me before the blessed shrine, and throwing herself down, and forcing me, as much by her evident desire as by her action, to kneel beside her, she exclaimed—

'"O Holy Virgin! you will never hearken to me again, but hear him; for you know him of old, that he does your bidding, and strives to heal broken hearts. Hear him!"'

'She turned to me.

'"She will hear you, if you will only pray. She never hears me: she and all the saints in Heaven cannot hear my prayers, for the Evil One carries them off, as he carried that first away. O Father Bernard, pray for me!"'

'I prayed for one in sore distress, of what nature I could not say; but the Holy Virgin would know. Bridget held me fast, gasping with eagerness at the sound of my words. When I had ended, I rose, and, making the sign of the Cross over her, I was going to bless her in the name of the Holy Church, when she shrank away like some terrified creature, and said—

"I am guilty of deadly sin, and am not shriven."

' " Arise, my daughter," said I, " and come with me."
And I led the way into one of the confessionals of St.
Jacques.

' She knelt; I listened. No words came. The evil
powers had stricken her dumb, as I heard afterwards
they had many a time before, when she approached
confession.

' She was too poor to pay for the necessary forms of
exorcism; and hitherto those priests to whom she had
addressed herself were either so ignorant of the meaning
of her broken French, or her Irish-English, or else
esteemed her to be one crazed—as, indeed, her wild and
excited manner might easily have led any one to think
—that they had neglected the sole means of loosening
her tongue, so that she might confess her deadly sin,
and after due penance, obtain absolution. But I knew
Bridget of old, and felt that she was a penitent sent to
me. I went through those holy offices appointed by
our Church for the relief of such a case. I was the more
bound to do this, as I found that she had come to Antwerp for the sole purpose of discovering me, and making
confession to me. Of the nature of that fearful confession I am forbidden to speak. Much of it you know;
possibly all.

' It now remains for her to free herself from mortal
guilt, and to set others free from the consequences
thereof. No prayers, no masses, will ever do it,
although they may strengthen her with that strength
by which alone acts of deepest love and purest self-
devotion may be performed. Her words of passion,
and cries for revenge—her unholy prayers could never
reach the ears of the Holy Saints! Other powers intercepted them, and wrought so that the curses thrown up
to Heaven have fallen on her own flesh and blood; and
so, through her very strength of love, have bruised and
crushed her heart. Henceforward her former self must
be buried,—yea, buried quick, if need be,—but never
more to make sign, or utter cry on earth! She has
become a Poor Clare, in order that, by perpetual penance and constant service of others, she may at length

so act as to obtain final absolution and rest for her soul. Until then, the innocent must suffer. It is to plead for the innocent that I come to you ; not in the name of the witch, Bridget Fitzgerald, but of the penitent and servant of all men, the Poor Clare, Sister Magdalen.'

'Sir,' said I, 'I listen to your request with respect ; only I may tell you it is not needed to urge me to do all that I can on behalf of one, love for whom is part of my very life. If for a time I have absented myself from her, it is to think and work for her redemption. I, a member of the English Church—my uncle, a Puritan— pray morning and night for her by name : the con- gregations of London, on the next Sabbath, will pray for one unknown, that she may be set free from the Powers of Darkness. Moreover, I must tell you, sir, that those evil ones touch not the great calm of her soul. She lives her own pure and loving life, unharmed and untainted, though all men fall off from her. I would I could have her faith !'

My uncle now spoke.

'Nephew,' said he, 'it seems to me that this gentle- man, although professing what I consider an erroneous creed, has touched upon the right point in exhorting Bridget to acts of love and mercy, whereby to wipe out her sin of hate and vengeance. Let us strive after our fashion, by almsgiving and visiting of the needy and fatherless, to make our prayers acceptable. Mean- while, I myself will go down into the north, and take charge of the maiden. I am too old to be daunted by man or demon. I will bring her to this house as to a home ; and let the Double come if it will ! A company of godly divines shall give it the meeting, and we will try issue.'

The kindly, brave old man ! But Father Bernard sat on musing.

'All hate,' said he, 'cannot be quenched in her heart ; all Christian forgiveness cannot have entered into her soul, or the demon would have lost its power— You said, I think, that her grandchild was still tor- mented ?'

'Still tormented!' I replied, sadly, thinking of
Mistress Clarke's last letter.

He rose to go. We afterwards heard that the occasion of his coming to London was a secret political
mission on behalf of the Jacobites.* Nevertheless, he
was a good and a wise man.

Months and months passed away without any change.
Lucy entreated my uncle to leave her where she was,—
dreading, as I learnt, lest if she came, with her fearful
companion, to dwell in the same house with me, that
my love could not stand the repeated shocks to which
I should be doomed. And this she thought from no
distrust of the strength of my affection, but from a kind
of pitying sympathy for the terror to the nerves which
she observed that the demoniac visitation caused in all.

I was restless and miserable. I devoted myself to
good works; but I performed them from no spirit of
love, but solely from the hope of reward and payment,
and so the reward was never granted. At length, I
asked my uncle's leave to travel; and I went forth, a
wanderer, with no distincter end than that of many
another wanderer—to get away from myself. A
strange impulse led me to Antwerp, in spite of the wars
and commotions then raging in the Low Countries*—or
rather, perhaps, the very craving to become interested
in something external, led me into the thick of the
struggle then going on with the Austrians. The cities
of Flanders were all full at that time of civil distur-
bances and rebellions, only kept down by force, and the
presence of an Austrian garrison in every place.

I arrived in Antwerp, and made inquiry for Father
Bernard. He was away in the country for a day or
two. Then I asked my way to the Convent of Poor
Clares; but, being healthy and prosperous, I could only
see the dim, pent-up, grey walls, shut closely in by
narrow streets, in the lowest part of the town. My
landlord told me, that had I been stricken by some
loathsome disease, or in desperate case of any kind, the
Poor Clares would have taken me, and tended me. He
spoke of them as an order of mercy of the strictest kind,

dressing scantily in the coarsest materials, going bare-foot, living on what the inhabitants of Antwerp chose to bestow, and sharing even those fragments and crumbs with the poor and helpless that swarmed all around; receiving no letters or communication with the outer world; utterly dead to everything but the alleviation of suffering. He smiled at my inquiring whether I could get speech of one of them; and told me that they were even forbidden to speak for the purposes of begging their daily food; while yet they lived, and fed others upon what was given in charity.

'But,' exclaimed I, 'supposing all men forgot them! Would they quietly lie down and die, without making sign of their extremity?'

'If such were their rule, the Poor Clares would willingly do it; but their founder appointed a remedy for such extreme case as you suggest. They have a bell—'tis but a small one, as I have heard, and has yet never been rung in the memory of man: when the Poor Clares have been without food for twenty-four hours, they may ring this bell, and then trust to our good people of Antwerp for rushing to the rescue of the Poor Clares, who have taken such blessed care of us in all our straits.'

It seemed to me that such rescue would be late in the day; but I did not say what I thought. I rather turned the conversation, by asking my landlord if he knew, or had ever heard, anything of a certain Sister Magdalen.

'Yes,' said he, rather under his breath, 'news will creep out, even from a convent of Poor Clares. Sister Magdalen is either a great sinner or a great saint. She does more, as I have heard, than all the other nuns put together; yet, when last month they would fain have made her mother-superior, she begged rather that they would place her below all the rest, and make her the meanest servant of all.'

'You never saw her?' asked I.

'Never,' he replied.

I was weary of waiting for Father Bernard, and yet

I lingered in Antwerp. The political state of things became worse than ever, increased to its height by the scarcity of food consequent on many deficient harvests. I saw groups of fierce, squalid men, at every corner of the street, glaring out with wolfish eyes at my sleek skin and handsome clothes.

At last Father Bernard returned. We had a long conversation, in which he told me that, curiously enough, Mr. Gisborne, Lucy's father, was serving in one of the Austrian regiments, then in garrison at Antwerp. I asked Father Bernard if he would make us acquainted; which he consented to do. But, a day or two afterwards, he told me that, on hearing my name, Mr. Gisborne had declined responding to any advances on my part, saying he had abjured his country, and hated his countrymen.

Probably he recollected my name in connection with that of his daughter Lucy. Anyhow, it was clear enough that I had no chance of making his acquaintance. Father Bernard confirmed me in my suspicions of the hidden fermentation, for some coming evil, working among the ' blouses '* of Antwerp, and he would fain have had me depart from out the city; but I rather craved the excitement of danger, and stubbornly refused to leave.

One day, when I was walking with him in the Place Verte, he bowed to an Austrian officer, who was crossing towards the cathedral.

'That is Mr. Gisborne,' said he, as soon as the gentleman was past.

I turned to look at the tall, slight figure of the officer. He carried himself in a stately manner, although he was past middle age, and from his years, might have had some excuse for a slight stoop. As I looked at the man, he turned round, his eyes met mine, and I saw his face. Deeply lined, sallow, and scathed was that countenance; scarred by passion as well as by the fortunes of war. 'Twas but a moment our eyes met. We each turned round, and went on our separate way.

But his whole appearance was not one to be easily forgotten ; the thorough appointment of the dress, and evident thought bestowed on it, made but an incongruous whole with the dark, gloomy expression of his countenance. Because he was Lucy's father, I sought instinctively to meet him everywhere. At last he must have become aware of my pertinacity, for he gave me a haughty scowl whenever I passed him. In one of these encounters, however, I chanced to be of some service to him. He was turning the corner of a street, and came suddenly on one of the groups of discontented Flemings of whom I have spoken. Some words were exchanged, when my gentleman out with his sword, and with a slight but skilful cut drew blood from one of those who had insulted him, as he fancied, though I was too far off to hear the words. They would all have fallen upon him had I not rushed forwards and raised the cry, then well known in Antwerp, of rally, to the Austrian soldiers who were perpetually patrolling the streets, and who came in numbers to the rescue. I think that neither Mr. Gisborne nor the mutinous group of plebeians owed me much gratitude for my interference. He had planted himself against a wall, in a skilful attitude of fence, ready with his bright glancing rapier to do battle with all the heavy, fierce, unarmed men, some six or seven in number. But when his own soldiers came up, he sheathed his sword ; and, giving some careless word of command, sent them away again, and continued his saunter all alone down the street, the workmen snarling in his rear, and more than half-inclined to fall on me for my cry for rescue. I cared not if they did, my life seemed so dreary a burden just then ; and, perhaps, it was this daring loitering among them that prevented their attacking me. Instead, they suffered me to fall into conversation with them ; and I heard some of their grievances. Sore and heavy to be borne were they, and no wonder the sufferers were savage and desperate.

The man whom Gisborne had wounded across his face would fain have got out of me the name of his

aggressor, but I refused to tell it.   Another of the
group heard his inquiry, and made answer :—
    ' I know the man.  He is one Gisborne, aide-de-camp
to the General-Commandant.   I know him well.'
He began to tell some story in connection with
Gisborne in a low and muttering voice ;  and while
he was relating a tale, which I saw excited their evil
blood, and which they evidently wished me not to
hear, I sauntered away and back to my lodgings.
    That night Antwerp was in open revolt.  The inhabi-
tants rose in rebellion against their Austrian masters.
The Austrians, holding the gates of the city, remained
at first pretty quiet in the citadel ;  only, from time to
time, the boom of a great cannon swept sullenly over
the town.   But if they expected the disturbance to
die away, and spend itself in a few hours' fury, they
were mistaken.   In a day or two, the rioters held
possession of the principal municipal buildings.   Then
the Austrians poured forth in bright flaming array,
calm and smiling, as they marched to the posts assigned,
as if the fierce mob were no more to them than the
swarms of buzzing summer flies.   Their practised
manœuvres, their well-aimed shot, told with terrible
effect ;  but in the place of one slain rioter, three sprang
up of his blood to avenge his loss.   But a deadly foe,
a ghastly ally of the Austrians, was at work.   Food,
scarce and dear for months, was now hardly to be
obtained at any price.   Desperate efforts were being
made to bring provisions into the city, for the rioters
had friends without.   Close to the city port nearest to
the Scheldt, a great struggle took place.   I was there,
helping the rioters, whose cause I had adopted.   We
had a savage encounter with the Austrians.   Numbers
fell on both sides ;  I saw them lie bleeding for a
moment ;  then a volley of smoke obscured them ;  and
when it cleared away, they were dead—trampled upon
or smothered, pressed down and hidden by the freshly-
wounded whom those last guns had brought low.   And
then a grey-robed and grey-veiled figure came right
across the flashing guns, and stooped over some one,

whose life-blood was ebbing away; sometimes it was
to give him drink from cans which they carried slung
at their sides, sometimes I saw the cross held above
a dying man, and rapid prayers were being uttered,
unheard by men in that hellish din and clangour, but
listened to by One above. I saw all this as in a dream:
the reality of that stern time was battle and carnage.
But I knew that these grey figures, their bare feet all
wet with blood, and their faces hidden by their veils,
were the Poor Clares—sent forth now because dire
agony was abroad and imminent danger at hand.
Therefore, they left their cloistered shelter, and came
into that thick and evil mêlée.

Close to me—driven past me by the struggle of
many fighters—came the Antwerp burgess with the
scarce-healed scar upon his face; and in an instant
more, he was thrown by the press upon the Austrian
officer Gisborne, and ere either had recovered the shock,
the burgess had recognized his opponent.

'Ha! the Englishman Gisborne!' he cried, and
threw himself upon him with redoubled fury. He had
struck him hard—the Englishman was down; when
out of the smoke came a dark-grey figure, and threw
herself right under the uplifted flashing sword. The
burgess's arm stood arrested. Neither Austrians nor
Anversois willingly harmed the Poor Clares.

'Leave him to me!' said a low stern voice. 'He
is mine enemy—mine for many years.'

Those words were the last I heard. I myself was
struck down by a bullet. I remember nothing more
for days. When I came to myself, I was at the
extremity of weakness, and was craving for food to
recruit my strength. My landlord sat watching me.
He, too, looked pinched and shrunken; he had heard
of my wounded state, and sought me out. Yes! the
struggle still continued, but the famine was sore; and
some, he had heard, had died for lack of food. The
tears stood in his eyes as he spoke. But soon he
shook off his weakness, and his natural cheerfulness
returned. Father Bernard had been to see me—no

one else. (Who should, indeed ?) Father Bernard
would come back that afternoon—he had promised.
But Father Bernard never came, although I was up
and dressed, and looking eagerly for him.

My landlord brought me a meal which he had cooked
himself : of what it was composed he would not say.
but it was most excellent, and with every mouthful
I seemed to gain strength. The good man sat looking
at my evident enjoyment with a happy smile of sympathy ; but, as my appetite became satisfied, I began
to detect a certain wistfulness in his eyes, as if craving
for the food I had so nearly devoured—for, indeed, at
that time I was hardly aware of the extent of the
famine. Suddenly, there was a sound of many rushing
feet past our window. My landlord opened one of the
sides of it, the better to learn what was going on. Then
we heard a faint, cracked, tinkling bell, coming shrill upon
the air, clear and distinct from all other sounds. ' Holy
Mother ! ' exclaimed my landlord, ' the Poor Clares ! '

He snatched up the fragments of my meal, and
crammed them into my hands, bidding me follow.
Downstairs he ran, clutching at more food, as the
women of his house eagerly held it out to him ; and
in a moment we were in the street, moving along with
the great current, all tending towards the Convent of
the Poor Clares. And still, as if piercing our ears with
its inarticulate cry, came the shrill tinkle of the bell.
In that strange crowd were old men trembling and
sobbing, as they carried their little pittance of food ;
women with the tears running down their cheeks, who
had snatched up what provisions they had in the
vessels in which they stood, so that the burden of these
was in many cases much greater than that which they
contained ; children, with flushed faces, grasping tight
the morsel of bitten cake or bread, in their eagerness
to carry it safe to the help of the Poor Clares ; strong
men—yea, both Anversois and Austrians—pressing
onwards with set teeth, and no word spoken ; and
over all, and through all, came that sharp tinkle—
that cry for help in extremity.

We met the first torrent of people returning with blanched and piteous faces; they were issuing out of the convent to make way for the offerings of others. 'Haste, haste!' said they. 'A Poor Clare is dying! A Poor Clare is dead for hunger! God forgive us, and our city!'

We pressed on. The stream bore us along where it would. We were carried through refectories, bare and crumbless; into cells over whose doors the conventual name of the occupant was written. Thus it was that I, with others, was forced into Sister Magdalen's cell. On her couch lay Gisborne, pale unto death, but not dead. By his side was a cup of water, and a small morsel of mouldy bread, which he had pushed out of his reach, and could not move to obtain. Over against his bed were these words, copied in the English version: 'Therefore, if thine enemy hunger, feed him; if he thirst, give him drink.'*

Some of us gave him of our food, and left him eating greedily, like some famished wild animal. For now it was no longer the sharp tinkle, but that one solemn toll, which in all Christian countries tells of the passing of the spirit out of earthly life into eternity; and again a murmur gathered and grew, as of many people speaking with awed breath, 'A Poor Clare is dying! a Poor Clare is dead!'

Borne along once more by the motion of the crowd, we were carried into the chapel belonging to the Poor Clares. On a bier before the high altar, lay a woman— lay Sister Magdalen—lay Bridget Fitzgerald. By her side stood Father Bernard, in his robes of office, and holding the crucifix on high while he pronounced the solemn absolution of the Church, as to one who had newly confessed herself of deadly sin. I pushed on with passionate force, till I stood close to the dying woman, as she received extreme unction amid the breathless and awed hush of the multitude around. Her eyes were glazing, her limbs were stiffening; but when the rite was over and finished, she raised her gaunt figure slowly up, and her eyes brightened to a strange intensity of joy, as, with the gesture of her finger and the trance-like gleam of her eye, she seemed like one who watched the disappearance of some loathed and fearful creature.

'She is freed from the curse!' said she, as she fell back dead.

# THE HALF-BROTHERS

My mother was twice married. She never spoke of
her first husband, and it is only from other people that
I have learnt what little I know about him. I believe
she was scarcely seventeen when she was married to
him : and he was barely one-and-twenty. He rented
a small farm up in Cumberland, somewhere towards
the sea-coast; but he was perhaps too young and
inexperienced to have the charge of land and cattle :
anyhow, his affairs did not prosper, and he fell into ill
health, and died of consumption before they had been
three years man and wife, leaving my mother a young
widow of twenty, with a little child only just able to
walk, and the farm on her hands for four years more
by the lease, with half the stock on it dead, or sold
off one by one to pay the more pressing debts, and
with no money to purchase more, or even to buy the
provisions needed for the small consumption of every
day. There was another child coming, too ; and sad
and sorry, I believe, she was to think of it. A dreary
winter she must have had in her lonesome dwelling,
with never another near it for miles around ; her sister
came to bear her company, and they two planned and
plotted how to make every penny they could raise go
as far as possible. I can't tell you how it happened
that my little sister, whom I never saw, came to sicken
and die ; but, as if my poor mother's cup was not full
enough, only a fortnight before Gregory was born the
little girl took ill of scarlet fever, and in a week she
lay dead. My mother was, I believe, just stunned
with this last blow. My aunt has told me that she
did not cry ; aunt Fanny would have been thankful
if she had ; but she sat holding the poor wee lassie's
hand, and looking in her pretty, pale, dead face, with-

out so much as shedding a tear. And it was all the same, when they had to take her away to be buried. She just kissed the child, and sat her down in the window-seat to watch the little black train of people (neighbours—my aunt, and one far-off cousin, who were all the friends they could muster) go winding away amongst the snow, which had fallen thinly over the country the night before. When my aunt came back from the funeral, she found my mother in the same place, and as dry-eyed as ever. So she continued until after Gregory was born; and, somehow, his coming seemed to loosen the tears, and she cried day and night, day and night, till my aunt and the other watcher looked at each other in dismay, and would fain have stopped her if they had but known how. But she bade them let her alone, and not be over-anxious, for every drop she shed eased her brain, which had been in a terrible state before for want of the power to cry. She seemed after that to think of nothing but her new little baby; she hardly appeared to remember either her husband or her little daughter that lay dead in Brigham churchyard—at least so aunt Fanny said; but she was a great talker, and my mother was very silent by nature, and I think aunt Fanny may have been mistaken in believing that my mother never thought of her husband and child just because she never spoke about them. Aunt Fanny was older than my mother, and had a way of treating her like a child; but, for all that, she was a kind, warm-hearted creature, who thought more of her sister's welfare than she did of her own; and it was on her bit of money that they principally lived, and on what the two could earn by working for the great Glasgow sewing-merchants. But by-and-by my mother's eyesight began to fail. It was not that she was exactly blind, for she could see well enough to guide herself about the house, and to do a good deal of domestic work; but she could no longer do fine sewing and earn money. It must have been with the heavy crying she had had in her day, for she was but a young creature at this time, and as pretty a young woman, I have heard people say, as any on the country side. She took it sadly to heart that she could no longer gain anything towards the keep of herself and her child. My aunt Fanny would fain have persuaded her that she had enough to do in managing their cottage and minding Gregory; but my mother knew that they were pinched, and that aunt Fanny herself had not as much to eat, even of the commonest kind of food, as she could have done with; and as for Gregory, he was not a strong lad, and needed, not more food—for he always had enough, whoever went short—but better nourishment, and more flesh-meat. One day—it was aunt Fanny who told me all this about my poor mother, long after her death—as the sisters were sitting together, aunt Fanny working, and my mother hushing Gregory to sleep, William Preston, who was afterwards my father, came in. He was reckoned an old bachelor; I suppose he was long past forty, and he was one of the wealthiest farmers thereabouts, and had known my grandfather well, and my mother and my aunt in their more prosperous days. He sat down, and began to twirl his hat by way of being agreeable; my aunt Fanny talked, and he listened and looked at my mother. But he said very little, either on that visit, or on many another that he paid before he spoke out what had been the real purpose of his calling so often all along, and from the very first time he came to their house. One Sunday, however, my aunt Fanny stayed away from church, and took care of the child, and my mother went alone. When she came back, she ran straight upstairs, without going into the kitchen to look at Gregory or speak any word to her sister, and aunt Fanny heard her cry as if her heart was breaking; so she went up and scolded her right well through the bolted door, till at last she got her to open it. And then she threw herself on my aunt's neck, and told her that William Preston had asked her to marry him, and had promised to take good charge of her boy, and to let him want for nothing, neither in the way of keep nor of education, and that she had consented. Aunt Fanny was a good deal shocked at this; for, as I have said, she had often thought that my mother had forgotten her first husband very quickly, and now here was proof positive of it, if she could so soon think of marrying again. Besides, as aunt Fanny used to say, she herself would have been a far more suitable match for a man of William Preston's age than Helen, who, though she was a widow, had not seen her four-and-twentieth summer. However, as aunt Fanny said, they had not asked her advice; and there was much to be said on the other side of the question. Helen's eyesight would never be good for much again, and as William Preston's wife she would never need to do anything, if she chose to sit with her hands before her; and a boy was a great charge to a widowed mother; and now there would be a decent, steady man to see after him. So, by-and-by, aunt Fanny seemed to take a brighter view of the marriage than did my mother herself, who hardly ever looked up, and never smiled after the day when she promised William Preston to be his wife. But much as she had loved Gregory before, she seemed to love him more now. She was continually talking to him when they were alone, though he was far too young to understand her moaning words, or give her any comfort, except by his caresses.

At last William Preston and she were wed; and she went to be mistress of a well-stocked house, not above half an hour's walk from where aunt Fanny lived. I believe she did all that she could to please my father; and a more dutiful wife, I have heard him himself say, could never have been. But she did not love him, and he soon found it out. She loved Gregory, and she did not love him. Perhaps, love would have come in time, if he had been patient enough to wait; but it just turned him sour to see how her eye brightened and her colour came at the sight of that little child, while for him who had given her so much, she had only gentle words as cold as ice.

He got to taunt her with the difference in her manner, as if that would bring love : and he took a positive dislike to Gregory,—he was so jealous of the ready love that always gushed out like a spring of fresh water when he came near. He wanted her to love him more, and perhaps that was all well and good ; but he wanted her to love her child less, and that was an evil wish. One day, he gave way to his temper, and cursed and swore at Gregory, who had got into some mischief, as children will ; my mother made some excuse for him ; my father said it was hard enough to have to keep another man's child, without having it perpetually held up in its naughtiness by his wife, who ought to be always in the same mind that he was ; and so from little they got to more ; and the end of it was, that my mother took to her bed before her time, and I was born that very day. My father was glad, and proud, and sorry, all in a breath ; glad and proud that a son was born to him ; and sorry for his poor wife's state, and to think how his angry words had brought it on. But he was a man who liked better to be angry than sorry, so he soon found out that it was all Gregory's fault, and owed him an additional grudge for having hastened my birth. He had another grudge against him before long. My mother began to sink the day after I was born. My father sent to Carlisle for doctors, and would have coined his heart's blood into gold to save her, if that could have been ; but it could not. My aunt Fanny used to say sometimes, that she thought that Helen did not wish to live, and so just let herself die away without trying to take hold on life ; but when I questioned her, she owned that my mother did all the doctors bade her do, with the same sort of uncomplaining patience with which she had acted through life. One of her last requests was to have Gregory laid in her bed by my side, and then she made him take hold of my little hand. Her husband came in while she was looking at us so, and when he bent tenderly over her to ask her how she felt now, and seemed to gaze on us two little half-brothers, with a grave sort of kindliness, she looked up in his face and smiled, almost her first smile at him; and such a sweet smile! as more besides aunt Fanny have said. In an hour she was dead. Aunt Fanny came to live with us. It was the best thing that could be done. My father would have been glad to return to his old mode of bachelor life, but what could he do with two little children? He needed a woman to take care of him, and who so fitting as his wife's elder sister? So she had the charge of me from my birth; and for a time I was weakly, as was but natural, and she was always beside me, night and day watching over me, and my father nearly as anxious as she. For his land had come down from father to son for more than three hundred years, and he would have cared for me merely as his flesh and blood that was to inherit the land after him. But he needed something to love, for all that, to most people, he was a stern, hard man, and he took to me as, I fancy, he had taken to no human being before—as he might have taken to my mother, if she had had no former life for him to be jealous of. I loved him back again right heartily. I loved all around me, I believe, for everybody was kind to me. After a time, I overcame my original weakliness of constitution, and was just a bonny, strong-looking lad whom every passer-by noticed, when my father took me with him to the nearest town.

At home I was the darling of my aunt, the tenderly-beloved of my father, the pet and plaything of the old domestic, the 'young master' of the farm-labourers, before whom I played many a lordly antic, assuming a sort of authority which sat oddly enough, I doubt not, on such a baby as I was.

Gregory was three years older than I. Aunt Fanny was always kind to him in deed and in action, but she did not often think about him, she had fallen so completely into the habit of being engrossed by me, from the fact of my having come into her charge as a delicate baby. My father never got over his grudging

dislike to his stepson, who had so innocently wrestled
with him for the possession of my mother's heart.
I mistrust me, too, that my father always considered
him as the cause of my mother's death and my early
delicacy ; and utterly unreasonable as this may seem,
I believe my father rather cherished his feeling of
alienation to my brother as a duty, than strove to
repress it.   Yet not for the world would my father
have grudged him anything that money could purchase.
That was, as it were, in the bond when he had wedded
my mother.  Gregory was lumpish and loutish, awkward and ungainly, marring whatever he meddled in,
and many a hard word and sharp scolding did he get
from the people about the farm, who hardly waited till
my father's back was turned before they rated the
stepson.   I am ashamed—my heart is sore to think
how I fell into the fashion of the family, and slighted
my poor orphan step-brother.   I don't think I ever
scouted him, or was wilfully ill-natured to him ;  but
the habit of being considered in all things, and being
treated as something uncommon and superior, made
me insolent in my prosperity, and I exacted more
than Gregory was always willing to grant, and then,
irritated, I sometimes repeated the disparaging words
I had heard others use with regard to him, without
fully understanding their meaning.   Whether he did
or not I cannot tell.   I am afraid he did.   He used
to turn silent and quiet—sullen and sulky, my father
thought it ;  stupid, aunt Fanny used to call it.   But
every one said he was stupid and dull, and this
stupidity and dullness grew upon him.   He would sit
without speaking a word, sometimes, for hours ;  then
my father would bid him rise and do some piece of
work, maybe, about the farm.   And he would take
three or four tellings before he would go.   When we
were sent to school, it was all the same.   He could
never be made to remember his lessons ;  the schoolmaster grew weary of scolding and flogging, and at
last advised my father just to take him away, and
set him to some farm-work that might not be above

his comprehension. I think he was more gloomy and stupid than ever after this, yet he was not a cross lad; he was patient and good-natured, and would try to do a kind turn for any one, even if they had been scolding or cuffing him not a minute before. But very often his attempts at kindness ended in some mischief to the very people he was trying to serve, owing to his awkward, ungainly ways. I suppose I was a clever lad; at any rate, I always got plenty of praise; and was, as we called it, the cock of the school. The schoolmaster said I could learn anything I chose, but my father, who had no great learning himself, saw little use in much for me, and took me away betimes, and kept me with him about the farm. Gregory was made into a kind of shepherd, receiving his training under old Adam, who was nearly past his work. I think old Adam was almost the first person who had a good opinion of Gregory. He stood to it that my brother had good parts, though he did not rightly know how to bring them out; and, for knowing the bearings of the Fells, he said he had never seen a lad like him. My father would try to bring Adam round to speak of Gregory's faults and shortcomings; but, instead of that, he would praise him twice as much as soon as he found out what was my father's object.

One winter-time, when I was about sixteen, and Gregory nineteen, I was sent by my father on an errand to a place about seven miles distant by the road, but only about four by the Fells. He bade me return by the road, whichever way I took in going, for the evenings closed in early, and were often thick and misty; besides which, old Adam, now paralytic and bedridden, foretold a downfall of snow before long. I soon got to my journey's end, and soon had done my business; earlier by an hour, I thought, than my father had expected, so I took the decision of the way by which I would return into my own hands, and set off back again over the Fells, just as the first shades of evening began to fall. It looked dark and gloomy enough; but everything was so still that I thought

I should have plenty of time to get home before the snow came down. Off I set at a pretty quick pace. But night came on quicker. The right path was clear enough in the daytime, although at several points two or three exactly similar diverged from the same place ; but when there was a good light, the traveller was guided by the sight of distant objects,—a piece of rock, —a fall in the ground—which were quite invisible to me now. I plucked up a brave heart, however, and took what seemed to me the right road. It was wrong, however, and led me whither I knew not, but to some wild boggy moor where the solitude seemed painful, intense, as if never footfall of man had come thither to break the silence. I tried to shout,—with the dimmest possible hope of being heard—rather to reassure myself by the sound of my own voice ; but my voice came husky and short, and yet it dismayed me ; it seemed so weird and strange in that noiseless expanse of black darkness. Suddenly the air was filled thick with dusky flakes, my face and hands were wet with snow. It cut me off from the slightest knowledge of where I was, for I lost every idea of the direction from which I had come, so that I could not even retrace my steps ; it hemmed me in, thicker, thicker, with a darkness that might be felt. The boggy soil on which I stood quaked under me if I remained long in one place, and yet I dared not move far. All my youthful hardiness seemed to leave me at once. I was on the point of crying, and only very shame seemed to keep it down. To save myself from shedding tears, I shouted—terrible, wild shouts for bare life they were. I turned sick as I paused to listen ; no answering sound came but the unfeeling echoes. Only the noiseless, pitiless snow kept falling thicker, thicker —faster, faster ! I was growing numb and sleepy. I tried to move about, but I dared not go far, for fear of the precipices which, I knew, abounded in certain places on the Fells. Now and then, I stood still and shouted again ; but my voice was getting choked with tears, as I thought of the desolate, helpless death I was to die, and how little they at home, sitting round the warm, red, bright fire, wotted what was become of me,—and how my poor father would grieve for me—it would surely kill him—it would break his heart, poor old man ! Aunt Fanny too—was this to be the end of all her cares for me ? I began to review my life in a strange kind of vivid dream, in which the various scenes of my few boyish years passed before me like visions. In a pang of agony, caused by such remembrance of my short life, I gathered up my strength and called out once more, a long, despairing, wailing cry, to which I had no hope of obtaining any answer, save from the echoes around, dulled as the sound might be by the thickened air. To my surprise, I heard a cry—almost as long, as wild as mine—so wild that it seemed unearthly, and I almost thought it must be the voice of some of the mocking spirits of the Fells, about whom I had heard so many tales. My heart suddenly began to beat fast and loud. I could not reply for a minute or two. I nearly fancied I had lost the power of utterance. Just at this moment a dog barked. Was it Lassie's bark—my brother's collie ?—an ugly enough brute, with a white, ill-looking face, that my father always kicked whenever he saw it, partly for its own demerits, partly because it belonged to my brother. On such occasions, Gregory would whistle Lassie away, and go off and sit with her in some outhouse. My father had once or twice been ashamed of himself, when the poor collie had yowled out with the suddenness of the pain, and had relieved himself of his self-reproach by blaming my brother, who, he said, had no notion of training a dog, and was enough to ruin any collie in Christendom with his stupid way of allowing them to lie by the kitchen fire. To all which Gregory would answer nothing, nor even seem to hear, but go on looking absent and moody.

Yes ! there again ! It was Lassie's bark ! Now or never ! I lifted up my voice and shouted 'Lassie ! Lassie ! For God's sake, Lassie !' Another moment, and the great white-faced Lassie was curving and gambolling with delight round my feet and legs, looking, however, up in my face with her intelligent, apprehensive eyes, as if fearing lest I might greet her with a blow, as I had done oftentimes before. But I cried with gladness, as I stooped down and patted her. My mind was sharing in my body's weakness, and I could not reason, but I knew that help was at hand. A grey figure came more and more distinctly out of the thick, close-pressing darkness. It was Gregory wrapped in his maud.*

'Oh, Gregory!' said I, and I fell upon his neck, unable to speak another word. He never spoke much, and made me no answer for some little time. Then he told me we must move, we must walk for the dear life— we must find our road home, if possible; but we must move or we should be frozen to death.

'Don't you know the way home?' asked I.

'I thought I did when I set out, but I am doubtful now. The snow blinds me, and I am feared that in moving about just now, I have lost the right gait homewards.'

He had his shepherd's staff with him, and by dint of plunging it before us at every step we took—clinging close to each other, we went on safely enough, as far as not falling down any of the steep rocks, but it was slow, dreary work. My brother, I saw, was more guided by Lassie and the way she took than anything else, trusting to her instinct. It was too dark to see far before us; but he called her back continually, and noted from what quarter she returned, and shaped our slow steps accordingly. But the tedious motion scarcely kept my very blood from freezing. Every bone, every fibre in my body seemed first to ache, and then to swell, and then to turn numb with the intense cold. My brother bore it better than I, from having been more out upon the hills. He did not speak, except to call Lassie. I strove to be brave, and not complain; but now I felt the deadly fatal sleep stealing over me.

'I can go no farther,' I said, in a drowsy tone. I remember I suddenly became dogged and resolved. Sleep I would, were it only for five minutes. If death were to be the consequence, sleep I would. Gregory stood still. I suppose, he recognized the peculiar phase of suffering to which I had been brought by the cold.

'It is of no use,' said he, as if to himself. 'We are no nearer home than we were when we started, as far as I can tell. Our only chance is in Lassie. Here! roll thee in my maud, lad, and lay thee down on this sheltered side of this bit of rock. Creep close under it, lad, and I'll lie by thee, and strive to keep the warmth in us. Stay! hast gotten aught about thee they'll know at home?"

I felt him unkind thus to keep me from slumber, but on his repeating the question, I pulled out my pocket-handkerchief, of some showy pattern, which aunt Fanny had hemmed for me—Gregory took it, and tied it round Lassie's neck.

'Hie thee, Lassie, hie thee home!' And the white-faced, ill-favoured brute was off like a shot in the darkness. Now I might lie down—now I might sleep. In my drowsy stupor I felt that I was being tenderly covered up by my brother; but what with I neither knew nor cared—I was too dull, too selfish, too numb to think and reason, or I might have known that in that bleak bare place there was naught to wrap me in, save what was taken off another. I was glad enough when he ceased his cares and lay down by me. I took his hand.

'Thou canst not remember, lad, how we lay together thus by our dying mother. She put thy small, wee hand in mine—I reckon she sees us now; and belike we shall soon be with her. Anyhow, God's will be done.'

'Dear Gregory,' I muttered, and crept nearer to him for warmth. He was talking still, and again about our mother, when I fell asleep. In an instant—or so it seemed—there were many voices about me—many faces hovering round me—the sweet luxury of warmth was stealing into every part of me. I was in my own little bed at home. I am thankful to say, my first word was 'Gregory?'

A look passed from one to another—my father's stern

old face strove in vain to keep its sternness; his mouth quivered, his eyes filled slowly with unwonted tears.

'I would have given him half my land—I would have blessed him as my son,—oh God! I would have knelt at his feet, and asked him to forgive my hardness of heart.'

I heard no more. A whirl came through my brain, catching me back to death.

I came slowly to my consciousness, weeks afterwards. My father's hair was white when I recovered, and his hands shook as he looked into my face.

We spoke no more of Gregory. We could not speak of him; but he was strangely in our thoughts. Lassie came and went with never a word of blame; nay, my father would try to stroke her, but she shrank away; and he, as if reproved by the poor dumb beast, would sigh, and be silent and abstracted for a time.

Aunt Fanny—always a talker—told me all. How, on that fatal night, my father, irritated by my prolonged absence, and probably more anxious than he cared to show, had been fierce and imperious, even beyond his wont, to Gregory: had upbraided him with his father's poverty, his own stupidity which made his services good for nothing—for so, in spite of the old shepherd, my father always chose to consider them. At last, Gregory had risen up, and whistled Lassie out with him—poor Lassie, crouching underneath his chair for fear of a kick or a blow. Some time before, there had been some talk between my father and my aunt respecting my return; and when Aunt Fanny told me all this, she said she fancied that Gregory might have noticed the coming storm, and gone out silently to meet me. Three hours afterwards, when all were running about in wild alarm, not knowing whither to go in search of me —not even missing Gregory, or heeding his absence, poor fellow—poor, poor fellow!—Lassie came home, with my handkerchief tied round her neck. They knew and understood, and the whole strength of the farm was turned out to follow her, with wraps, and blankets, and brandy, and everything that could be thought of.

I lay in chilly sleep, but still alive, beneath the rock that Lassie guided them to. I was covered over with my brother's plaid, and his thick shepherd's coat was carefully wrapped round my feet. He was in his shirt-sleeves—his arm thrown over me—a quiet smile (he had hardly ever smiled in life) upon his still, cold face.

My father's last words were, 'God forgive me my hardness of heart towards the fatherless child!'

And what marked the depth of his feeling of repentance, perhaps more than all, considering the passionate love he bore my mother, was this: we found a paper of directions after his death, in which he desired that he might lie at the foot of the grave, in which, by his desire, poor Gregory had been laid with OUR MOTHER.

# MR. HARRISON'S CONFESSIONS

## CHAPTER I

THE fire was burning gaily. My wife had just gone
upstairs to put baby to bed. Charles sat opposite to
me, looking very brown and handsome. It was
pleasant enough that we should feel sure of spending
some weeks under the same roof, a thing which we had
never done since we were mere boys. I felt too lazy
to talk, so I ate walnuts and looked into the fire. But
Charles grew restless.

'Now that your wife is gone upstairs, Will, you must
tell me what I've wanted to ask you ever since I saw
her this morning. Tell me all about the wooing and
winning. I want to have the receipt for getting such
a charming little wife of my own. Your letters only
gave the barest details. So set to, man, and tell me
every particular.'

'If I tell you all, it will be a long story.'

'Never fear. If I get tired, I can go to sleep, and
dream that I am back again, a lonely bachelor, in Ceylon;
and I can waken up when you have done, to know that
I am under your roof. Dash away, man! "Once upon
a time, a gallant young bachelor"—— There's a
beginning for you!'

'Well, then, "Once upon a time, a gallant young
bachelor" was sorely puzzled where to settle, when he
had completed his education as a surgeon*—I must speak
in the first person; I cannot go on as a gallant young
bachelor. I had just finished walking the hospitals
when you went to Ceylon, and, if you remember,
I wanted to go abroad like you, and thought of offering
myself as a ship-surgeon; but I found I should rather
lose caste in my profession; so I hesitated, and while

I was hesitating, I received a letter from my father's cousin, Mr. Morgan—that old gentleman who used to write such long letters of good advice to my mother, and who tipped me a five-pound note when I agreed to be bound apprentice to Mr. Howard, instead of going to sea. Well, it seems the old gentleman had all along thought of taking me as his partner, if I turned out pretty well ; and as he heard a good account of me from an old friend of his, who was a surgeon at Guy's, he wrote to propose this arrangement : I was to have a third of the profits for five years ; after that, half ; and eventually I was to succeed to the whole. It was no bad offer for a penniless man like me, as Mr. Morgan had a capital country practice, and, though I did not know him personally, I had formed a pretty good idea of him, as an honourable, kind-hearted, fidgety, meddlesome old bachelor ; and a very correct notion it was, as I found out in the very first half-hour of seeing him. I had had some idea that I was to live in his house, as he was a bachelor and a kind of family friend ; and I think he was afraid that I should expect this arrangement, for when I walked up to his door, with the porter carrying my portmanteau, he met me on the steps, and while he held my hand and shook it, he said to the porter, " Jerry, if you'll wait a moment, Mr. Harrison will be ready to go with you to his lodgings, at Jocelyn's, you know " ; and then turning to me, he addressed his first words of welcome. I was a little inclined to think him inhospitable, but I got to understand him better afterwards. " Jocelyn's," said he, " is the best place I have been able to hit upon in a hurry, and there is a good deal of fever about, which made me desirous that you should come this month—a low kind of typhoid, in the oldest part of the town. I think you'll be comfortable there for a week or two. I have taken the liberty of desiring my housekeeper to send down one or two things which give the place a little more of a home aspect—an easy-chair, a beautiful case of preparations, and one or two little matters in the way of eatables ; but if you'll take my advice, I've a plan in my head which we will talk about to-morrow morning. At present, I don't like to keep you standing out on the steps here, so I'll not detain you from your lodgings, where I rather think my housekeeper is gone to get tea ready for you."

'I thought I understood the old gentleman's anxiety for his own health, which he put upon care for mine, for he had on a kind of loose grey coat, and no hat on his head. But I wondered that he did not ask me indoors, instead of keeping me on the steps. I believe, after all, I made a mistake in supposing he was afraid of taking cold; he was only afraid of being seen in deshabille. And for his apparent inhospitality, I had not been long in Duncombe before I understood the comfort of having one's house considered as a castle into which no one might intrude, and saw good reason for the practice Mr. Morgan had established of coming to his door to speak to every one. It was only the effect of habit that made him receive me so. Before long, I had the free run of his house.

'There was every sign of kind attention and fore-thought on the part of some one, whom I could not doubt to be Mr. Morgan, in my lodgings. I was too lazy to do much that evening, and sat in the little bow-window which projected over Jocelyn's shop, looking up and down the street. Duncombe calls itself a town, but I should call it a village. Really, looking from Jocelyn's, it is a very picturesque place. The houses are anything but regular; they may be mean in their details; but altogether they look well; they have not that flat, unrelieved front, which many towns of far more pretensions present. Here and there a bow-window—every now and then a gable, cutting up against the sky—occasionally a projecting upper story—throws good effect of light and shadow along the street; and they have a queer fashion of their own of colouring the whitewash of some of the houses with a sort of pink blotting-paper tinge, more like the stone of which Mayence* is built than anything else. It may be very bad taste, but to my mind it gives a rich warmth to the colouring. Then, here and there a dwelling-house has a court in front, with a grass-plot on each side of the flagged walk, and a large tree or two—limes or horse chestnuts—which send their great, projecting upper branches over into the street, making round dry places of shelter on the pavement in the times of summer showers.

'While I was sitting in the bow-window, thinking of the contrast between this place and the lodgings in the heart of London, which I had left only twelve hours before—the window open here, and, although in the centre of the town, admitting only scents from the mignonette boxes on the sill, instead of the dust and smoke of —— Street—the only sound heard in this, the principal street, being the voices of mothers calling their playing children home to bed, and the eight o'clock bell of the old parish church bim-bomming in remembrance of the curfew; while I was sitting thus idly, the door opened, and the little maid-servant, dropping a curtsy, said—

' "Please, sir, Mrs. Munton's compliments, and she would be glad to know how you are after your journey."

'There! was not that hearty and kind? Would even the dearest chum I had at Guy's have thought of doing such a thing? while Mrs. Munton, whose name I had never heard of before, was doubtless suffering anxiety till I could relieve her mind by sending back word that I was pretty well.

' "My compliments to Mrs. Munton, and I am pretty well: much obliged to her." It was as well to say only "pretty well", for "very well" would have destroyed the interest Mrs. Munton evidently felt in me. Good Mrs. Munton! Kind Mrs. Munton! Perhaps, also, young—handsome—rich—widowed Mrs. Munton! I rubbed my hands with delight and amusement, and, resuming my post of observation, began to wonder at which house Mrs. Munton lived.

' Again the little tap, and the little maid-servant—

' "Please, sir, the Miss Tomkinsons' compliments, and they would be glad to know how you feel yourself after your journey."

'I don't know why, but the Miss Tomkinsons' name had not such a halo about it as Mrs. Munton's. Still it was very pretty in the Miss Tomkinsons to send and inquire. I only wished I did not feel so perfectly robust. I was almost ashamed that I could not send word I was quite exhausted by fatigue, and had fainted twice since my arrival. If I had but had a headache, at least! I heaved a deep breath : my chest was in perfect order ; I had caught no cold ; so I answered again—

' " Much obliged to the Miss Tomkinsons ; I am not much fatigued ; tolerably well : my compliments."

'Little Sally could hardly have got downstairs, before she returned, bright and breathless—

' " Mr. and Mrs. Bullock's compliments, sir, and they hope you are pretty well after your journey."

'Who would have expected such kindness from such an unpromising name ? Mr. and Mrs. Bullock were less interesting, it is true, than their predecessors ; but I graciously replied—

' " My compliments ; a night's rest will perfectly recruit me."

'The same message was presently brought up from one or two more unknown kind hearts. I really wished I were not so ruddy-looking. I was afraid I should disappoint the tender-hearted town when they saw what a hale young fellow I was. And I was almost ashamed of confessing to a great appetite for supper when Sally came up to inquire what I would have. Beefsteaks were so tempting ; but perhaps I ought rather to have water-gruel, and go to bed. The beefsteak carried the day, however. I need not have felt such a gentle elation of spirits, as this mark of the town's attention is paid to every one when they arrive after a journey. Many of the same people have sent to inquire after you—great, hulking, brown fellow as you are—only Sally spared you the infliction of devising interesting answers.

## CHAPTER II

'THE next morning Mr. Morgan came before I had
finished breakfast.  He was the most dapper little man
I ever met.   I see the affection with which people cling
to the style of dress that was in vogue when they were
beaux and belles, and received the most admiration.
They are unwilling to believe that their youth and
beauty are gone, and think that the prevailing mode is
unbecoming.  Mr. Morgan will inveigh by the hour
together against frock-coats, for instance, and whiskers.
He keeps his chin close shaven, wears a black dress-
coat, and dark-grey pantaloons ; and in his morning
round to his town patients, he invariably wears the
brightest and blackest of Hessian boots,* with dangling
silk tassels on each side.  When he goes home, about
ten o'clock, to prepare for his ride to see his country
patients, he puts on the most dandy top-boots I ever
saw, which he gets from some wonderful bootmaker
a hundred miles off.  His appearance is what one calls
" jemmy "*; there is no other word that will do for it.
He was evidently a little discomfited when he saw me
in my breakfast costume, with the habits which I
brought with me from the fellows at Guy's ; my feet
against the fireplace, my chair balanced on its hind legs
(a habit of sitting which I afterwards discovered he
particularly abhorred) ; slippers on my feet (which,
also, he considered a most ungentlemanly piece of un-
tidiness " out of a bedroom ") ; in short, from what
I afterwards learned, every prejudice he had was out-
raged by my appearance on this first visit of his.   I put
my book down, and sprang up to receive him.  He
stood, hat and cane in hand.

' " I came to inquire if it would be convenient for you
to accompany me on my morning's round, and to be
introduced to a few of our friends."  I quite detected
the little tone of coldness, induced by his disappointment
at my appearance, though he never imagined that it

was in any way perceptible.  " I will be ready directly,
sir," said I ;  and bolted into my bedroom, only too
happy to escape his scrutinizing eye.

'When I returned, I was made aware, by sundry
indescribable little coughs and hesitating noises, that
my dress did not satisfy him.  I stood ready, hat and
gloves in hand ;  but still he did not offer to set off on our
round.  I grew very red and hot.  At length he said—

' " Excuse me, my dear young friend, but may I ask
if you have no other coat besides that—' cut-away ',
I believe you call them ?  We are rather sticklers for
propriety, I believe, in Duncombe ;  and much depends
on a first impression.  Let it be professional, my dear sir.
Black is the garb of our profession.  Forgive my speaking
so plainly, but I consider myself *in loco parentis*."*

'He was so kind, so bland, and, in truth, so friendly,
that I felt it would be most childish to take offence ;
but I had a little resentment in my heart at this way of
being treated.  However, I mumbled, " Oh, certainly,
sir, if you wish it " ;  and returned once more to change
my coat—my poor cut-away.

' " Those coats, sir, give a man rather too much of
a sporting appearance, not quite befitting the learned
professions ;  more as if you came down here to hunt
than to be the Galen or Hippocrates*of the neighbourhood."  He smiled graciously, so I smothered a sigh ;
for, to tell you the truth, I had rather anticipated—
and, in fact, had boasted at Guy's of—the runs I hoped
to have with the hounds ;  for Duncombe was in a
famous hunting district.  But all these ideas were quite
dispersed when Mr. Morgan led me to the inn-yard,
where there was a horse-dealer on his way to a neighbouring fair, and " strongly advised me "—which in our
relative circumstances was equivalent to an injunction
—to purchase a little, useful, fast-trotting, brown cob,
instead of a fine, showy horse, " who would take any
fence I put him to," as the horse-dealer assured me.
Mr. Morgan was evidently pleased when I bowed to his
decision, and gave up all hopes of an occasional hunt.
He opened out a great deal more after this purchase.

He told me his plan of establishing me in a house of my own, which looked more respectable, not to say professional, than being in lodgings ; and then he went on to say that he had lately lost a friend, a brother surgeon in a neighbouring town, who had left a widow with a small income, who would be very glad to live with me, and act as mistress to my establishment ; thus lessening the expense.

' " She is a lady-like woman," said Mr. Morgan, " to judge from the little I have seen of her ; about forty-five or so ; and may really be of some help to you in the little etiquettes of our profession ; the slight, delicate attentions which every man has to learn, if he wishes to get on in life. This is Mrs. Munton's, sir," said he, stopping short at a very unromantic-looking green door, with a brass knocker.

' I had no time to say, " Who is Mrs. Munton ? " before we had heard Mrs. Munton was at home, and were following the tidy elderly servant up the narrow carpeted stairs into the drawing-room. Mrs. Munton was the widow of a former vicar, upwards of sixty, rather deaf ; but, like all the deaf people I have ever seen, very fond of talking ; perhaps because she then knew the subject, which passed out of her grasp when another began to speak. She was ill of a chronic complaint, which often incapacitated her from going out ; and the kind people of the town were in the habit of coming to see her and sit with her, and of bringing her the newest, freshest, tit-bits of news ; so that her room was the centre of the gossip of Duncombe—not of scandal, mind ; for I make a distinction between gossip and scandal. Now you can fancy the discrepancy between the ideal and the real Mrs. Munton. Instead of any foolish notion of a beautiful, blooming widow, tenderly anxious about the health of the stranger, I saw a homely, talkative, elderly person, with a keen, observant eye, and marks of suffering on her face ; plain in manner and dress, but still unmistakably a lady. She talked to Mr. Morgan, but she looked at me ; and I saw that nothing I did escaped her notice. Mr. Morgan annoyed me by his anxiety to show me off ; but he was kindly anxious to bring out every circumstance to my credit in Mrs. Munton's hearing, knowing well that the town-crier had not more opportunities to publish all about me than she had.

'"What was that remark you repeated to me of Sir Astley Cooper's ? "* asked he.    It had been the most trivial speech in the world that I had named as we walked along, and I felt ashamed of having to repeat it : but it answered Mr. Morgan's purpose, and before night all the town had heard that I was a favourite pupil of Sir Astley's (I had never seen him but twice in my life) ; and Mr. Morgan was afraid that as soon as he knew my full value I should be retained by Sir Astley to assist him in his duties as surgeon to the Royal Family.    Every little circumstance was pressed into the conversation which could add to my importance.

'"As I once heard Sir Robert Peel* remark to Mr. Harrison, the father of our young friend here—The moons in August are remarkably full and bright."— If you remember, Charles, my father was always proud of having sold a pair of gloves to Sir Robert, when he was staying at the Grange, near Biddicombe, and I suppose good Mr. Morgan had paid his only visit to my father at the time ; but Mrs. Munton evidently looked at me with double respect after this incidental remark, which I was amused to meet with, a few months afterwards, disguised in the statement that my father was an intimate friend of the Premier's, and had, in fact, been the adviser of most of the measures taken by him in public life.    I sat by, half indignant and half amused.    Mr. Morgan looked so complacently pleased at the whole effect of the conversation, that I did not care to mar it by explanations ; and, indeed, I had little idea at the time how small sayings were the seeds of great events in the town of Duncombe.    When we left Mrs. Munton's, he was in a blandly communicative mood.

'"You will find it a curious statistical fact, but five-sixths of our householders of a certain rank in Duncombe are women.    We have widows and old maids in rich abundance. In fact, my dear sir, I believe that you and I are almost the only gentlemen in the place— Mr. Bullock, of course, excepted. By gentlemen, I mean professional men. It behoves us to remember, sir, that so many of the female sex rely upon us for the kindness and protection which every man who is worthy of the name is always so happy to render."

'Miss Tomkinson, on whom we next called, did not strike me as remarkably requiring protection from any man. She was a tall, gaunt, masculine-looking woman, with an air of defiance about her, naturally; this, however, she softened and mitigated, as far as she was able, in favour of Mr. Morgan. He, it seemed to me, stood a little in awe of the lady, who was very *brusque* and plain-spoken, and evidently piqued herself on her decision of character and sincerity of speech.

' " So, this is the Mr. Harrison we have heard so much of from you, Mr. Morgan ? I must say, from what I had heard, that I had expected something a little more— hum—hum ! But he's young yet ; he's young. We have been all anticipating an Apollo, Mr. Harrison, from Mr. Morgan's description, and an Aesculapius*combined in one ; or, perhaps, I might confine myself to saying Apollo, as he, I believe, was the god of medicine ! "

' How could Mr. Morgan have described me without seeing me ? I asked myself.

' Miss Tomkinson put on her spectacles, and adjusted them on her Roman nose. Suddenly relaxing from her severity of inspection, she said to Mr. Morgan—" But you must see Caroline. I had nearly forgotten it ; she is busy with the girls, but I will send for her. She had a bad headache yesterday, and looked very pale ; it made me very uncomfortable."

' She rang the bell, and desired the servant to fetch Miss Caroline.

' Miss Caroline was the younger sister—younger by twenty years ; and so considered as a child by Miss Tomkinson, who was fifty-five, at the very least. If she was considered as a child, she was also petted and caressed, and cared for as a child ; for she had been left as a baby to the charge of her elder sister; and when the father died, and they had to set up a school, Miss Tomkinson took upon herself every difficult arrangement, and denied herself every pleasure, and made every sacrifice in order that "Carry" might not feel the change in their circumstances. My wife tells me she once knew the sisters purchase a piece of silk, enough, with management, to have made two gowns; but Carry wished for flounces, or some such fal-lals; and, without a word, Miss Tomkinson gave up her gown to have the whole made up as Carry wished, into one handsome one; and wore an old, shabby affair herself as cheerfully as if it were Genoa velvet. That tells the sort of relationship between the sisters as well as anything, and I consider myself very good to name it thus early, for it was long before I found out Miss Tomkinson's real goodness; and we had a great quarrel first. Miss Caroline looked very delicate and die-away when she came in; she was as soft and sentimental as Miss Tomkinson was hard and masculine; and had a way of saying, "Oh, sister, how can you?" at Miss Tomkinson's startling speeches, which I never liked—especially as it was accompanied by a sort of protesting look at the company present, as if she wished to have it understood that she was shocked at her sister's *outré* manners. Now, that was not faithful between sisters. A remonstrance in private might have done good—though, for my own part, I have grown to like Miss Tomkinson's speeches and ways; but I don't like the way some people have of separating themselves from what may be unpopular in their relations. I know I spoke rather shortly to Miss Caroline when she asked me whether I could bear the change from "the great metropolis" to a little country village. In the first place, why could not she call it "London", or "town", and have done with it? And in the next place, why should she not love the place that was her home well enough to fancy that every one would like it when they came to know it as well as she did?

'I was conscious I was rather abrupt in my

conversation with her, and I saw that Mr. Morgan was watching me, though he pretended to be listening to Miss Tomkinson's whispered account of her sister's symptoms. But when we were once more in the street, he began, " My dear young friend "——

' I winced; for all the morning I had noticed that when he was going to give a little unpalatable advice, he always began with " My dear young friend ". He had done so about the horse.

' " My dear young friend, there are one or two hints I should like to give you about your manner. The great Sir Everard Home* used to say, " A general practitioner should either have a very good manner, or a very bad one." Now, in the latter case, he must be possessed of talents and acquirements sufficient to ensure his being sought after, whatever his manner might be. But the rudeness will give notoriety to these qualifications. Abernethy*is a case in point. I rather, myself, question the taste of bad manners. I, therefore, have studied to acquire an attentive, anxious politeness, which combines ease and grace with a tender regard and interest. I am not aware whether I have succeeded (few men do) in coming up to my ideal; but I recommend you to strive after this manner, peculiarly befitting our profession. Identify yourself with your patients, my dear sir. You have sympathy in your good heart, I am sure, to really feel pain when listening to their account of their sufferings, and it soothes them to see the expression of this feeling in your manner. It is, in fact, sir, manners that make the man in our profession. I don't set myself up as an example—far from it; but—— This is Mr. Hutton's, our vicar; one of the servants is indisposed, and I shall be glad of the opportunity of introducing you. We can resume our conversation at another time."

' I had not been aware that we had been holding a conversation, in which, I believe, the assistance of two persons is required. Why had not Mr. Hutton sent to ask after my health the evening before, according to the custom of the place ? I felt rather offended.

## CHAPTER III

'THE vicarage was on the north side of the street, at
the end opening towards the hills. It was a long low
house, receding behind its neighbours; a court was
between the door and the street, with a flag-walk and
an old stone cistern on the right-hand side of the door;
Solomon's seal growing under the windows. Some one
was watching from behind the window-curtain; for the
door opened, as if by magic, as soon as we reached it;
and we entered a low room, which served as hall, and
was matted all over, with deep, old-fashioned window-
seats, and Dutch tiles in the fireplace; altogether it
was very cool and refreshing, after the hot sun in the
white and red street.

' " Bessie is not so well, Mr. Morgan," said the sweet
little girl of eleven or so, who had opened the door.
" Sophy wanted to send for you; but papa said he was
sure you would come soon this morning, and we were
to remember that there were other sick people wanting
you."

' " Here 's Mr. Morgan, Sophy," said she, opening the
door into an inner room, to which we descended a step,
as I remember well; for I was nearly falling down it,
I was so caught by the picture within.* It was like
a picture—at least, seen through the door-frame. A
sort of mixture of crimson and sea-green in the room,
and a sunny garden beyond, a very low casement
window, open to the amber air; clusters of white roses
peeping in, and Sophy sitting on a cushion on the
ground, the light coming from above on her head, and
a little, sturdy, round-eyed brother kneeling by her, to
whom she was teaching the alphabet. It was a mighty
relief to him when we came in, as I could see; and I am
much mistaken if he was easily caught again to say
his lesson, when he was once sent off to find papa.
Sophy rose quietly, and of course we were just introduced, and that was all, before she took Mr. Morgan

upstairs to see her sick servant. I was left to myself in the room. It looked so like a home, that it at once made me know the full charm of the word. There were books and work about, and tokens of employment; there was a child's plaything on the floor; and against the sea-green walls there hung a likeness or two, done in water-colours; one, I was sure, was that of Sophy's mother. The chairs and sofa were covered with chintz, the same as the curtains—a little pretty red rose on a white ground. I don't know where the crimson came from, but I am sure there was crimson somewhere; perhaps in the carpet. There was a glass door besides the window, and you went up a step into the garden. This was, first, a grass plot, just under the windows, and beyond that, straight gravel walks, with box-borders and narrow flower-beds on each side, most brilliant and gay at the end of August, as it was then; and behind the flower-borders were fruit-trees trained over woodwork, so as to shut out the beds of kitchen-garden within.

'While I was looking round, a gentleman came in, who, I was sure, was the Vicar. It was rather awkward, for I had to account for my presence there.

'"I came with Mr. Morgan; my name is Harrison," said I, bowing. I could see he was not much enlightened by this explanation, but we sat down and talked about the time of year, or some such matter, till Sophy and Mr. Morgan came back. Then I saw Mr. Morgan to advantage. With a man whom he respected, as he did the Vicar, he lost the prim, artificial manner he had in general, and was calm and dignified; but not so dignified as the Vicar. I never saw any one like him. He was very quiet and reserved, almost absent at times; his personal appearance was not striking; but he was altogether a man you would talk to with your hat off whenever you met him. It was his character that produced this effect—character that he never thought about, but that appeared in every word, and look, and motion.

'"Sophy," said he, "Mr. Morgan looks very warm;

could you not gather a few jargonelle pears off the south
wall ? I fancy there are some ripe there. Our jargonelle
pears are remarkably early this year."

'Sophy went into the sunny garden, and I saw her
take a rake and tilt at the pears, which were above her
reach, apparently. The parlour had become chilly
(I found out afterwards it had a flag floor, which
accounts for its coldness), and I thought I should like
to go into the warm sun. I said I would go and help
the young lady ; and without waiting for an answer,
I went into the warm, scented garden, where the bees
were rifling the flowers, and making a continual, busy
sound. I think Sophy had begun to despair of getting
the fruit, and was glad of my assistance. I thought
I was very senseless to have knocked them down so
soon, when I found we were to go in as soon as they
were gathered. I should have liked to have walked round
the garden, but Sophy walked straight off with the
pears, and I could do nothing but follow her. She took
up her needlework while we ate them : they were very
soon finished, and when the Vicar had ended his conversation with Mr. Morgan about some poor people, we
rose up to come away. I was thankful that Mr. Morgan
had said so little about me. I could not have endured
that he should have introduced Sir Astley Cooper or
Sir Robert Peel at the vicarage ; nor yet could I have
brooked much mention of my " great opportunities for
acquiring a thorough knowledge of my profession ",
which I had heard him describe to Miss Tomkinson,
while her sister was talking to me. Luckily, however,
he spared me all this at the Vicar's. When we left, it
was time to mount our horses and go the country rounds,
and I was glad of it.

## CHAPTER IV

'By and by the inhabitants of Duncombe began to have parties in my honour.  Mr. Morgan told me it was on my account, or I don't think I should have found it out.  But he was pleased at every fresh invitation, and rubbed his hands, and chuckled, as if it was a compliment to himself, as in truth it was.

'Meanwhile, the arrangement with Mrs. Rose had been brought to a conclusion.  She was to bring her furniture, and place it in a house, of which I was to pay the rent.  She was to be the mistress, and, in return, she was not to pay anything for her board. Mr. Morgan took the house, and delighted in advising and settling all my affairs.  I was partly indolent, and partly amused, and was altogether passive.  The house he took for me was near his own : it had two sitting-rooms downstairs, opening into each other by folding-doors, which were, however, kept shut in general.  The back room was my consulting room ("the library," he advised me to call it), and he gave me a skull to put on the top of my bookcase, in which the medical books were all ranged on the conspicuous shelves ; while Miss Austen, Dickens, and Thackeray* were, by Mr. Morgan himself, skilfully placed in a careless way, upside down or with their backs turned to the wall.  The front parlour was to be the dining-room, and the room above was furnished with Mrs. Rose's drawing-room chairs and table, though I found she preferred sitting downstairs in the dining-room close to the window, where, between every stitch, she could look up and see what was going on in the street.  I felt rather queer to be the master of this house, filled with another person's furniture, before I had even seen the lady whose property it was.

'Presently she arrived.  Mr. Morgan met her at the inn where the coach stopped, and accompanied her to my house.  I could see them out of the drawing-room window, the little gentleman stepping daintily along, flourishing his cane, and evidently talking away. She was a little taller than he was, and in deep widow's mourning; such veils and falls, and capes and cloaks, that she looked like a black crape haycock. When we were introduced, she put up her thick veil, and looked around and sighed.

' " Your appearance and circumstances, Mr. Harrison, remind me forcibly of the time when I was married to my dear husband, now at rest. He was then, like you, commencing practice as a surgeon. For twenty years I sympathized with him, and assisted him by every means in my power, even to making up pills when the young man was out. May we live together in like harmony for an equal length of time ! May the regard between us be equally sincere, although, instead of being conjugal, it is to be maternal and filial ! "

' I am sure she had been concocting this speech in the coach, for she afterwards told me she was the only passenger. When she had ended, I felt as if I ought to have had a glass of wine in my hand, to drink, after the manner of toasts. And yet I doubt if I should have done it heartily, for I did not hope to live with her for twenty years ; it had rather a dreary sound. However, I only bowed and kept my thoughts to myself. I asked Mr. Morgan, while Mrs. Rose was upstairs taking off her things, to stay to tea ; to which he agreed, and kept rubbing his hands with satisfaction, saying—

' " Very fine woman, sir ; very fine woman ! And what a manner ! How she will receive patients, who may wish to leave a message during your absence. Such a flow of words to be sure ! "

' Mr. Morgan could not stay long after tea, as there were one or two cases to be seen. I would willingly have gone, and had my hat on, indeed, for the purpose, when he said it would not be respectful, "not the thing," to leave Mrs. Rose the first evening of her arrival.

' " Tender deference to the sex—to a widow in the first months of her loneliness—requires a little consideration, my dear sir. I will leave that case at

Miss Tomkinson's for you; you will perhaps call early to-morrow morning. Miss Tomkinson is rather particular, and is apt to speak plainly if she does not think herself properly attended to."

'I had often noticed that he shuffled off the visits to Miss Tomkinson's on me, and I suspect he was a little afraid of the lady.

'It was rather a long evening with Mrs. Rose. She had nothing to do, thinking it civil, I suppose, to stop in the parlour, and not go upstairs and unpack. I begged I might be no restraint upon her if she wished to do so; but (rather to my disappointment) she smiled in a measured, subdued way, and said it would be a pleasure to her to become better acquainted with me. She went upstairs once, and my heart misgave me when I saw her come down with a clean folded pocket-handkerchief. Oh, my prophetic soul !—she was no sooner seated, than she began to give me an account of her late husband's illness, and symptoms, and death. It was a very common case, but she evidently seemed to think it had been peculiar. She had just a smattering of medical knowledge, and used the technical terms so very mala-propos that I could hardly keep from smiling; but I would not have done it for the world, she was evidently in such deep and sincere distress. At last she said—

' " I have the ' dognoses ' of my dear husband's com-plaint in my desk, Mr. Harrison, if you would like to draw up the case for the *Lancet*.* I think he would have felt gratified, poor fellow, if he had been told such a compliment would be paid to his remains, and that his case should appear in those distinguished columns."

'It was rather awkward; for the case was of the very commonest, as I said before. However, I had not been even this short time in practice without having learnt a few of those noises which do not compromise one, and yet may bear a very significant construction if the listener chooses to exert a little imagination.

'Before the end of the evening, we were such friends that she brought me down the late Mr. Rose's picture to look at. She told me she could not bear herself to

gaze upon the beloved features; but that if I would
look upon the miniature, she would avert her face.
I offered to take it into my own hands, but she seemed
wounded at the proposal, and said she never, never could
trust such a treasure out of her own possession; so she
turned her head very much over her left shoulder, while
I examined the likeness held by her extended right arm.

'The late Mr. Rose must have been rather a good-
looking, jolly man; and the artist had given him such
a broad smile, and such a twinkle about the eyes, that it
really was hard to help smiling back at him. However,
I restrained myself.

'At first Mrs. Rose objected to accepting any of the
invitations which were sent her to accompany me to the
tea-parties in the town. She was so good and simple,
that I was sure she had no other reason than the one
which she alleged—the short time that had elapsed
since her husband's death; or else, now that I had had
some experience of the entertainments which she
declined so pertinaciously, I might have suspected that
she was glad of the excuse. I used sometimes to wish
that I was a widow. I came home tired from a hard
day's riding, and if I had but felt sure that Mr. Morgan
would not come in, I should certainly have put on my
slippers and my loose morning coat, and have indulged
in a cigar in the garden. It seemed a cruel sacrifice to
society to dress myself in tight boots, and a stiff coat,
and go to a five-o'clock tea. But Mr. Morgan read me
such lectures upon the necessity of cultivating the
goodwill of the people among whom I was settled, and
seemed so sorry, and almost hurt, when I once complained of the dullness of these parties, that I felt I could
not be so selfish as to decline more than one out of
three. Mr. Morgan, if he found that I had an invitation
for the evening, would often take the longer round, and
the more distant visits. I suspected him at first of the
design, which I confess I often entertained, of shirking
the parties; but I soon found out he was really making
a sacrifice of his inclinations for what he considered to
be my advantage.

## CHAPTER V

'THERE was one invitation which seemed to promise
a good deal of pleasure. Mr. Bullock (who is the
attorney of Duncombe) was married a second time to
a lady from a large provincial town; she wished to
lead the fashion—a thing very easy to do, for every
one was willing to follow her. So instead of giving a
tea-party in my honour, she proposed a picnic to some
old hall in the neighbourhood; and really the arrangements sounded tempting enough. Every patient we
had seemed full of the subject; both those who were
invited and those who were not. There was a moat
round the house, with a boat on it; and there was
a gallery in the hall, from which music sounded delight-
fully. The family to whom the place belonged were
abroad, and lived at a newer and grander mansion
when they were at home; there were only a farmer
and his wife in the old hall, and they were to have the
charge of the preparations. The little, kind-hearted
town was delighted when the sun shone bright on the
October morning of our picnic; the shopkeepers and
cottagers all looked pleased as they saw the cavalcade
gathering at Mr. Bullock's door. We were somewhere
about twenty in number; a "silent few", she called us;
but I thought we were quite enough. There were the
Miss Tomkinsons, and two of their young ladies—one
of them belonged to a "county family", Mrs. Bullock
told me in a whisper; then came Mr. and Mrs. and
Miss Bullock, and a tribe of little children, the offspring
of the present wife. Miss Bullock was only a step-
daughter. Mrs. Munton had accepted the invitation
to join our party, which was rather unexpected by the
host and hostess, I imagine, from little remarks that
I overheard; but they made her very welcome.
Miss Horsman (a maiden lady who had been on a visit
from home till last week) was another. And last, there
were the Vicar and his children. These, with Mr.

Morgan and myself, made up the party. I was very much pleased to see something more of the Vicar's family. He had come in occasionally to the evening parties, it is true; and spoken kindly to us all; but it was not his habit to stay very long at them. And his daughter was, he said, too young to visit. She had had the charge of her little sisters and brother since her mother's death, which took up a good deal of her time, and she was glad of the evenings to pursue her own studies. But to-day the case was different; and Sophy, and Helen, and Lizzie, and even little Walter, were all there, standing at Mrs. Bullock's door; for we none of us could be patient enough to sit still in the parlour with Mrs. Munton and the elder ones, quietly waiting for the two chaises and the spring-cart, which were to have been there by two o'clock, and now it was nearly a quarter past. "Shameful! the brightness of the day would be gone." The sympathetic shop-keepers, standing at their respective doors with their hands in their pockets, had, one and all, their heads turned in the direction from which the carriages (as Mrs. Bullock called them) were to come. There was a rumble along the paved street; and the shopkeepers turned and smiled, and bowed their heads congratulat-ingly to us; all the mothers and all the little children of the place stood clustering round the door to see us set off. I had my horse waiting; and, meanwhile, I assisted people into their vehicles. One sees a good deal of management on such occasions. Mrs. Munton was handed first into one of the chaises; then there was a little hanging back, for most of the young people wished to go in the cart—I don't know why. Miss Hors-man, however, came forward, and as she was known to be the intimate friend of Mrs. Munton, so far was satisfactory. But who was to be third—bodkin* with two old ladies, who liked the windows shut? I saw Sophy speaking to Helen; and then she came forward and offered to be the third. The two old ladies looked pleased and glad (as every one did near Sophy); so that chaise-full was arranged. Just as it was going off,

however, the servant from the vicarage came running
with a note for her master. When he had read it, he
went to the chaise door, and I suppose told Sophy,
what I afterwards heard him say to Mrs. Bullock,
that the clergyman of a neighbouring parish was ill,
and unable to read the funeral service for one of his
parishioners, who was to be buried that afternoon.
The Vicar was, of course, obliged to go, and said he
should not return home that night. It seemed a relief
to some, I perceived, to be without the little restraint
of his dignified presence. Mr. Morgan came up just
at the moment, having ridden hard all the morning to
be in time to join our party; so we were resigned, on
the whole, to the Vicar's absence. His own family
regretted him the most, I noticed, and I liked them all
the better for it. I believe that I came next in being
sorry for his departure; but I respected and admired
him, and felt always the better for having been in his
company. Miss Tomkinson, Mrs. Bullock, and the
"county" young lady, were in the next chaise. I
think the last would rather have been in the cart with
the younger and merrier set, but I imagine that was
considered *infra dig*. The remainder of the party
were to ride and tie;* and a most riotous, laughing set
they were. Mr. Morgan and I were on horseback; at
least I led my horse, with little Walter riding on him;
his fat, sturdy legs standing stiff out on each side of
my cob's broad back. He was a little darling, and
chattered all the way, his sister Sophy being the heroine
of all his stories. I found he owed this day's excursion
entirely to her begging papa to let him come; nurse was
strongly against it—" cross old nurse ! " he called her
once, and then said, "No, not cross; kind nurse ; Sophy
tells Walter not to say cross nurse." I never saw so
young a child so brave. The horse shied at a log of
wood. Walter looked very red, and grasped the mane,
but sat upright like a little man, and never spoke all the
time the horse was dancing. When it was over he
looked at me, and smiled—

' " You would not let me be hurt, Mr. Harrison,

would you ? " He was the most winning little fellow I ever saw.

'There were frequent cries to me from the cart, " Oh, Mr. Harrison ! do get us that branch of blackberries ; you can reach it with your whip handle." "Oh, Mr. Harrison ! there were such splendid nuts on the other side of that hedge ; would you just turn back for them ? " Miss Caroline Tomkinson was once or twice rather faint with the motion of the cart, and asked me for my smelling bottle, as she had forgotten hers. I was amused at the idea of my carrying such articles about with me. Then she thought she should like to walk, and got out, and came on my side of the road ; but I found little Walter the pleasanter companion, and soon set the horse off into a trot, with which pace her tender constitution could not keep up.

'The road to the old hall was along a sandy lane, with high hedge-banks ; the wych-elms almost met overhead. "Shocking farming ! " Mr. Bullock called out ; and so it might be, but it was very pleasant and picturesque-looking. The trees were gorgeous, in their orange and crimson hues, varied by great, dark-green holly-bushes, glistening in the autumn sun. I should have thought the colours too vivid, if I had seen them in a picture, especially when we wound up the brow, after crossing the little bridge over the brook (what laughing and screaming there was as the cart splashed through the sparkling water !)—and I caught the purple hills beyond. We could see the old hall, too, from that point, with its warm rich woods billowing up behind, and the blue waters of the moat lying still under the sunlight.

'Laughing and talking is very hungry work, and there was a universal petition for dinner when we arrived at the lawn before the hall, where it had been arranged that we were to dine. I saw Miss Carry take Miss Tomkinson aside, and whisper to her ; and presently the elder sister came up to me, where I was busy, rather apart, making a seat of hay, which I had fetched from the farmer's loft for my little friend Walter, who, I had noticed, was rather hoarse, and for whom I was afraid of a seat on the grass, dry as it appeared to be.

' " Mr. Harrison, Caroline tells me she has been feeling very faint, and she is afraid of a return of one of her attacks. She says she has more confidence in your medical powers than in Mr. Morgan's. I should not be sincere if I did not say that I differ from her; but as it is so, may I beg you to keep an eye upon her? I tell her she had better not have come if she did not feel well; but, poor girl, she had set her heart upon this day's pleasure. I have offered to go home with her; but she says, if she can only feel sure you are at hand, she would rather stay."

' Of course I bowed, and promised all due attendance on Miss Caroline; and in the meantime, until she did require my services, I thought I might as well go and help the Vicar's daughter, who looked so fresh and pretty in her white muslin dress, here, there, and everywhere, now in the sunshine, now in the green shade, helping every one to be comfortable, and thinking of every one but herself.

' Presently, Mr. Morgan came up.

' " Miss Caroline does not feel quite well. I have promised your services to her sister."

' " So have I, sir. But Miss Sophy cannot carry this heavy basket."

' I did not mean her to have heard this excuse; but she caught it up and said—

' " Oh, yes, I can ! I can take the things out one by one. Go to poor Miss Caroline, pray, Mr. Harrison."

' I went; but very unwillingly, I must say. When I had once seated myself by her, I think she must have felt better. It was, probably, only a nervous fear, which was relieved when she knew she had assistance near at hand; for she made a capital dinner. I thought she would never end her modest requests for " just a little more pigeon-pie, or a merry-thought of chicken ". Such a hearty meal would, I hope, effectually revive her; and so it did; for she told me she thought she could manage to walk round the garden, and see the old peacock yews, if I would kindly give her my arm. It was very provoking; I had so set my heart upon being with the Vicar's children. I advised Miss Caroline strongly to lie down a little, and rest before tea, on the sofa in the farmer's kitchen; you cannot think how persuasively I begged her to take care of herself. At last she consented, thanking me for my tender interest; she should never forget my kind attention to her. She little knew what was in my mind at the time. However, she was safely consigned to the farmer's wife, and I was rushing out in search of a white gown and a waving figure, when I encountered Mrs. Bullock at the door of the hall. She was a fine, fierce-looking woman. I thought she had appeared a little displeased at my (unwilling) attentions to Miss Caroline at dinner-time; but now, seeing me alone, she was all smiles.

' "Oh, Mr. Harrison, all alone! How is that? What are the young ladies about to allow such churlishness? And, by the way, I have left a young lady who will be very glad of your assistance, I am sure—my daughter, Jemima' (her step-daughter, she meant). 'Mr. Bullock is so particular, and so tender a father, that he would be frightened to death at the idea of her going into the boat on the moat unless she was with some one who could swim. He is gone to discuss the new wheel-plough with the farmer (you know agriculture is his hobby, although law, horrid law, is his business). But the poor girl is pining on the bank, longing for my permission to join the others, which I dare not give unless you will kindly accompany her, and promise, if any accident happens, to preserve her safe."

' Oh, Sophy, why was no one anxious about you?

## CHAPTER VI

'MISS BULLOCK was standing by the waterside,
looking wistfully, as I thought, at the water party; the
sound of whose merry laughter came pleasantly enough
from the boat, which lay off (for, indeed, no one knew
how to row, and she was of a clumsy, flat-bottomed
build) about a hundred yards, "weatherbound," as
they shouted out, among the long stalks of the water-
lilies.

'Miss Bullock did not look up till I came close to her;
and then, when I told her my errand, she lifted up her
great, heavy, sad eyes, and looked at me for a moment.
It struck me, at the time, that she expected to find
some expression on my face which was not there, and
that its absence was a relief to her. She was a very pale,
unhappy-looking girl, but very quiet, and, if not agreeable in manner, at any rate not forward or offensive.
I called to the party in the boat, and they came slowly
enough through the large, cool, green lily-leaves towards
us. When they got near, we saw there was no room for
us, and Miss Bullock said she would rather stay in the
meadow and saunter about, if I would go into the boat;
and I am certain from the look on her countenance
that she spoke the truth; but Miss Horsman called
out, in a sharp voice, while she smiled in a very disagreeable, knowing way—

' "Oh, mamma will be displeased if you don't come
in, Miss Bullock, after all her trouble in making such a
nice arrangement."

'At this speech the poor girl hesitated, and at last,
in an undecided way, as if she was not sure whether she
was doing right, she took Sophy's place in the boat.
Helen and Lizzie landed with their sister, so that there
was plenty of room for Miss Tomkinson, Miss Horsman,
and all the little Bullocks; and the three vicarage girls
went off strolling along the meadow side, and playing
with Walter, who was in a high state of excitement.

The sun was getting low, but the declining light was beautiful upon the water ; and, to add to the charm of the time, Sophy and her sisters, standing on the green lawn in front of the hall, struck up the little German canon,* which I had never heard before—

Oh wie wohl ist mir am abend, &c.

At last we were summoned to tug the boat to the landing-steps on the lawn, tea and a blazing wood fire being ready for us in the hall. I was offering my arm to Miss Horsman, as she was a little lame, when she said again, in her peculiar disagreeable way, " Had you not better take Miss Bullock, Mr. Harrison ? It will be more satisfactory."

' I helped Miss Horsman up the steps, however, and then she repeated her advice ; so, remembering that Miss Bullock was in fact the daughter of my entertainers, I went to her ; but though she accepted my arm, I could perceive she was sorry that I had offered it.

' The hall was lighted by the glorious wood fire in the wide old grate ; the daylight was dying away in the west ; and the large windows admitted but little of what was left, through their small leaded frames, with coats of arms emblazoned upon them. The farmer's wife had set out a great long table, which was piled with good things ; and a huge black kettle sang on the glowing fire, which sent a cheerful warmth through the room as it crackled and blazed. Mr. Morgan (who I found had been taking a little round in the neighbourhood among his patients) was there, smiling and rubbing his hands as usual. Mr. Bullock was holding a conversation with the farmer at the garden-door on the nature of different manures, in which it struck me that if Mr. Bullock had the fine names and the theories on his side, the farmer had all the practical knowledge and the experience, and I know which I would have trusted. I think Mr. Bullock rather liked to talk about Liebig* in my hearing ; it sounded well, and was knowing. Mrs. Bullock was not particularly placid in her mood. In the first place, I wanted to sit by the Vicar's daughter,

and Miss Caroline as decidedly wanted to sit on my
other side, being afraid of her fainting fits, I imagine.
But Mrs. Bullock called me to a place near her daughter.
Now I thought I had done enough civility to a girl who
was evidently annoyed rather than pleased by my
attentions, and I pretended to be busy stooping under
the table for Miss Caroline's gloves, which were missing ;
but it was of no avail ; Mrs. Bullock's fine, severe eyes
were awaiting my reappearance, and she summoned
me again.

'"I am keeping this place on my right hand for you,
Mr. Harrison. Jemima, sit still ! "

'I went up to the post of honour and tried to busy
myself with pouring out coffee to hide my chagrin ; but
after forgetting to empty the water put in ("to warm
the cups", Mrs. Bullock said), and omitting to add any
sugar, the lady told me she would dispense with my
services, and turn me over to my neighbour on the
other side.

'"Talking to the younger lady was, no doubt, more
Mr. Harrison's vocation than assisting the elder one."
I dare say it was only the manner that made the words
seem offensive. Miss Horsman sat opposite to me,
smiling away. Miss Bullock did not speak, but seemed
more depressed than ever. At length, Miss Horsman
and Mrs. Bullock got to a war of innuendoes, which were
completely unintelligible to me, and I was very much
displeased with my situation ; while, at the bottom of
the table, Mr. Morgan and Mr. Bullock were making
the young ones laugh most heartily. Part of the joke
was Mr. Morgan insisting upon making tea at that end ;
and Sophy and Helen were busy contriving every
possible mistake for him. I thought honour was a
very good thing, but merriment a better. Here was
I in the place of distinction, hearing nothing but cross
words. At last the time came for us to go home. As
the evening was damp, the seats in the chaises were
the best and most to be desired. And now Sophy offered
to go in the cart ; only she seemed anxious, and so was
I, that Walter should be secured from the effects of the

white wreaths of fog rolling up from the valley; but the little violent affectionate fellow would not be separated from Sophy. She made a nest for him on her knee in one corner of the cart, and covered him with her own shawl; and I hoped that he would take no harm. Miss Tomkinson, Mr. Bullock, and some of the young ones walked; but I seemed chained to the windows of the chaise, for Miss Caroline begged me not to leave her, as she was dreadfully afraid of robbers; and Mrs. Bullock implored me to see that the man did not overturn them in the bad roads, as he had certainly had too much to drink.

'I became so irritable before I reached home, that I thought it was the most disagreeable day of pleasure I had ever had, and could hardly bear to answer Mrs. Rose's never-ending questions. She told me, however, that from my account the day was so charming that she thought she should relax in the rigour of her seclusion, and mingle a little more in the society of which I gave so tempting a description. She really thought her dear Mr. Rose would have wished it; and his will should be law to her after his death, as it had ever been during his life. In compliance, therefore, with his wishes, she would even do a little violence to her own feelings.

'She was very good and kind; not merely attentive to everything which she thought could conduce to my comfort, but willing to take any trouble in providing the broths and nourishing food which I often found it convenient to order, under the name of kitchen-physic, for my poorer patients; and I really did not see the use of her shutting herself up, in mere compliance with an etiquette, when she began to wish to mix in the little quiet society of Duncombe. Accordingly I urged her to begin to visit, and even when applied to as to what I imagined the late Mr. Rose's wishes on that subject would have been, answered for that worthy gentleman, and assured his widow that I was convinced he would have regretted deeply her giving way to immoderate grief, and would have been rather grateful than otherwise at seeing her endeavour to divert her thoughts by a few quiet visits. She cheered up, and said, "As I really thought so, she would sacrifice her own inclinations, and accept the very next invitation that came."

## CHAPTER VII

'I was roused from my sleep in the middle of the night by a messenger from the vicarage. Little Walter had got the croup, and Mr. Morgan had been sent for into the country. I dressed myself hastily, and went through the quiet little street. There was a light burning upstairs at the vicarage. It was in the nursery. The servant, who opened the door the instant I knocked, was crying sadly, and could hardly answer my inquiries as I went upstairs, two steps at a time, to see my little favourite.

'The nursery was a great large room. At the farther end it was lighted by a common candle, which left the other end, where the door was, in shade, so I suppose the nurse did not see me come in, for she was speaking very crossly.

'"Miss Sophy!" said she, "I told you over and over again it was not fit for him to go, with the hoarseness that he had, and you would take him. It will break your papa's heart, I know; but it's none of my doing."

'Whatever Sophy felt, she did not speak in answer to this. She was on her knees by the warm bath, in which the little fellow was struggling to get his breath, with a look of terror on his face that I have often noticed in young children when smitten by a sudden and violent illness. It seems as if they recognized something infinite and invisible, at whose bidding the pain and the anguish come, from which no love can shield them. It is a very heart-rending look to observe, because it comes on the faces of those who are too young to receive comfort from the words of faith, or the promises of religion. Walter had his arms tight round Sophy's neck, as if she, hitherto his paradise-angel, could save him from the dread shadow of Death. Yes! of Death! I knelt down by him on the other side, and examined him. The very robustness of his little frame gave violence to the disease, which is always one of the most fearful by which children of his age can be attacked.

' "Don't tremble, Watty," said Sophy, in a soothing tone; "it's Mr. Harrison, darling, who let you ride on his horse." I could detect the quivering in the voice, which she tried to make so calm and soft to quiet the little fellow's fears. We took him out of the bath, and I went for leeches.* While I was away, Mr. Morgan came. He loved the vicarage children as if he were their uncle; but he stood still and aghast at the sight of Walter—so lately bright and strong—and now hurrying alone to the awful change—to the silent mysterious land, where, tended and cared for as he had been on earth, he must go—alone. The little fellow! the darling!

' We applied the leeches to his throat. He resisted at first; but Sophy, God bless her! put the agony of her grief on one side, and thought only of him, and began to sing the little songs he loved. We were all still. The gardener had gone to fetch the Vicar; but he was twelve miles off, and we doubted if he would come in time. I don't know if they had any hope; but the first moment Mr. Morgan's eyes met mine, I saw that he, like me, had none. The ticking of the house-clock sounded through the dark, quiet house. Walter was sleeping now, with the black leeches yet hanging to his fair, white throat. Still Sophy went on singing little lullabies, which she had sung under far different and happier circumstances. I remember one verse, because it struck me at the time as strangely applicable.

> " Sleep, baby, sleep !
> Thy rest shall angels keep;
> While on the grass the lamb shall feed,
> And never suffer want or need.
>                 Sleep, baby, sleep."*

The tears were in Mr. Morgan's eyes. I do not think either he or I could have spoken in our natural tones ; but the brave girl went on, clear though low. She stopped at last, and looked up.

' " He is better, is he not, Mr. Morgan ? "

' " No, my dear. He is—ahem "—he could not speak all at once. Then he said—" My dear ! he will be better soon. Think of your mamma, my dear Miss Sophy. She will be very thankful to have one of her darlings safe with her, where she is."

' Still she did not cry. But she bent her head down on the little face, and kissed it long and tenderly.

' " I will go for Helen and Lizzie. They will be sorry not to see him again." She rose up and went for them. Poor girls, they came in, in their dressing-gowns, with eyes dilated with sudden emotion, pale with terror, stealing softly along, as if sound could disturb him. Sophy comforted them by gentle caresses. It was over soon.

' Mr. Morgan was fairly crying like a child. But he thought it necessary to apologize to me, for what I honoured him for. " I am a little overdone by yesterday's work, sir. I have had one or two bad nights, and they rather upset me. When I was your age I was as strong and manly as any one, and would have scorned to shed tears."

' Sophy came up to where we stood.

' " Mr. Morgan ! I am so sorry for papa. How shall I tell him ? " She was struggling against her own grief for her father's sake. Mr. Morgan offered to await his coming home ; and she seemed thankful for the proposal. I, new friend, almost stranger, might stay no longer. The street was as quiet as ever ; not a shadow was changed ; for it was not yet four o'clock. But during the night a soul had departed.

' From all I could see, and all I could learn, the Vicar and his daughter strove which should comfort the other the most. Each thought of the other's grief— each prayed for the other rather than for themselves. We saw them walking out, countrywards ; and we

heard of them in the cottages of the poor. But it was
some time before I happened to meet either of them
again. And then I felt, from something indescribable in
their manner towards me, that I was one of the

"Peculiar people, whom Death had made dear."

That one day at the old hall had done this. I was,
perhaps, the last person who had given the little fellow
any unusual pleasure. Poor Walter ! I wish I could
have done more to make his short life happy !


## CHAPTER VIII

'There was a little lull, out of respect to the Vicar's
grief, in the visiting. It gave time to Mrs. Rose to
soften down the anguish of her weeds.

'At Christmas, Miss Tomkinson sent out invitations
for a party. Miss Caroline had once or twice apologized
to me because such an event had not taken place before ;
but, as she said, "the avocations of their daily life
prevented their having such little *réunions* except in
the vacations." And, sure enough, as soon as the holidays began, came the civil little note—

'"The Misses Tomkinson request the pleasure of
Mrs. Rose's and Mr. Harrison's company at tea, on the
evening of Monday, the 23rd inst. Tea at five o'clock."

'Mrs. Rose's spirit roused, like a war-horse at the
sound of the trumpet, at this. She was not of a repining
disposition, but I do think she believed the party-giving
population of Duncombe had given up inviting her, as
soon as she had determined to relent, and accept the
invitations, in compliance with the late Mr. Rose's
wishes.

'Such snippings of white love-ribbon as I found
everywhere, making the carpet untidy ! One day, too,
unluckily, a small box was brought to me by mistake.
I did not look at the direction, for I never doubted it
was some hyoscyamus* which I was expecting from
London ; so I tore it open, and saw inside a piece of

paper, with "No more grey hair", in large letters, upon it. I folded it up in a hurry, and sealed it afresh, and gave it to Mrs. Rose ; but I could not refrain from asking her, soon after, if she could recommend me anything to keep my hair from turning grey, adding that I thought prevention was better than cure. I think she made out the impression of my seal on the paper after that ; for I learned that she had been crying, and that she talked about there being no sympathy left in the world for her since Mr. Rose's death ; and that she counted the days until she could rejoin him in the better world. I think she counted the days to Miss Tomkinson's party, too ; she talked so much about it.

' The covers were taken off Miss Tomkinson's chairs, and curtains, and sofas ; and a great jar full of artificial flowers was placed in the centre of the table, which, as Miss Caroline told me, was all her doing, as she doted on the beautiful and artistic in life. Miss Tomkinson stood, erect as a grenadier, close to the door, receiving her friends, and heartily shaking them by the hands as they entered : she said she was truly glad to see them. And so she really was.

' We had just finished tea, and Miss Caroline had brought out a little pack of conversation cards— sheaves of slips of cardboard, with intellectual or sentimental questions on one set, and equally intellectual and sentimental answers on the other ; and as the answers were fit to any and all the questions, you may think they were a characterless and "wersh"*set of things. I had just been asked by Miss Caroline—

' " *Can you tell what those dearest to you think of you at this present time ?* " and had answered—

' " *How can you expect me to reveal such a secret to the present company !* " when the servant announced that a gentleman, a friend of mine, wished to speak to me downstairs.

' " Oh, show him up, Martha ; show him up ! " said Miss Tomkinson, in her hospitality.

' " Any friend of our friend's is welcome," said Miss Caroline, in an insinuating tone.

'I jumped up, however, thinking it might be some one on business ; but I was so penned in by the spider-legged tables, stuck out on every side, that I could not make the haste I wished ; and before I could prevent it, Martha had shown up Jack Marshland, who was on his road home for a day or two at Christmas.

'He came up in a hearty way, bowing to Miss Tom-kinson, and explaining that he had found himself in my neighbourhood, and had come over to pass a night with me, and that my servant had directed him where I was.

'His voice, loud at all times, sounded like Stentor's* in that little room, where we all spoke in a kind of purring way. He had no swell in his tones ; they were *forte* from the beginning. At first it seemed like the days of my youth come back again, to hear full, manly speaking ; I felt proud of my friend, as he thanked Miss Tomkinson for her kindness in asking him to stay the evening. By and by he came up to me, and I dare say he thought he had lowered his voice, for he looked as if speaking confidentially, while in fact the whole room might have heard him.

' " Frank, my boy, when shall we have dinner at this good old lady's ? I'm deuced hungry."

'Dinner ! Why, we had had tea an hour ago. While he yet spoke, Martha came in with a little tray, on which was a single cup of coffee and three slices of wafer bread-and-butter. His dismay, and his evident submission to the decrees of Fate, tickled me so much, that I thought he should have a further taste of the life I led from month's end to month's end, and I gave up my plan of taking him home at once, and enjoyed the anticipation of the hearty laugh we should have to-gether at the end of the evening. I was famously punished for my determination.

' " Shall we continue our game ? " asked Miss Caroline, who had never relinquished her sheaf of questions.

'We went on questioning and answering, with little gain of information to either party.

' " No such thing as heavy betting in this game, eh,

Frank ? " asked Jack, who had been watching us.
" You don't lose ten pounds at a sitting, I guess, as you
used to do at Short's.   Playing for love, I suppose you
call it ? "

' Miss Caroline simpered, and looked down.   Jack
was not thinking of her.   He was thinking of the days
we had had at the " Mermaid ".*   Suddenly he said,
" Where were you this day last year, Frank ? "

' " I don't remember ! " said I.

' " Then I'll tell you.   It 's the 23rd—the day you
were taken up for knocking down the fellow in Long
Acre, and that I had to bail you out ready for Christmas
Day.   You are in more agreeable quarters to-night."

' He did not intend this reminiscence to be heard,
but was not in the least put out when Miss Tomkinson,
with a face of dire surprise, asked—

' " Mr. Harrison taken up, sir ? "

' " Oh, yes, ma'am ;  and you see it was so common
an affair with him to be locked up that he can't remember the dates of his different imprisonments."

' He laughed heartily ;  and so should I, but that I
saw the impression it made.   The thing was, in fact,
simple enough, and capable of easy explanation.   I
had been made angry by seeing a great hulking fellow,
out of mere wantonness, break the crutch from under
a cripple ;  and I struck the man more violently than
I intended, and down he went, yelling out for the
police, and I had to go before the magistrate to be
released.   I disdained giving this explanation at the
time.   It was no business of theirs what I had been
doing a year ago ;  but still Jack might have held his
tongue.   However, that unruly member of his was set
a-going, and he told me afterwards he was resolved to
let the old ladies into a little of life ;  and accordingly
he remembered every practical joke we had ever had,
and talked and laughed, and roared again.   I tried to
converse with Miss Caroline—Mrs. Munton—any one ;
but Jack was the hero of the evening, and every one
was listening to him.

' " Then he has never sent any hoaxing letters since

he came here, has he ? Good boy ! He has turned over
a new leaf.   He was the deepest dog at that I ever met
with.   Such anonymous letters as he used to send !
Do you remember that to Mrs. Walbrook, eh, Frank ?
That was too bad ! " (the wretch was laughing all the
time).   " No ;  I won't tell about it—don't be afraid.
Such a shameful hoax ! " (laughing again).

' " Pray do tell," I called out ;  for he made it seem
far worse than it was.

' " Oh no, no ;  you've established a better character
—I would not for the world nip your budding efforts.
We'll bury the past in oblivion."

' I tried to tell my neighbours the story to which he
alluded ;  but they were attracted by the merriment of
Jack's manner, and did not care to hear the plain
matter of fact.

' Then came a pause ;  Jack was talking almost quietly
to Miss Horsman.   Suddenly he called across the
room—" How many times have you been out with the
hounds ?   The hedges were blind very late this year,
but you must have had some good mild days since."

' " I have never been out," said I shortly.

' " Never !—whew !——   Why, I thought that was
the great attraction to Duncombe."

' Now was not he provoking ?   He would condole with
me, and fixed the subject in the minds of every one
present.

' The supper trays were brought in, and there was a
shuffling of situations.   He and I were close together again.

' " I say, Frank, what will you lay me that I don't
clear that tray before people are ready for their second
helping ?   I'm as hungry as a hound."

' " You shall have a round of beef and a raw leg cf
mutton when you get home.   Only do behave yourself
here."

' " Well, for your sake ;  but keep me away from those
trays, or I'll not answer for myself.   ' Hould me, or I'll
fight,' as the Irishman said.   I'll go and talk to that
little old lady in blue, and sit with my back to those
ghosts of eatables."

' He sat down by Miss Caroline, who would not have liked his description of her ; and began an earnest, tolerably quiet conversation. I tried to be as agreeable as I could, to do away with the impression he had given of me ; but I found that every one drew up a little stiffly at my approach, and did not encourage me to make any remarks.

' In the middle of my attempts, I heard Miss Caroline beg Jack to take a glass of wine, and I saw him help himself to what appeared to be port ; but in an instant he set it down from his lips, exclaiming, " Vinegar, by Jove ! " He made the most horribly wry face : and Miss Tomkinson came up in a severe hurry to investigate the affair. It turned out it was some black-currant wine, on which she particularly piqued herself ; I drank two glasses of it to ingratiate myself with her, and can testify to its sourness. I don't think she noticed my exertions, she was so much engrossed in listening to Jack's excuses for his malapropos observation. He told her, with the gravest face, that he had been a teetotaller so long that he had but a confused recollection of the distinction between wine and vinegar, particularly eschewing the latter, because it had been twice fermented ; and that he had imagined Miss Caroline had asked him to take toast-and-water, or he should never have touched the decanter.

## CHAPTER IX

' As we were walking home, Jack said, " Lord, Frank ! I've had such fun with the little lady in blue. I told her you wrote to me every Saturday, telling me the events of the week. She took all in." He stopped to laugh ; for he bubbled and chuckled so that he could not laugh and walk. " And I told her you were deeply in love " (another laugh) ; " and that I could not get you to tell me the name of the lady, but that she had light brown hair—in short, I drew from life, and gave

her an exact description of herself; and that I was
most anxious to see her, and implore her to be merciful
to you, for that you were a most timid, faint-hearted
fellow with women." He laughed till I thought he
would have fallen down. "I begged her, if she could
guess who it was from my description—I'll answer for
it she did—I took care of that; for I said you described
a mole on the left cheek in the most poetical way, saying
Venus had pinched it out of envy at seeing any one
more lovely—oh, hold me up, or I shall fall—laughing
and hunger make me so weak;—well, I say, I begged
her, if she knew who your fair one could be, to implore
her to save you. I said I knew one of your lungs had
gone after a former unfortunate love-affair, and that
I could not answer for the other if the lady here were
cruel. She spoke of a respirator; but I told her that
might do very well for the odd lung; but would it
minister to a heart diseased?* I really did talk fine.
I have found out the secret of eloquence—it's believing
what you've got to say; and I worked myself well up
with fancying you married to the little lady in blue."

'I got to laughing at last, angry as I had been; his
impudence was irresistible. Mrs. Rose had come home
in the sedan, and gone to bed; and he and I sat up
over the round of beef and brandy-and-water till two
o'clock in the morning.

'He told me I had got quite into the professional
way of mousing about a room, and mewing and purring
according as my patients were ill or well. He mimicked
me, and made me laugh at myself. He left early the
next morning.

'Mr. Morgan came at his usual hour; he and
Marshland would never have agreed, and I should have
been uncomfortable to see two friends of mine disliking
and despising each other.

'Mr. Morgan was ruffled; but with his deferential
manner to women, he smoothed himself down before
Mrs. Rose—regretted that he had not been able to come
to Miss Tomkinson's the evening before, and consequently had not seen her in the society she was so well

calculated to adorn.   But when we were by ourselves, he said—

' " I was sent for to Mrs. Munton's this morning—the old spasms.   May I ask what is this story she tells me about—about prison, in fact ?   I trust, sir, she has made some little mistake, and that you never were;——— that it is an unfounded report."   He could not get it out— "that you were in Newgate for three months ! "   I burst out laughing ;   the story had grown like a mushroom indeed.   Mr. Morgan looked grave.   I told him the truth.   Still he looked grave.   "I've no doubt, sir, that you acted rightly ;   but it has an awkward sound. I imagined from your hilarity just now that there was no foundation whatever for the story.   Unfortunately, there is."

' " I was only a night at the police-station.   I would go there again for the same cause, sir."

' " Very fine spirit, sir—quite like Don Quixote ;   but don't you see you might as well have been to the hulks* at once ? "

' " No, sir ;   I don't."

' " Take my word, before long the story will have grown to that.   However, we won't anticipate evil. *Mens conscia recti,** you remember, is the great thing. The part I regret is, that it may require some short time to overcome a little prejudice which the story may excite against you.   However, we won't dwell on it.   *Mens conscia recti !*   Don't think about it, sir."

' It was clear he was thinking a good deal about it.

## CHAPTER X

' Two or three days before this time, I had had an invitation from the Bullocks to dine with them on Christmas Day.   Mrs. Rose was going to spend the week with friends in the town where she formerly lived ; and I had been pleased at the notion of being received into a family, and of being a little with Mr. Bullock, who struck me as a bluff, good-hearted fellow.

' But this Tuesday before Christmas Day, there came an invitation from the Vicar to dine there ; there were to be only their own family and Mr. Morgan. " Only their own family." It was getting to be all the world to me. I was in a passion with myself for having been so ready to accept Mr. Bullock's invitation—coarse and ungentlemanly as he was ; with his wife's airs of pretension and Miss Bullock's stupidity. I turned it over in my mind. No ! I could not have a bad headache, which should prevent me going to the place I did not care for, and yet leave me at liberty to go where I wished. All I could do was to join the vicarage girls after church, and walk by their side in a long country ramble. They were quiet ; not sad, exactly ; but it was evident that the thought of Walter was in their minds on this day. We went through a copse where there were a good number of evergreens planted as covers for game. The snow was on the ground ; but the sky was clear and bright, and the sun glittered on the smooth holly-leaves. Lizzie asked me to gather her some of the very bright red berries, and she was beginning a sentence with—

' " Do you remember,"——when Helen said " *Hush* ", and looked towards Sophy, who was walking a little apart, and crying softly to herself. There was evidently some connexion between Walter and the holly-berries, for Lizzie threw them away at once when she saw Sophy's tears. Soon we came to a stile which led to an open, breezy common, half covered with gorse. I helped the little girls over it, and set them to run down the slope ; but I took Sophy's arm in mine, and though I could not speak, I think she knew how I was feeling for her. I could hardly bear to bid her good-bye at the vicarage gate ; it seemed as if I ought to go in and spend the day with her.

## CHAPTER XI

'I VENTED my ill humour in being late for the Bullocks' dinner. There were one or two clerks, towards whom Mr. Bullock was patronizing and pressing. Mrs. Bullock was decked out in extraordinary finery. Miss Bullock looked plainer than ever; but she had on some old gown or other, I think, for I heard Mrs. Bullock tell her she was always making a figure of herself. I began to-day to suspect that the mother would not be sorry if I took a fancy to the step-daughter. I was again placed near her at dinner, and when the little ones came in to dessert I was made to notice how fond of children she was, and indeed when one of them nestled to her, her face did brighten; but the moment she caught this loud-whispered remark the gloom came back again, with something even of anger in her look; and she was quite sullen and obstinate when urged to sing in the drawing-room. Mrs. Bullock turned to me—

'"Some young ladies won't sing unless they are asked by gentlemen." She spoke very crossly. "If you ask Jemima, she will probably sing. To oblige me, it is evident she will not."

'I thought the singing, when we got it, would probably be a great bore; however, I did as I was bid, and went with my request to the young lady, who was sitting a little apart. She looked up at me with eyes full of tears, and said, in a decided tone (which, if I had not seen her eyes, I should have said was as cross as her mamma's), "No, sir, I will not." She got up, and left the room. I expected to hear Mrs. Bullock abuse her for her obstinacy. Instead of that, she began to tell me of the money that had been spent on her education; of what each separate accomplishment had cost. "She was timid," she said, "but very musical. Wherever her future home might be, there would be no want of music." She went on praising her till I hated her. If they thought I was going to marry that great lubberly

girl, they were mistaken. Mr. Bullock and the clerks
came up. He brought out Liebig, and called me to him.

' " I can understand a good deal of this agricultural
chemistry," said he, " and have put it in practice—
without much success, hitherto, I confess. But these
unconnected letters puzzle me a little. I suppose they
have some meaning, or else I should say it was mere
book-making to put them in."

' " I think they give the page a very ragged appearance," said Mrs. Bullock, who had joined us. " I inherit a little of my late father's taste for books, and
must say I like to see a good type, a broad margin, and
an elegant binding. My father despised variety; how
he would have held up his hands aghast at the cheap
literature of these times! He did not require many
books, but he would have twenty editions of those
that he had; and he paid more for binding than he did
for the books themselves. But elegance was everything
with him. He would not have admitted your Liebig,
Mr. Bullock; neither the nature of the subject, nor
the common type, nor the common way in which your
book is got up, would have suited him."

' " Go and make tea, my dear, and leave Mr. Harrison
and me to talk over a few of these manures."

' We settled to it; I explained the meaning of the
symbols, and the doctrine of chemical equivalents. At
last he said, " Doctor! you're giving me too strong
a dose of it at one time. Let's have a small quantity
taken ' hodie ';* that's professional, as Mr. Morgan
would call it. Come in and call when you have leisure,
and give me a lesson in my alphabet. Of all you've
been telling me I can only remember that C means
carbon and O oxygen; and I see one must know the
meaning of all these confounded letters before one can
do much good with Liebig."

' " We dine at three," said Mrs. Bullock. " There
will always be a knife and fork for Mr. Harrison.
Bullock! don't confine your invitation to the evening!'

' " Why, you see, I've a nap always after dinner, so
I could not be learning chemistry then."

' " Don't be so selfish, Mr. B. Think of the pleasure
Jemima and I shall have in Mr. Harrison's society."

' I put a stop to the discussion by saying I would come
in in the evenings occasionally, and give Mr. Bullock
a lesson, but that my professional duties occupied me
invariably until that time.

' I liked Mr. Bullock. He was simple, and shrewd ;
and to be with a man was a relief, after all the feminine
society I went through every day.

## CHAPTER XII

' THE next morning I met Miss Horsman.

' " So you dined at Mr. Bullock's yesterday, Mr.
Harrison ? Quite a family party, I hear. They are
quite charmed with you, and your knowledge of
chemistry. Mr. Bullock told me so, in Hodgson's shop,
just now. Miss Bullock is a nice girl, eh, Mr. Harrison ? "
She looked sharply at me. Of course, whatever I
thought, I could do nothing but assent. " A nice little
fortune, too—three thousand pounds, Consols, from
her own mother."

' What did I care ? She might have three millions
for me. I had begun to think a good deal about money,
though, but not in connexion with her. I had been
doing up our books ready to send out our Christmas
bills, and had been wondering how far the Vicar would
consider three hundred a year, with a prospect of
increase, would justify me in thinking of Sophy. Think
of her I could not help ; and the more I thought of how
good, and sweet, and pretty she was, the more I felt
that she ought to have far more than I could offer.
Besides, my father was a shopkeeper, and I saw the
Vicar had a sort of respect for family. I determined
to try and be very attentive to my profession. I was
as civil as could be to every one ; and wore the nap off
the brim of my hat by taking it off so often.

' I had my eyes open to every glimpse of Sophy. I am

overstocked with gloves now that I bought at that time, by way of making errands into the shops where I saw her black gown. I bought pounds upon pounds of arrowroot, till I was tired of the eternal arrowroot puddings Mrs. Rose gave me. I asked her if she could not make bread of it, but she seemed to think that would be expensive; so I took to soap as a safe purchase. I believe soap improves by keeping.

## CHAPTER XIII

'THE more I knew of Mrs. Rose, the better I liked her. She was sweet, and kind, and motherly, and we never had any rubs. I hurt her once or twice, I think, by cutting her short in her long stories about Mr. Rose. But I found out that when she had plenty to do she did not think of him quite so much; so I expressed a wish for Corazza shirts,* and in the puzzle of devising how they were to be cut out she forgot Mr. Rose for some time. I was still more pleased by her way about some legacy her elder brother left her. I don't know the amount, but it was something handsome, and she might have set up housekeeping for herself: but, instead, she told Mr. Morgan (who repeated it to me), that she should continue with me, as she had quite an elder sister's interest in me.

'The "county young lady", Miss Tyrrell, returned to Miss Tomkinson's after the holidays. She had an enlargement of the tonsils, which required to be frequently touched with caustic, so I often called to see her. Miss Caroline always received me, and kept me talking in her washed-out style, after I had seen my patient. One day she told me she thought she had a weakness about the heart, and would be glad if I would bring my stethoscope the next time, which I accordingly did; and while I was on my knees listening to the pulsations, one of the young ladies came in. She said—

' " Oh, dear ! I never ! I beg your pardon, ma'am," and scuttled out. There was not much the matter with Miss Caroline's heart : a little feeble in action or so, a mere matter of weakness and general languor. When I went down I saw two or three of the girls peeping out of the half-closed schoolroom door, but they shut it immediately, and I heard them laughing. The next time I called, Miss Tomkinson was sitting in state to receive me.

' " Miss Tyrrell's throat does not seem to make much progress. Do you understand the case, Mr. Harrison, or should we have further advice ? I think Mr. Morgan would probably know more about it."

' I assured her it was the simplest thing in the world ; that it always implied a little torpor in the constitution, and that we preferred working through the system, which of course was a slow process, and that the medicine the young lady was taking (iodide of iron) was sure to be successful, although the progress would not be rapid. She bent her head and said, " It might be so ; but she confessed she had more confidence in medicines which had some effect."

' She seemed to expect me to tell her something ; but I had nothing to say, and accordingly I bade good-bye. Somehow, Miss Tomkinson always managed to make me feel very small, by a succession of snubbings ; and whenever I left her I had always to comfort myself under her contradictions by saying to myself, " Her saying it is so, does not make it so." Or I invented good retorts which I might have made to her brusque speeches if I had but thought of them at the right time. But it was provoking that I had not had the presence of mind to recollect them just when they were wanted.

## CHAPTER XIV

'On the whole, things went on smoothly. Mr.
Holden's legacy came in just about this time ; and
I felt quite rich. Five hundred pounds would furnish
the house, I thought, when Mrs. Rose left and Sophy
came. I was delighted, too, to imagine that Sophy perceived the difference of my manner to her from what
it was to any one else, and that she was embarrassed
and shy in consequence, but not displeased with me for
it. All was so flourishing that I went about on wings
instead of feet. We were very busy, without having
anxious cares. My legacy was paid into Mr. Bullock's
hands, who united a little banking business to his profession of law. In return for his advice about invest-
ments (which I never meant to take, having a more
charming, if less profitable, mode in my head), I went
pretty frequently to teach him his agricultural chemistry.
I was so happy in Sophy's blushes that I was universally
benevolent, and desirous of giving pleasure to every
one. I went, at Mrs. Bullock's general invitation, to
dinner there one day unexpectedly : but there was such
a fuss of ill-concealed preparation consequent upon my
coming, that I never went again. Her little boy came
in, with an audibly given message from the cook, to ask—
' " If this was the gentleman as she was to send in
the best dinner-service and dessert for ? "
' I looked deaf, but determined never to go again.
' Miss Bullock and I, meanwhile, became rather
friendly. We found out that we mutually disliked each
other ; and were contented with the discovery. If
people are worth anything, this sort of non-liking is
a very good beginning of friendship. Every good
quality is revealed naturally and slowly, and is a
pleasant surprise. I found out that Miss Bullock was
sensible, and even sweet-tempered, when not irritated
by her stepmother's endeavours to show her off. But
she would sulk for hours after Mrs. Bullock's offensive

praise of her good points. And I never saw such a
black passion as she went into when she suddenly came
into the room when Mrs. Bullock was telling me of all
the offers she had had.

'My legacy made me feel up to extravagance. I
scoured the country for a glorious nosegay of camellias,
which I sent to Sophy on Valentine's Day. I durst not
add a line, but I wished the flowers could speak, and
tell her how I loved her.

'I called on Miss Tyrrell that day. Miss Caroline
was more simpering and affected than ever; and full
of allusions to the day.

' "Do you affix much sincerity of meaning to the
little gallantries of this day, Mr. Harrison?" asked
she, in a languishing tone. I thought of my camellias,
and how my heart had gone with them into Sophy's
keeping; and I told her I thought one might often
take advantage of such a time to hint at feelings one
dared not fully express.

'I remembered afterwards the forced display she
made, after Miss Tyrrell left the room, of a valentine.
But I took no notice at the time; my head was full of
Sophy.

'It was on that very day that John Brouncker, the
gardener to all of us who had small gardens to keep in
order, fell down and injured his wrist severely (I don't
give you the details of the case, because they would not
interest you, being too technical; if you've any curiosity,
you will find them in the *Lancet* of August in that year).
We all liked John, and this accident was felt like a
town's misfortune. The gardens, too, just wanted
doing up. Both Mr. Morgan and I went directly to
him. It was a very awkward case, and his wife and
children were crying sadly. He himself was in great
distress at being thrown out of work. He begged us to
do something that would cure him speedily, as he could
not afford to be laid up, with six children depending
on him for bread. We did not say much before him,
but we both thought the arm would have to come off,
and it was his right arm. We talked it over when we

came out of the cottage. Mr. Morgan had no doubt of
the necessity. I went back at dinner-time to see the
poor fellow. He was feverish and anxious. He had
caught up some expression of Mr. Morgan's in the
morning, and had guessed the measure we had in contemplation. He bade his wife leave the room, and spoke
to me by myself.

' " If you please, sir, I'd rather be done for at once
than have my arm taken off, and be a burden to my
family. I'm not afraid of dying, but I could not
stand being a cripple for life, eating bread, and not able
to earn it."

' The tears were in his eyes with earnestness. I had
all along been more doubtful about the necessity of the
amputation than Mr. Morgan. I knew the improved
treatment in such cases. In his days there was much
more of the rough and ready in surgical practice ; so
I gave the poor fellow some hope.

' In the afternoon I met Mr. Bullock.

' " So you're to try your hand at an amputation to-
morrow, I hear. Poor John Brouncker ! I used to tell
him he was not careful enough about his ladders.
Mr. Morgan is quite excited about it. He asked me to
be present, and see how well a man from Guy's could
operate ; he says he is sure you'll do it beautifully.
Pah ! no such sights for me, thank you."

' Ruddy Mr. Bullock went a shade or two paler at the
thought.

' " Curious ! how professionally a man views these
things. Here 's Mr. Morgan, who has been all along as
proud of you as if you were his own son, absolutely
rubbing his hands at the idea of this crowning glory,
this feather in your cap ! He told me just now he knew
he had always been too nervous to be a good operator ;
and had therefore preferred sending for White from
Chesterton. But now any one might have a serious
accident who liked, for you would be always at hand."

' I told Mr. Bullock, I really thought we might avoid
the amputation ; but his mind was preoccupied with
the idea of it, and he did not care to listen to me.

The whole town was full of it. That is a charm in a little town, everybody is so sympathetically full of the same events. Even Miss Horsman stopped me to ask after John Brouncker with interest ; but she threw cold water upon my intention of saving the arm.

'"As for the wife and family, we'll take care of them. Think what a fine opportunity you have of showing off, Mr. Harrison!"

'That was just like her. Always ready with her suggestions of ill-natured or interested motives.

'Mr. Morgan heard my proposal of a mode of treatment by which I thought it possible that the arm might be saved.

'"I differ from you, Mr. Harrison," said he. "I regret it, but I differ *in toto* from you. Your kind heart deceives you in this instance. There is no doubt that amputation must take place—not later than to-morrow morning, I should say. I have made myself at liberty to attend upon you, sir ; I shall be happy to officiate as your assistant. Time was when I should have been proud to be principal, but a little trembling in my arm incapacitates me."

'I urged my reasons upon him again ; but he was obstinate. He had, in fact, boasted so much of my acquirements as an operator, that he was unwilling I should lose this opportunity of displaying my skill. He could not see that there would be greater skill evinced in saving the arm ; nor did I think of this at the time. I grew angry at his old-fashioned narrow-mindedness, as I thought it ; and I became dogged in my resolution to adhere to my own course. We parted very coolly ; and I went straight off to John Brouncker to tell him I believed that I could save the arm, if he would refuse to have it amputated. When I calmed myself a little, before going in and speaking to him, I could not help acknowledging that we should run some risk of locked jaw ; but, on the whole, and after giving most earnest, conscientious thought to the case, I was sure that my mode of treatment would be best.

'He was a sensible man. I told him the difference of opinion that existed between Mr. Morgan and myself.

I said that there might be some little risk attending the non-amputation ; but that I should guard against it, and I trusted that I should be able to preserve his arm.

' " Under God's blessing," said he reverently. I bowed my head. I don't like to talk too frequently of the dependence which I always felt on that holy blessing, as to the result of my efforts ; but I was glad to hear that speech of John's, because it showed a calm and faithful heart ; and I had almost certain hopes of him from that time.

' We agreed that he should tell Mr. Morgan the reason of his objections to the amputation, and his reliance on my opinion. I determined to recur to every book I had relating to such cases, and to convince Mr. Morgan, if I could, of my wisdom. Unluckily, I found out afterwards that he had met Miss Horsman in the time that intervened before I saw him again at his own house that evening ; and she had more than hinted that I shrank from performing the operation, " for very good reasons, no doubt. She had heard that the medical students in London were a bad set, and were not remarkable for regular attendance in the hospitals. She might be mistaken ; but she thought it was, perhaps, quite as well poor John Brouncker had not his arm cut off by—— Was there not such a thing as mortification coming on after a clumsy operation ? It was, perhaps, only a choice of deaths ! "

' Mr. Morgan had been stung at all this. Perhaps I did not speak quite respectfully enough ; I was a good deal excited. We only got more and more angry with each other ; though he, to do him justice, was as civil as could be all the time, thinking that thereby he concealed his vexation and disappointment. He did not try to conceal his anxiety about poor John. I went home weary and dispirited. I made up and took the necessary applications to John ; and, promising to return with the dawn of day (I would fain have stayed, but I did not wish him to be alarmed about himself), I went home, and resolved to sit up and study the treatment of similar cases.

' Mrs. Rose knocked at the door.

' " Come in ! " said I sharply.

' She said she had seen I had something on my mind all day, and she could not go to bed without asking if there was nothing she could do. She was good and kind ; and I could not help telling her a little of the truth. She listened pleasantly ; and I shook her warmly by the hand, thinking that though she might not be very wise, her good heart made her worth a dozen keen, sharp, hard people, like Miss Horsman.

' When I went at daybreak, I saw John's wife for a few minutes outside of the door. She seemed to wish her husband had been in Mr. Morgan's hands rather than mine ; but she gave me as good an account as I dared to hope for of the manner in which her husband had passed the night. This was confirmed by my own examination.

' When Mr. Morgan and I visited him together later on in the day, John said what we had agreed upon the day before ; and I told Mr. Morgan openly that it was by my advice that amputation was declined. He did not speak to me till we had left the house. Then he said—" Now, sir, from this time, I consider this case entirely in your hands. Only remember the poor fellow has a wife and six children. In case you come round to my opinion, remember that Mr. White could come over, as he has done before, for the operation."

' So ! Mr. Morgan believed I declined operating because I felt myself incapable. Very well ! I was much mortified.

' An hour after we parted, I received a note to this effect—

' " Dear Sir,—I will take the long round to-day, to leave you at liberty to attend to Brouncker's case, which I feel to be a very responsible one.

" ' J. Morgan."

' This was kindly done. I went back, as soon as I could, to John's cottage. While I was in the inner room with him, I heard the Miss Tomkinsons' voices outside. They had called to inquire. Miss Tomkinson came in, and evidently was poking and snuffing about. (Mrs. Brouncker told her that I was within; and within I resolved to be till they had gone.)

'"What is this close smell?" asked she. "I am afraid you are not cleanly. Cheese!—cheese in this cupboard! No wonder there is an unpleasant smell. Don't you know how particular you should be about being clean when there is illness about?"

'Mrs. Brouncker was exquisitely clean in general, and was piqued at these remarks.

'"If you please, ma'am, I could not leave John yesterday to do any house-work, and Jenny put the dinner-things away. She is but eight years old."

'But this did not satisfy Miss Tomkinson, who was evidently pursuing the course of her observations.

'"Fresh butter, I declare! Well now, Mrs. Brouncker, do you know I don't allow myself fresh butter at this time of the year? How can you save, indeed, with such extravagance!"

'"Please, ma'am," answered Mrs. Brouncker, "you'd think it strange, if I was to take such liberties in your house as you're taking here."

'I expected to hear a sharp answer. No! Miss Tomkinson liked true plain-speaking. The only person in whom she would tolerate round-about ways of talking was her sister.

'"Well, that's true," she said. "Still, you must not be above taking advice. Fresh butter is extravagant at this time of the year. However, you're a good kind of woman, and I've a great respect for John. Send Jenny for some broth as soon as he can take it. Come, Caroline, we have got to go on to Williams's."

'But Miss Caroline said that she was tired, and would rest where she was till Miss Tomkinson came back. I was a prisoner for some time, I found. When she was alone with Mrs. Brouncker, she said—

'"You must not be hurt by my sister's abrupt manner. She means well. She has not much imagination or sympathy, and cannot understand the distraction of mind produced by the illness of a worshipped husband." I could hear the loud sigh of commiseration which followed this speech. Mrs. Brouncker said—

' "Please, ma'am, I don't worship my husband. I would not be so wicked."

' "Goodness! You don't think it wicked, do you? For my part, if . . . I should worship, I should adore him." I thought she need not imagine such improbable cases. But sturdy Mrs. Brouncker said again—

' "I hope I know my duty better. I've not learned my Commandments for nothing. I know whom I ought to worship."

' Just then the children came in, dirty and unwashed, I have no doubt. And now Miss Caroline's real nature peeped out. She spoke sharply to them, and asked them if they had no manners, little pigs as they were, to come brushing against her silk gown in that way? She sweetened herself again, and was as sugary as love when Miss Tomkinson returned for her, accompanied by one whose voice, "like winds in summer sighing," I knew to be my dear Sophy's.

' She did not say much; but what she did say, and the manner in which she spoke, was tender and compassionate in the highest degree; and she came to take the four little ones back with her to the Vicarage, in order that they might be out of their mother's way; the older two might help at home. She offered to wash their hands and faces; and when I emerged from my inner chamber, after the Miss Tomkinsons had left, I found her with a chubby child on her knees, bubbling and spluttering against her white wet hand, with a face bright, rosy, and merry under the operation. Just as I came in, she said to him, "There, Jemmy, now I can kiss you with this nice clean face."

' She coloured when she saw me. I liked her speaking, and I liked her silence. She was silent now, and I " lo'ed her a' the better". I gave my directions to Mrs. Brouncker, and hastened to overtake Sophy and the children; but they had gone round by the lanes, I suppose, for I saw nothing of them.

'I was very anxious about the case. At night I went again. Miss Horsman had been there; I believe she was really kind among the poor, but she could not help leaving a sting behind her everywhere. She had been frightening Mrs. Brouncker about her husband; and been, I have no doubt, expressing her doubts of my skill; for Mrs. Brouncker began—

'"Oh, please, sir, if you'll only let Mr. Morgan take off his arm, I will never think the worse of you for not being able to do it.'

'I told her it was from no doubt of my own competency to perform the operation that I wished to save the arm; but that he himself was anxious to have it spared.

'"Aye, bless him! he frets about not earning enough to keep us, if he's crippled; but, sir, I don't care about that. I would work my fingers to the bone, and so would the children; I'm sure we'd be proud to do for him, and keep him; God bless him! it would be far better to have him only with one arm, than to have him in the churchyard, Miss Horsman says"——

'"Confound Miss Horsman!" said I.

'"Thank you, Mr. Harrison," said her well-known voice behind me. She had come out, dark as it was, to bring some old linen to Mrs. Brouncker; for, as I said before, she was very kind to all the poor people of Duncombe.

'"I beg your pardon;" for I really was sorry for my speech, or rather, that she had heard it.

'"There is no occasion for any apology," she replied, drawing herself up, and pinching her lips into a very venomous shape.

'John was doing pretty well; but of course the danger of locked jaw was not over. Before I left, his wife entreated me to take off the arm; she wrung her hands in her passionate entreaty. "Spare him to me, Mr. Harrison," she implored. Miss Horsman stood by. It was mortifying enough; but I thought of the power which was in my hands, as I firmly believed, of saving the limb; and I was inflexible.

'You cannot think how pleasantly Mrs. Rose's sympathy came in on my return. To be sure, she did not understand one word of the case, which I detailed to her; but she listened with interest, and as long as she held her tongue I thought she was really taking it in; but her first remark was as malapropos as could be.

'"You are anxious to save the tibia—I see completely how difficult that will be. My late husband had a case exactly similar, and I remember his anxiety; but you must not distress yourself too much, my dear Mr. Harrison; I have no doubt it will end well."

'I knew she had no grounds for this assurance, and yet it comforted me.

'However, as it happened, John did fully as well as I could hope; of course, he was long in rallying his strength: and, indeed, sea-air was evidently so necessary for his complete restoration, that I accepted with gratitude Mrs. Rose's proposal of sending him to Highport for a fortnight or three weeks. Her kind generosity in this matter made me more desirous than ever of paying her every mark of respect and attention.

## CHAPTER XV

'ABOUT this time there was a sale at Ashmeadow, a pretty house in the neighbourhood of Duncombe. It was likewise an easy walk, and the spring days tempted many people thither who had no intention of buying anything, but who liked the idea of rambling through the woods, gay with early primroses and wild daffodils, and of seeing the gardens and house, which till now had been shut up from the ingress of the townspeople. Mrs. Rose had planned to go, but an unlucky cold prevented her. She begged me to bring her a very particular account, saying she delighted in details, and always questioned the late Mr. Rose as to the side dishes of the dinners to which he went. The late Mr. Rose's conduct was always held up as a model to me, by the way. I walked to Ashmeadow, pausing or loitering

with different parties of townspeople, all bound in the
same direction.   At last I found the Vicar and Sophy,
and with them I stayed.   I sat by Sophy and talked
and listened.   A sale is a very pleasant gathering after
all.   The auctioneer, in a country place, is privileged
to joke from his rostrum ; and having a personal knowledge of most of the people, can sometimes make a very
keen hit at their circumstances, and turn the laugh
against them.   For instance, on the present occasion,
there was a farmer present, with his wife, who was
notoriously the grey mare.   The auctioneer was selling
some horse-cloths, and called out to recommend the
article to her, telling her, with a knowing look at the
company, that they would make her a dashing pair of
trousers, if she was in want of such an article.   She
drew herself up with dignity, and said, " Come, John,
we've had enough of these."   Whereupon there was
a burst of laughter, and in the midst of it John meekly
followed his wife out of the place.   The furniture in the
sitting-rooms was, I believe, very beautiful, but I did
not notice it much.   Suddenly I heard the auctioneer
speaking to me, " Mr. Harrison, won't you give me a bid
for this table ? "

' It was a very pretty little table of walnut-wood.
I thought it would go into my study very well, so I gave
him a bid.   I saw Miss Horsman bidding against me, so I
went off with full force, and at last it was knocked down
to me.   The auctioneer smiled, and congratulated me.

' " A most useful present for Mrs. Harrison, when that
lady comes."

' Everybody laughed.   They like a joke about
marriage ; it is so easy of comprehension.   But the
table which I had thought was for writing, turned out
to be a work-table, scissors and thimble complete.   No
wonder I looked foolish.   Sophy was not looking at
me, that was one comfort.   She was busy arranging
a nosegay of wood-anemone and wild sorrel.

' Miss Horsman came up, with her curious eyes.

' " I had no idea things were far enough advanced for
you to be purchasing a work-table, Mr. Harrison."

' I laughed off my awkwardness.

' " Did not you, Miss Horsman ? You are very much behindhand. You have not heard of my piano, then ? "

' " No, indeed," she said, half uncertain whether I was serious or not. " Then it seems there is nothing wanting but the lady."

' " Perhaps she may not be wanting either," said I, for I wished to perplex her keen curiosity.

## CHAPTER XVI

' WHEN I got home from my round, I found Mrs. Rose in some sorrow.

' " Miss Horsman called after you left," said she. "Have you heard how John Brouncker is at Highport ?"

' " Very well," replied I. " I called on his wife just now, and she had just got a letter from him. She had been anxious about him, for she had not heard for a week. However, all 's right now ; and she has pretty well of work, at Mrs. Munton's, as her servant is ill. Oh, they'll do, never fear."

' " At Mrs. Munton's ? Oh, that accounts for it, then. She is so deaf, and makes such blunders."

' " Accounts for what ? " asked I.

' " Oh, perhaps I had better not tell you," hesitated Mrs. Rose.

' " Yes, tell me at once. I beg your pardon, but I hate mysteries."

' " You are so like my poor dear Mr. Rose. He used to speak to me just in that sharp, cross way. It is only that Miss Horsman called. She had been making a collection for John Brouncker's widow and "——

' " But the man 's alive ! " said I.

' " So it seems. But Mrs. Munton had told her that he was dead. And she has got Mr. Morgan's name down at the head of the list, and Mr. Bullock's."

' Mr. Morgan and I had got into a short, cool way of speaking to each other ever since we had differed so

much about the treatment of Brouncker's arm; and
I had heard once or twice of his shakes of the head over
John's case. He would not have spoken against my
method for the world, and fancied that he concealed
his fears.

' "Miss Horsman is very ill-natured, I think," sighed
forth Mrs. Rose.

' I saw that something had been said of which I had
not heard, for the mere fact of collecting money for
the widow was good-natured, whoever did it; so I
asked, quietly, what she had said.

' " Oh, I don't know if I should tell you. I only
know she made me cry; for I'm not well, and I can't
bear to hear any one that I live with abused."

' Come! this was pretty plain.

' " What did Miss Horsman say of me ? " asked I, half
laughing, for I knew there was no love lost between us.

' " Oh, she only said she wondered you could go to
sales, and spend your money there, when your ignorance
had made Jane Brouncker a widow, and her children
fatherless."

' " Pooh! pooh! John's alive, and likely to live as
long as you or I, thanks to you, Mrs. Rose.'

' When my work-table came home, Mrs. Rose was so
struck with its beauty and completeness, and I was so
much obliged to her for her identification of my interests
with hers, and the kindness of her whole conduct about
John, that I begged her to accept of it. She seemed
very much pleased; and, after a few apologies, she
consented to take it, and placed it in the most conspicuous part of the front parlour, where she usually
sat. There was a good deal of morning calling in
Duncombe after the sale, and during this time the fact
of John's being alive was established to the conviction
of all except Miss Horsman, who, I believe, still doubted.
I myself told Mr. Morgan, who immediately went to
reclaim his money; saying to me, that he was thankful
of the information; he was truly glad to hear it; and
he shook me warmly by the hand for the first time for
a month.

## CHAPTER XVII

'A FEW days after the sale, I was in the consulting-room. The servant must have left the folding-doors a little ajar, I think. Mrs. Munton came to call on Mrs. Rose; and the former being deaf, I heard all the speeches of the latter lady, as she was obliged to speak very loud in order to be heard. She began—

'"This is a great pleasure, Mrs. Munton, so seldom as you are well enough to go out."

'Mumble, mumble, mumble, through the door.

'"Oh, very well, thank you. Take this seat, and then you can admire my new work-table, ma'am; a present from Mr. Harrison."

'Mumble, mumble.

'"Who could have told you, ma'am? Miss Horsman? Oh, yes, I showed it Miss Horsman."

'Mumble, mumble.

'"I don't quite understand you, ma'am.'

'Mumble, mumble.

'"I'm not blushing, I believe. I really am quite in the dark as to what you mean."

'Mumble, mumble.

'"Oh, yes, Mr. Harrison and I are most comfortable together. He reminds me so of my dear Mr. Rose—just as fidgety and anxious in his profession."

'Mumble, mumble.

'"I'm sure you are joking now, ma'am." Then I heard a pretty loud—

'"Oh, no"; mumble, mumble, mumble, for a long time.

'"Did he really? Well, I'm sure I don't know. I should be sorry to think he was doomed to be unfortunate in so serious an affair; but you know my undying regard for the late Mr. Rose."

'Another long mumble.

'"You're very kind, I'm sure. Mr. Rose always thought more of my happiness than his own"—a little crying—"but the turtle-dove has always been my ideal, ma'am."

'Mumble, mumble.

' " No one could have been happier than I. As you say, it is a compliment to matrimony."

'Mumble.

' " Oh, but you must not repeat such a thing. Mr. Harrison would not like it. He can't bear to have his affairs spoken about."

'Then there was a change of subject; an inquiry after some poor person, I imagine. I heard Mrs. Rose say—

' " She has got a mucous membrane, I'm afraid, ma'am."

'A commiserating mumble.

' " Not always fatal. I believe Mr. Rose knew some cases that lived for years after it was discovered that they had a mucous membrane." A pause. Then Mrs. Rose spoke in a different tone.

' " Are you sure, ma'am, there is no mistake about what he said ? "

'Mumble.

' " Pray don't be so observant, Mrs. Munton ; you find out too much. One can have no little secrets."

'The call broke up ; and I heard Mrs. Munton say in the passage, " I wish you joy, ma'am, with all my heart. There's no use denying it ; for I've seen all along what would happen."

'When I went in to dinner, I said to Mrs. Rose—

' " You've had Mrs. Munton here, I think. Did she bring any news ? " To my surprise, she bridled and simpered, and replied, " Oh, you must not ask, Mr. Harrison : such foolish reports."

'I did not ask, as she seemed to wish me not, and I knew there were silly reports always about. Then I think she was vexed that I did not ask. Altogether she went on so strangely that I could not help looking at her ; and then she took up a hand-screen, and held it between me and her. I really felt rather anxious.

' " Are you not feeling well ? " said I innocently.

' " Oh, thank you, I believe I'm quite well ; only the room is rather warm, is it not ? "

' " Let me put the blinds down for you ? the sun begins to have a good deal of power." I drew down the blinds.

' " You are so attentive, Mr. Harrison. Mr. Rose himself never did more for my little wishes than you do."

' " I wish I could do more—I wish I could show you how much I feel "——her kindness to John Brouncker, I was going on to say ; but I was just then called out to a patient. Before I went I turned back, and said——

' " Take care of yourself, my dear Mrs. Rose ; you had better rest a little."

' " For your sake, I will," said she tenderly.

' I did not care for whose sake she did it. Only I really thought she was not quite well, and required rest. I thought she was more affected than usual at tea-time ; and could have been angry with her non-sensical ways once or twice, but that I knew the real goodness of her heart. She said she wished she had the power to sweeten my life as she could my tea. I told her what a comfort she had been all during my late time of anxiety, and then I stole out to try if I could hear the evening singing at the Vicarage, by standing close to the garden-wall.

## CHAPTER XVIII

' THE next morning I met Mr. Bullock by appoint-ment, to talk a little about the legacy which was paid into his hands. As I was leaving his office, feeling full of my riches, I met Miss Horsman. She smiled rather grimly, and said—

' " Oh ! Mr. Harrison, I must congratulate I be-lieve. I don't know whether I ought to have known, but as I do, I must wish you joy. A very nice little sum, too. I always said you would have money."

' So she had found out my legacy, had she ? Well, it was no secret, and one likes the reputation of being a person of property. Accordingly I smiled, and said

I was much obliged to her, and if I could alter the figures to my liking, she might congratulate me still more.

'She said, "Oh, Mr. Harrison, you can't have everything. It would be better the other way, certainly. Money is the great thing, as you've found out. The relation died most opportunely, I must say."

'"He was no relative," said I; "only an intimate friend."

'"Dear-ah-me! I thought it had been a brother! Well, at any rate, the legacy is safe."

'I wished her good morning, and passed on. Before long I was sent for to Miss Tomkinson's.

'Miss Tomkinson sat in severe state to receive me. I went in with an air of ease, because I always felt so uncomfortable.

'"Is this true that I hear?" asked she, in an inquisitorial manner.

'I thought she alluded to my five hundred pounds: so I smiled, and said that I believed it was.

'"Can money be so great an object with you, Mr. Harrison?" she asked again.

'I said I had never cared much for money, except as an assistance to any plan of settling in life; and then, as I did not like her severe way of treating the subject, I said that I hoped every one was well; though of course I expected some one was ill, or I should not have been sent for.

'Miss Tomkinson looked very grave and sad. Then she answered: "Caroline is very poorly—the old palpitations at the heart; but of course that is nothing to you."

'I said I was very sorry. She had a weakness there, I knew. Could I see her? I might be able to order something for her.

'I thought I heard Miss Tomkinson say something in a low voice about my being a heartless deceiver. Then she spoke up. "I was always distrustful of you, Mr. Harrison. I never liked your looks. I begged Caroline again and again not to confide in you. I foresaw how it would end. And now I fear her precious life will be a sacrifice."

'I begged her not to distress herself, for in all probability there was very little the matter with her sister. Might I see her?

'"No!" she said shortly, standing up as if to dismiss me. "There has been too much of this seeing and calling. By my consent, you shall never see her again."

'I bowed. I was annoyed, of course. Such a dismissal might injure my practice just when I was most anxious to increase it.

'"Have you no apology, no excuse to offer?"

'I said I had done my best; I did not feel that there was any reason to offer an apology. I wished her good morning. Suddenly she came forwards.

'"Oh, Mr. Harrison," said she, 'if you have really loved Caroline, do not let a little paltry money make you desert her for another."

'I was struck dumb. Loved Miss Caroline! I loved Miss Tomkinson a great deal better, and yet I disliked her. She went on—

'"I have saved nearly three thousand pounds. If you think you are too poor to marry without money, I will give it all to Caroline. I am strong, and can go on working; but she is weak, and this disappointment will kill her." She sat down suddenly, and covered her face with her hands. Then she looked up.

'"You are unwilling, I see. Don't suppose I would have urged you if it had been for myself; but she has had so much sorrow." And now she fairly cried aloud. I tried to explain; but she would not listen, but kept saying, "Leave the house, sir! leave the house!" But I would be heard.

'"I have never had any feeling warmer than respect for Miss Caroline, and I have never shown any different feeling. I never for an instant thought of making her my wife, and she has had no cause in my behaviour to imagine I entertained any such intention."

'"This is adding insult to injury," said she. "Leave the house, sir, this instant!"

## CHAPTER XIX

'I WENT, and sadly enough. In a small town such an occurrence is sure to be talked about, and to make a great deal of mischief. When I went home to dinner I was so full of it, and foresaw so clearly that I should need some advocate soon to set the case in its right light, that I determined on making a confidante of good Mrs. Rose. I could not eat. She watched me tenderly, and sighed when she saw my want of appetite.

'"I am sure you have something on your mind, Mr. Harrison. Would it be—would it not be—a relief to impart it to some sympathizing friend?"

'It was just what I wanted to do.

'"My dear kind Mrs. Rose," said I, "I must tell you, if you will listen."

'She took up the fire-screen, and held it, as yesterday, between me and her.

'"The most unfortunate misunderstanding has taken place. Miss Tomkinson thinks that I have been paying attentions to Miss Caroline; when, in fact—may I tell you, Mrs. Rose?—my affections are placed elsewhere. Perhaps you have found it out already?" for indeed I thought I had been too much in love to conceal my attachment to Sophy from any one who knew my movements as well as Mrs. Rose.

'She hung down her head, and said she believed she had found out my secret.

'"Then only think how miserably I am situated. If I have any hope—oh, Mrs. Rose, do you think I have any hope"——

'She put the hand-screen still more before her face, and after some hesitation she said she thought "if I persevered—in time—I might have hope". And then she suddenly got up and left the room.

## CHAPTER XX

'THAT afternoon I met Mr. Bullock in the street. My mind was so full of the affair with Miss Tomkinson that I should have passed him without notice, if he had not stopped me short, and said that he must speak to me ; about my wonderful five hundred pounds, I supposed. But I did not care for that now.

' " What is this I hear," said he severely, " about your engagement with Mrs. Rose ? "

' " With Mrs. Rose ! " said I, almost laughing, although my heart was heavy enough.

' " Yes ! with Mrs. Rose ! " said he sternly.

' " I'm not engaged to Mrs. Rose," I replied. " There is some mistake."

' " I'm glad to hear it, sir," he answered, " very glad. It requires some explanation, however. Mrs. Rose has been congratulated, and has acknowledged the truth of the report. It is confirmed by many facts. The work-table you bought, confessing your intention of giving it to your future wife, is given to her. How do you account for these things, sir ? "

'I said I did not pretend to account for them. At present, a good deal was inexplicable ; and when I could give an explanation, I did not think that I should feel myself called upon to give it to him.

' " Very well, sir ; very well," replied he, growing very red. " I shall take care and let Mr. Morgan know the opinion I entertain of you. What do you think that man deserves to be called who enters a family under the plea of friendship, and takes advantage of his intimacy to win the affections of the daughter, and then engages himself to another woman ? "

'I thought he referred to Miss Caroline. I simply said I could only say that I was not engaged ; and that Miss Tomkinson had been quite mistaken in supposing I had been paying any attentions to her sister beyond those dictated by mere civility.

' " Miss Tomkinson ! Miss Caroline ! I don't understand to what you refer. Is there another victim to your perfidy ? What I allude to are the attentions you have paid to my daughter, Miss Bullock."

'Another ! I could but disclaim, as I had done in the case of Miss Caroline ; but I began to be in despair. Would Miss Horsman, too, come forward as a victim to my tender affections ? It was all Mr. Morgan's doing, who had lectured me into this tenderly deferential manner. But on the score of Miss Bullock, I was brave in my innocence. I had positively disliked her ; and so I told her father, though in more civil and measured terms, adding that I was sure the feeling was reciprocal.

'He looked as if he would like to horsewhip me. I longed to call him out.

'"I hope my daughter has had sense enough to despise you ; I hope she has, that's all. I trust my wife may be mistaken as to her feelings."

'So, he had heard all through the medium of his wife. That explained something, and rather calmed me. I begged he would ask Miss Bullock if she had ever thought I had any ulterior object in my intercourse with her, beyond mere friendliness (and not so much of that, I might have added). I would refer it to her.

'"Girls," said Mr. Bullock, a little more quietly, "do not like to acknowledge that they have been deceived and disappointed. I consider my wife's testimony as likely to be nearer the truth than my daughter's, for that reason. And she tells me she never doubted but that, if not absolutely engaged, you understood each other perfectly. She is sure Jemima is deeply wounded by your engagement to Mrs. Rose."

'"Once for all, I am not engaged to anybody. Till you have seen your daughter, and learnt the truth from her, I will wish you farewell."

'I bowed in a stiff, haughty manner, and walked off homewards. But when I got to my own door, I remembered Mrs. Rose, and all that Mr. Bullock had said about her acknowledging the truth of the report of my engage-

ment to her.   Where could I go to be safe ?  Mrs. Rose,
Miss Bullock, Miss Caroline—they lived as it were at
the three points of an equilateral triangle ;  here was
I in the centre.   I would go to Mr. Morgan's, and drink
tea with him.   There, at any rate, I was secure from
any one wanting to marry me ;  and I might be as
professionally bland as I liked, without being misunderstood.   But there, too, a *contretemps* awaited me.

## CHAPTER XXI

' MR. MORGAN was looking grave.   After a minute or
two of humming and hawing, he said—

' " I have been sent for to Miss Caroline Tomkinson,
Mr. Harrison.   I am sorry to hear of this.   I am
grieved to find that there seems to have been some
trifling with the affections of a very worthy lady.
Miss Tomkinson, who is in sad distress, tells me that
they had every reason to believe that you were
attached to her sister.   May I ask if you do not intend
to marry her ? '

' I said, nothing was farther from my thoughts.

' " My dear sir," said Mr. Morgan, rather agitated,
" do not express yourself so strongly and vehemently.
It is derogatory to the sex to speak so.   It is more
respectful to say, in these cases, that you do not venture
to entertain a hope ;  such a manner is generally understood, and does not sound like such positive objection."

' " I cannot help it, sir ;  I must talk in my own
natural manner.   I would not speak disrespectfully of
any woman ;  but nothing should induce me to marry
Miss Caroline Tomkinson ;  not if she were Venus
herself, and Queen of England into the bargain.   I cannot understand what has given rise to the idea."

' " Indeed, sir ;  I think that is very plain.   You
have a trifling case to attend to in the house, and you
invariably make it a pretext for seeing and conversing
with the lady."

' "That was her doing, not mine ! " said I vehemently.

' " Allow me to go on. You are discovered on your knees before her—a positive injury to the establishment, as Miss Tomkinson observes ; a most passionate valentine is sent ; and when questioned, you acknowledge the sincerity of meaning which you affix to such things." He stopped, for in his earnestness he had been talking more quickly than usual, and was out of breath. I burst in with my explanations—

' " The valentine I know nothing about."

' " It is in your handwriting," said he coldly. " I should be most deeply grieved to—in fact, I will not think it possible of your father's son. But I must say, it is in your handwriting."

' I tried again, and at last succeeded in convincing him that I had been only unfortunate, not intentionally guilty of winning Miss Caroline's affections. I said that I had been endeavouring, it was true, to practise the manner he had recommended, of universal sympathy, and recalled to his mind some of the advice he had given me. He was a good deal hurried.

' " But, my dear sir, I had no idea that you would carry it out to such consequences. ' Philandering,' Miss Tomkinson called it. That is a hard word, sir. My manner has been always tender and sympathetic ; but I am not aware that I ever excited any hopes ; there never was any report about me. I believe no lady was ever attached to me. You must strive after this happy medium, sir."

' I was still distressed. Mr. Morgan had only heard of one, but there were three ladies (including Miss Bullock) hoping to marry me. He saw my annoyance.

' " Don't be too much distressed about it, my dear sir ; I was sure you were too honourable a man, from the first. With a conscience like yours, I would defy the world."

' He became anxious to console me, and I was hesitating whether I would not tell him all my three dilemmas, when a note was brought in to him. It was from Mrs. Munton. He threw it to me, with a face of dismay.

' "MY DEAR MR. MORGAN,—I most sincerely congratulate you on the happy matrimonial engagement I hear you have formed with Miss Tomkinson. All previous circumstances, as I have just been remarking to Miss Horsman, combine to promise you felicity. And I wish that every blessing may attend your married life.—Most sincerely yours,

' "JANE MUNTON."

' I could not help laughing, he had been so lately congratulating himself that no report of the kind had ever been circulated about himself. He said—

' "Sir ! this is no laughing matter ; I assure you it is not."

' I could not resist asking, if I was to conclude that there was no truth in the report.

' "Truth, sir ! it's a lie from beginning to end. I don't like to speak too decidedly about any lady ; and I've a great respect for Miss Tomkinson ; but I do assure you, sir, I'd as soon marry one of Her Majesty's Life Guards. I would rather ; it would be more suitable. Miss Tomkinson is a very worthy lady ; but she's a perfect grenadier."

' He grew very nervous. He was evidently insecure. He thought it not impossible that Miss Tomkinson might come and marry him, *vi et armis.** I am sure he had some dim idea of abduction in his mind. Still, he was better off than I was ; for he was in his own house, and report had only engaged him to one lady ; while I stood, like Paris,* among three contending beauties. Truly, an apple of discord had been thrown into our little town. I suspected at the time, what I know now, that it was Miss Horsman's doing ; not intentionally, I will do her the justice to say. But she had shouted out the story of my behaviour to Miss Caroline up Mrs. Munton's trumpet ; and that lady, possessed with the idea that I was engaged to Mrs. Rose, had imagined the masculine pronoun to relate to Mr. Morgan, whom she had seen only that afternoon *tête à tête* with Miss Tomkinson, condoling with her in some tender deferential manner, I'll be bound.

## CHAPTER XXII

'I WAS very cowardly. I positively dared not go home ; but at length I was obliged to. I had done all I could to console Mr. Morgan, but he refused to be comforted. I went at last. I rang at the bell. I don't know who opened the door, but I think it was Mrs. Rose. I kept a handkerchief to my face, and muttering something about having a dreadful toothache, I flew up to my room and bolted the door. I had no candle ; but what did that signify. I was safe. I could not sleep ; and when I did fall into a sort of doze, it was ten times worse wakening up. I could not remember whether I was engaged or not. If I was engaged, who was the lady ? I had always considered myself as rather plain than otherwise ; but surely I had made a mistake. Fascinating I certainly must be ; but perhaps I was handsome. As soon as day dawned, I got up to ascertain the fact at the looking-glass. Even with the best disposition to be convinced, I could not see any striking beauty in my round face, with an unshaven beard and a nightcap like a fool's cap at the top. No ! I must be content to be plain, but agreeable. All this I tell you in confidence. I would not have my little bit of vanity known for the world. I fell asleep towards morning. I was awakened by a tap at my door. It was Peggy : she put in a hand with a note. I took it.

' "It is not from Miss Horsman ? " said I, half in joke, half in very earnest fright.

' "No, sir ; Mr. Morgan's man brought it."

' I opened it. It ran thus—

' "MY DEAR SIR,—It is now nearly twenty years since I have had a little relaxation, and I find that my health

requires it.  I have also the utmost confidence in you, and
I am sure this feeling is shared by our patients.  I have,
therefore, no scruple in putting in execution a hastily
formed plan, and going to Chesterton to catch the early
train on my way to Paris.  If your accounts are good,
I shall remain away probably a fortnight.  Direct to
Meurice's.—Yours, most truly,

" ' J. MORGAN.

' " PS.—Perhaps it may be as well not to name where
I am gone, especially to Miss Tomkinson."

' He had deserted me.  He—with only one report—
had left me to stand my ground with three.

' " Mrs. Rose's kind regards, sir, and it 's nearly
nine o'clock.  Breakfast has been ready this hour, sir."

' " Tell Mrs. Rose I don't want any breakfast.  Or
stay " (for I was very hungry), " I will take a cup of
tea and some toast up here."

' Peggy brought the tray to the door.

' " I hope you're not ill, sir ? " said she kindly.

' " Not very.  I shall be better when I get into the
air."

' " Mrs. Rose seems sadly put about," said she ;
" she seems so grieved like."

' I watched my opportunity, and went out by the
side door in the garden.


CHAPTER XXIII

' I HAD intended to ask Mr. Morgan to call at the
vicarage, and give his parting explanation before they
could hear the report.  Now, I thought that if I could
see Sophy, I would speak to her myself ; but I did not
wish to encounter the Vicar.  I went along the lane at
the back of the vicarage, and came suddenly upon
Miss Bullock.  She coloured, and asked me if I would
allow her to speak to me.  I could only be resigned ;
but I thought I could probably set one report at rest
by this conversation.

'She was almost crying.

' " I must tell you, Mr. Harrison, I have watched you here in order to speak to you. I heard with the greatest regret of papa's conversation with you yesterday." She was fairly crying. " I believe Mrs. Bullock finds me in her way, and wants to have me married. It is the only way in which I can account for such a complete misrepresentation as she had told papa. I don't care for you in the least, sir. You never paid me any attentions. You've been almost rude to me ; and I have liked you the better. That 's to say, I never have liked you."

' " I am truly glad to hear what you say," answered I. " Don't distress yourself. I was sure there was some mistake."

' But she cried bitterly.

' " It is so hard to feel that my marriage—my absence —is desired so earnestly at home. I dread every new acquaintance we form with any gentleman. It is sure to be the beginning of a series of attacks on him, of which everybody must be aware, and to which they may think I am a willing party. But I should not much mind if it were not for the conviction that she wishes me so earnestly away. Oh, my own dear mamma, you would never "——

' She cried more than ever. I was truly sorry for her, and had just taken her hand, and began—" My dear Miss Bullock "——when the door in the wall of the vicarage garden opened. It was the Vicar letting out Miss Tomkinson, whose face was all swelled with crying. He saw me ; but he did not bow, or make any sign. On the contrary, he looked down as from a severe eminence, and shut the door hastily. I turned to Miss Bullock.

' " I am afraid the Vicar has been hearing something to my disadvantage from Miss Tomkinson, and it is very awkward "—— She finished my sentence—" To have found us here together. Yes, but as long as we understand that we do not care for each other, it does not signify what people say."

' " Oh, but to me it does," said I.      " I may, perhaps, tell you—but do not mention it to a creature—I am attached to Miss Hutton."

' " To Sophy ! Oh, Mr. Harrison, I am so glad ; she is such a sweet creature.   Oh, I wish you joy."

' " Not yet ;  I have never spoken about it."

' " Oh, but it is certain to happen."   She jumped with a woman's rapidity to a conclusion.   And then she began to praise Sophy.   Never was a man yet who did not like to hear the praises of his mistress.   I walked by her side ;  we came past the front of the vicarage together.   I looked up, and saw Sophy there, and she saw me.

' That afternoon she was sent away ; sent to visit her aunt ostensibly ;  in reality, because of the reports of my conduct, which were showered down upon the Vicar, and one of which he saw confirmed by his own eyes.

## CHAPTER XXIV

' I HEARD of Sophy's departure as one heard of everything, soon after it had taken place.   I did not care for the awkwardness of my situation, which had so perplexed and amused me in the morning.   I felt that something was wrong ;  that Sophy was taken away from me.   I sank into despair.   If anybody liked to marry me they might.   I was willing to be sacrificed. I did not speak to Mrs. Rose.   She wondered at me, and grieved over my coldness, I saw ;  but I had left off feeling anything.   Miss Tomkinson cut me in the street ;  and it did not break my heart.   Sophy was gone away ;  that was all I cared for.   Where had they sent her to ?   Who was her aunt, that she should go and visit her ?   One day I met Lizzie, who looked as though she had been told not to speak to me, but could not help doing so.

' " Have you heard from your sister ? " said I.

' " Yes."

' " Where is she ? I hope she is well."

' " She is at the Leoms "—I was not much wiser.
" Oh yes, she is very well. Fanny says she was at the
Assembly last Wednesday, and danced all night with
the officers."

' I thought I would enter myself a member of the
Peace Society at once. She was a little flirt, and a
hard-hearted creature. I don't think I wished Lizzie
good-bye.

## CHAPTER XXV

' WHAT most people would have considered a more
serious evil than Sophy's absence, befell me. I found
that my practice was falling off. The prejudice of the
town ran strongly against me. Mrs. Munton told me
all that was said. She heard it through Miss Horsman.
It was said—cruel little town—that my negligence or
ignorance had been the cause of Walter's death ; that
Miss Tyrrell had become worse under my treatment ;
and that John Brouncker was all but dead, if he
was not quite, from my mismanagement. All Jack
Marshland's jokes and revelations, which had, I thought,
gone to oblivion, were raked up to my discredit. He himself, formerly, to my astonishment, rather a favourite
with the good people of Duncombe, was spoken of as
one of my disreputable friends.

' In short, so prejudiced were the good people of
Duncombe that I believe a very little would have made
them suspect me of a brutal highway robbery, which
took place in the neighbourhood about this time.
Mrs. Munton told me, apropos of the robbery, that she
had never yet understood the cause of my year's
imprisonment in Newgate ; she had no doubt, from
what Mr. Morgan had told her, there was some good
reason for it ; but if I would tell her the particulars, she
should like to know them.

' Miss Tomkinson sent for Mr. White, from Chesterton,
to see Miss Caroline ; and, as he was coming over, all

our old patients seemed to take advantage of it, and send for him too.

'But the worst of all was the Vicar's manner to me. If he had cut me, I could have asked him why he did so. But the freezing change in his behaviour was indescribable, though bitterly felt. I heard of Sophy's gaiety from Lizzie. I thought of writing to her. Just then Mr. Morgan's fortnight of absence expired. I was wearied out by Mrs. Rose's tender vagaries, and took no comfort from her sympathy, which indeed I rather avoided. Her tears irritated, instead of grieving me. I wished I could tell her at once that I had no intention of marrying her.

## CHAPTER XXVI

'MR. MORGAN had not been at home above two hours before he was sent for to the Vicarage. Sophy had come back, and I had never heard of it. She had come home ill and weary, and longing for rest : and the *rest* seemed approaching with awful strides. Mr. Morgan forgot all his Parisian adventures, and all his terror of Miss Tomkinson, when he was sent for to see her. She was ill of a fever, which made fearful progress. When he told me, I wished to force the Vicarage door, if I might but see her. But I controlled myself ; and only cursed my weak indecision, which had prevented my writing to her. It was well I had no patients : they would have had but a poor chance of attention. I hung about Mr. Morgan, who might see her, and did see her. But from what he told me, I perceived that the measures he was adopting were powerless to check so sudden and violent an illness. Oh ! if they would but let me see her. But that was out of the question. It was not merely that the Vicar had heard of my character as a gay Lothario,* but that doubts had been thrown out of my medical skill. The accounts grew worse. Suddenly my resolution was taken. Mr. Morgan's very regard for Sophy made him more than usually timid in his practice. I had my horse saddled, and galloped to Chesterton. I took the express train to town. I went to Dr. ——. I told him every particular of the case. He listened; but shook his head. He wrote down a prescription; and recommended a new preparation, not yet in full use; a preparation of a poison, in fact.

' " It may save her," said he. " It is a chance, in such a state of things as you describe. It must be given on the fifth day, if the pulse will bear it. Crabbe makes up the preparation most skilfully. Let me hear from you, I beg."

' I went to Crabbe's; I begged to make it up myself; but my hands trembled, so that I could not weigh the quantities. I asked the young man to do it for me. I went, without touching food, to the station, with my medicine and my prescription in my pocket. Back we flew through the country. I sprang on Bay Maldon, which my groom had in waiting, and galloped across the country to Duncombe.

' But I drew bridle when I came to the top of the hill —the hill above the old hall, from which we catch the first glimpse of the town, for I thought within myself that she might be dead; and I dreaded to come near certainty. The hawthorns were out in the woods, the young lambs were in the meadows, the song of the thrushes filled the air; but it only made the thought the more terrible.

' " What, if in this world of hope and life she lies dead ! " I heard the church bells soft and clear. I sickened to listen. Was it the passing bell ? No ! it was ringing eight o'clock. I put spurs to my horse, down hill as it was. We dashed into the town. I turned him, saddle and bridle, into the stable-yard, and went off to Mr. Morgan's.

' " Is she —— ? " said I. " How is she ? "

' " Very ill. My poor fellow, I see how it is with you. She may live—but I fear. My dear sir, I am very much afraid."

' I told him of my journey and consultation with Dr. ——, and showed him the prescription. His hands trembled as he put on his spectacles to read it.

' " This is a very dangerous medicine, sir," said he, with his finger under the name of the poison.

' " It is a new preparation," said I. " Dr. —— relies much upon it."

' " I dare not administer it," he replied. " I have never tried it. It must be very powerful. I dare not play tricks in this case."

' I believe I stamped with impatience ; but it was all of no use. My journey had been in vain. The more I urged the imminent danger of the case requiring some powerful remedy, the more nervous he became.

' I told him I would throw up the partnership. I threatened him with that, though, in fact, it was only what I felt I ought to do, and had resolved upon before Sophy's illness, as I had lost the confidence of his patients. He only said—

' " I cannot help it, sir. I shall regret it for your father's sake ; but I must do my duty. I dare not run the risk of giving Miss Sophy this violent medicine— a preparation of a deadly poison."

' I left him without a word. He was quite right in adhering to his own views, as I can see now ; but at the time I thought him brutal and obstinate.

## CHAPTER XXVII

' I WENT home. I spoke rudely to Mrs. Rose, who awaited my return at the door. I rushed past, and locked myself in my room. I could not go to bed.

' The morning sun came pouring in, and enraged me, as everything did since Mr. Morgan refused. I pulled the blind down so violently that the string broke. What did it signify ? The light might come in. What was the sun to me ? And then I remembered that that sun might be shining on her—dead.

' I sat down and covered my face. Mrs. Rose knocked at the door. I opened it. She had never been in bed, and had been crying too.

' " Mr. Morgan wants to speak to you, sir."

' I rushed back for my medicine, and went to him. He stood at the door, pale and anxious.

' " She's alive, sir," said he, " but that's all. We have sent for Dr. Hamilton. I'm afraid he will not come in time. Do you know, sir, I think we should venture—with Dr. ——'s sanction—to give her that medicine. It is but a chance ; but it is the only one, I'm afraid." He fairly cried before he had ended.

' " I've got it here," said I, setting off to walk ; but he could not go so fast.

' " I beg your pardon, sir," said he, " for my abrupt refusal last night."

' " Indeed, sir," said I ; " I ought much rather to beg your pardon. I was very violent."

' " Oh ! never mind ! never mind ! Will you repeat what Dr. —— said ? "

' I did so ; and then I asked, with a meekness that astonished myself, if I might not go in and administer it.

' " No, sir," said he, " I'm afraid not. I am sure your good heart would not wish to give pain. Besides, it might agitate her, if she has any consciousness before death. In her delirium she has often mentioned your name ; and, sir, I'm sure you won't name it again, as it may, in fact, be considered a professional secret ; but I did hear our good Vicar speak a little strongly about you ; in fact, sir, I did hear him curse you. You see the mischief it might make in the parish, I'm sure, if this were known."

' I gave him the medicine, and watched him in, and saw the door shut. I hung about the place all day. Poor and rich all came to inquire. The county people drove up in their carriages—the halt and the lame came on their crutches. Their anxiety did my heart good. Mr. Morgan told me that she slept, and I watched Dr. Hamilton into the house. The night came on. She slept. I watched round the house. I saw the light high up, burning still and steady. Then I saw it moved. It was the crisis, in one way or other.

## CHAPTER XXVIII

' Mr. Morgan came out. Good old man ! The tears
were running down his cheeks : he could not speak ;
but kept shaking my hands. I did not want words.
I understood that she was better.

' " Dr. Hamilton says, it was the only medicine that
could have saved her. I was an old fool, sir. I beg
your pardon. The Vicar shall know all. I beg your
pardon, sir, if I was abrupt."

' Everything went on brilliantly from this time.

' Mr. Bullock called to apologize for his mistake, and
consequent upbraiding. John Brouncker came home,
brave and well.

' There was still Miss Tomkinson in the ranks of the
enemy ; and Mrs. Rose too much, I feared, in the ranks
of the friends.

## CHAPTER XXIX

' One night she had gone to bed, and I was thinking
of going. I had been studying in the back room, where
I went for refuge from her in the present position of
affairs (I read a good number of surgical books about
this time, and also *Vanity Fair*)*—when I heard a loud,
long-continued knocking at the door, enough to waken
the whole street. Before I could get to open it, I heard
that well-known bass of Jack Marshland's, once heard
never to be forgotten, pipe up the negro song—

Who's dat knocking at de door ?

' Though it was raining hard at the time, and I stood
waiting to let him in, he would finish his melody in the
open air ; loud and clear along the street it sounded.
I saw Miss Tomkinson's night-capped head emerge from
a window. She called out " Police ! police ! "

' Now there were no police, only a rheumatic constable in the town ; but it was the custom of the ladies,

when alarmed at night, to call an imaginary police,
which had, they thought, an intimidating effect; but
as every one knew the real state of the unwatched town,
we did not much mind it in general.  Just now, however,
I wanted to regain my character.  So I pulled Jack in,
quavering as he entered.

'"You've spoilt a good shake," said he, "that's
what you have.  I'm nearly up to Jenny Lind;* and
you see I'm a nightingale, like her."

'We sat up late; and I don't know how it was, but
I told him all my matrimonial misadventures.

'"I thought I could imitate your hand pretty well,"
said he.  "My word! it was a flaming valentine!  No
wonder she thought you loved her!"

'"So that was your doing, was it?  Now I'll tell you
what you shall do to make up for it.  You shall write me
a letter confessing your hoax—a letter that I can show."

'"Give me pen and paper, my boy! you shall dictate.
'With a deeply penitent heart'—— Will that do for
a beginning?"

'I told him what to write; a simple, straightforward
confession of his practical joke.  I enclosed it in a few
lines of regret that, unknown to me, any of my friends
should have so acted.

## CHAPTER XXX

'ALL this time I knew that Sophy was slowly recovering.  One day I met Miss Bullock, who had seen her.

'"We have been talking about you," said she, with
a bright smile; for since she knew I disliked her, she
felt quite at her ease, and could smile very pleasantly.
I understood that she had been explaining the misunderstanding about herself to Sophy; so that when Jack
Marshland's note had been sent to Miss Tomkinson's,
I thought myself in a fair way to have my character
established in two quarters.  But the third was my
dilemma.  Mrs. Rose had really so much of my true

regard for her good qualities, that I disliked the idea of a formal explanation, in which a good deal must be said on my side to wound her. We had become very much estranged ever since I had heard of this report of my engagement to her. I saw that she grieved over it. While Jack Marshland stayed with us, I felt at my ease in the presence of a third person. But he told me confidentially he durst not stay long, for fear some of the ladies should snap him up, and marry him. Indeed I myself did not think it unlikely that he would snap one of them up if he could. For when we met Miss Bullock one day, and heard her hopeful, joyous account of Sophy's progress (to whom she was a daily visitor), he asked me who that bright-looking girl was? And when I told him she was the Miss Bullock of whom I had spoken to him, he was pleased to observe that he thought I had been a great fool, and asked me if Sophy had anything like such splendid eyes. He made me repeat about Miss Bullock's unhappy circumstances at home, and then became very thoughtful—a most unusual and morbid symptom in his case.

'Soon after he went, by Mr. Morgan's kind offices and explanations, I was permitted to see Sophy. I might not speak much; it was prohibited, for fear of agitating her. We talked of the weather and the flowers; and we were silent. But her little white thin hand lay in mine; and we understood each other without words. I had a long interview with the Vicar afterwards; and came away glad and satisfied.

'Mr. Morgan called in the afternoon, evidently anxious, though he made no direct inquiries (he was too polite for that), to hear the result of my visit at the vicarage. I told him to give me joy. He shook me warmly by the hand; and then rubbed his own together. I thought I would consult him about my dilemma with Mrs. Rose, who, I was afraid, would be deeply affected by my engagement.

'"There is only one awkward circumstance," said I— "about Mrs. Rose." I hesitated how to word the fact of her having received congratulations on her supposed

engagement with me, and her manifest attachment ;
but, before I could speak, he broke in—

'My dear sir, you need not trouble yourself about
that ; she will have a home. In fact, sir," said he,
reddening a little, " I thought it would, perhaps, put
a stop to those reports connecting my name with Miss
Tomkinson's, if I married some one else. I hoped it
might prove an efficacious contradiction. And I was
struck with admiration for Mrs. Rose's undying memory
of her late husband. Not to be prolix, I have this
morning obtained Mrs. Rose's consent to—to marry
her, in fact, sir ! " said he, jerking out the climax.

'Here was an event ! Then Mr. Morgan had never
heard the report about Mrs. Rose and me. (To this
day, I think she would have taken me, if I had proposed.) So much the better.

'Marriages were in the fashion that year. Mr. Bullock met me one morning, as I was going to ride with
Sophy. He and I had quite got over our misunderstanding, thanks to Jemima, and were as friendly as ever.
This morning he was chuckling aloud as he walked.

' " Stop, Mr. Harrison ! " he said, as I went quickly
past. " Have you heard the news ? Miss Horsman has
just told me Miss Caroline has eloped with young
Hoggins ! She is ten years older than he is ! How can her
gentility like being married to a tallow-chandler ? It is
a very good thing for her, though," he added, in a more
serious manner ; "old Hoggins is very rich ; and though
he's angry just now, he will soon be reconciled."

'Any vanity I might have entertained on the score
of the three ladies who were, at one time, said to be
captivated by my charms, was being rapidly dispersed.
Soon after Mr. Hoggins's marriage, I met Miss Tomkinson face to face, for the first time since our memorable
conversation. She stopped me, and said—

' " Don't refuse to receive my congratulations,
Mr. Harrison, on your most happy engagement to
Miss Hutton. I owe you an apology, too, for my behaviour when I last saw you at our house. I really did
think Caroline was attached to you then ; and it

irritated me, I confess, in a very wrong and unjustifiable way. But I heard her telling Mr. Hoggins only yesterday that she had been attached to him for years ; ever since he was in pinafores, she dated it from ; and when I asked her afterwards how she could say so, after her distress on hearing that false report about you and Mrs. Rose, she cried, and said I never had understood her ; and that the hysterics which alarmed me so much were simply caused by eating pickled cucumber. I am very sorry for my stupidity, and improper way of speaking ; but I hope we are friends now, Mr. Harrison, for I should wish to be liked by Sophy's husband."

' Good Miss Tomkinson ! to believe the substitution of indigestion for disappointed affection. I shook her warmly by the hand ; and we have been all right ever since. I think I told you she is baby's godmother.

## CHAPTER XXXI

' I HAD some difficulty in persuading Jack Marshland to be groomsman ; but when he heard all the arrangements, he came. Miss Bullock was bridesmaid. He liked us all so well, that he came again at Christmas, and was far better behaved than he had been the year before. He won golden opinions indeed. Miss Tomkinson said he was a reformed young man. We dined all together at Mr. Morgan's (the Vicar wanted us to go there ; but, from what Sophy told me, Helen was not confident of the mincemeat, and rather dreaded so large a party). We had a jolly day of it. Mrs. Morgan was as kind and motherly as ever. Miss Horsman certainly did set out a story that the Vicar was thinking of Miss Tomkinson for his second ; or else, I think, we had no other report circulated in consequence of our happy, merry Christmas Day ; and it is a wonder, considering how Jack Marshland went on with Jemima.'

Here Sophy came back from putting baby to bed ; and Charles wakened up.

# APPENDIX

## Round the Sofa

[The decision to publish a collection of her recent stories in the 'chain' format, whether made by Mrs Gaskell or by Sampson Low, compelled her to create an introduction giving an appropriate setting and group for the telling of the stories in the chain. The idea she came up with was that of a regular weekly evening gathering of friends round the sofa of an invalid, Margaret Dawson, to whom the narrator had been introduced 'long ago' when sent to Edinburgh for medical treatment. It is the unidentified narrator who introduces Margaret Dawson, induces her to recount the story of Lady Ludlow, and provides the descriptive links between the other stories. The device gave Mrs Gaskell an opportunity to use some personal recollections. For the Edinburgh scene in general she drew, at least in bare outline, on the time she spent there as a young woman in 1831. For Margaret Dawson she drew on a much later acquaintance, Mrs Fletcher, the widow of an Edinburgh advocate, whose salon when she was a young wife had been a centre for Edinburgh literary society, including Gaskell's own father, William Stevenson. The other members of the group reflect something of the cosmopolitan flavour of Edinburgh society at the time, and they are, by and large, appropriate to their stories, although the links are the briefest of connecting passages, and make a minimal gesture of developing individual personalities.]

## Round the Sofa

LONG ago I was placed by my parents under the medical treatment of a certain Mr. Dawson, a surgeon in Edinburgh, who had obtained a reputation for the cure of a particular class of diseases. I was sent with my governess into lodgings near his house, in the Old Town. I was to combine lessons from the excellent Edinburgh masters, with the medicines and exercises needed for my indisposition. It was at first rather dreary to leave my brothers and sisters, and to give up our merry out-of-doors life with our country home, for dull lodgings, with only poor grave Miss Duncan for a companion; and to exchange our romps in the garden and rambles through the fields for stiff walks in the streets, the decorum of which obliged me to tie my bonnet-strings neatly, and put on my shawl with some regard to straightness.

The evenings were the worst. It was autumn, and of course they daily grew longer: they were long enough, I am sure, when we first settled down in those gray and drab lodgings. For, you must know, my father and mother were not rich, and there were a great many of us, and the medical expenses to be incurred by my being placed under Mr. Dawson's care were expected to be considerable; therefore, one great point in our search after lodgings was economy. My father, who was too true a gentleman to feel false shame, had named this necessity for cheapness to Mr. Dawson; and in return, Mr. Dawson had told him of those at No. 6 Cromer Street, in which we were finally settled. The house belonged to an old man, at one time a tutor to young men preparing for the University, in which capacity he had become known to Mr. Dawson. But his pupils had dropped off; and when we went to lodge with him, I imagine that his principal support was derived from a few occasional lessons which he gave, and from letting the rooms that we took, a drawing-room opening into a bed-room, out of which a smaller chamber led. His daughter was his housekeeper: a son, whom we never saw, was supposed to be leading the same life that his father had done before him, only we never saw or heard of any pupils; and there was one hard-working, honest little Scottish maiden, square, stumpy, neat, and plain, who might have been any age from eighteen to forty.

Looking back on the household now, there was perhaps much to admire in their quiet endurance of decent poverty; but at this time, their poverty grated against many of my tastes, for I could not recognize the fact, that in a town the simple graces of fresh flowers, clean white muslin curtains, pretty bright chintzes, all cost money, which is saved by the adoption of dust-coloured moreen,* and mud-coloured carpets. There was not a penny spent on mere elegance in that room; yet there was everything considered necessary to comfort: but after all, such mere pretences of comfort! a hard, slippery, black horse-hair sofa, which was no place of rest; an old piano, serving as a sideboard; a grate, narrowed by an inner supplement, till it hardly held a handful of the small coal which could scarcely ever be stirred up into a genial blaze. But there were two evils worse than even this coldness and bareness of the rooms: one was that we were provided with a latch-key, which allowed us to open the front door whenever we came home from a walk, and go upstairs without meeting any face of welcome, or hearing the sound of a human voice in the apparently deserted house— Mr. Mackenzie piqued himself on the noiselessness of his establishment; and the other, which might almost seem to neutralize the first, was the danger we were always exposed to on going out, of the old man—sly, miserly, and intelligent—popping out upon us from his room, close to the left hand of the door, with some civility which we learnt to distrust as a mere pretext for extorting more money, yet which it was difficult to refuse: such as the offer of any books out of his library, a great temptation, for we could see into the shelf-lined room; but just as we were on the point of yielding, there was a hint of the 'consideration' to be expected for the loan of books of so much higher a class than any to be obtained at the circulating library, which made us suddenly draw back. Another time he came out of his den to offer us written cards, to distribute among our acquaintance, on which he undertook to teach the very things I was to learn; but I would rather have been the most ignorant woman that ever lived than tried to learn anything from that old fox in breeches. When we had declined all his proposals, he went apparently into dudgeon. Once when we had forgotten our latch-key we rang in vain for many times at the door, seeing our landlord standing all the time at the window to the right, looking out of it in an absent and philosophical state of mind, from which no signs and gestures of ours could arouse him.

The women of the household were far better, and more really respectable, though even on them poverty had laid her heavy left hand, instead of her blessing right. Miss Mackenzie kept us as short in our food as she decently could—we paid so much a week for our board, be it observed; and if one day we had less appetite than another, our meals were docked to the smaller standard, until Miss Duncan ventured to remonstrate. The sturdy maid-of-all-work was scrupulously honest, but looked discontented, and scarcely vouchsafed us thanks, when on leaving we gave her what Mrs. Dawson had told us would be considered handsome in most lodgings. I do not believe Phenice ever received wages from the Mackenzies.

But that dear Mrs. Dawson! The mention of her comes into my mind like the bright sunshine into our dingy little drawing-room came on those days;—as a sweet scent of violets greets the sorrowful passer among the woodlands.

Mrs. Dawson was not Mr. Dawson's wife, for he was a bachelor. She was his crippled sister, an old maid, who had, what she called, taken her brevet rank.*

After we had been about a fortnight in Edinburgh, Mr. Dawson said, in a sort of half-doubtful manner, to Miss Duncan:

'My sister bids me say, that every Monday evening a few friends come in to sit round her sofa for an hour or so,— some before going to gayer parties—and that if you and Miss Greatorex would like a little change, she would only be too glad to see you. Any time from seven to eight to-night; and I must add my injunctions, both for her sake, and for that of my little patient's, here, that you leave at nine o'clock. After all, I do not know if you will care to come; but Margaret bade me ask you;' and he glanced up suspiciously and sharply at us. If either of us had felt the slightest reluctance, however well disguised by manner, to accept this invitation, I am sure he would have at once detected our feelings, and withdrawn it; so jealous and chary was he of anything pertaining to the appreciation of this beloved sister.

But if it had been to spend an evening at a dentist's, I believe I should have welcomed the invitation, so weary was I of the monotony of the nights in our lodgings; and as for Miss Duncan, an invitation to tea was of itself a pure and unmixed honour, and one to be accepted with all becoming form and gratitude: so Mr. Dawson's sharp glances over his spectacles failed to detect anything but the truest pleasure, and he went on.

'You'll find it very dull, I dare say. Only a few old fogies like myself, and one or two good sweet young women: I never know who'll come. Margaret is obliged to lie in a darkened room,—only half-lighted, I mean—because her eyes are weak,—oh, it will be very stupid, I dare say: don't thank me till you've been once and tried it, and then, if you like it, your best thanks will be to come again every Monday, from half-past seven to nine, you know. Good-bye, good-bye.

Hitherto I had never been out to a party of grown-up people; and no court ball to a London young lady could seem more redolent of honour and pleasure than this Monday evening to me.

Dressed out in new stiff book-muslin,* made up to my throat,—a frock which had seemed to me and my sisters the height of earthly grandeur and finery—Alice, our old nurse, had been making it at home, in contemplation of the possibility of such an event during my stay in Edinburgh, but which had then appeared to me a robe too lovely and angelic to be ever worn short of heaven—I went with Miss Duncan to Mr. Dawson's at the appointed time. We entered through one small lofty room, perhaps I ought to call it an antechamber, for the house was old-fashioned, and stately and grand, the large square drawing-room, into the centre of which Mrs. Dawson's sofa was drawn. Behind her a little was placed a table with a great cluster candlestick upon it, bearing seven or eight wax-lights;* and that was all the light

in the room, which looked to me very vast and indistinct
after our pinched-up apartment at the Mackenzies'. Mrs.
Dawson must have been sixty; and yet her face looked very
soft and smooth and child-like. Her hair was quite gray: it
would have looked white but for the snowiness of her cap,
and satin ribbon. She was wrapped in a kind of dressing-
gown of French grey merino: the furniture of the room was
deep rose-colour, and white and gold,—the paper which
covered the walls was Indian,* beginning low down with a
profusion of tropical leaves and birds and insects, and
gradually diminishing in richness of detail till at the top it
ended in the most delicate tendrils and most filmy insects.

Mr. Dawson had acquired much riches in his profession,
and his house gave one this impression. In the corners of the
rooms were great jars of Eastern china, filled with flower-
leaves and spices; and in the middle of all this was placed the
sofa, on which poor Mrs. Margaret Dawson passed whole
days, and months, and years, without the power of moving
by herself. By-and-by Mrs. Dawson's maid brought in tea
and macaroons for us, and a little cup of milk and water and
a biscuit for her. Then the door opened. We had come very
early, and in came Edinburgh professors, Edinburgh
beauties, and celebrities  all on their way to some other
gayer and later party, but coming first to see Mrs. Dawson,
and tell her their *bon-mots*, or their interests, or their plans.
By each learned man, by each lovely girl, she was treated as
a dear friend, who knew something more about their own individual selves, independent of their reputation and general
society-character, than any one else.

It was very brilliant and very dazzling, and gave enough
to think about and wonder about for many days.

Monday after Monday we went, stationary, silent; what
could we find to say to any one but Mrs. Margaret herself?
Winter passed, summer was coming, still I was ailing, and
weary of my life; but still Mr. Dawson gave hopes of my
ultimate recovery. My father and mother came and went;
but they could not stay long, they had so many claims upon
them. Mrs. Margaret Dawson had become my dear friend,

although, perhaps, I had never exchanged as many words with her as I had with Miss Mackenzie, but then with Mrs. Dawson every word was a pearl or a diamond.

People began to drop off from Edinburgh, only a few were left, and I am not sure if our Monday evenings were not all the pleasanter.

There was Mr. Sperano, the Italian exile, banished even from France, where he had long resided, and now teaching Italian with meek diligence in the northern city; there was Mr. Preston, the Westmoreland squire, or, as he preferred to be called, statesman,* whose wife had come to Edinburgh for the education of their numerous family, and who, whenever her husband had come over on one of his occasional visits, was only too glad to accompany him to Mrs. Dawson's Monday evenings, he and the invalid lady having been friends from long ago. These and ourselves kept steady visitors, and enjoyed ourselves all the more for having the more of Mrs. Dawson's society.

One evening I had brought the little stool close to her sofa, and was caressing her thin white hand, when the thought came into my head and out I spoke it.

'Tell me, dear Mrs. Dawson,' said I, 'how long you have been in Edinburgh; you do not speak Scotch, and Mr. Dawson says he is not Scotch.'

'No, I am Lancashire—Liverpool-born,' said she, smiling. 'Don't you hear it in my broad tongue?'

'I hear something different to other people, but I like it because it is just you; is that Lancashire?'

'I dare say it is; for, though I am sure Lady Ludlow took pains enough to correct me in my younger days, I never could get rightly over the accent.'

'Lady Ludlow,' said G 'what had she to do with you? I heard you talking about her to Lady Madeline Stuart the first evening I ever came here; you and she seemed so fond of Lady Mǐdlow; who is she?'

'She is dead, my child; dead long ago.'

I felt sorry I had spoken about her, Mrs. Dawson looked so grave and sad. I suppose she perceived my sorrow, for she went on and said:

'My dear, I like to talk and to think of Lady Ludlow: she was my true, kind friend and benefactress for many years; ask me what you like about her, and do not think you give me pain.'

I grew bold at this.

'Will you tell me all about her then, please, Mrs. Dawson?'

'Nay,' said she, smiling, 'that would be too long a story. Here are Signor Sperano, and Miss Duncan, and Mr. and Mrs. Preston are coming to-night, Mr. Preston told me; how would they like to hear an old-world story which, after all, would be no story at all, neither beginning, nor middle, nor end, only a bundle of recollections.'

'If you speak of me, madame,' said Signor Sperano, 'I can only say you do me one great honour by recounting in my presence anything about any person that has ever interested you.'

Miss Duncan tried to say something of the same kind. In the middle of her confused speech, Mr. and Mrs. Preston came in. I sprang up; I went to meet them.

'Oh,' said I, 'Mrs. Dawson is just going to tell us all about Lady Ludlow, and a great deal more, only she is afraid it won't interest anybody: do say you would like to hear it!'

Mrs. Dawson smiled at me, and in reply to their urgency she promised to tell us all about Lady Ludlow, on condition that each one of us should, after she had ended, narrate something interesting, which we had either heard, or which had fallen within our own experience. We all promised willingly, and then gathered round her sofa to hear what she could tell us about my Lady Ludlow.

### Link to 'An Accursed Race'*

As any one may guess, it had taken Mrs. Dawson several Monday evenings to narrate all this history of the days of her youth. Miss Duncan thought it would be a good exercise for me, both in memory and composition, to write out on Tuesday mornings all that I had heard the night before; and thus it came to pass that I have the manuscript of 'My Lady Ludlow' now lying by me.

MR. DAWSON had often come in and out of the room during the time that his sister had been telling us about Lady Ludlow. He would stop, and listen a little, and smile or sigh as the case might be. The Monday after the dear old lady had wound up her tale (if tale it could be called), we felt rather at a loss what to talk about, we had grown so accustomed to listen to Mrs. Dawson. I remember I was saying, 'Oh, dear! I wish some one would tell us another story!' when her brother said, as if in answer to my speech, that he had drawn up a paper all ready for the Philosophical Society, and that perhaps we might care to hear it before it was sent off: it was in a great measure compiled from a French book,* published by one of the Academies, and rather dry in itself; but to which Mr. Dawson's attention had been directed, after a tour he had made in England during the past year, in which he had noticed small walled-up doors in unusual parts of some old parish churches, and had been told that they had formerly been appropriated to the use of some half-heathen race, who, before the days of gipsies, held the same outcast pariah position in most of the countries of western Europe. Mr. Dawson had been recommended to the French book which he named, as containing the fullest and most authentic account of this mysterious race, the Cagots.* I did not think I should like hearing this paper as much as a story; but, of course, as he meant it kindly, we were bound to submit, and I found it, on the whole, more interesting than I anticipated.

### 'AN ACCURSED RACE'

#### Link to 'The Doom of the Griffiths'

FOR some time past I had observed that Miss Duncan made a good deal of occupation for herself in writing, but that she did not like me to notice her employment. Of course, this made me all the more curious; and many were my silent conjectures—some of them so near the truth that

I was not much surprised when, after Mr. Dawson had finished reading his Paper to us, she hesitated, coughed, and abruptly introduced a little formal speech, to the effect that she had noted down an old Welsh story, the particulars of which had often been told her in her youth, as she lived close to the place where the events occurred. Everybody pressed her to read the manuscript, which she now produced from her reticule; but, when on the point of beginning, her nervousness seemed to overcome her, and she made so many apologies for its being the first and only attempt she had ever made at that kind of composition, that I began to wonder if we should ever arrive at the story at all. At length, in a high-pitched, ill-assured voice, she read out the title:

'THE DOOM OF THE GRIFFITHS.'

### Link to 'Half a Life-Time Ago'*

YOU cannot think how kindly Mrs. Dawson thanked Miss Duncan for writing and reading this story. She shook my poor, pale governess so tenderly by the hand that the tears came into her eyes, and the colour into her cheeks.

'I thought you had been so kind; I liked hearing about Lady Ludlow; I fancied perhaps I could do something to give a little pleasure,' were the half-finished sentences Miss Duncan stammered out. I am sure it was the wish to earn similar kind words from Mrs. Dawson, that made Mrs. Preston try and rummage through her memory to see if she could not recollect some fact, or event, or history, which might interest Mrs. Dawson and the little party that gathered round her sofa. Mrs. Preston it was who told us the following tale:

'HALF A LIFE-TIME AGO.'

### Link to 'The Poor Clare'

WHEN this narrative was finished, Mrs. Dawson called on our two gentlemen, Signor Sperano and Mr. Preston,

and told them that they had hitherto been amused or interested, but that it was now their turn to amuse or interest.
They looked at each other as if this application of hers took
them by surprise, and seemed altogether as much abashed
as well-grown men can ever be. Signor Sperano was the first
to recover himself: after thinking a little, he said:—

'Your will, dear lady, is law. Next Monday evening, I will
bring you an old, old story, which I found among the papers
of the good old priest who first welcomed me to England. It
was but a poor return for his generous kindness; but I had
the opportunity of nursing him through the cholera, of
which he died. He left me all that he had—no money—but
his scanty furniture, his book of prayers, his crucifix and
rosary, and his papers. How some of those papers came into
his hands I know not. They had evidently been written
many years before the venerable man was born; and I doubt
whether he had ever examined the bundles, which had come
down to him from some old ancestor, or in some strange
bequest. His life was too busy to leave any time for the
gratification of mere curiosity; I, alas! have only had too
much leisure.'

Next Monday, Signor Sperano read to us the story which
I will call

'The Poor Clare.'

## Link to 'The Half-Brothers'

NOW, of all our party who had first listened to 'My Lady
Ludlow', Mr. Preston was the only one who had not told
us something, either of information, tradition, history, or
legend. We naturally turned to him; but we did not like asking him directly for his contribution, for he was a grave,
reserved, and silent man.

He understood us, however, and, rousing himself as it
were, he said—

'I know you wish me to tell you, in my turn, of something
which I have learnt or heard during my life. I could tell you

something of my own life, and of a life dearer still to my memory; but I have shrunk from narrating anything so purely personal. Yet, shrink as I will, no other but those sad recollections will present themselves to my mind. I call them sad ×hen I think of the end of it all. However, I am not going to moralize. If my dear brother's life and death does not speak for itself, no words of mine will teach you what may be learnt from it.

# EXPLANATORY NOTES

## My Lady Ludlow

The story was first published in *Household Words*, from 19 June to 25 September, 1858. In 1859 it was vol. 1 of *Round the Sofa*. (There was an unauthorized American publication by Harper and Brothers in 1858.) The text used is 1859, which differs only in minor editorial tidying-up from the periodical version. (See note to p. 1).

1 *as I said*: the phrase was inserted in the 1859 publication to echo and emphasize the introduction written for *Round the Sofa*.

2 *coat of arms*: the 'lozenge' or diamond-shaped shield is reserved for females. A 'quartered' coat will have one or more distinct sections instead of a single overall design. Quarters may show the coat of another family; in this case the Hanbury arms quartered in the Ludlow arms. The motto is in old French, *Foy et Loy* (Faith and Law). The brief description, by its use of precise and correct terms, indicates Lady Ludlow's conscious pride in her status as a woman of the nobility in her own right as well as by marriage (see also 163).

5 *Christ's Hospital*: known as the Bluecoat school because of the traditional uniform. Originally founded for poor scholars, it became a leading school with entry places in the gift of patrons.

7 *Hampton Court*: the palace built in the reign of Henry VIII.

8 *mode gown*: this describes a fashionable, rich, and sweeping style of dress, but the ingenious way of hitching up its length shows a practical side of Lady Ludlow's character.

9 *dimity*: a strong cotton cloth.

11 *Mr. Raikes*: Robert Raikes (1735–1811). His Sunday School founded in 1780 developed into a national movement.

15 *John Wesley*: (1703–91) the founder of Methodism.

16 *the Rump*: the remnant of the 'Long Parliament' (1640–60) that defied Charles I, and was finally dissolved by General Monk before the Restoration of Charles II (see also 135).

17 *Moravian Methodist*: the Moravians were a German pietistic sect which influenced John Wesley.

18 *Guy Faux' day*: the Gunpowder Plot was hatched in 1605 by a

group of malcontent Roman Catholics. Guido Fawkes was captured in the act of igniting barrels of gunpowder in the cellars of Parliament, which was in session.

19 *'Spectator'*: Joseph Addison (1672–1719) was a leading politician and author. *The Spectator*, a periodical he began (with Richard Steele) in 1711, set the standard for urbane style and for comment on social, moral, and literary matters.

*'Sturm's Reflections'*: Guides to behaviour and moral improvement were a standard feature in the education of the young, particularly girls. The examples quoted were among the most popular, and were constantly reprinted well into the nineteenth century: (i) Christoph Christian Sturm (1740–86), *Reflections on the works of God and of his Providence throughout all nature, for every day of the year*. Translated from the German into French . . . and into English. By a lady, 1788. (ii) Hester Mulso Chapone (1727–1801), *Letters on the Improvement of the Mind, addressed to a Young Lady*, 1773. (iii) Dr John Gregory (1724–73), *A Father's Legacy to his Daughters*, 1774. The Chapone and Gregory items were often published as one book.

21 *Lord George Gordon*: (1751–93) instigated the vicious 'no Popery' riots in London in 1780.

*sans-culottism*: (and see 61). Sansculottes (French, 'without breeches') was a term given to the ragged and more violent mob element of the French Revolution.

30 *St. Stephen's*: correctly the name for the old House of Commons building, here used for Parliament as a whole.

37 *Mr. Hogarth's*: William Hogarth (1697–1764), whose great and popular series of paintings included 'The Harlot's Progress' and 'The Rake's Progress'.

40 *'Bacon's Essays'*: Sir Francis Bacon (1561–1620), lawyer and philosopher who became Lord Chancellor. His brief essays are models of witty and aphoristic thought.

*Childers or Eclipse*: famous racehorses. The bet of 'Eclipse first and the rest nowhere', made by his owner (Colonel O'Kelly) at his first race, became a popular saying.

41 *Mrs. Nickleby*: in Dickens's *Nicholas Nickleby* (1838–39) the hero's mother, whose flow of speech is a comic feature of the novel.

45 *catechism*: the Church Catechism is a question-and-answer

instruction manual used by the Church of England.

46 *dictionary*: Nathaniel Bailey's dictionary (1721) was superseded by Dr Johnson's great dictionary of 1755, which became the standard reference.

48 *battants*: the French term for the leaf of a door.

50 *tree . . . Genesis*: the reference is to the tree of knowledge in the Garden of Eden.

58 *Mr. Fox*: Charles James Fox (1749–1806), a leading politician and a man of considerable culture, was also a notorious gambler. The reference is double-edged.

61 *Christopher Sly*: the drunk tinker in Shakespeare's *The Taming of the Shrew*, who is bathed, dressed in fine clothes, and carried away to wake up in luxury.

67 *Jean-Jacques Rousseau*: (1712–78) 'infamous' because his works questioned existing social conditions and attitudes, and were a major influence on revolutionary thought in France.

*Encyclopédistes*: *L'Encyclopédie*, published in France between 1751 and 1776, established the philosophic spirit of the period. It promoted rational enquiry and attacked superstition.

68 *Mademoiselle Necker*: known by her married name as Madame de Staël (1766–1817), wrote important political and literary books, as well as two popular novels translated into English.

70 *Æneas*: Trojan hero and legendary founder of Rome. In Virgil's *Aeneid* (30–19 BC) he is called 'pious Aeneas' because of his care for his father and his sense of filial duty after the fall of Troy.

71 *Cassandra*: daughter of King Priam of Troy. She rejected the god Apollo; in revenge he doomed her to be a prophetess whose prophecies would never be believed.

80 *the Lanterne*: prison and death. In the early days of the Revolution one method of summary execution was to use the crossbeam of a convenient skylight (*une lanterne*) as a gallows for unfortunate victims; hence the expression '*mettre à la lanterne*'.

84 *galette*: thin cake or biscuit.

*Beaumarchais*: Pierre Augustin Caron de Beaumarchais (1732–99), a popular dramatist whose satirical comedies *The Barber of Seville* and *The Marriage of Figaro* were turned into operas by Rossini and Mozart.

84 *Adam*: Adolphe Adam (1803–56) was a popular composer whose *Giselle* is still performed. But this is an anachronism; his reorchestration of an earlier opera, *Richard Cœur de Lion* by André Grétry (1741–1813), was not made, as *Richard en Palestine*, until 1844. Mrs Gaskell has confused the contemporary work with the original.

109 *canaille*: (Fr.) rabble, mob.

128 *Xantippe*: Xanthippe, wife of the philosopher Socrates (469–399 BC) and a reputed scold.

129 *For Satan . . . to do*: from the popular *Divine Songs for Children* (no. 21 'Against Evil Company') by Isaac Watts (1674–1748).

131 *Doctor Burney*: Charles Burney (1726–1814), the music critic and author of the authoritative *History of Music*. His daughter, Frances (Fanny) Burney, later Mme d'Arblay (1752–1840), became famous with her first novel, *Evelina* (1778), and remained popular as a writer.

133 *mended my pens*: pens were fashioned from goose quills, and the writing end needed frequent reshaping as it became worn.

135 *fifth of November and on the thirtieth of January*: as a royalist and traditionalist member of the Church of England, Lady Ludlow would observe Guy Fawkes Day (see note to 18) and the anniversary of the execution of Charles I, for whom a special occasional service was appended to the prayer book from 1662 to 1859.

136 *potters*: (dialect), bothers, troubles.

*Susannah . . . Dragon*: *The History of Susanna* and *The History of the Destruction of Bel and the Dragon* are two short, melodramatic books of the Old Testament *Apocrypha*.

137 *sugar . . . blood*: the Evangelical movement led the opposition to the slave trade which supplied labour to the sugar plantations in the West Indies.

138 *Martha and Mary*: in Luke 10: 35–41, Martha is the practical sister who busied herself looking after Jesus, although he praised Mary, the contemplative sister.

149 *Hall, the Bang-beggar*: I cannot trace this reference.

159 *Gulliver*: in Jonathan Swift's *Gulliver's Travels* (1726), Part One.

163 *Hatchments*: a corruption of the term 'achievement' (coat of arms), a large diamond 'shield' carrying the coat of arms of the deceased, set over the main entrance.

171 *Trafalgar*: the naval battle of 1805, when Nelson destroyed the French fleet.

173 *Greenwich Hospital*: Sir Christopher Wren (1631–1723) designed a magnificent building for a seamen's hospital, by the Thames near London; now the Royal Naval College and Naval Museum.

191 *'Tours'*: Arthur Young (1741–1820), agricultural theorist and author of several 'Tours', whose most popular work was his *Travels in France* (1792).

193 *Dodwell's heresy*: Henry Dodwell the younger (1701?–84), a deist and nationalist whose pamphlet *Christianity not founded on Argument* (1741), stirred up a controversy.

195 *Mr. Coke*: Thomas William Coke (1752–1842), later first Earl of Leicester, known as Coke of Norfolk or Coke of Holkham, his Norfolk base. A leader in new and improved farming methods, he increased the yearly value of his farms tenfold, and attracted visitors from all over Europe to his model estates.

207 *Grecian*: a boy in the highest class, both a classical scholar and school leader, at Christ's Hospital (see note to 5).

## An Accursed Race

First published in *Household Words*, 25 August 1855, then in vol. 2 of *Round the Sofa*, 1859. The book version shows careful editing. The punctuation is heavier, and there are a number of verbal changes to improve the style which substitute more precise words and tighten up some loose phrasing. One substantive omission is worth noting, a rather naïve appeal dropped from the final paragraph: '. . . recently persecuted. [Gentle reader, am I not rightly representing your feelings? If so,] The moral history . . .'
The 1859 text is used in this edition.

212 *Crestiaa*: possibly a corruption of 'Chrestien'.

*Martinmas*: 11 November, the feast day of the great missionary bishop, St Martin of Tours.

214 *bénitier*: font.

218 *alcaldes*: (Span.) a justice official.

221 *'He that's . . . still'*: *Hudibras*. Part 1. 547–8. A satirical mock epic by Samuel Butler (1612–80). The correct version is:

'He that complies against his will / Is of his own opinion still.'

223 *Perlute*: possibly related to the Latin 'perlustrare', with a general meaning of 'watch out'.

   *King Clovis*: (AD 465–511.) Clovis unified much of the early Frankish kingdom, and was converted to Christianity. One tradition makes the Cagots descendants of the Visigoths, regarded as heretics and defeated by Clovis.

224 *Charlemagne*: (AD 742–814.) The Frankish king who, in 800, became Emperor of the West.

225 *tarantella*: a rapid and whirling South Italian dance.

   *Berserker*: a type of Norse warrior noted for fury in battle; hence the phrase 'to go berserk'.

227 *jurat*: a municipal official of the period.

### The Doom of the Griffiths

First published in *Harper's New Monthly Magazine* (USA), January 1858, then in *Round the Sofa*, 1859. There was some minor editorial work on the opening paragraphs to adapt the story for English publication. The only other change to be noted was the omission of the word 'wittol' (see note to 252).

229 *Owen Glendower*: (*c*.1359–*c*.1416) was the leader of the last major armed struggle for Welsh independence. He is an important figure in Welsh legend, and a major character in Shakespeare's *1 Henry IV*: the quotation is from III. i.

   *Sir David Gam*: Davy Gam is listed as one of the English dead in *Henry V*, IV. viii. There is no historical record of the attempted murder.

232 *Dr. Pugh*: William Owen Pughe (1789–1835), noted Welsh scholar and antiquarian.

240 '*stretched . . . repose*': cf. James Thomson (1700–48), *The Castle of Indolence*, canto 2, stanza 50: 'Renown is not the child of indolent repose.'

241 *Œdipus Tyrannus*: more familiarly *Œdipus Rex*, a tragedy by the Greek dramatist Sophocles (496–406 BC).

243 *cwrw*: ale.

247 *Sorbus aucuparia*: the mountain ash.

249  *Undine*: a water nymph. The German writer de la Motte
     Fouqué (1777–1843) published a tragic romance, *Undine*
     (1811), that became very popular and was widely translated.

252  *yr buten*: a harlot.

     *Fool—poor fool!*: in the *Harper's* version this is 'Fool—poor wit-
     tol fool' ('wittol' is an archaic or dialect word for a cuckold).
     Possibly a quiet bit of censoring by the publisher.

264  *drookit*: (dialect), drenched, soaked.

### The Poor Clare

First published in *Household Words*, 13–24 December 1856.
Reprinted in *Round the Sofa*, vol. 2, 1859. There are minor editorial
corrections. The 1859 text is used.

272  *Heptarchy*: the seven kingdoms formed by the end of the fifth
     century AD following the Anglo-Saxon invasions of England.

273  *the old faith*: James II, an avowed Roman Catholic, attempted
     to restore the position of Roman Catholics, who were severely
     penalized by rigidly pro-Anglican legislation, when he came to
     the throne in 1685. He was defeated and exiled after the
     'Glorious Revolution' of 1688. Roman Catholics had to wait
     until the Catholic Emancipation Act of 1828 to regain full
     rights of citizenship.

285  *Gray's Inn*: the various Inns of Court in London are tradi-
     tionally, and in important ways officially, the centre of the
     legal profession.

289  *Her teeth . . . near together*: the traditional image of a witch.

304  *Sir Matthew Hale*: (1609–76) a famous lawyer who became Lord
     Chief Justice.

308  *that rank*: see note to 273.

311  *strange New England cases*: they provide the basis for one of
     Gaskell's finest stories, 'Lois the Witch' (in *Cousin Phillis and
     Other Tales*, World's Classics, 1981).

     *Mr. Defoe*: Daniel Defoe (1660?–1731), the author of *Robinson
     Crusoe*. The reference is to his *A True Relation of the Apparition
     of Mrs. Veal* (1706).

315  *the law . . . burnt*: the law against witchcraft was not repealed
     until 1736.

320 *Stoney Hurst*: an old-established Catholic foundation and famous Catholic school, now Stonyhurst College.

325 *Jacobites*: these were followers of James Stuart, the Old Pretender (1688–1766), who were behind the first Jacobite rising in Scotland in 1715.

*wars and commotions . . . Low Countries*: no particular historical incident can be traced, but Antwerp was one of the focal points of popular resistance to Austrian rule of the Low Countries.

327 '*blouses*': (French) workmen's tunics. The term is used to refer to the working class.

332 *Therefore . . . drink*: Romans 12: 20. Only half of this New Testament verse is given. The second half—which readers of the period would be well aware of—is a brilliant omission by Mrs Gaskell since it points up, by its very absence, the whole action of the story: '. . . for in so doing thou shalt heap coals of fire on his head'.

## The Half Brothers

The Preface to *Round the Sofa* refers to one story that 'has obtained only a limited circulation'. Vol. 2 appears to be its first publication. Geoffrey Sharps surmises MS circulation for the 'limited circulation'.

345 *maud*: a grey-striped plaid.

## Mr. Harrison's Confessions

First published in the *Ladies' Companion and Monthly Magazine*, February–April 1851. Reprinted in *Lizzie Leigh and Other Tales*, (London, Chapman and Hall, 1855). There has been a little corrective editing. The text used is 1855.

349 *surgeon*: the terms 'surgeon' and 'doctor' were then largely interchangeable.

351 *Mayence*: the French form of the West German town of Mainz.

352 *Guy's*: Guy's hospital in London was famous for its medical school.

354 *Hessian boots*: a style of high boot copied from the uniform of the troops of Hesse in Germany.

'*jemmy*': (dialect) dandified, spruce.

355 *in loco parentis*: (Latin) in the place of a parent.

355 *Galen or Hippocrates*: Galen (AD *c.*130–201) was a Greek physician whose books on medicine were accepted as authoritative into the eighteenth century. Hippocrates (*c.*460–*c.*375 BC) was the Greek physician regarded as the 'father' of medicine, whose code of ethics, the Hippocratic oath, was affirmed when doctors qualified.

357 *Sir Astley Cooper*: (1768–1841) President of the College of Surgeons, and one of the initiators of the medical school at Guy's Hospital; he was probably the best-known surgeon of the time.

*Sir Robert Peel*: (1788–1850) leader of the Conservative party and Prime Minister, 1841–6.

358 *Aesculapius*: in Greek mythology, the god of healing and son of Apollo, god of medicine and handsomest of the gods.

360 *Sir Everard Home*: (1756–1832) professor at the College of Surgeons and first to be named President, in 1821.

*Abernethy*: John Abernethy (1764–1831), surgeon and professor at St Batholomew's Hospital, noted as an outstanding teacher.

361 *the picture within*: the scene 'framed' is of a type familiar in domestic and 'story-telling' genre paintings of the period.

364 *Miss Austen, Dickens, and Thackeray*: given the date of this story, the three novelists represent major influences, one of the recent past (Jane Austen, 1775–1817), one contemporary (Charles Dickens, 1812–70), and one a new star (W. M. Thackeray, 1811–63—see note to 428).

366 *the Lancet*: Britain's leading medical journal was founded in 1823.

369 *bodkin*: to travel bodkin is to be a third person squeezed between the occupants of a seat for two ('bodkin' is a long thin needle).

370 *to 'ride and tie'* is when one horse is shared by two or more riders. One rider covers an agreed distance, then dismounts and ties up the horse for the next rider, being then overtaken while walking to the next 'tie' point, and so on.

375 *German canon*: a 'canon' is a musical round or part-song. The one quoted (trans. 'Oh! how well I feel in the evening') is a traditional hymn-like folk song.

*Liebig*: Justus Freiherr von Liebig (1803–73), a German

chemist whose researches into animal chemistry led to the invention of meat extracts and baby foods.

379 *leeches*: blood-letting by the use of live leeches was a basic element of medical practice at the time.

*'Sleep, baby, sleep!'*: translated from German, attributed to the American, Elizabeth Payson Prentiss (1818–78).

381 *hyoscyamus*: henbane, a poisonous narcotic drug.

382 *'wersh'*: (dialect, also 'wairsh') insufficiently salted, insipid, sickly.

383 *Stentor*: in Homer's *Iliad*, the Greek herald who shouted as loud as fifty men.

384 *the 'Mermaid'*: the Mermaid Tavern in London was famous as the haunt of Shakespeare and others. Keats celebrated it in 'Lines to the Mermaid Tavern'.

387 *minister to a heart diseased?*: parodies *Macbeth*, V. iii, 'Cans't thou not minister to a mind diseased?'

388 *hulks*: dismantled ships, used as floating prisons.

*Mens conscia recti*: (Latin) 'mens sibi conscia recti'. Virgil, *The Aeneid*, 1.604: A mind conscious of the right.

391 *'hodie'*: (Latin) daily; a standard term in prescriptions.

393 *Corazza shirts*: a sleeveless shirt in the style of a cuirass. The Italian name (*corraza* = cuirass) indicates the interest in things Italian during Italy's wars of independence under Mazzini, Garibaldi, and Cavour.

418 *vi et armis*: (Latin) by force and arms.

*Paris*: in Greek myth, Paris, the son of King Priam of Troy, was called on to judge between the goddesses Hera, Athena, and Aphrodite. He awarded the coveted golden apple to Aphrodite, the goddess of love, who later helped him to carry off Helen, the act that caused the Trojan War.

424 *gay Lothario*: the 'gay Lothario' is a libertine character in *The Fair Penitent* (1703), by the dramatist Nicholas Rowe (1674–1718). The name became proverbial.

428 *Vanity Fair*: the novel that made Thackeray famous (see note to 364) was published in 1848.

429 *Jenny Lind*: (1820–87), the most popular singer of her time, was known as the Swedish Nightingale.

### Appendix: Round the Sofa

First published as an introductory narrative to the two-volume *Round the Sofa* collection of 1859.

435 *moreen*: a durable curtain material, of wool or wool and cotton.

436 *brevet rank*: nominal rank in army, officially awarded but not attached to regular professional duties; generally an honorary rank.

437 *book-muslin*: a fine muslin that was folded like a book for retail sale.

*wax-lights*: wax candles were brighter, more elegant, and more expensive than ordinary tallow candles.

438 *Indian*: Indian wallpaper would show fashionable taste as well as wealth. Indian artefacts and art were being introduced by those who went out to India, generally with the East India Company, to create careers and fortunes (Elizabeth Gaskell's only brother, John, vanished on one of his trips to India).

439 *statesman*: the word was commonly used to describe an independent farmer or small landowner in the Lake District.

### Link to 'An Accursed Race'

440 This first link in the chain of stories is more closely tied to the context of 'Round the Sofa' than later ones, and is appropriately given to Mrs Dawson's brother, the specialist in contagious diseases, to lead off the sequence.

441 *French book*: A. W. Ward suggests Francisque Michel's *Histoire des races maudites de la France et d'Espagne* (Paris, 1847).

*Cagots*: the etymology is uncertain, as is that of the alternative terms mentioned on 222, 'Malandrins' and 'Oiseliers'.

### Link to 'Half a Life-time Ago'

442 This story is now published in the *Cousin Phillis* volume of the current World's Classics series.

Memoirs from the House of the Dead
*Translated by Jessie Coulson*
*Edited by Ronald Hingley*

ARTHUR CONAN DOYLE:
Sherlock Holmes: Selected Stories
*With an introduction by S. C. Roberts*

ALEXANDRE DUMAS *fils*: La Dame aux Camélias
*Translated and edited by David Coward*

MARIA EDGEWORTH: Castle Rackrent
*Edited by George Watson*

GEORGE ELIOT: The Mill on the Floss
*Edited by Gordon S. Haight*

JOHN EVELYN: Diary
*Selected and edited by John Bowle*

SUSAN FERRIER: Marriage
*Edited by Herbert Foltinek*

HENRY FIELDING: Joseph Andrews *and* Shamela
*Edited by Douglas Brooks-Davies*

GUSTAVE FLAUBERT: Madame Bovary
*Translated by Gerard Hopkins*
*With an introduction by Terence Cave*

THEODOR FONTANE: Before the Storm
*Translated with an introduction by R. J. Hollingdale*

JOHN GALT: Annals of the Parish
*Edited by James Kinsley*

The Entail
*Edited by Ian A. Gordon*

The Provost
*Edited by Ian A. Gordon*

ELIZABETH GASKELL: Cousin Phillis and Other Tales
*Edited by Angus Easson*

RUDYARD KIPLING: The Day's Work
*Edited by Thomas Pinney*

The Jungle Book (in two volumes)
*Edited by W. W. Robson*

Kim
*Edited by Alan Sandison*

Life's Handicap
*Edited by A. O. J. Cockshut*

The Man Who Would be King and Other Stories
*Edited by Louis L. Cornell*

Plain Tales From the Hills
*Edited by Andrew Rutherford*

Stalky & Co.
*Edited by Isobel Quigly*

A complete list of Oxford Paperbacks, including The World's Classics, Twentieth-Century Classics, OPUS, Past Masters, Oxford Authors, Oxford Shakespeare, and Oxford Paperback Reference, is available in the UK from the General Publicity Department (JH), Oxford University Press, Walton Street, Oxford OX2 6DP.

In the USA, complete lists are available from the Paperbacks Marketing Manager, Oxford University Press, 200 Madison Avenue, New York, NY 10016.

Oxford Paperbacks are available from all good bookshops. In case of difficulty, customers in the UK can order direct from Oxford University Press Bookshop, Freepost, 116 High Street, Oxford, OX1 4BR, enclosing full payment. Please add 10 per cent of published price for postage and packing.

# THE WORLD'S CLASSICS

## *A Select List*